daughters who walk this path

~ A NOVEL ~

YEJIDE KILANKO

PINTAIL

PINTAIL
a member of Penguin Group (USA)

Published by the Penguin Group
Penguin Group (Canada)
90 Eglinton Avenue East, Suite 700, Toronto, Ontario, Canada M4P 2Y3

Penguin Group (USA) Inc., 375 Hudson Street, New York, New York 10014, U.S.A.
Penguin Books Ltd, 80 Strand, London WC2R 0RL, England
Penguin Ireland, 25 St Stephen's Green, Dublin 2, Ireland (a division of Penguin Books Ltd)
Penguin Group (Australia), 707 Collins Street, Melbourne, Victoria 3008, Australia
(a division of Pearson Australia Group Pty Ltd)
Penguin Books India Pvt Ltd, 11 Community Centre, Panchsheel Park,
New Delhi – 110 017, India
Penguin Group (NZ), 67 Apollo Drive, Rosedale, Auckland 0632, New Zealand
(a division of Pearson New Zealand Ltd)
Penguin Books (South Africa) (Pty) Ltd, 24 Sturdee Avenue, Rosebank,
Johannesburg 2196, South Africa

Penguin Books Ltd, Registered Offices: 80 Strand, London WC2R 0RL, England

First published in Penguin softcover by Penguin Canada, 2012.

Published in this edition, 2013

1 2 3 4 5 6 7 8 9 10   (RRD)

Copyright © Yejide Kilanko, 2012

Manufactured in the U.S.A.

978-0-14-318643-4

Visit the Penguin US website at **www.penguin.com**

ALWAYS LEARNING   PEARSON

To my mother,
Catherine Bamidele Alonge,
for listening to my many childhood dreams
and telling me I could do them all.

Prologue

My first memory was of Eniayo. I was five years old. When Mummy explained to me that the big bump in her stomach meant I was getting a baby sister or brother to play with, I jumped up and down with happiness. "Please can you make sure it's a girl?"

Mummy's brown eyes crinkled at the sides as she smiled. "That is God's decision," she said and continued to knit a large baby shawl. I watched closely as her silver knitting pins expertly pulled the yellow wool in and out, in and out. I sent up a little prayer and ran out of the room.

On a bright afternoon not too long after, Daddy's company driver, Mr. Bello, came to pick me up at school. Looking out of my classroom window, I saw his lanky figure bouncing up the short flight of steps. "Madam just had the baby," he said to my teacher, Mrs. Abe. "She wants to see Morayo."

After asking me to pack up my school bag, Mrs. Abe sent me off. "Please greet your mother for me."

"Yes, Ma."

I sat in the back of the red Peugeot 505, kicking the seat in front of me until Mr. Bello turned around. "Morayo, that is enough," he said with a stern look.

Lifting up my head, I gave Mr. Bello an apologetic look. "It is just that it is taking too long."

His face softened. "Don't worry, we will soon be there."

I squirmed in my seat as waves of hot air fanned my face from the open window. There was a traffic jam in front of Bodija Market. Several cows, swishing their tails from side to side, walked majestically across the road. Car horns blared as one of the cows slowly lowered herself to the ground in the middle of the road. After a few minutes of being prodded with the cowherds' long wooden sticks, the beast rose awkwardly to her feet and ambled to the side of the road to chew the long grass on the verge.

Daddy always said cows were the real kings of the road, since it was impossible for a car to win an argument against them.

When Mr. Bello finally turned the car into the main road leading to the huge University College Hospital complex, I saw my grandmother standing in the distance. Mama Ejiwunmi lived in Oyo but had arrived a week earlier to help Mummy with the birth—and now she was waiting for me by the entrance. She wore an *iro* and *buba* made from a deep blue *adire* material. Her round ebony face broke into a bright smile when she saw me and I ran into her arms.

I held on tightly to Mama Ejiwunmi's hand as we walked down the corridor to see Mummy and my new sister, my stomach turning from the strong smell of bleach. The pungent odour filled my nose, clinging to the short hairs in my nostrils. I stared as nurses in short white dresses and pinned white hats walked by.

We were halfway down the corridor when a woman's high-pitched screams halted my steps. I stopped to look at my grandmother. She squeezed my hand, smiled at me, and said softly, "Don't worry, my child. Those are just the cries of a woman giving birth. Very soon, the pain will pass and joy will come." I nodded, but I was relieved when we walked into the nursery and left those screams behind.

Mama Ejiwunmi pointed out my new sister through the nursery window. I turned to her in confusion. How could this be my sister? I turned back to look at the baby. She looked nothing like me. She was more like the blond, blue-eyed doll Daddy had bought for me from Leventis the last time he went to Lagos. Our baby was—white?

My grandmother pulled on my arm. "Morayo, do you want to hold your sister?"

"Hold her?"

She nodded. "Yes. You should welcome your sister into the world."

I dragged my feet after her as she walked into the nursery.

One of the nurses lifted an eyebrow when she saw us. "Mama, we don't allow children inside." Her thin voice held a tinge of annoyance.

"This little child just wants to see her sister," Mama Ejiwunmi pleaded.

I clutched onto Mama Ejiwunmi's wrapper, hoping that the nurse would say no. But the nurse pursed her lips. "She cannot stay long."

"God bless you for your kindness."

Mama Ejiwunmi picked up Eniayo from the small wooden crib and placed her in my arms. When Eniayo opened her eyes, I froze. They were pink, and not at all like the warm rich brown of my own and of everyone I knew. Eniayo looked like no one in our family.

That was the day the word *afin* exploded into my world.

The news of Eniayo's birth and albinism quickly travelled among our family when Mummy returned from the hospital.

Following Yoruba traditions, Eniayo's naming ceremony was held eight days after her birth. After the ceremony, I overheard two neighbours talking. "Where do you think this *afin* child came from?" the first woman asked.

"How would I know?" the other answered with a cough that shook her triple chins. "I just know that this is not a good thing. My friend's junior sister gave birth to an *afin* last year. Three months after the child's birth, the father lost his job. The following month, my friend's sister fell off an *okada* and broke her arm. Some children bring wealth and promotion. These *afin* children," the woman hissed, snapping her fingers to ward off any lurking evil, "all they bring is bad luck."

A few days later, my father's great-grand aunt, Iya Agba, came to our house to meet Eniayo. She was the oldest person in Daddy's family.

I stood unseen by the entryway into the sitting room and watched my sombre mother gently place Eniayo in Iya Agba's frail arms. Iya Agba, hunched over from old age, held Eniayo unsteadily. She peered closely at my sister's face through milky eyes.

Mummy, Daddy, and Mama Ejiwunmi sat close by, as still as if they were all holding their breath.

Iya Agba shook her head slowly, letting out a deep, sad sigh that echoed in the room. "So it is true," she muttered to herself. *"Paga!"*

"During the pregnancy"—she paused and turned to Mummy, catching her breath—"did you walk outside when the sun was up high in the sky?"

My sweaty back itched and I rubbed it slowly on the rough wall paint. I moved a little closer to the entryway to hear the answer.

Mummy gave Daddy a quick look. She then turned to Iya Agba and mumbled something under her breath.

"Eh?" Iya Agba snapped.

"Yes, Ma," Mummy said quietly.

Iya Agba's mouth fell open. "Ha! Bisoye!" She turned to Daddy. "Owolabi, did you hear what your wife just said? Did you?"

Daddy nodded, but wisely kept quiet. Mummy got up from her chair and knelt in front of Iya Agba on the thinning brown carpet. She clasped her hands behind her back and hung her head low. Then she raised her head and I saw the tears running down her face. My eyes twitched.

Iya Agba hissed loudly, shaking her legs. "Bisoye! Bisoye!"

Eniayo, who now hung precariously in Iya Agba's arms, started crying.

Mama Ejiwunmi rose shakily from her seat, stretching out to take Eniayo from Iya Agba. But Iya Agba ignored the outstretched hands; she continued to scold Mummy as if she were a little child. The furrows on her forehead deepened as her croaky voice shook. "Bisoye, did I not warn you? Did I not warn you that those mischievous evil spirits walk about at noontime, looking for a human body to occupy? Now, see what you have caused!" She paused again, catching her breath. "Your disobedience has brought bad luck to this poor child and to our entire family." Her hunched-over body swayed as she moved in her seat. The baby swung forward in her arms. I held my breath, praying that she would not drop my little sister on the floor. "Did we do something wrong by bringing yams to your father's house to ask for your hand in marriage? Tell me, did we?"

Mama Ejiwunmi's deep sigh echoed in the room. She gently pried Eniayo from Iya Agba and held her closely to her own age-flattened breasts, watching as silent tears rolled down her daughter's face.

The dim fluorescent lights in the corridor where I stood suddenly became menacing. The decorative wooden masks on the walls came alive, their fiery eyes staring down at me. I shivered, feeling goosebumps rise all over my body.

This new baby sister, this *afin*—she was really a spirit child!

That evening, to show her great and continued displeasure with Mummy, Iya Agba refused to eat the food set on the table before her. Knowing that Iya Agba was coming, Mummy had prepared her favourite *amala* and *gbegiri* soup filled with an assortment of bush meat, dried fish, and cow-tail.

Mummy reminded her that the food was getting cold, but Iya Agba hissed and turned away. "Owolabi, go and get my bags. I am going to sleep at Gbadebo's house. Your wife has shown that she does not respect my words. They probably have no elders in her family."

Mummy flinched. Mama Ejiwunmi fanned her legs at a furious pace. Daddy, silent until this moment, prostrated flat on the floor before Iya Agba. "Please don't go. We are very sorry."

Iya Agba turned her face away. When all his entreaties failed, Daddy relented and took her to his cousin's house for the night.

After they left I heard Mummy crying softly in her bedroom. When I tried to open the door, Mama Ejiwunmi appeared in the passage. "Go!" She waved sharply, chasing me away.

I sat alone in the empty sitting room, my heart pounding hard. Before this baby came our house had been full of laughter and happiness. Suddenly it was full of tears and shouting and sadness. It was all Eniayo's fault.

In those early weeks, I refused to go near Eniayo. When Mummy would ask me to hold the baby's bottle, I suddenly complained of stomach aches and ran off to use the toilet. The times when she danced with Eniayo around the sitting room to quiet her cries, I would go to Aunty Adunni in the kitchen. She is one of Mummy's relatives and had come to live with us after Mama Ejiwunmi returned home. And whenever Mummy brought Eniayo into the kitchen to find out what Aunty Adunni was cooking for our nightly meal, I would escape down the stairs into the backyard.

But no matter how fast I moved, those strange pale pink eyes followed me everywhere. And when Aunty Adunni carried Eniayo on her back as she did her housework, I could not escape my sister's stare as I ran from room to room.

Finally, Mummy grabbed my arm one day as I was slipping past her. "Morayo, what is wrong? What is chasing you?"

"I am scared of Eniayo," I said in a small voice, shifting from one foot to the other.

She looked puzzled. "Why?"

I repeated what I had heard Iya Agba say during her visit.

The puzzled look on Mummy's face changed into an angry one. On another occasion, my confession would surely have earned me some kind of punishment. I knew that children were not to eavesdrop on adult conversations. But that day Mummy just sighed. "Come," she said, sitting down with me in her bedroom while Eniayo slept in the other room. She put her arm around me. "My dear Morayo," she said gently, "your sister is not a spirit child. She is an *afin* due to some things the doctors call recessive genes. Okay?" For several minutes, Mummy continued to explain what the doctors had told them, waving her hands as she spoke. I did not understand most of what she said, but I was overjoyed to know that I did not have to sleep at night with one eye open anymore.

I looked up at Mummy's face. She reached over and patted me on the head. But there was one more thing I still needed to know. "Do we have to hide Eniayo inside the house?"

Her forehead furrowed. "Hide Eniayo?"

I dropped my voice. "Like Bolude."

Bolude was our neighbour's deaf and dumb son who rarely left their flat. Many mornings he would stand by their sitting room window and watch as his younger sister and I walked to school. Once, he returned my tentative wave. His sister looked around with wide eyes and pulled my hand down. "Stop it," she said in a fierce whisper. "People are watching."

"Bolude's matter is different," Mummy said with a dismissive shake of her head. "We have nothing to be ashamed of."

But I wasn't satisfied. "Do you mean that Bolude's parents did something wrong? What did they do?"

Mummy clicked her tongue. "You ask too many questions," she chided, pulling me close to her side. "Remember that you are the big sister. This means you must always take care of Eniayo. Have you heard me?"

"Yes, Mummy."

She gave me a pleased smile. "Come, let us go and see if Adunni needs some help making our dinner."

Somehow, as the days and months passed, I no longer noticed my sister's pale pink eyes. All I saw was Eniayo, an annoying little girl, calling my name, determined to follow me everywhere I went. And as the years passed, Eniayo's features, which had once looked so strange—her yellowish hair, her pink eyes, and her milky white skin—became as familiar and welcome to me as the sun in the sky.

Part One

MORAYO AND ENIAYO
1982~1988

"Rain, rain, go away.
Come again another day;
little Eniayo and Morayo want to play."

*H*olding hands, Eniayo and I danced around in our compound. Falling raindrops drummed out playful tunes on the colourful cotton dresses plastered to our bodies. With pink tongues sticking out to taste the rain, we laughed at the display of heavenly fireworks that lit up the wide open skies above the city of Ibadan.

I was ten years old. Eniayo was almost five. We lived near the Ibadan Polytechnic in a block of six flats right along the busy Poly-Sango Road. Our three-bedroom flat was up on the second floor of an old building with fading green paint and a rusty brown roof. Bold red letters painted above the front door told visitors they were entering Remilekun House. Remilekun was Baba Landlord's late mother.

Eniayo and I shared a bedroom. Mummy and Daddy each had theirs. Aunty Adunni was bothered by our night chattering and so she slept in the sitting room on a little foam mattress that she rolled up each morning.

We woke to the shouts of minibus conductors calling out their next destinations outside our window: "Sango, Mokola, Oke Padre!" Their regular calls were our alarm clock. Lake Eleyele, our source of drinking water, was on the other side of the road. The still green waters of the lake peeked through giant baobab trees standing guard along its banks.

By early afternoon, school was over and we often walked home in a group made up of other children from our street. After completing our homework and siesta, Eniayo and I were free to roam the streets with our friends. Our parents were rarely home in the afternoons—Daddy was a pharmaceutical salesman and often travelled, while Mummy had her tailor shop at Amunigun Market. She did not come back until late in the evening. Aunty Adunni stayed home with us but was usually busy with household chores. She was more than happy to have us out of her way.

One of our favourite things was to wave at the trains that ran right by the outskirts of our neighbourhood. Beside the train tracks, tall, dark Hausa traders with cat whisker–like tribal marks sold dried catfish impaled on short black sticks. They waved back when we walked by their tables. On the other side of the train tracks was the dusty little field we called "no man's land." That was where the schoolboys settled their disputes. There were no houses nearby and no adults to break up their fights.

On our way to the train tracks, Eniayo and I often stopped at my friend Tomi's house. Tomi lived in a little brick bungalow surrounded by a big compound. There was a swing in her yard. She was the only girl in our neighbourhood who had a swing. But she was also the only girl who did not have a father; he had died when she was three years old. The only other child we knew without a father was a boy named Babarinsa. His name meant "my father saw me and ran." His father had died just weeks before he was born.

"Morayo, can you imagine if that were my name?" Tomi once asked with a shudder while I pushed her on the swing. "Everybody would think it was my fault."

Most times, Tomi could be found waiting outside her house gate, chattering to her ever-smiling *mai-guard* who listened to her lively conversation but rarely said a word.

On clear afternoons, from Tomi's house we could see the smoke of the locomotive trains swirling high up in the air. Then we would run to the nearby ridge to watch the trains go by.

The first time Eniayo joined us she tugged frantically at my arm, her tiny glasses bouncing on her red, glowing face. "Morayo! Morayo! Look, look, the train is coming!" We watched and waved as the train slowly chugged by the grassy ridge where we stood. It overflowed with people, and some passengers sat on top of the train with their luggage strapped down beside them. We stared in wonder at a scowling man who held tightly onto a squealing baby goat in his lap.

Children with curious dark eyes peeked out of the train cab windows. One of them waved back at us. How we envied them! Tomi gazed longingly at the passing cabs. "I wish *we* could go on the train," she said.

I nodded. "Me too." We clasped our hands together and sighed.

The trains were going to the northern part of the country, and I had always wanted to know what the north looked like. Although Daddy, who travelled there all the time, said it was very hot, I could not imagine anywhere hotter than Ibadan.

Eniayo turned towards us. "Why can't we just go?" she asked.

Tomi and I looked at each other and burst into laughter. The thought of the serious *koboko* whipping that would await us at home was enough to drive away such foolish thoughts.

On our way back home, Eniayo and I stopped at Tomi's house for a short visit. Mrs. Adigun, Tomi's mother, was a caterer and she always offered us something wonderful to eat. The mouth-watering smell of frying fish pie greeted us when Tomi opened their front door. We trooped into the hot kitchen. "Good evening, Ma," we chorused as we fell to our knees in greeting.

Mrs. Adigun looked up from the pan of sizzling oil. "Good evening, girls. Morayo, how are your parents? It has been a while since I saw your mother."

"They are fine, Ma," I said. "Mummy has been very busy at her shop." Mrs. Adigun smiled at me, wiping the sweat on her forehead with the sleeve of her *buba*. Drifting black fumes from the smoking kerosene stove made my eyes sting.

Tomi signalled with her fingers that we should go back to the sitting room. Shortly after, Mrs. Adigun came out of the kitchen with a chipped porcelain plate piled high with golden-brown fish pies. "Morayo and Eniayo, I am sure you would like to eat some fish pie?"

Before Eniayo could say anything, I quickly spoke up. "No, Ma. Thank you, Ma. We ate just before leaving home."

Even as I refused the offer, the aroma from the fish pies reached my nose and my mouth flooded. I silently prayed that Mrs. Adigun would make the offer a second time so that I could say yes. Accepting Mrs. Adigun's first offer would have suggested that Mummy had failed to teach us good manners.

When Tomi visited our house, Mummy expected the same behaviour from her. I gave Mrs. Adigun a big smile when she repeated her offer. The warm flaky crust melted in my mouth.

Though I loved spending time with Tomi, I had another reason to want to visit her: a boy named Dotun. He was a friend of Tomi's older brother, Gbayi.

Dotun! So handsome, with large brown eyes framed by dark eyelashes that fluttered any time he laughed. He also had a few scraggly hairs growing above his light pink upper lip. Gbayi would chase us into the house whenever he caught us staring at his friend. But from Tomi's bedroom window, she and I took turns peeking at Dotun while the boys played.

"Morayo, guess what?" Tomi asked during an afternoon visit to her house. We were sitting on her bed, going through a pile of Macmillan Pacesetter novels. Tomi slid closer and whispered. "I found out that Gbayi and Dotun have been growing their moustaches by rubbing methylated spirits on their faces."

We both rolled with laughter while the thin silver bangles on my wrist clanged together.

Although he never said anything, Tomi and I were absolutely convinced that Dotun liked us too. He had to—he was always winking at us. Tomi and I kept a tally of who earned the most winks. Years later, we were stunned to find out that Dotun was not winking at us after all. The object of our affections had an uncontrollable facial tic. But even so, Tomi insisted that hers were real winks mixed in with the tics.

Clutching the novels I had picked out, I stood up. "I have to go. I promised that I would not stay long because of Eniayo." She was at home sulking because Aunty Adunni would not let her leave the house in a short dress.

Tomi nodded. "Let me see you off."

Mummy worried about exposing Eniayo's delicate skin to the
harsh sun, and always insisted that my sister wear long-flowing,
long-sleeved dresses. Eniayo hated the dresses since she could
not easily climb any of the three guava trees in our compound.
She so desperately wanted to see the colourful lights of the
Premier Hotel flashing afar from the top of Mokola Hill. At
night, the bright lights left a shimmering glow on the rusty
brown rooftops that dotted our neighbourhood. Once, when
she had managed to scale the nearby cement fence to launch
herself up, she slipped off the smooth bark of the tree. She
lay in a heap at the bottom of the tree and cried bitterly at her
bruised nose.

As Eniayo grew older, she found new ways to rebel against
the dress code. Hiding behind the house, she would cut up the
long dresses with a pair of scissors and wear the shorter gowns
she had already outgrown. To teach her a lesson, Mummy
took the scraps and sewed them together into funny-looking
patchwork dresses. At first Eniayo refused to wear them, but
Mummy took away her other clothes, and Eniayo had no choice.

The other children on the street laughed when they saw
her. "Here comes Lady Eniayo in her London dress," someone
shouted one day as Eniayo and I walked past a group of children
playing *ten-ten*.

"Unfortunate European, did you buy your dress when you
went to London to see the Queen?" one of the girls asked with
a mocking laugh.

"This one? *London dress?*" another child said, "I am sure
even the blind beggars in London would throw this dress back
in your face if you gave it to them!"

"Unfortunate European." "Blind Bat." The children threw these insults at my *afin* sister, but Eniayo would not let them see her cry. She would walk past them on the street with her head raised high and let her tears flow only after we walked into our compound. There were days when I wanted to punch those children, but if Daddy heard that I had fought, his *koboko* whip would come down from its place of honour on top of the fridge. "A child from a good home does not fight on the street," he would tell us with a wag of his finger.

Eventually, Mummy agreed that Eniayo could wear shorter dresses. That day my sister danced around the house, her face flushed red with happiness. "Morayo, see my dress," she said with a laugh, clapping her hands as she spun around the room. I could not help laughing along with her. Mummy and Aunty Adunni also had smiles on their tired faces.

Large black freckles and moles soon covered Eniayo's face, neck, and arms, but she did not care. She just wanted to do all the things that I could, and feel the sun's warm rays on her face.

I gave Eniayo a warning look and slowly pushed open the front door. We jumped when we saw Aunty Adunni standing by the door. She planted her hands on her hips. "Where are you two coming from?"

We kept quiet.

Rainwater dripped from our dresses and formed a small puddle of water around our feet. It had been my idea to sneak out of the house to dance in the rain. I had brought chicken pox home from school and Eniayo caught it from me. After five days of staying inside our bedroom, we were ready to escape.

Aunty Adunni clucked her tongue. "What is wrong with both of you? So you want to catch pneumonia too?"

She faced me. "Morayo, don't you realize that you are too old for this kind of behaviour?"

My eyes followed her downward gaze. My wet blouse had plastered itself to the little mounds on my chest. I quickly crossed my arms over them.

She gave me a pitiful look. "Quick! Go and dry yourselves."

Eniayo and I ran for our bedroom.

After towelling ourselves dry, we dipped our fingers into the big bottle of calamine lotion Daddy had brought home and painted each other's pox marks.

Eniayo flinched when I painted the pox marks on her arm. "Morayo, they hurt."

I gently dabbed at one that looked more like a blister. "I know. But you should not have been scratching them."

Tears slid down Eniayo's face. "They are so itchy."

"Mine itches too, but your skin is too delicate." I replaced the lid on the bottle and gently squeezed her hand. "Try and sleep."

Most nights, Eniayo and I talked about our day until one of us fell asleep. That evening, when Eniayo stayed quiet on her bed, I knew something was wrong. It was hard for me to see her face in the darkness. "Eniayo, what is it?"

The bedsprings creaked and I saw her sit up. "Morayo," she said, her voice sad and small. "Is it true that I was adopted as a baby?"

I was stunned. "Who said that you were adopted?" I blurted out.

Eniayo was silent. Despite my repeated badgering, she refused to tell me any name. The only person I could think of was one of those wicked children with loose lips living on our street.

"But Morayo," Eniayo insisted, "no one else in our family looks like me."

She was right.

"Listen to me, whoever told you that you were adopted is a liar," I said firmly. "Did I not see you with my own two eyes the day you were born? Think about it. Where would Mummy and Daddy find another child with our pointed ears?"

When I saw Eniayo's teeth flash in the darkness, I smiled.

Turning my head towards Eniayo's bed on the other side of the room, I saw her snuggle under her cover cloth. Minutes later, she was fast asleep. I laid my head on my pillow, and soon Eniayo's familiar soft snores lulled me to sleep.

2

It is from a small seed that the giant iroko *tree has its beginning.*

*E*niayo and I loved those quiet evenings when Daddy was home. Sometimes, if Mummy had a bad report for him, he would get angry with us and correct our behaviour, but mostly he made us laugh. We each had nicknames: Eniayo was *arewa,* beauty. Mine was *sisi,* young lady.

When we had stomach aches, Daddy would put his lips close to our stomachs and whisper softly. He called the words *incantations.* "I learned them from my father," Daddy explained—his father, who had been the medicine man at their village of Elewure, died long before we were born. Our grandfather's incantations always worked. Within minutes our stomach aches would vanish. Sometimes I would pretend to have one just so Daddy would put his warm lips on my stomach. But no matter how hard I tried, I could never make out the words he whispered.

Because our Daddy was *eni ti o ti apata dide,* a person who arose from a rock, that hard place, he was often at work travelling. But on those quiet evenings he was home, Eniayo and I would listen to him tell stories in the sitting room. Most evenings we sat under the bright blue lights of our Aladdin kerosene lamps. Electricity supply across the country was unreliable. The National Electric Power Authority (NEPA) was famous for blackouts. Any time the lights flickered out, Eniayo and I would raise our fists in the air and shout with frustration, "NEPA!" Outside, we heard our neighbours shouting too.

Mummy sat next to Daddy while he told us stories, and she would hum softly as she knitted.

Aunty Adunni often joined us after clearing up the kitchen. She would sit on one of the chairs across from Daddy, her stout legs neatly tucked away under a long wrapper while her soft brown eyes gleamed in the blue lights of the Aladdin lamps.

Most times, Daddy told us about the many adventures of Ijapa, the greedy, cunning tortoise, and his long-suffering wife, Yanibo. Other times, Daddy told us about his childhood in Elewure. Having spent all our lives in the city, the stories of village life sounded to us like folktales.

One evening, Daddy told us a folktale about a young man named Alao.

Daddy's deep voice filled the room as he began: *"Alo-o,"* he said.

"Alo!" Eniayo and I shouted back.

"*Oruku tindi tindi, oruku tindi tindi;* my story rumbles, flies straight like an arrow and lands on the head of Alao. Alao was a handsome, hard-working young man. When he walked through the village, he made the young maidens giggle shyly behind their fingers. On the days that Alao went to the stream to take his bath, the maidens would line his path with their specially marked loofah sponges. They waited, each anxious for Alao to pick up their sponge as a sign of his interest. But to their dismay, Alao would walk by the sponges with his head held up high."

Looking at each other with twinkling eyes, Eniayo and I giggled behind our palms. Pausing, Daddy smiled at us.

"One morning, Alao woke up to a terrible surprise. A sheep horn had grown right on top of his head! A panicked Alao ran, ran, and ran to the home of the village medicine man. The long ears of the *abetiaja* cap he wore to hide the horn flopped around his face. The medicine man, Baba Oloogun, took one look at Alao and shook his head. Baba Oloogun told Alao that there was only one remedy for the abomination growing on his head. That remedy was a potion made from the fresh excrement of an earthworm and the blood of a newborn flea. A desperate Alao searched high and low for the items, but all his searches were in vain.

"To the dismay of the village maidens, Alao no longer took his baths at the stream. Friends asked why Alao no longer wanted to participate in the wrestling matches where he had excelled.

"But how could he? Alao wondered. What if his cap fell off his head during one of the wrestling matches?

"Finally, when he could no longer bear the heavy weight of his secret, he shared it with his best friend. For months, Alao's friend kept the secret. However, as time passed by, keeping the secret became more and more difficult. In desperation, Alao's friend ran into the forest at the edge of the village and whispered the secret into the hollow of a large *odan* tree. Relieved, he quickly filled the hole with dead leaves and went back to the village."

Eniayo and I shifted in our seats. The fading blue lights of the kerosene lamp left shadows on Daddy's thin face.

"All was well until the day a great windstorm blew though the village. The powerful wind shook the trees vigorously until their heads bowed in submission. The dead leaves that Alao's friend had stuffed into the hollow of the *odan* tree fell out, scattering in the wind. Alao's secret rose among the tree branches, filling the pores of the broad leaves. The dancing leaves started chanting softy, Alao *wu iwo,* Alao *wu iwo,* Alao has a horn, Alao has a horn. Swift winds carrying the words blew them right over the village huts. Soon, the whole village knew Alao's shocking secret.

"The adoring looks on the faces of the village maidens changed to looks of disgust. Who wanted a monster for a husband? Little children ran, hiding under their mother's wrappers when Alao walked by. Only the gods could have cursed Alao, the villagers whispered in little groups that dispersed as soon as they saw him coming. One by one, his friends stopped going to his hut to drink palm wine and to play the *ayo* game.

"One day, the villagers woke up to find that Alao had packed up his belongings in the middle of the night and left. His footsteps led them straight to the edge of the river. His fishing canoe was gone. They never saw him again."

When Daddy finished the story, we sat there quietly. Even Mummy's knitting fingers stayed still for a while.

Eniayo suddenly spoke up. "Daddy?" She looked puzzled.

"Yes, Arewa."

I watched my sister's pale face as she searched for the questions. "Why … What does it mean?"

Daddy had once told us that folk stories were the mediums by which our ancestors taught life lessons. Now, as he smiled proudly at Eniayo, I wished I had been the one to ask the question.

"The lesson," he said, "is that if you don't want everyone to know your secret, don't share it with anyone."

Despite our age difference, Eniayo—who had inherited Daddy's tall, lean body—quickly towered over me. I was stuck with a shorter, rounder body. To add insult to injury, I also had rickets. My thin legs almost made a perfect zero from my hips down.

All through primary school, the boys in my class teased me mercilessly. They walked behind me, mimicking my awkward steps. They even double-dared each other as to who had the courage to squeeze themselves through the space between my legs. One day, out in the schoolyard, a boy actually tried. Our teacher, Mrs. Oni, had to run and rescue him, for I had sat down hard on his head. The satisfaction of hearing him squeal was worth the pain of having my knuckles rapped with the back of a wooden blackboard eraser. That night, I whispered the story to Aunty Adunni while she prepared our meal, and we both laughed until we heard Mummy in the sitting room.

While one of my legs did straighten out by the time I was thirteen, the other leg remained bent in at the knee. Instead of a perfect zero, my legs then looked like the letter K.

One afternoon, Mummy caught me staring unhappily in the full-length mirror in her bedroom. Smiling, she put her arm around my shoulders. "Morayo, *kilo de*? Why is your face so long?"

"Eniayo said that I look like a bottle of Imperial Stout."

Mummy frowned. "Don't mind her. Did your father not tell you that you look exactly like his mother? Have I not told you that she was a very beautiful woman?"

Daddy did say that all the time, but I was not so sure. We had only one grainy black-and-white picture of her in the house. The picture was from Daddy's graduation day. Mother and son stood beside each other, their arms held stiffly at their sides. Daddy, tall and thin, was dressed in his graduation gown; my grandmother, who barely reached her son's shoulders, had a big *gele* wrapped around her head, partially covering her face. Daddy was the only one out of his thirteen siblings to attend university. Many times, I stared at the grainy picture and wondered what her face must have looked like.

Mummy shook her head. "Eniayo, on the other hand, is just like your father's sister."

I agreed. Daddy's younger sister did have a sharp tongue. The good thing was that she lived in far-away Abidjan and did not visit Nigeria often. During her last visit to our house, she had looked me up and down and clucked. "It will be difficult for you to find a husband with those bowed legs." She said this as if commenting on a bad smell, then turned and went to the kitchen for a drink. From the look on her face, one would have thought that was the worst thing that could happen to me.

Mummy pursed her lips. "Come, my dear. Let us go look for your sharp-tongued sister. I have told her many times that that big mouth of hers will get her into trouble one day."

It was rare to see Mummy get angry, or hear her raised voice. Eniayo and I knew we were in big trouble if we ever heard her shouting our names. She stood at the top of the steps leading to the backyard. "Eniayo!"

In the sitting room, Eniayo's eyes widened when she heard her punishment. "I should frog-jump around the room ten times?"

I too gave Mummy a surprised look. She usually asked us to do "angle ninety." To do the punishment, we had to rest our backs straight against the wall and pretend we were sitting on a chair. In the elevated squat stance, our arms were stretched out at an angle of ninety degrees to our bodies. If our arms dropped or we sat on our buttocks, we received more punishment time.

Mummy gave Eniayo an unsympathetic look. "Yes. Next time, before your mouth shoots off like a runaway train, you will remember the pain."

Eniayo crouched on the floor, held onto her ears, and jumped. She only made it around the room four times before she started crying. "I am so sorry, Mummy," she begged.

"Are you going to call your sister names next time?" Mummy asked. By this time the tips of Eniayo's ears were bright red from all the pulling. She wiped a dripping nose with her blouse sleeve. "No, Ma."

"Good! Go to the bathroom and wash your face."

Head bowed, I waited for Eniayo outside the bathroom. When she opened the door, I gave her an apologetic smile. "How are your ears?"

Eniayo scowled. "Leave me alone." She slammed the door shut. I got my toes out of the way just in time.

The sound of the blaring honk from the ice-cream vendor riding past the house brought a slow smile to my face. I ran downstairs.

"Wait! Wait!"

The bicycle came to a halt. The twenty-five kobo Aunty Adunni had given me for helping to loosen her hair was still in my pocket. I handed over the coin. The vendor adjusted his wide-brimmed straw hat, opened the little metal cooler welded to his bicycle, and gave me a bar of Wall's French vanilla ice cream.

"Please, sir, can you cut it into two?" I asked. Nodding, he fished out a long rusty razor from his bag.

Back inside, I looked for Eniayo. When I found her in our bedroom, I sat beside her and handed over a half bar. For a minute Eniayo hesitated, and then she accepted my gift. We sat quietly, licking drops of vanilla from our fingers.

"Christmas is coming, New Year will follow.
Mama buy shoe for me, Papa buy dress for me.
O ya ya, o ya ya.
O ya ya, o ya ya."

Eniayo sang the song at the top of her lungs as she skipped around the room. It was the Saturday before Christmas.

Our cousin, Brother Tayo—Bros T—and his mother,

Aunty Tope, had come to Ibadan to spend the holiday with us. My grandmother Mama Ejiwunmi was also visiting—she was napping in the bedroom. Aunty Tope and Mummy had left the house earlier in the day. Mummy had gone to the shop to finish working on our Christmas dresses while Aunty Tope visited an old school friend.

I was in the sitting room, waiting for Aunty Adunni to straighten my hair with the hot comb that was heating up on top of the stove. When she applied a coat of Vaseline to the comb, I could hear the sizzle as the grease melted against the hot metal. I cried out in pain when a tiny drop of hot grease landed on my earlobe.

"*Pele,* Morayo. Sorry. Don't rub it," Aunty Adunni said, carefully running the hot comb through my kinky curls. I watched as a cloud of smoke rose from my hair.

Bros T walked into the living room. He stopped when he saw us. "Morayo, you are frying your hair *again?*" he asked with a smile. "I don't understand why you can't just perm the hair and stop punishing yourself."

The smell of scorched hair drifted to my nose. I sneezed. "Mummy said that I am too young to perm my hair."

"I see." Bros T turned to Eniayo. "Do you want to play *ayo* with me?" Eniayo, who had already had her hair straightened, ran off to get the wooden board.

Bros T's father had died in a car accident when he was just three years old. Aunty Tope, who did not remarry, poured all her love into their only child. He spent half of his long school holidays with us in Ibadan and the other half with his father's family in Ilesha. I once heard Aunty Adunni mutter to another cousin, "It would have done Tayo some good if his mother had held back some of that love." I didn't understand why.

Eniayo and I were always happy to have Bros T in the house. Aunty Tope had a successful business selling textiles and shoes in Jos, and made sure that her son had more than enough money to spend. He indulged us by paying for anything we wanted, and upon his arrival, we immediately started having visions of endless buckets of Fan Milk ice cream.

During his visits, Bros T would entertain us with exciting stories about his life in Jos. Once he told us that he was friends with one of the Sultan of Sokoto's sons. He said the Sultan's son had invited him on a caravan ride across the Sahara Desert with a band of Tuaregs from the neighbouring country of Niger. He described their daring escape from the bandits attacking their caravan. I could easily picture the jostling camels and the distinctive blue robes of the nomads. Most of his stories were highly exaggerated—or outright lies—but we loved Bros T anyway. His handsome face and infectious laugh always brought a smile to the females in the house.

Even Daddy the authoritarian was not immune to his charm. Somehow, Bros T always managed to talk himself out of getting a *koboko* whipping, even when everyone around could see that he truly deserved one.

I remember the day Bros T drove Mummy's car. Not only had he not asked for permission, he did not have a driver's licence. When he came back and met Daddy at home, he quickly prostrated. "Good afternoon, sir. I am so sorry about the car. I was just trying to surprise Aunty Bisoye so that I can drive if there is any emergency when you are not home."

Daddy's angry expression changed. "That is very thoughtful of you, Tayo. That will really help your aunty. But we have to get you a learner's permit first, okay?"

"Yes, sir."

Eniayo and I watched in amazement, for we were never so lucky!

Later that day, as Aunty Adunni prepared to go to the market, we heard her knocking things over in the kitchen. She soon came out to the sitting room. "Who took the money I left on the table?"

Money? Eniayo and I looked at each other and shook our heads.

"Not me," I answered.

"Me neither," Eniayo said.

Bros T kept quiet as Mama Ejiwunmi walked into the room and spoke up. "Adunni, how much is this money you are looking for?"

"Two hundred naira, Ma," Aunty Adunni answered, holding out the notes in her hand. "I left four hundred naira on the table. I found only half."

Mama Ejiwunmi turned to Bros T. "Tayo, did I not see you take some money from the kitchen just now?"

Bros T's mouth dropped. "Me? Mama, you saw me take money? I did not!"

Aunty Adunni looked at him with dimmed eyes. I held my breath, and beside me I felt Eniayo freeze. We knew Bros T had just returned from the kitchen with a bottle of Fanta.

"Tayo, empty your pockets. Empty them now," Aunty Adunni commanded.

Bros T stood to his feet quickly. "Why should I? I said that I did not take any money."

"Tayo." Aunty Adunni's voice was low. "Eh, I am warning you-o. If you don't empty your pockets right away, I will come and empty them for you."

Bros T gave her a defiant look.

Aunty Adunni took a step towards him.

Mama Ejiwunmi held up her hand. "Adunni, wait." She turned to Bros T. "Tayo, you know it's not a good thing to take things that don't belong to you." She beckoned him with her hand. "Please, my child, hand over the money to Adunni so that she can go to the market."

Bros T's face grew dark. "But I said that I did not take any money!"

Aunty Tope walked into a sitting room thick with silence. She looked around in surprise. "What is going on here?" she asked.

Mama Ejiwunmi faced her daughter. "Tope, thank God you are back. I saw Tayo take some money from the kitchen table. Adunni needs to go to market and Tayo has refused to give her the money he took."

"You saw Tayo take money?" Aunty Tope repeated, dropping her handbag on the settee.

My eyes followed the handbag as it fell to the floor—it was an Yves St. Laurent bag. I liked the shiny black leather and wanted to touch it. Mummy did not have any designer bags. "We don't have money for me to waste on such frivolous things," she had told me with a sigh when I asked why she did not have nice things like Aunty Tope. "It's the end of the month. Your father's people will soon be here to ask for money to pay their children's school fees or to start a new business." She gave a bitter laugh. "They forget that he too has a family to feed. When he begged them to go to school so that they could better their own lives, how many of them listened? Now we are the ones paying for their decisions. My child, truly a man of means in the midst of fifty paupers is a pauper too."

Aunty Tope's pencilled-in eyebrows met when she frowned.

"Why would he do that? He can ask for money any time he wants." She turned to her son. "Tayo, did you take any money from the kitchen?"

He pouted. "No, Mummy. I did not."

"See." Sitting down next to Mama Ejiwunmi, Aunty Tope smiled confidently. "Tayo did not take anything. Adunni, are you sure you did not misplace the money?"

Aunty Adunni shook her head. "I am very sure. Please, Ma, ask Tayo to empty his pockets."

Frowning, Aunty Tope sat back up. "Adunni, have you gone mad? So what if he has his own money in his pocket? Do you know the serial numbers of the money you are looking for?"

Aunty Adunni kept quiet, looking down at her toes.

"Tope, I saw Tayo take the money with my own eyes," Mama Ejiwunmi said quietly.

Aunty Tope gave her mother a pained smile. "Mama, didn't you tell me yesterday you have been having some problem with your eyesight?"

Mama Ejiwunmi's mouth dropped. "Ha! Tope! So my eyes are now too old to see the truth *abi*?" She shook her head. "Tope, you are spoiling this child. It will not end well."

Aunty Tope's face darkened. "I am not spoiling him, Mama. Is Tayo the only child in this house?" She pointed at me and Eniayo—and my sister shrank back behind me. "Why is it that when anything goes missing or wrong, he is the only child everybody points their finger at?"

Mama Ejiwunmi's voice was sad. "Is he not my child too?"

Aunty Tope glared in silence.

Sighing, Mama Ejiwunmi loosened the top of her wrapper to reveal the cloth money pouch tied around her waist. She unzipped it and counted out some money. Then she beckoned to Aunty Adunni. "Come, add this to your money so you can go to the market."

Aunty Adunni took the scrunched-up notes from Mama Ejiwunmi's hand. She left for the market in silence, avoiding the glares from Aunty Tope and Bros T.

Hissing, Aunty Tope got up from the chair and walked out of the house. Bros T followed behind his mother.

Mama Ejiwunmi shook her head, watching her daughter and grandson march out of the house with identical frowns on their faces. She sighed. "This world has evil and good living side by side, my children," she said. She stood slowly and walked towards the kitchen. "But sometimes it is difficult to tell where one ends and the other begins."

I had heard much about evil growing up, for we were often told that evil is the barren, one-toothed step-grandmother whose food we were never to eat. That evil is the no-good stranger lurking at the marketplace, waiting patiently for a chance to steal little children right from under the noses of distracted caregivers. "Run away the instant a stranger offers you a smile," Mummy would tell us. But no one told us that sometimes evil is found much closer to home, and that those who want to harm us can have the most soothing and familiar of voices.

3

The blame does not belong to the person with the protruding teeth. It is the god that created them that failed to cover their mouth with enough skin.

In February of 1984, we moved out of our three-bedroom flat into a new two-storey house on Eleyele Road, just minutes from our old neighbourhood.

Like Remilekun House, the house was painted light green, but its rooms were bigger and the louvres on the windows opened completely inside their black, burglar-proof metal casing.

For weeks, Mummy danced around the house with a smile on her face. "Finally. Something to show for all our years of hard work."

Daddy had started building the house not too long after Eniayo was born. Whenever he told Eniayo with a big smile that she had brought our family good luck, I remembered what those women said when she was an infant. They were wrong after all.

What I liked most about the new house was that we had our own bedrooms. Eniayo did not like sleeping alone, so she still came to my room at night. She would drag Aunty Adunni's old mattress and place it on the floor beside my bed. "Can I move to your room?" she begged one night. "Mummy said I can if you agree. I promise I won't make too much trouble." Eniayo stuck out her pink lips and batted long pale eyelashes behind her glasses.

Trying not to smile, I shook my head. "No."

"Please ..."

"Go and sleep in your own room. You should be thankful. How many other children have a room to themselves?"

"But something is calling my name at night," Eniayo whined.

I pursed my lips in disbelief. "When it calls, don't answer."

Eniayo's seventh birthday took place three months after we moved into the new house. Soon after we got home from school, our second cousin Aunty Morenike and her son Damilare arrived. An excited Eniayo ran and opened door. "Aunty Morenike! Damilare!"

Aunty Morenike's heart-shaped face lit up with a big smile. "Here comes the Birthday Girl." As usual, her petite figure was swimming inside a baggy blue-jean dungaree. I noticed how her neatly trimmed fingernails, painted a soft lavender colour, matched her lace blouse.

We knelt down to greet her. "Good evening, Aunty."

"Good evening," she replied, carrying in a big wicker basket. Three-year-old Damilare ran into the sitting room and tugged on Eniayo's arm. "Mummy made you a cake."

If our birthdays fell during the time she was home from teacher training college, Aunty Morenike baked cakes for us.

On my last birthday, she made me a pink and purple butterfly cake. "That is because you are beautiful like a butterfly," she said with a smile. Aunty Adunni rolled her eyes. "She is also as restless as one."

I collected the wicker basket from Aunty Morenike and set it down on the dining table. She lifted the blue-checkered kitchen towel and revealed a round chocolate cake decorated with multicoloured Smarties.

Eniayo's face turned red when she saw the cake. She wrapped her arms around Aunty Morenike's waist. "It is so beautiful. Thank you!"

Mummy, who had come home early from her shop for the celebration, gave Aunty Morenike a pleased smile. "Morenike, this is really nice."

Aunty Morenike waved her hand. "It is nothing, Aunty."

After we sang the birthday song, Damilare swiped the side of the cake and filled his mouth with Smarties.

Aunty Morenike wagged a finger at her son and scowled. "Damilare!"

Laughing, Damilare ran to the other side of the room. Aunty Morenike caught him and picked him up. "*Oya*, tell your cousin that you are sorry for spoiling her cake."

The rest of us turned and found Eniayo's cheeks bulging from the Smarties she had scooped from her side. Damilare's eyes widened and he shook his head. "Eniayo bad," he said in a small accusing voice. We all laughed.

After a dinner of *jollof* rice and chicken, Mummy persuaded Aunty Morenike to spend the night with us.

The following morning, I sat at the back of the house peeling a bowl of black-eyed beans. Aunty Adunni sat close by starching Daddy and Mummy's clothes.

Damilare was outside with us. He ran around the backyard chasing Mummy's prized chickens. Every few minutes, he shrieked and held onto my legs when the mother hen angrily flapped her wings at him. She chased him to the big rock at the corner of the compound. He clambered on top while she circled around it. His cries made Aunty Adunni look up from her task with a smile.

Hearing a car honking loudly at the house gates, I quickly rinsed off my hands. Who could be visiting us this early in the day? I opened the padlock and was surprised to see Aunty Tope's driver pull into the compound. As soon as Aunty Tope opened the car door, I knelt down in the warm sand to greet her.

"*Ekaaro*, Aunty Tope. How was your journey from Jos?"

"Morayo, *kaaro*. Our journey went very well," Aunty Tope said, looking up at the house. She seemed distracted, but she studied me. "You are a big girl now. You are almost as tall as me. How old are you now?"

I smiled proudly. "I am twelve, Ma."

I hadn't seen Aunty Tope in almost two years. I reached for her handbag and we headed for the house. She looked around the compound and noticed that there were no parked cars. "Is your Mummy home?"

"Yes, Ma, she is," I answered. "Daddy is travelling on a business trip to Gboko."

Mummy must have heard Aunty Tope's voice through the open windows, because she ran out of the house with a wide smile on her chubby face. Eniayo skipped behind her with her half-plaited head.

"Sister *mi*!" Mummy shouted with joy, giving Aunty Tope a big hug. "I hope everything is okay. But you did not say that you were coming to see us when we spoke last week."

"I know, I know. The whole journey just happened at the last minute, my dear *aburo*." Then Aunty stepped back, her mouth wide open in surprise. "It is a lie! Eniayo, is this you?" She pulled Eniayo up to her feet. "I would not have recognized you on the street. Ha, Bisoye, you have done a very good job with my girls."

Mummy beamed. "Sister *mi,* I am trying my best. Please come in."

Luckily, NEPA had given us electricity overnight and the soft drinks in the fridge were still cold. Aunty Adunni helped me gather bottles of Coke and Mirinda, and by the time I came back with some clean tumblers and a bottle opener, Mummy and Aunty Tope were in the sitting room. Mummy gave me a quiet smile of approval as I poured a bottle of Coke for Aunty Tope. Aunty Tope took a long drink. I could hear the liquid going down her throat.

Aunty Tope turned to me. "Thank you, my dear Morayo. I did not know that I was this thirsty."

Eniayo and I brought in Aunty Tope's luggage and opened the presents she had brought. Soon I was back to peeling the swollen beans behind the house. Aunty Adunni had yam cooking on the stove, and she was busy chopping up fresh spinach leaves for *egusi* soup. Mummy and Aunty Tope disappeared into Mummy's bedroom, and I was about to knock on her door when I heard the sound of crying behind it. My hand hovered in front of the door handle. I did not want to get into trouble for interrupting, so I moved closer and pressed my ear against the door.

Someone *was* crying.

I heard Mummy's soft voice. "Sister *mi,* please. We will figure out what to do. I do not like all this crying. After all, nobody died."

"Ah Bisoye, I am finished. Tayo has finished me," Aunty Tope wailed. "Imagine the audacity to slap your own school principal! *Kilo de?* And this past long holidays, he and his friend Abu stole a suitcase full of foreign currency from Abu's father. That boy almost slept in prison! This headstrong …" She paused, and then continued, "What is he now, a half-man, half-boy?"

"Sister *mi,*" my mother said softly. I could imagine her stroking her sister's shoulders to comfort her.

"Bisoye, I have nowhere else to turn. I cannot send him to live with his father's people with this kind of behaviour. What would they think of me? I know Owolabi is still angry, but I want Tayo to finish his education here. He has to go to university. What else I am working for? But he needs the firm hand of a man to guide him."

When I heard footsteps coming towards me, I fled to my bedroom.

Two years earlier, Bros T had finally managed to get into Daddy's bad books. We were watching the NTA national nightly news when we heard loud screaming coming from the bathroom. Mummy bolted up from her chair. Seconds later, Aunty Adunni ran into the sitting room. She had a short bath towel wrapped around her soapy body. "Tayo!" she blurted out. "That wayward boy, he was spying while I took my bath!"

Mummy shuddered, both hands flying to the top of her head. "Are you sure?" she asked. Aunty Adunni nodded. She started crying.

Daddy had been listening from his chair. He bellowed, "Tayo!" His eyes smouldered. "Come here now!"

Bros T ran into the sitting room. When he saw Daddy's face, he stopped in his tracks.

"Tayo, is it true?" Daddy asked.

Bros T's face changed and his dimpled chin quivered.

"Aunty Adunni, me?" He quickly prostrated on the carpeted floor. "Sir, as God is my witness, I did not go into the bathroom to spy on Sister Adunni. I was urinating when she pushed back the shower curtain to look at *me*." Bros T pointed to some wet spots on his trousers. "See. I don't understand why she is telling a lie against me, sir." Shaking his head, he added, "But she has never liked me."

Aunty Adunni charged across the room and gave him a hot slap. She managed to scratch his face before Mummy pulled her away from him. Mummy had to hold her down.

The next day, Mummy called Aunty Tope in Jos. She arrived in Ibadan three days later. When Mummy told her what had happened, Aunty Tope insisted that it all had to be a misunderstanding. Eniayo and I could hear her shouting from Mummy's room.

"Bisoye, please tell me why Tayo would want to see Adunni naked? Are they not blood relatives?"

"Sister *mi*," Mummy said calmly, "all the years Adunni has been living with us, I have never known her to tell a lie."

"So you brought me all the way from Jos to insult me?" Aunty Tope yelled. "So I am the one with a liar for a son. Because he was caught lying one time? Just once?" Eniayo and

I exchanged knowing looks. The number of times we had heard Bros T lie was more than both our fingers and toes combined.

"And now you fling my shame in my face! Thank you very much, my dear sister. I am taking my child home today."

Mummy did not try to change her mind, and when Aunty Tope left with Bros T, the whole house heaved a deep sigh of relief.

Later that year, we heard that Bros T was no longer at his private school. A female student in his class reported that he tried to force his way into her bedroom late one night. When Aunty Adunni heard the news, she just shook her head and hissed in disgust. "Character is like smoke, and no matter how much his mother tries to cover it, that boy's character will eventually rise to the surface."

Now, two years later, Aunty Tope was back in our house, asking Mummy to forgive the past and take in her son.

By the time Mummy and Aunty Tope emerged from Mummy's room that morning, Aunty Morenike and Damilare had left. Looking at Aunty Tope's freshly powdered face, you would not have guessed she had just been crying. She stayed with us for two days before she returned to Jos. Daddy was coming back from Gboko later that week.

After Aunty Tope left for Jos, I told Aunty Adunni that Bros T might be coming back to the house. Her eyes widened. "Who told you?" she asked with a dark look on her face. I was not going to admit I had been eavesdropping. "I just have a feeling." I said, backing out of the kitchen. She narrowed her eyes, but I kept my mouth shut.

Whenever Mummy needed a favour from Daddy, she would ask Eniayo and me to go down the street to buy two bottles of Guinness from Mama Kachi's wooden kiosk. This time, she made sure both bottles were chilled and waiting for Daddy before his nightly meal. She served his food herself, waiting patiently until he was halfway through the first bottle before presenting her petition.

But the Guinness was not working its customary magic with Daddy. When Mummy came back to the kitchen without her usual satisfied smile, we knew she had been unsuccessful. Aunty Adunni, Eniayo, and I all escaped to our bedrooms. No one wanted to be the scapegoat.

The next day, Mummy launched a campaign that would have made any army general envious. For weeks she prepared Daddy's favourite meals. She subjected him to long stretches of silent treatment. Then she slid into bouts of crying, until Daddy finally caved. It took her over three months, but she finally got her way.

Yes. Bros T could come and live with us.

When Aunty Adunni found out, I knew she was not happy. She would probably have returned to her parents' house if she had a choice in the matter. But instead, she begged Mummy to let her go and live in one of the rooms in the Boys' Quarters.

She knelt before Mummy with tears in her eyes. "Please, Ma," she begged. "If Tayo is coming back to the house, I will feel better if I move outside."

The Boys' Quarters was the little building behind the main house. It had two rooms and a little kitchen. When they built the house, Mummy and Daddy had planned to rent them out, but the rooms were still empty.

Looking at Aunty Adunni's anxious face, Mummy sighed.

"I will talk to Daddy Morayo when he gets back home next week."

Three weeks later, Eniayo and I helped Aunty Adunni move her things to the Boys' Quarters.

The following week, Bros T's six-foot frame swaggered into our house with a Brother Johnson afro, two large blue suitcases, and his handsome, cocky smile. Aunty Tope did not come with him. She had sent him with her driver instead.

Daddy was home when he arrived. He took one look at Bros T's lopsided afro and decreed an immediate trip to the barbershop. "No wonder you have been misbehaving," Daddy said. "Your brain is not getting enough oxygen with all that hair on your head."

Daddy bundled Bros T into the car and drove him to his barbershop, Marindoti at Mokola. An hour later, a sombre-looking young man returned to the house. I could almost see my reflection in his shiny *gorimapa* head. The cocky smile was gone and his eyes burned like hot coals. Mummy called Eniayo and me aside. "You had better stay out of Tayo's way tonight," she warned.

Finishing her work in the kitchen, Aunty Adunni greeted Mummy good night and escaped to her room.

"Tayo, your food is on the table."

A sullen Bros T looked up. "Thank you, Ma, but I am not hungry."

Mummy gave him a surprised look. "You are not hungry? But you have not eaten anything since you came from Jos. *Oya dide.* I said stand up. The food is getting cold."

Bros T quietly declined again.

Daddy sat behind his newspaper, pretending that he could not hear Mummy begging Bros T.

Eniayo and I exchanged looks. We knew better than to refuse food because we were angry. A proper *koboko* whipping would drive the food-refusing spirit out of us. Then we would hear the speech about the hungry street orphans who would have gladly exchanged places with us. Lastly, we would sit at the dining table with tears wiped from our faces to clean our plates with the proper display of gratitude.

Some time back, due to the Structural Adjustment Program's austerity measures, we had to eat beans every afternoon for three weeks straight. Mummy kept telling us they would make us grow taller, but we were not convinced. Finally, one evening Eniayo looked at her watery bowl of beans and back at Aunty Adunni's face. "Aunty, the weevils are more than the beans!" she wailed. Daddy's glare was reply enough. We both finished our beans quickly.

If Bros T knew that Daddy was just getting started, he would have caught the next bus back to Jos. The following Monday, Daddy took Bros T to the free, government-run secondary school within walking distance of our house and enrolled him in classes. He had to repeat the final year of secondary school.

Mummy was not happy about the school because it was rundown and had no windows. During the rainy season, the teachers used buckets to catch the water dripping on the students. Students had to bring their own wooden tables and chairs from home.

Daddy hired a teacher, named Mr. Bada, from the school to serve as Bros T's private tutor. Mr. Bada came to the house every day after school. Between school, private lessons, and house chores, Daddy was determined that Bros T would have no time on his hands to make mischief. And he did not. Within one week, Bros T went from a pampered child driven to his expensive private school to a boy who walked to public school every morning. On Saturday mornings he rose early to wash the cars, cut the grass, and do other duties around the house.

On Bros T's first day of school, the sight of his long hairy legs sticking out from his grey khaki school shorts sent Eniayo and me rolling with laughter. We both forgot Mummy's warning. Bros T scowled. "What are you two laughing about?"

We instantly quieted. For a minute, I was sure he would knock us on our heads. But he must have realized that he did look funny in the uniform, because he tried to hide his own smile—and for a moment, I could see the Bros T I remembered from years before.

As the months passed, Daddy became impressed with Bros T's hard work and diligence. And the worried look on Mummy's face gradually faded away. It seemed as if Bros T's actions during his last visit were not going to define his new relationship with Daddy. Even Aunty Adunni stopped escaping to her room behind the house at every opportunity.

One Saturday afternoon, Bros T took us to the Trans Amusement Park. On the half-hour bus ride from Eleyele to the outdoor park near the University of Ibadan, Eniayo could barely contain her excitement. She whispered, "Morayo, are you sure they will still be open by the time we get there?"

After we arrived at the park gates and bought our tickets Eniayo ran off towards the bumper cars. Bros T started laughing. "Eniayo, come back!"

With an impatient look on her face, Eniayo stopped. "But you people are too slow," she said. "Hurry!"

Two hours later, Bros T asked, "Are you girls ready to go home?" We had gone on the carousel ride, the dragon roller coaster, and the bumper cars more than three times each.

"Home?" Eniayo shook her head. "I don't want to go home yet."

I sat on Bros T's lap at the picnic area. He fiddled with my braids. "Do we have to go home now?" Eniayo asked. "It is not yet dark."

I turned to look at Bros T. I did not want to go home either. The park would be open for another three hours. Since it was a Saturday evening, there were many children running around. At the table next to ours, a little boy was blowing out candles on his birthday cake.

"Please, can we go for one more ride on the bumper cars?" I asked.

Bros T gave me a wink. "Okay, girls. Just one more time."

By the time Aunty Tope came to visit her son at the end of the first school term, he was much changed from the discontented-looking young man her driver had dropped off four months earlier. She stayed with us for the duration of the first-term holidays and observed Mr. Bada's tutorials. Bros T's university entrance examinations were coming up fast, and Daddy regularly reminded him that failing his examinations was not an acceptable option.

Aunty Tope was delirious with happiness at Bros T's progress. She held Mummy's hands and danced around the room. To show her gratitude, she took Eniayo and me to

Adamasingba Shopping Complex. "So what kind of dresses do you want? And which store should we go to?"

On several occasions Eniayo and I had been to the complex with Mummy. Tomi had a maxi chiffon gown with an empire waistline that I had admired. I knew where she had bought the dress at the complex. "Can we go to International Clothing?" Mummy had said the dresses at the store were too expensive, but I didn't tell Aunty Tope that. Aunty Tope had money.

She smiled at me. "I don't see why not. Eniayo, do you like that store too?"

Eniayo nodded. "Yes, Ma. They have very nice dresses."

"Morayo, when we get to the complex, you can lead the way," Aunty Tope said. She bought us five imported dresses each. I even found the same dress Tomi had, only mine had a floral green pattern while hers was yellow.

"Thank you, Ma," we chorused as Aunty Tope paid for the dresses. We proudly held the bags with our dresses to our chests.

Inside the car, we were surprised when Aunty Tope asked her driver to take us to the Bata store. "Girls, we are not yet done. I think your new dresses deserve new shoes."

Eniayo and I looked at each other in amazement. New dresses and shoes—all in one day? When Aunty Tope allowed me to pick the shining patent shoes with two buckles at the side, I was happy beyond words. It was Christmas, Easter, and our birthdays all rolled into one special day.

Mummy smiled gently as Eniayo and I danced around the house, modelling our dresses and shoes. And with her mind finally at rest that her son was going to finish secondary school and go on to attend university, Aunty Tope returned to Jos.

4

*The enemy lurks in the courtyard,
the evildoer lives within the home.*

"Good morning, class!"

"Good morning, sir!" we shouted back from our desks.

Our J.S.S. 3 biology teacher, Mr. Ojo, stood in front of the class with his legs wide apart, his thumbs tucked in the tight waistband of his Bongo trousers. The black hair on Mr. Ojo's chest curled over the neckline of his pink shirt. The hair snaked around his neck to join the hairy bush covering half of his face. He even had long hairs growing out of his ears and on each finger knuckle. Behind his back, we called him "Missing Link."

The boy sitting in front of me, who had been sleeping, nodded his head into the concrete wall beside him. He jerked awake and rubbed his head without a sound while the rest of us waited for instruction. That boy was always falling asleep at school. Tomi and I thought that perhaps a tsetse fly had bitten him, giving him the sleeping sickness. Looking at the back of his head, I could see the numbers 666 clearly written on the shining scalp with a black permanent marker—Bembe's handiwork—and I muffled a giggle.

Mr. Ojo walked over to the teacher's desk. He cleared his throat. "Open your textbooks to chapter eleven. Today we are going to talk about meiosis and sexual reproduction." He picked up a piece of chalk and wrote the topic on the blackboard.

We quickly flipped through the pages of our *Modern Biology* textbook, keeping straight faces as Mr. Ojo rushed through the chapter. He cleared his throat and tugged at his shirt collar endlessly; it was obvious he was embarrassed. When he asked if we had any questions, no one raised a hand.

Twice I looked up to find my friend Kachi, who sat on the other side of the class, sneaking glances at me. Kachi's mother owned the little wooden kiosk at the end of our street where she sold food, drinks, and kerosene. It was where Eniayo and I always bought Daddy's bottles of Guinness. I kept my face turned away from the slanted brown eyes shining from Kachi's light-skinned, oblong face.

During the first morning break, I sat with a group of girls on the tree stumps behind our classroom. Tomi, who did not mind getting the bottom of her red-checkered school uniform dirty, sat cross-legged on the thick layer of sandy creeping fern. Ireti was the class expert on the matters we had learned in biology that day, since she was thirteen and repeating the grade. She was also the first girl to grow breasts.

Tomi whispered, "Ireti, is it true that if you let a boy touch them"—she pointed to Ireti's breasts—"they will keep growing bigger and bigger?"

We all watched Ireti expectantly. Our mothers had told us this—could it be untrue? Ireti rolled her eyes and smiled knowingly. "It is not true," she said in a loud whisper. Looking around, she moved closer. "I know because I let Bembe touch them and nothing happened."

We all gasped with a mixture of shock and grudging respect. Ireti was always so fearless. But how could she have let a boy touch her? And *there*? As if that was not bad enough, of all the boys in the world—why, oh why, Bembe!?

Wide-eyed, Tomi and I looked at each other. We both remembered our mother's promises. "If you let a boy touch any part of your body," Mummy had told me once as she knitted, "I will find out. I will smell it on you and I will know." She stopped and raised her silver needle. "If I catch you, Morayo, I will kill you before you bring shame to this family!" She narrowed her eyes. "Yes, I brought your life into this world and I can snuff it without batting an eyelash!"

I wanted to ask Ireti how it felt when Bembe touched her there. But seeing the faces of the other girls, I kept quiet. I giggled with them when Ireti described how Bembe's eyes had grown as large as a teacup saucer when he slipped his hand under her school blouse.

That evening after school, I saw Kachi at his mother's kiosk. I was buying a bottle of palm oil, and as he handed me the change, his long warm fingers lingered over mine. I snatched my hand away, remembering the disturbing looks from him during biology class. Mumbling a quick thank you, I turned to hurry home.

"Morayo," he called.

I stopped.

"Are you coming to watch me play at the soccer match tomorrow evening?"

Kachi had never asked me that before.

The boys in our neighbourhood were on the soccer field

rain or shine—and we girls were their unofficial supporters club. We pretended to be near the school field to pick the juicy wild mangoes that littered the ground, but it was obvious that we came to watch them play. After their game, the boys climbed the tall mango trees to pick fresh fruit for us.

But until that day, no boy had ever invited me to watch a game.

Before I could answer, a brown-and-yellow taxi pulled up and parked in front of the kiosk. Mama Kachi stepped out, so I greeted her and ran home as fast as my legs could carry me.

My fingers still tingled from Kachi's touch.

The next evening, the soccer match was held at our school's football field. Since it was a Friday and there was no school the next day, we all sat on the grass to talk and eat the wild mangoes from the nearby trees. The hot afternoon sun had cooled considerably and we were in no hurry to go home. Kachi sat with the boys. I sat with the girls. Several times, I caught Kachi staring at me as he absent-mindedly pulled out the long yellow dandelions growing around him.

Bembe, the team's goalkeeper, started the *yabis*. His real name was Bambo but we all called him Bembe, like the drum, because of his huge pot belly. What Bembe lacked in height, he made up for with his sharp tongue. His *yabis* were very funny but often cruel. Thankfully, we girls were rarely his targets.

Bembe soon started describing the latest escapade of Biyi's father, who was legendary for his ability to sniff out a family still eating their night meal as he passed by. He always managed to knock on a door just when the food was brought to the table.

When the other men went to work in the morning, he was often seen lounging about, a chewing stick in his mouth and a wrapper tied loosely around his waist.

"Biyi's father will easily win the award for the most shameless man on our street!" Bembe said, laughing. I felt sorry for Biyi when I saw the shame that clouded his eyes before he too joined awkwardly in the other boys' laughter.

Kachi must have seen the look on Biyi's face too, because he quickly spoke up. "By the way, Bembe, last week I saw your father at Bere Market hawking *kan kan* sponges he made from his beard. Are things really that bad at home now?"

The boys howled and rolled with laughter in the grass. Biyi's laughter was the loudest. Bembe's father grew his beard so long and bushy that it was almost impossible to see his mouth when he spoke. Not to be outdone, Bembe laughed dryly. "Yes, things are bad. You know we are not all rich like your tycoon office-messenger father. The good thing about my father selling his beard is that mad people—like your mother!—are always at the market looking for good sponges to buy."

The laughter died instantly. The air stood still.

Mothers were never meant to be part of the *yabis*.

Immediately, Kachi stood and marched towards Bembe. The other boys jumped up, planting themselves between the two boys. They all seemed to be shouting at Bembe at once.

"Bembe, why now?"

"Bembe, how could you?"

"Bembe, that is not good."

For a moment, I thought Kachi might punch Bembe. Kachi towered over the rest of the boys and could have easily beaten Bembe if he wanted to.

Hiding behind the other boys, Bembe's mouth was still

running at full force. "*Eyin* boys, please leave Kachi alone. Let him come and meet his master. If he thinks that because he chews raw cassava every evening he can fight me and win, he had better think again."

Biyi gently laid his hand on Kachi's arm. "Kachi, don't mind Bembe. You know he has a big mouth." Kachi turned away from the group and started walking back towards his house.

After that day, Kachi stopped coming to the soccer field. I still saw him at school and at his mother's kiosk. But I found it was not the same watching the games without seeing Kachi's tall, slim figure running across the field.

A couple of months after the incident on the soccer field, I was on my way to Tomi's house when I heard a familiar voice call my name.

"Morayo! Wait."

Kachi ran towards me. Panting slightly, he stopped at my side. "Where are you going?"

"And why are you asking?" I replied, lifting my eyebrow.

Kachi smiled. "What is it with you Nigerians? Why must you always answer a question with a question?"

I rolled my eyes. "See the pot calling the kettle black. Did you not just answer my own question with a question?"

He laughed and moved closer to where I stood.

Tugging at my skirt, I gave Kachi a look from the side of my eyes. I suddenly felt uncomfortable at the way he was staring at me. "Well if you must know," I said, "I am going to Tomi's house."

Kachi scratched his head and licked his lips nervously. "Are you going to stay there for a long time? I want to talk to you. I can wait for you near Sesan's house if you are not going to be long."

Trying to mask my excitement, I said coolly, "I am not going to be there long. You can wait if you'd like."

Tomi and I were studying for our geography test, but I could not concentrate and kept jumbling up the answers. "Morayo, what are you thinking about?" Tomi asked with a frown. "Please tell me, when did Conakry become the capital of Ghana?"

Smiling sheepishly, I closed my textbook and swung my feet off the bed. The truth was that I could not wait to hear what Kachi had to tell me. "I am sorry. I think I should start for home. We can go over the answers again tomorrow during our first break." I stood and picked up my school bag.

"Okay. Let me go and tell Mummy that I am seeing you off."

Tomi was surprised when I insisted she did not need to escort me halfway home. This was our usual routine, but I did not want her to see Kachi waiting for me. Shrugging her shoulders, Tomi walked me to the front of their gate and turned back.

I found Kachi and Sesan sitting outside Sesan's house. When the boys saw me, Sesan got up and went inside his bungalow.

"You did not stay long at all," Kachi said as he approached.

"I told you."

Kachi held a polythene bag of *agbalumo* that he had picked from the star-apple tree behind Sesan's house. We walked slowly towards the train tracks adjacent to our street. It was starting to get dark, but I wanted to hear what Kachi had to say. I knew a place where we could sit and talk—the same grassy ridge where Tomi, Eniayo, and I went to wave at the trains.

Sitting with my legs tucked under my skirt, I rubbed an *agbalumo* with both hands to soften it. I split the ripe fruit open and ate the pulp, wincing at the sweet and sour taste.

Kachi was still rubbing his own *agbalumo* between his palms. He seemed tongue-tied. He finally spoke up. "Em ... Em ... I just wanted to say—that I like you." He looked at me expectantly.

Inside my heart sang: *He likes me, he likes me!*

Outwardly, I calmly removed the seeds of the *agbalumo* from the pulp, sucking hard and spitting them into the grass. After making Kachi wait for a couple of minutes, I smiled. "I like you too." Kachi beamed.

Next morning, I told Tomi what had happened. She laughed. "I said so. The two of you are always making cow eyes at each other in class."

When Tomi started singing my name and Kachi's, I quickly covered her mouth with my hand. "Tomi!" My heart was beating fast. Mummy was home and I knew that if she heard Tomi pairing my name with a boy's she would question me. Mummy had said that I could not have a boyfriend until I was in university. Tomi's mother had told her the same.

Laughing, Tomi gently nipped my hand. Tomi liked Kachi because he was always nice to the girls in our class. Unlike most of the other boys, he had never tried to see our underwear by rolling a mirrored pencil sharpener under our desks.

But soon Tomi complained that I used my visits to her house as an excuse to see Kachi at his mother's kiosk. I brushed this off, but I had to admit I often begged Tomi to come along with me to the kiosk so that I could see Kachi after school.

On the days when I could not get Tomi to leave her house with me, Eniayo would come. Her price was usually a bottle of Fanta and one packet of Okin biscuits. She would sit happily at one end of the wooden bench sipping on her cold Fanta while Kachi and I sat at the other end giggling and whispering.

Whenever Mummy or Auntie Adunni sent me to Kachi's mother's kiosk to buy something, I would put Vaseline petroleum jelly on my lips to make them shine. On the days when Mama Kachi was not at the kiosk, Kachi would ask one of his younger sisters—either Adanna or Ogadinma—to mind the kiosk while he walked me halfway home. If it was getting dark Kachi would hold my hand. When we saw a car approaching, he would quickly drop it and walk ahead of me. We could not risk being caught in the headlights of the car. One evening the headlights belonged to Daddy's car. I thought my heart was going to stop beating from the fear, but luckily, he did not see me.

When our classmates realized that Kachi and I were *in like* with each other, they teased us endlessly. I laughed with them, but in truth, something was going on inside of me and I did not know how to put my new emotions into words. I was growing hair in new places, too, and thinking about Kachi all the time. I was afraid to share these feelings with my friends—even Tomi. What if my secret got out? What if my mother heard about it?

Once, I built up my courage and tried talking to Mummy about it. We were alone in her bedroom. I was folding her newly washed clothes and she was arranging them inside the wardrobe.

"Mummy?"

"Yes, Morayo. What is it?"

"Em … I have been feeling … funny." Biting my lip, I stopped. I was not sure how to describe what I was feeling for Kachi.

A worried look flitted across Mummy's face as she touched my forehead. "Are you feeling sick?"

I shook my head. "No, Ma. I am not feeling sick." I took a deep breath. "In biology class, our teacher talked about how our bodies change during puberty and how we start having new feelings about boys …"

Mummy suddenly slammed the wardrobe door shut. The wooden door rattled on its hinges. Startled, I jumped back.

"Morayo, what kind of nonsense talk is this?" She wagged her finger. "Listen. Your job right now is to focus on your books and behave like the well-brought-up child you are. Have you heard me?"

"Yes, Mummy." I bit down hard on the inside of my cheek and picked up the empty laundry basket. I left the room. I should have known better than to ask her anything.

During this time, it suddenly felt strange when Bros T pulled me onto his lap when we sat in the sitting room. Some days, he would sneak up behind me and hug me tightly, laughing as if we were playing a game. But it was starting to feel like a game whose rules I did not know. Sometimes in the car, he would stretch his arms across my back, brushing his hands against the sides of my chest. I knew that something did not feel right, but Bros T was always physically affectionate. When Mummy returned from the salon, he often put his arm around her shoulders and complimented her on her newly set jerry curls. With her forehead still shining with the gel activator, she chided his sweet mouth even as a pleased smile crossed her face.

Mummy never said anything when Bros T pulled Eniayo or me onto his lap, but one evening, Daddy walked in and saw Bros T playing with us. He stopped suddenly and looked strangely at me. Then he snapped, "Morayo, are you not too old for this kind of behaviour? Get off Tayo's lap now."

Mummy had been present in the room all the while. She just looked up at Bros T and me and smiled. "Your father is right, Morayo. You are turning into a young *sisi* now. I am sure you won't want your friends to see you sitting on your brother's lap?"

As far as Mummy was concerned, her sister's child was her child too. Eniayo, who had been sitting beside Mummy, hopped over and sat on Bros T's lap. "*Shebi,* I am not too old to sit on Bros T's lap, am I Mummy?" she asked with her cheeky grin.

Daddy narrowed his eyes but said nothing. Mummy and Eniayo started laughing. I moved over to the other side of the room, and could not help noticing Bros T's eyes following me.

Aunty Morenike was different from my other female cousins. She did not treat me as if I was an annoying child. Even when she did not answer my questions directly, she never scolded me for being too inquisitive. Maybe it was because of her *experience.* Years ago, I overheard another cousin say that Aunty Morenike's child Damilare was a result of her *experience with men.* That it was a shame that Damilare had no father to speak of.

Aunty Morenike reminded me of an *agbalumo* fruit. The sourness of the first bite would make me clench my teeth, but as I chewed on its fleshy pulp it would became sweeter, and remind me of why I had bothered to climb its tree in the first place. Getting to know Aunty Morenike was like that. At first Eniayo and I were scared of her because of her no-nonsense attitude and prickly demeanour. But as she spent more and more time with us, we grew to love her kindness and sweet generosity.

At family gatherings, Aunty Morenike sat at the back of our house and helped the hired cooks who were always grateful for an extra hand. She did not easily fit in with the different groups of women in our family. The married women felt that as a spinster, she should not be part of their conversation. She had little in common with her own age group but was too old to sit with us, her younger cousins.

Aunt Morenike often had a faraway look in her eyes, as if her mind was elsewhere while her body sat still. Some days she had an impatient air about her, as if she could not afford to waste even a second on us. She would answer in abrupt monosyllables: "No." "Yes." "Why?" But other times, when she spoke about something she was passionate about, like her son Damilare, her teaching work, or Nigerian politics, it was impossible to get a word in edgewise.

Just when Kachi and I were growing closer, Aunty Morenike came for a visit. We were sitting alone in the sitting room while she plaited my hair. Eniayo was playing outside with Damilare.

"Aunty Morenike?"

"Yes, Morayo." Her slight lisp sometimes caused her to change the sound of my name, though most times she managed to say it properly.

"When you were my age, did you like a boy?"

Even with my back turned to her, I could hear the smile in her voice. "Yes, I did."

Surprised, I turned around to look at her. She was trying to conceal a smile. "You did? Is that not a bad thing?"

Her fingers stopped weaving my hair. "Why do you think it is a bad thing?" she asked.

"Because everybody says that it is."

Aunty Morenike laid a soft arm on my shoulder. "Morayo, tell me the truth. Is there a boy that you like?"

Dropping my eyes, I nodded.

"What do you do when you are with this boy?" she asked gently.

I could feel my face and neck getting hot. Kachi and I had *almost* kissed several times, and sometimes I thought about taking his hand and pushing it under my blouse. I longed to feel his warm bare hand against my skin so much that my toes curled tight from the tingling sensations that ran through my body. In those moments, I did not care about what Mummy said. I did not want that feeling to stop. Now I knew why the women in the films bent one calf up in the air when they were kissed; they probably could not stand on their curled-up toes!

"Well, sometimes we hold hands ..." I paused. "But sometimes I feel ..."

Aunty Morenike frowned. "Funny?"

"I don't know."

But I did know. Looking around, I whispered, "Sometimes, I want him to put his arms around me."

"Ah ..." Aunty Morenike's expression softened. "Morayo, listen to me. Those feelings are part of growing up. But sometimes they make you want to do things that you are too young to do. My dear, it is not yet time. Do you understand what I mean?"

I nodded. I knew exactly what she meant: those things Ireti told us girls about, the things she said no one would ever know.

I looked at Aunty Morenike gratefully. "Okay, Aunty."

When I did finally kiss Kachi, it was New Year's Day, 1985.

Every New Year's Eve the children in the neighbourhood walked to the nearby church for the watch-night service. The cold Harmattan air usually had us girls huddled together as we tried to get away from the boys, who were always looking for every opportunity to throw a banger in our midst. The small, powerful fireworks exploded with deafening noises that sounded like gunshots. When we saw the brightly lit ends of the bangers we would scatter, running in different directions while those naughty boys chased us. The smell of gunpowder from the exploding bangers would cling to our clothes and follow us to church.

That year, the watch-night service started at ten P.M. and ended at two in the morning. As soon as the clock chimed twelve, shouts of "Happy New Year" echoed through the whole city. The service closed with a giving of thanks. All the people danced to the front of the church, with their offering money tightly crunched up in their hands and a song of thanks on their lips.

Under cover of the loud New Year thanksgiving, Kachi and I slipped away from our families. We met outside the church building and walked back home. Holding hands, we stayed in the shadows in case somebody was watching. Kachi stopped in front of his house and then pulled me over to sit on the little wooden bench by his mother's kiosk.

After staring at my face for a short while, Kachi cleared his throat. "Morayo, can I kiss you?" he asked, holding on tightly to my hand. When I nodded, he smiled brightly and dug a shaking hand into his trouser pocket.

I was puzzled when Kachi brought out a Tom-Tom sweet. He unwrapped it and popped it in his mouth. He sucked furiously on it for a moment and then spat it back inside its striped orange-and-black wrapper. I smiled.

I kept my eyes open. I wanted to see what would happen. In the dim light of the house security lights, I could only see Kachi's gleaming eyes.

When he brought his face closer to mine, I smelled the menthol flavour from the sweet on his quickened breath. His pointed nose poked right into my broad flat one. I could not breathe. Kachi had to tilt his head to one side. I decided to keep my lips together since he had his own lips pressed together. When our lips touched, we pressed them hard together for about a minute and then sprang apart. We looked at each other and began to laugh. I decided that the next time Kachi kissed me, I would keep my eyes closed.

When I got home, Bros T was there alone. I must have walked in with a funny look because he kept glancing at me as I sat at the dining table cutting up carrots and green peppers for our New Year's Day fried rice. The rest of the family soon arrived from church. In the excitement of entering the New Year, Mummy did not ask me where I had disappeared to after the service. Eniayo did.

"Morayo, where did you go?" she asked as she sat next to me. "Tomi and I were looking for you outside the church."

Looking around, I put a finger to my lips and glared at her. Eniayo cocked her head to one side with a questioning look.

I smiled to myself. It was going to be a good year.

5

If one has been told that a bird can eat one's eyes,
when one sees the tiniest of birds, one takes to one's heels.

Soon Bros T was bringing girls from his school to our house when Mummy and Daddy were out. Sometimes they would go into his bedroom with beer and food. Eniayo and I exchanged glances when we heard the girls giggle. Aunty Adunni and Bros T seemed to have an unspoken agreement to stay out of each other's way. They tiptoed around each other in the house, and when Bros T brought his girls home, Aunty Adunni hissed at them and ignored their greetings.

On other days, she would grab her handbag and ask Eniayo and me to come with her to the market. "Go and put on your shoes," she said to us one afternoon. "I need to go and buy some items for our night meal."

When Eniayo pointed out that the meal was already cooked, Aunty Adunni snapped at her, "I said go and put on your shoes!" Eniayo did not have to be told twice.

One afternoon, Kachi and Sesan walked Eniayo and me

home from school. Eniayo saw me lingering, and called over her shoulder, "Morayo, I am going inside to find something to eat." She ran into the house.

"I am coming soon." I stayed outside to chat with the boys.

We sat on a pile of cement blocks from a nearby construction site, trying to talk above the *ejika ni shop,* the mobile tailor who walked up and down the street with his Singer sewing machine perched on one shoulder calling, "Tailoring services! Tailoring services!"

Mummy said the mobile tailors walked around because they didn't have money to rent a shop space. After a few moments of yelling, he found a customer in one of the three-storey, multi-tenanted "face me, I face you" buildings across the road.

We chatted amiably until we saw Bros T approach. His face darkened. He barely acknowledged our greetings—he just marched past us into the compound. Kachi and Sesan quickly said their goodbyes.

When I went inside, Bros T was waiting in the sitting room. "Who are those boys?"

Surprised at the angry tone of his voice, I said, "They are my friends. You know them. They both live down the street."

He scowled. "Your friends? What kind of foolish talk is that? Who told you boys and girls can be friends?"

I was silent, unsure how to respond.

"You mean your boyfriends?"

My heart dropped. What did Bros T know about Kachi and me? But as quickly as these fears came, I dismissed them with a shake of my head. "Boyfriends?" I laughed nervously. "I don't have a boyfriend."

"Good girl," Bros T said. He took a breath and seemed to calm down. "I hope you know that you are too young for that kind of nonsense. Don't let me catch you with any boy, or else ..." He turned and went into the kitchen.

Later, in the sitting room, I was surprised when Bros T told Mummy that he had seen me in the midst of a group of boys on my way back from school. "Aunty, Morayo was even laughing when one of the boys put his arm around her shoulder."

I nearly dropped my book. "I—"

Mummy's withering stare silenced me. "Shut up. I say shut up. Have you no shame?" she snapped. Mummy always told Eniayo and me that having no shame was a terrible flaw. Adjusting her wrapper, she wagged her finger. "Morayo, I have told you. A woman who has no shame will lie and steal. A woman who is a thief and a liar will sleep around with different men. Tell me, who would want such a woman as a wife?"

"But Mummy ..." I paused, trying to ignore Bros T, who was standing behind her. There was a strange satisfied smile on his face as he watched Mummy scold me. "I did not walk around with a group of boys. I was just standing outside the house with two of my classmates."

Mummy hissed. "Does it matter whether Tayo saw you with five boys or two boys? A good girl does not let the whole street see her walking and talking with boys when she should be home helping her mother with house chores. Tell me, what kind of example are you setting for Eniayo? I do not want to hear any such report from your brother again. Do you hear me?"

I lowered my eyes. "Yes, Ma."

That evening as I dished Bros T's food, I spat repeatedly into his soup. I made sure I mixed it properly with my finger before I carried out his bowl from the kitchen. I pursed my lips.

"Bros T, your food is ready," I announced with downcast eyes.

Sitting across from him at the dining table, I watched with a smile as he licked the soup off his fingers.

Later that night as I lay curled in my bed, frustrated tears filled my eyes. I knew Mummy would now be watching me like a hawk. It would it make it much harder for me to see Kachi after school.

My bedroom door creaked open and Eniayo came into the room. She never bothered with knocking before coming in. She sat beside me on the bed with a worried look on her face. "Morayo?"

"Yes."

"Why is Bros T angry with you?" Eniayo did not like it when there was any argument in the house.

I looked at my sister in surprise. "Why do you think he is angry with me?"

Eniayo shrugged her shoulders. "I don't know." She blinked rapidly behind her glasses. "It is just that his eyes look like this"—Eniayo narrowed her eyes—"when he is looking at you."

Bros T's recent behaviour puzzled me too. But I was too tired to think about it that night. "That is his business. It's past our bedtime. You better go to your room."

For weeks afterwards, I spoke to Bros T only when I needed to. Many times I would look up to find him watching me with a strange expression. I found myself following Aunty Adunni around the house, helping her in the kitchen or washing clothes with her behind the house. We chatted and laughed together. And together, we avoided Bros T.

One night, Bros T came to my bedroom. I had just finished clearing up the kitchen with Aunty Adunni and was getting ready for bed. Naked, I had my nightgown poised right above my head when Bros T walked into the room without knocking.

Embarrassed, I quickly pulled down my nightgown, but I knew that he had already seen my body.

Bros T acted as if nothing out of the ordinary had happened. He walked over and sat calmly at the small wooden desk in the room. Sitting at the edge of my bed, I tried not to look at him.

"Morayo, are you still fighting with me?" he asked.

I kept quiet. After all, what did he expect?

Tapping his long fingers on the table, he leaned forward so that he could catch my eye, and gave me a smile. "Morayo, is it that bad now? Okay, I am sorry. I should not have mentioned anything to Aunty Bisoye about those boys."

I was surprised to hear his apology. He never said he was sorry for anything. Seeing that he had my attention, he gave me another charming smile. "Is my apology accepted?"

Temporarily blinded by his brilliant white teeth, I felt my anger recede. My lip curved into a smile. "Yes."

He looked pleased. "In that case, will you come and give me a hug?"

Still embarrassed that he had seen me naked, I reluctantly dragged myself from the bed. I bent down to give him a quick hug. But Bros T pulled me down onto his lap. "So no more silent treatment?" he asked with an exaggerated wink. The expression was so funny, I started laughing—until I felt his rough palm caress the side of my breast through the short sleeves of my nightgown.

I jumped up.

Before I could say anything, Eniayo burst in. Oblivious to the tension in the room, she said, "Bros T! I have been looking for you everywhere. Daddy is calling you."

Bros T did not look at me as he left. Eniayo skipped out of the room behind him.

I stood for a moment, dumbfounded. I was not exactly sure about what had happened. Had Bros T meant to touch me? Was it an accident? My heart pounding, I touched the spot his fingers had caressed.

I thought about Mummy's face when she found out I had walked home with the boys. What exactly would I say now? She would think that I was just trying to get Bros T into trouble.

I sat on my bed for a long time, listening to the night sounds.

✄

As the weeks passed, I concluded that the incident must have been a simple mistake. Bros T kept his distance from me and I felt for sure that it was because he was sorry about what had happened. Like me, he did not know how to talk about it.

After all, Bros T was like my older brother.

✄

Kachi and I continued to see each other outside school. When I was with Kachi, I did not have to think about what was going on at home. At first, I thought of telling him about what had happened with Bros T. But then I reasoned that he might not understand it had been a mistake. As Kachi and I spent more and more time alone, Aunty Morenike's warning and Mummy's threats were never far from my mind. Most of the time, Kachi and I sat and talked. I would not let him put his hands under my clothes.

Two weeks before the end of the school year, a sombre-looking Kachi told me that his family was moving back to the

East. His father was starting a civil service job at the Anambra State Ministry of Works and Transport office at Awka. Kachi, who was from Anambra State, said that his parents were happy to be moving closer to their families.

We looked at each other with reddened eyes. What would happen to us?

The evening before they left for Awka, Kachi came to find me to say goodbye. He could not just knock on the front door to ask for me, so he sent his younger sister Adanna to ask for Eniayo.

Adanna told Mummy that she had come to say goodbye to Eniayo since they were leaving for Awka in the morning. Eniayo knew that Kachi would be waiting for me outside, so when Adanna was leaving, Eniayo asked Mummy if I could escort her since it was getting dark. I made sure that I followed behind the two girls with a slightly irritated look so as not to arouse Mummy's suspicions.

Kachi was waiting for us by the side of the house fence. Light from the full moon reflected on his long sad face. He was throwing pebbles into a little puddle of water by the side of the road.

Eniayo and Adanna walked ahead of us while Kachi and I walked quietly behind. Finally, I broke the awkward silence. "So, what time are you leaving tomorrow?"

"Nne said that the driver will come around eight in the morning. She wants us to be in Awka before it gets dark."

"Okay."

Kachi stopped walking. "Is that all you are going to say?" He reached for my hand. "Morayo, are you not going to miss me?"

I glanced at Kachi's face. I had grown to like him so much. But we both knew that the chance of us ever meeting again was very slim. I tightened my hold on his hand. "Kachi, of course I am going to miss you. Will you write me when you get to Awka?"

Kachi's face brightened. "I will! But how will I send the letters to you?"

He could not send them to our post office box. Daddy would read the letters before he brought them home.

"Maybe you can send the letters to Sesan and he can give them to me?"

Kachi smiled. "Okay."

Adanna and Eniayo soon noticed that Kachi and I had stopped walking. They sat on a log by the side of the road to wait for us. It was getting late. I told Kachi that Eniayo and I had to go back home.

Kachi and I faced each other. I could feel tears in my eyes. Unexpectedly, Kachi reached for my hand and pulled me to him for a quick, tight hug. He whispered, "I love you, Morayo" in my ear. Then he ran off to join his sister. All the way back home, I smiled through my tears.

I got only two letters from Kachi. Two months after he moved away, Sesan squeezed a crumpled-up airmail envelope into my hand when we were walking back to our classroom after the morning school assembly. I quickly hid the envelope inside my skirt pocket. It was all I could think about during morning class. During our first break, I locked myself into one of the cubicles in the girls' toilet and opened the envelope. Kachi had written the four-page letter on lined paper he must have torn out from the middle of his school exercise book. I smiled when I saw the irregular heart shapes drawn around the edges of the pages and read the first paragraph.

My sweetest paragon of beauty a.k.a Morayo,

I hope this letter meets you in an extraordinary state of health and peace. My principal aim in writing this letter is to tell you how much I have missed you since we moved to Awka. Even as I write these words to you, my body temperature is rising and visions of your face are dancing right before my eyes.

Kachi wrote that while Ibadan had seven hills, the town of Awka lay in a valley. His father had taken him to visit the famous Awka *uzu-ike* blacksmith quarters and he had watched while the blacksmith made him a little plane. He had also made friends with two boys on his street with whom he was playing soccer. I smiled when I read that he had scored the winning goal in the first match he played. Kachi asked after Eniayo and wrote about how much he missed Ibadan just because of me.

Over the next couple of days, when I was alone in my room, I laboured over the letter I was going to send in reply. In my letter, I told Kachi how I kept walking past his old house thinking that I was going to see him. I wrote that I was happy he had new friends and was playing soccer again. I asked after his sisters and told him to greet them for me. I almost told him what happened with Bros T, but I changed my mind at the last minute. I drew neat heart shapes all around the edges of my letter and sealed it with a kiss.

A few months later, I received one more letter from Kachi. Late at night, while everybody slept, I read the last paragraph again with a fading torchlight.

Morayo, I really miss you. Even though Awka is only 375 kilometres from Ibadan, it is like a planet away. I know a planet is really really far away but that is what it feels like. I wish I had a picture of you so that I could stop squeezing my eyes tight to see your face. My friends say that I am stupid for thinking that you will wait for me. They say that we are too young. But I never argue with them. It is because they don't know you.

I quickly sent a reply, but nothing else ever came from Kachi. Eventually I stopped looking expectantly at Sesan when I saw him at school. Kachi's name remained unspoken between us. With each passing month, my memories of Kachi grew fainter and fainter, like the ink markings on his letters that remained stuffed—hidden from Mummy—inside a little opening in my mattress.

6

The wicked one forgets kinship ties,
the tormentor forgets tomorrow.

When the results for the West African Examinations were released, Bros T got five A's and three C's, and officially redeemed himself in Daddy's eyes. To celebrate, Daddy took all of us to the Koko Dome restaurant. Eniayo and I sat beside the packed pool, slowly drinking our Chapman's. We felt on top of the world as Mummy's face beamed with a happy smile.

As the weeks went by, Daddy and Bros T laughed together over the funny items in the news and analyzed the English premier soccer league matches. The rest of the school year quickly flew past. By the time the school holidays ended, Bros T had completed all his examinations.

With a lot of spare time on his hands, Bros T began spending more time with two friends he had met at Havana, the beer parlour on the next street over from ours. During the day the young men would go to Havana to drink Heineken beer and eat fried snails. Eniayo and I heard whispers that other things happened there—but we never went inside. If we had to go fetch Bros T, we would stand by the swinging, beaded doorway curtain until somebody noticed us and asked who we were looking for. The only thing that deterred Eniayo from going inside was the stench of cigarette smoke. It always made her feel sick. The only thing that stopped me was the promise of Mummy's wrath.

I am not sure if Mummy and Daddy noticed Bros T's behaviour. If they did, I did not hear them talk about it. Maybe they felt that he deserved some reward for all his hard work at school.

I cannot remember any clear warning signs. I did not stub my left big toe that week. Neither did I hear the owl hoot in the night among the trees. But I did wake up drenched in sticky sweat one morning. By ten o'clock I was burning up with fever and shaking with chills. From the way my body ached and from the bitter taste in my mouth, I knew I had malaria. Because of my AA genotype, I was prone to malarial attacks. Eniayo had Daddy's AS genotype, so she was lucky. She fell sick maybe once a year.

My sickness could not have come at a more inconvenient time. Aunty Adunni's older sister was getting married in Ilorin on the weekend. Aunty Adunni had left Ibadan the week before so that she could help her mother prepare for the wedding. Mummy, Eniayo, and I were to leave that afternoon for Ilorin—Daddy was away on a business trip. Bros T had told Mummy that he did not want to attend the wedding, so he was staying behind at home.

Mummy quickly started me on chloroquine tablets. I was not sure what I hated more, the bitterness of the pills or the ache in my bones. When Mummy found me shivering, she looked as if she was unsure what to do. Eniayo was in the bridal train as one of the flower girls. She had to take Eniayo to the wedding, but how could she leave a sick child at home?

When Bros T said he would take care of me, I saw the reluctance in Mummy's eyes. But I knew how much Eniayo wanted to be a flower girl, and I reminded Mummy that our neighbour Mama Comfort was also around if I needed help. Mummy seemed relieved. She said she would ask Mama Comfort to visit the house and promised that they would leave for Ibadan immediately after the wedding reception. "We will be gone only one night," she said gently before they left.

Bros T came back to the house later that afternoon with his beer parlour comrades, Bros Niran and Bros Jimi. He also brought back a polythene bag full of roasted, spicy *suya* meat and a carton of Guinness. I was in the sitting room, watching television in the silent house. When I saw the little group, I realized Bros T must have been planning this little rendezvous since the day he knew we were all going to Ilorin for the wedding. I did not like these friends—and the smell of the spicy meat only made me feel even more nauseated—so I finally decided to go to bed.

"Good night, Bros T." By now, Bros T and his friends had almost finished the carton of beer. Empty bottles littered the floor beside them. Bros T wove his hand in the air in response. I could feel Bros Niran's eyes on me as I walked out of the room.

As I changed into my nightgown, I could hear raised voices coming from the sitting room. I wrapped my cover cloth around myself and made my way quietly down the corridor. I could hear Bros T's loud, angry voice.

"Niran, what kind of nonsense talk is this? My friend, face your beer and shut your mouth. Morayo is still a small girl. Do you think she is one of those Havana prostitutes you parade as your girlfriends?"

I rubbed my pounding head. Why were they arguing about me?

Bros Jimi's drunken laughter drifted out into the corridor. "Small girl? Is it because we did not tell you we saw Morayo sneaking around with that Igbo boy who used to live down the street?"

I froze. They had seen Kachi and me?

"Tayo, didn't you sleep with my little sister? *Abeg*, leave Niran alone."

"Jimi, please leave that one. You and I know that half of Eleyele has slept with your sister." Bros T laughed scornfully.

I heard another drunken laugh. "Fine, I agree with you about my sister, but I can bet you that Morayo is no longer a virgin, so what is your problem?"

"Thank you, my brother!" said Bros Niran. "I don't know why he is suddenly being stingy." His voice became softer. "Or Tayo, is it that you want her for yourself?"

I jumped when I heard a loud bang on the table and the sound of a bottle crashing to the floor. Bros T swore loudly. "God punish the two of you! Is this nonsense talk my reward for buying beer for you two fools? Before I get back, you had better find your way to your houses."

Hearing the sound of a chair pushed back, I made a silent dash for my bedroom, where I lay in bed for a while. No wonder Bros T warned me against being too friendly with his friends. I shivered, promising myself never to be alone with them.

Just before I drifted off to sleep, I smiled, remembering Eniayo's excitement earlier in the day as they left for Ilorin. It was the first time she would be in a bridal train. I realized then how much I missed her constant chatter. This was also the first time we were spending the night apart. I reassured myself that Mummy and Eniayo would be back the next day.

I dozed off—

And then woke to the firm pressure of a large, coarse hand across my mouth.

My cover cloth was yanked away and flung to the floor. My heart raced and I could hear the blood rushing through my brain. It had finally happened. One of my recurring nightmares—armed robbers in the house!

For the past month, a gang of armed robbers had stormed a block of flats in our housing estate. First, they posted a letter by the estate gates announcing that they were coming and warning against any police involvement. At night, the gunshots from the neighbourhood vigilante group who patrolled the estate kept us up. The armed robbers still attacked, killing two members of the vigilante group and tying their bodies to the streetlight poles. The robbers, angry that several tenants did not have large sums of money at home, punished them by forcing some of the male tenants to sleep with their neighbours' wives while their husbands watched. By daybreak, the block of flats was empty. Under cover of night, the tenants had fled the building. After the incident Mummy had begged Daddy to keep a little stash of money at home. Just in case we needed it.

Where was Bros T? Was he asleep or was he lying dead somewhere? Bile rose up in my throat. I was going to faint. I ignored all the warnings flashing in my head about the dangers of looking at an armed robber's face. I wanted to see my attacker. I turned to look.

It was Bros T.

I froze. Then, angry and betrayed, I sank my teeth deep

into his palm, determined to bite out a chunk of flesh. Bros T immediately clamped his other hand tightly around my throat. I gasped. He leaned over and whispered harshly into my ear, his breath sour with beer and meat. "Stop this nonsense or I will break your little neck. It is time a real man makes you a woman before one of your little boyfriends tries and spoils you for good."

Inside my head a shrill voice screamed, *What little boyfriends?*

Bros T forced his tongue into my mouth, and I gagged. I could taste alcohol and cigarettes. But the hand pressed firmly around my neck did not allow me to throw up. Desperate to free myself, I struggled under his weight.

He whispered softly into my ear. "Stop this nonsense or I will call Jimi and Niran to come. I am sure they will be very happy to join us. Is that what you want?"

I shook my head wildly side to side. *Please.*

I stilled my thrashing limbs. I heard the metal rings of the bed creak as Bros T stretched out his long, heavy body on top of mine. One of his hands roughly pushed up my nightgown. As he moved on top of me, my chest tightened. I felt as if I was suffocating. He pushed his hand between my thighs. When he ripped apart my underwear, my body shook. I needed to scream, but I could hardly breathe. When he lifted his mouth from mine, all I could do was squeak. His warm breath fanned my face and his glazed eyes shone in the dark.

My legs were thrown apart. I felt a sharp pain go right through my centre. As Bros T pushed into my unwelcoming body, my spirit floated high up to the ceiling. Looking down, I saw a child with a familiar face on the bed below. Her terror-filled eyes stared away into nothingness, her mouth open wide in a silent scream.

Then, as quickly as I had left that trembling body, I was back inside. I felt a pain deep, deep inside me. Bros T panted and grunted for an eternity, until he suddenly jerked and then was still. Without one word he got up from my bed, pulled on his trousers, and staggered out of the room.

I lay there shaking, my eyes filled with tears that refused to flow. My throat was on fire. My bruised lips trembled. I whimpered.

"Mummy ..."

I called again. But she was not there. I was alone in the dark of the room. A tear rolled down the side of my face. Others followed. I was terrified that Bros T would change his mind and come back with his friends. I wanted to drag myself out of bed and lock the door, but my legs refused to move.

I could not move.

From the corner of my right eye, I saw something pale dash across the ceiling. It was a wall gecko. It stood, as if transfixed to the spot, staring and slowing nodding its head as if to tell me that everything was going to be okay. I am not sure how long I stared back until, mercifully, sleep took me. It came and took me away to a safe, happy place. A place with Eniayo.

*

"Bisi, I found her! I found her!" Eniayo shouted, clapping her hands with excitement. It was a beautiful sunny day and we were playing hide-and-seek in our grandfather's compound in Oyo. Laughing, I pulled away from her grasp, running into the large corn field beside the house. When I glanced back I saw that Eniayo was not running after me. She was waiting for our playmate Bisi to catch up.

Giggling, I ran between the long cornstalks and hid in the middle of the field. I could feel the hot sun's rays shining right onto the middle of my head, melting the heavy pomade used to grease the lines in my woven hair. I was sure that it would take Eniayo and Bisi some time to find where I was. Then I heard something hissing behind me.

My blood instantly ran cold. I slowly turned around to find a black-necked spitting cobra. Staring open-mouthed at the snake, I noticed that there was something very peculiar about it. While the cobra had the body of a snake, it had a familiar face. Bros T. I screamed.

From a distance, I heard Eniayo shouting my name. "Morayo, where are you? What is wrong? Morayo, please, where are you?"

The snake reared its head and dug its fangs into the fleshy part of my leg. I felt myself falling, falling into a deep and endless hole.

7

The kite does not die and the partridge is anxious;
the eagle watches the snail from the corner of its eye.

I bolted up in bed. My heart pounded hard against my rib cage. Looking around at the familiar yellow walls of my bedroom, I realized that I had been dreaming. The early morning sunlight streamed into the room through the sheer window curtains.

I felt a strange stiffness in my lower body. For a moment, my mind was blank. Then I looked up and I saw the wall gecko. It was still staring down from that same spot on the ceiling. Memories of the night came rushing back. Suddenly, I felt nauseated. I squeezed my eyes shut, and when I opened them again the gecko was gone.

I dragged myself to the door, listening for any sounds. All I could hear was the grandfather clock in the sitting room. I slowly undressed, wrapped myself in a towel, and then gathered up my torn underwear, my nightgown, and the bloodstained bedsheet. I quietly opened my bedroom door. Bros T's door was wide open but I did not see him. I was alone in the house.

Walking stiffly to the bathroom, I threw my clothes into a metal bucket. I needed to wash them, but first I needed a bath. I had to wash his taste and smell off me.

After a long cold bath, I dragged myself to the backyard to wash my clothes. I sat on a little wooden stool under the pawpaw tree beside the house. My chest tightened as I stared at the bloodstains on the clothes. The more I scrubbed them, the brighter they grew. I scrubbed furiously at the red spots until my fingers became raw from the caustic soda soap.

"Sisi Morayo."

Startled, I jerked around. I almost fell off my low wooden stool.

Our neighbour Mama Comfort stood behind me. I had not heard her come in through the side gate. "How are you feeling this morning?" Her daughter Comfort was strapped snugly to her back. Comfort plucked a thumb out of her mouth and gave me a gummy smile.

I stood up, giving Comfort a weak smile in return. "Mama Comfort, good morning," I greeted. "I am better. I think the fever has finally gone."

To my horror, I realized Mama Comfort was staring at the reddish tint of the soapy water. She smiled at me with a kind look. "I am happy to hear you are feeling better, Morayo. I will come and see you later."

Watching her walk away, I wondered why she smiled. Was it just me, or was the world turning upside down? As I hung the clothes on the line, my stomach suddenly heaved and I doubled over, vomiting in the long grass.

Thankfully, Bros T was not yet back when I went inside. I curled up on the settee in the sitting room and soon fell asleep.

I woke up to loud knocking on the front door. My heart began racing again—but settled when I heard a familiar voice call out. "Morayo, it's me, Mama Comfort."

I opened the door. She held a wicker basket and a striped black-and-white polythene bag. She set the basket on the dining table and brought out two half-filled plastic containers. One had cooked *ofada* rice, the other, palm oil stew and fried mackerel. All the while, Mama Comfort was talking softly. "I am sure you must be feeling some discomfort. It is very natural. I remember my own first time. You will probably need to take some Panadol. It gets easier after each episode, and it is something every woman has to go through."

I looked at her in confusion.

Mama Comfort handed me the polythene bag. Looking inside, I finally understood. The bag held a pack of sanitary pads.

"Ma ... Mama Comfort ...," I stammered, unsure of what to say. "Thank you, Ma."

"It is nothing, my dear." She smiled, patting my shoulder. "I could tell from the way you looked this morning that it was your first time. I was not sure if your mother had any pads in the house, so I brought you these. Have you eaten yet? Did you take your medicine this morning?"

"No, Ma."

The truth was that I was not even sure I could force any food down my throat today.

Mama Comfort frowned. "That is not good now. How are you going to get better if you don't eat?" She pulled out a dining chair. "*Oya,* sit down and eat some rice."

To please her, I sat down and forced two spoons of rice into my mouth. She patted me gently on the shoulder. "Try and eat everything, you hear? I will come back and check on you later."

As soon as Mama Comfort left, I laid down my spoon. I was not hungry, but I was touched by Mama Comfort's generosity. She and her husband worked hard and sometimes had only enough to feed Comfort.

Sighing, I stood up and carried the uneaten plate of rice to the kitchen.

Late in the afternoon, I heard a car honking at the gate. Daddy was back!

Jumping up, I ran out of the house. When I opened the gate I saw it was Mummy, Eniayo, and Aunty Adunni arriving in a brown-and-yellow taxicab. A shrieking Eniayo flew out of the car and ran towards me. "Morayo! We are back," she said as she put her arms around my neck. "Mummy brought you some *dankwa*. Can I have some?" Laughing, Aunty Adunni shook her head.

Looking at her glowing face, I could tell that Eniayo had enjoyed her time in Ilorin. We were still bringing out their travelling bags from the boot of the taxicab when Daddy's car pulled into the compound.

Not too long after, Bros T arrived in front of the house on an *okada,* and from the look on his face, he was clearly not sure of the reception that would be waiting for him. When he walked in through the gate and saw Mummy's smile, he prostrated flat on the ground, greeting Mummy and Daddy.

I picked up Mummy's travelling bag and quickly walked towards the house. Bros T picked up Daddy's suitcase and followed. Catching up with me, he casually draped his arm across my shoulder. I froze. With our backs to the rest, he leaned closer and whispered, "Listen, if you say anything to Aunty Bisoye, you will be responsible for what happens to Eniayo."

Jerking my head around, I studied his face. He looked blankly at me and continued inside the house. That afternoon, at every moment, Bros T seemed to hover a few steps between me and Mummy. When I followed Mummy into the kitchen, he followed to get a soft drink. When Mummy asked me to bring her some water, Bros T sat close by her in the sitting room until I returned. When Aunty Adunni and I sat at the back of the house shelling melon seeds, Bros T came outside to weed Mummy's vegetable garden.

Later we all sat in the sitting room, listening to Eniayo and Mummy talk about the wedding. I was thinking about what Bros T had said. Would he go into her room too? I could not let such a thing happen to Eniayo. That kind of horror—it would kill her.

From then on, I watched Eniayo and Bros T like a hawk. When Daddy was not home, Bros T would pull Eniayo onto his lap— "Come here, my little wife!"—all the while looking at me with that curious smile. Some days I would hear them giggling in his bedroom while I stood in the corridor with my heart beating in my mouth.

Bros T stayed away from my room for two months. Just when I began telling myself that perhaps the horror was over, he came back one night. Daddy and Mummy were upstairs in their room and Aunty Adunni had gone to her room in the Boys' Quarter. He did it to me again and again. He even started calling me to his room during the afternoon as Eniayo played right outside his window.

During those months, I kept waiting for Mummy to notice something different about me. A different way of walking. A new scent. Had she not said that she could smell a boy's touch on me?

One day Mummy found me standing in the corridor leading to Bros T's bedroom. He was calling my name. "Morayo, Morayo, please come and help me find something under the bed."

I stood where I was. "Find it yourself," I mumbled.

Mummy heard me. "Morayo! What kind of behaviour is that? Go to Tayo's room right now and see what he wants." Shaking her head, she watched me drag my reluctant feet to his room before climbing the stairs to her own bedroom.

When I entered his room, Bros T pushed me roughly onto his bed. "So you think you can escape from me?"

That day, I felt a deep anger towards Mummy start to bubble inside of me.

Three months later, I had my first menstrual period. I did not tell Mummy. I still had Mama Comfort's sanitary pads— and Mummy was not going to notice anyway, I told myself. But I was wrong. This time, she *did* notice. That afternoon, Mummy walked into the kitchen. "Morayo, when you are done washing those plates, please come to my room. I want to talk to you."

She was sitting on her bed when I came in. "Morayo, I saw a bloodstain on your nightgown this morning. Has your period come?"

"Yes, Ma," I answered quietly.

"When?" She looked puzzled. "Why didn't you tell me? What have you been using?"

I kept quiet.

Mummy sighed and sat me down on the bed beside her. She repeated the same instructions Mama Comfort had given me about changing the pads. Then, moving closer, she added one more instruction with a very serious look. "Morayo, listen carefully. This is very important. You must not let any boy at school touch you. If they do, you will get pregnant. Do you understand?"

I nodded. "Yes, Ma."

"Please, my daughter, don't bring disgrace to our family's name."

I almost burst out into bitter laugher. I wanted to tell her she did not have to worry about the boys at school.

That day, to celebrate my transition into womanhood, Mummy asked Bros T to kill one of her prized chickens for our nightly meal. On another night I might have waved that chicken drumstick in a victory dance while basking in the warmth of Mummy's affection—and Eniayo's envy!—but that night I ate the drumstick in silence. It was like eating moulded sawdust.

The following night, when Bros T came to my room and touched my body, he drew back quickly. He made a disgusted noise and left. I smiled in the darkness as he closed the door behind him. I discovered that there was something good about becoming a woman after all.

My reprieve was short-lived. Bros T came back on many other nights. Only he now used a condom. Nothing else changed.

Eight months after it all began, I woke up with tender, heavy breasts. That same week I had to rush to the toilet after eating my breakfast. I vomited. Bros T found me sitting on the floor when he came to use the toilet.

"Morayo, what is wrong with you?"

"I think I am sick," I answered weakly, getting up to vomit again. Scratching his head, Bros T closed the toilet door behind him and watched me. He moved closer and whispered, "When was the last time you saw your period?"

My period had not come the month before. I did not see why this was any business of his, but he grabbed my arm tightly and asked again. "Morayo—when?"

"I have not seen it for almost two months," I murmured, looking sideways. I felt very uncomfortable talking to him about this.

I saw instant panic in Bros T's eyes. But I was not worried; I had heard from the girls at school that sometimes it takes a while to get a regular menstrual pattern.

That afternoon, I was outside gathering laundry from the clothesline at the back of the house when Bros T walked up to me. He looked around nervously. Through the screen door, I could see Aunty Adunni moving about in the kitchen.

"Morayo, I have something for you." Bros T stuck his palm out. He held two small white tablets. "Here, take these."

Alarm bells went off in my mind. Silently, I shook my head. "No, I do not want any tablets."

Bros T ran his hand over his head. Beads of sweat gathered rapidly on his brow. "YOU STUPID GIRL!" he shouted. He lowered his voice and whispered furiously. "Listen to me. Do you want to have a baby?"

I muttered, *"A baby?"*

"Yes!" He looked incredulous. "A baby! Don't you know that you can get pregnant?"

I felt the ground move underneath my feet. I held on tightly to the metal post of the clothesline.

Pregnant.

The heavy word hung in the air as my head spun.

Pregnant.

I could be pregnant from my own cousin. A cold shiver ran through me. I could not even begin to think of the implications of being pregnant. Without saying a word, I took the white tablets from his sweaty palm with trembling fingers and threw them in my mouth.

Bros T watched me and then turned away, walking back to the house with a look of relief. But I did not swallow the tablets. I spat them out into the grass and smiled bitterly to myself. If he thought he could get rid of me that easily, he had to think again. I was not yet ready to die. There was no way I could be pregnant. He was just saying that to scare me. After all, what could a tablet do to a pregnancy?

Over the next couple of days, I caught Bros T's dark eyes watching me expectantly. I knew that he was waiting for me to drop dead, but he was not going to get his wish. Still, my period did not come. I told myself it did not matter. It would come soon. It had to.

Three weeks after the tablet incident, I was walking home from school alone. Despite Mummy's repeated warnings to avoid taking shortcuts and to walk on the main road where there was more foot traffic, I took a shortcut through a building site. I was tired and wanted to get home as quickly as I could.

The building site was deserted. The construction workers

had finished work for the day. As I walked slowly through the site, I heard a stick breaking behind me. Startled, I looked back and saw two young men who looked very much like Bros Jimi and Bros Niran. Both wore hats and seemed to quicken their pace as I quickened mine.

My heart began beating so fast I was afraid it was going to jump out of my chest. Bros T must have grown tired of waiting for me to die; he had sent his friends to finish the job!

I started sprinting. They gave chase. I ran even faster, looking around in desperation for help. I should have listened to Mummy, I thought in a panic.

Distracted by constantly looking over my shoulder, I walked right into an open gutter. I felt my legs stepping into air as I tumbled, banging my head against the slimy green concrete. The stench of the putrid water filled my nostrils. I felt something crawl over my leg. I screamed.

I heard hurrying footsteps approach. I started to shout at the top of my lungs. "Help! Somebody please help me!"

Two concerned pairs of eyes looked down at me. They belonged to the young men following me, but I realized then that they were complete strangers—definitely not Bros Niran and Jimi. They reached into the gutter and pulled me out, wrinkling their noses at the smell. "Why were you running?" one of them asked. "We started walking fast because we saw you running. What did you see behind us?"

"I did not see anything," I said. I was gasping for air. "I was running because I was in a hurry to get home." It was partly the truth, but I could tell they did not believe me. Shaking their heads, they went on their way.

When I finally dragged myself home, I treated my scrapes with iodine and took some Panadol Extra. My body was aching all over. Surely everything had to be fine now. I had cheated death again.

Later that night, I felt cramping in my stomach. The cramps intensified, coming rapidly in waves. I clutched my stomach in pain, curling up in my bed. Eventually I got up and rolled on the tiled floor of my room. Dampness was seeping between my thighs. Puzzled, I reached down. My fingers were covered in blood.

I dragged myself to the bathroom. Bending over the bathtub, I felt my stomach clench and a flood came gushing down my leg. I climbed into the bathtub—forcing myself to swallow my cries. With each stomach cramp the bleeding came heavier, the clots larger. Soon the bathtub was filled with a dark red pool around me.

From the bathroom, I heard the loud chime of the clock. Around five in the morning, the bleeding finally started to slow down—until I realized it had stopped. I bit hard on my lip when I turned on the tap and it ran dry. There was no water in the overhead tank. I lifted the lid to the water drum in the bathroom. Luckily, there was just enough water for me to wash away the blood and take a cold shower.

Back in my room, as soon as my head touched the pillow, I fell into a deep sleep.

Eniayo woke me two hours later. It was time for our morning chores.

Outside, when I started sweeping the compound, I felt the ground rise up to meet me. When I came to I realized that only a few moments had passed, for everyone was still inside. I could hear Eniayo chattering with Aunty Adunni in the kitchen. No one had even noticed.

The day dragged on painfully, and by evening, I could not wait for bed. I could not yet bear the thought of saying anything to Mummy and Daddy. But suddenly that changed. Maybe I was just tired of the silent screams in my head. Or maybe it was the sight I walked in on later that afternoon.

Mummy had just finished her afternoon meal. She asked me to take her plate and tumbler to Eniayo, who was washing dishes in the kitchen. When I walked in, Bros T was standing right behind Eniayo, rubbing his body against her back. Eniayo was standing at the sink with her hands in soapy water, laughing, trying to push him away with her elbow. "Bros T! Please!"

I recognized that look on his face.

The porcelain plate dropped from my hand. It hit the cement and shattered into little pieces all over the floor. Bros T jerked quickly away from Eniayo. Startled, he glared at me. Then he left the kitchen through the back door.

Mummy hurried in. She found me staring at the shards on the floor. "Morayo, what happened?" she asked in annoyance. When I was silent, she just sighed and asked me to get the broom. "Your daydreaming is just getting worse and worse. What are you always thinking of?"

That evening, we sat at the dining table quietly eating our night meal. Aunty Adunni was in the kitchen—she had once told me, "I prefer eating alone, you know? I don't want anyone staring at my mouth as I chew." The only sounds in the dining room were our spoons scraping our plates. "Mealtimes are for eating and not talking," Daddy always said. I was about to lift a spoonful of rice and beans to my mouth when I suddenly laid the spoon down.

I looked around the table. Then my voice rang out clearly in the silence: "Bros T has been coming to my room at night."

A spoon clattered to the table.

Daddy's face hardened, Mummy gasped. A puzzled look clouded Eniayo's face. On the opposite side of the table, the vein on the side of Bros T's head was pulsating so fast I was afraid it would explode and spray us all with blood.

I exhaled, sitting back in my chair.

Mummy's eyes filled with tears. She placed both her shaking hands on top of her head. Daddy's spoonful of rice and beans hung halfway to his mouth as if it were suddenly unsure of its destination. We all watched as he slowly dropped it and picked up his tumbler of water.

Bros T flinched as if he thought Daddy might fling the tumbler in his direction. He crouched back in his chair, holding both arms in front of his face. Daddy took a long sip and gently set the tumbler down. While his face gave nothing away, his trembling hands told a different story. He was a man fighting hard for composure.

Daddy's tumbler had red streaks around the rim. His blood pressure had shot up quickly and his gums were bleeding. Mummy's eyes widened when she saw the bloody streaks. Getting up from her chair at the other end of the table, she walked over to his side. She laid her hand on Daddy's arm, silently pleading with him.

The brownish-white ceiling fan above the dining table continued to turn slowly like an old woman carefully stirring a pot. Its familiar creaking was the only sound in the humid

room. "Morayo. Eniayo. Go to your rooms now," Daddy
ordered quietly.

Poor Eniayo—looking baffled—quickly got to her feet and
headed for the entryway. She looked around, still unsure as
to what had just happened. Reluctantly, I followed her. As we
exited the room, I took a quick look back.

Daddy was standing. He held tightly onto the dining table,
looking down at Bros T, who was now prostrated, face flat,
on the floor before him. Mummy was kneeling beside Daddy's
feet, tugging at his trousers, silently pleading for her nephew.

In that moment, my anger towards Mummy reignited. She
should have been worried about *me*! She should have been
coming after *me*!

I followed a pale Eniayo back to her bedroom. By now, she
knew something was very wrong. She kept asking, "Morayo,
why is Daddy angry with Bros T?" but I refused to answer. After
a while she started to cry. I wanted to scream at her, to shout
"Shut up!" but seeing her tears melted my anger. I snuggled
with her under her cover cloth, linking my fingers through hers.
"Don't be angry. Do you want me to tell you a story?" Eniayo
nodded.

"Alo-o," I said.

"Alo," Eniayo's small voice whispered back. I swallowed the
lump in my throat.

> "One day, Ijapa the tortoise woke up and declared that
> he was going to be the wisest creature in the whole
> world. He decided to gather up all the wisdom in the
> world to keep for him only. So Ijapa hung a big gourd
> around his neck and went around gathering wisdom
> across the lands. After he was done, he decided to hide

the gourd at the top of a very tall palm tree, but every time Ijapa tried to climb up the tree, the gourd would get between him and the palm tree and he would fall off. An ant strolling by stopped and watched the tortoise. 'Why don't you hang the gourd on your back so that you can climb the tree?' the ant asked Ijapa. When Ijapa realized that the ant was right, he became very angry. He did not have all the wisdom in the world after all. He flung the gourd on the ground and all the wisdom he had gathered went back into the world."

Eniayo fell asleep. Even in her slumber, she was troubled. She kept mumbling, rolling, and kicking me with her feet and arms.

Straining my ears, I listened for any noise from the dining room. It was eerily quiet. I wanted to leave the room and find out what was happening, but I remembered Daddy's command. I got up from Eniayo's bed and stood by the window, staring into the starless night. I heard the compound gate open and the sound of an engine—Daddy's car? Where was he going so late at night?

I kept staring at the door. I waited for Mummy. I was sure she would come and look for me. Finally, just before dawn, I fell asleep on the floor beside Eniayo's bed. When I woke up, I was alone in the room. I soon found out that Mummy and Daddy had left the house during the night with Bros T in tow.

8

*A child does not die because
the mother's breasts are dry.*

Sitting on Eniayo's bed that morning, a story Daddy told us a few years back came to my mind.

The story started with a rich man dragging a poor man before the king's court. Respectfully removing his beaded velvet cap, the rich man prostrated before the king. He explained that one of his housemen had found the poor man lurking behind his kitchen walls.

"Great King, earlier this afternoon, my dear wife's pot of chicken stew was simmering on the stove. The aroma was drifting out of the kitchen window."

Pointing a trembling finger at the man grovelling on the ground before the king, the rich man continued whilst anger dripped from his every word. "This wretched man was cowering beside my wall like the pathetic thief that he is. Not only did he have the audacity to stand behind my kitchen window uninvited, he proceeded to eat his morsels of cassava *fufu* with the smell of my wife's stew!"

An audible gasp went up from the spectators at the king's court. The poor man hid his face in the sleeve of his *buba* in shame.

"Surely, Great King, you agree that this man is a blatant thief. Lazy men like him are an unwanted blight on our illustrious community. Who knows where he stole the *fufu* he is clutching in his hands? He deserves to be flogged. Better still, he should be thrown into the dungeons for a week. I know that you are a fair ruler and I have come to you to seek justice. Great King, may the crown stay long on your head and the royal shoes on your feet."

The rich man gathered his beautifully patterned *agbada* around himself and marched to his seat with a pious expression. Those sitting close by patted his shoulder in sympathy.

The poor man, hearing his accuser's speech, cried out in a weak voice. "Mercy! Mercy, Great King! Have mercy on your wretched servant! It is true that I stole the smell of his wife's stew, but please believe me that I did not steal this *fufu* in my hand. I received it as a payment for my work on Baba Ojikutu's farm. Please do not send me to the maddening darkness of the dungeons. Tomorrow, I must work as a hired labourer. If I do not work, my children will not eat. I am all they have. Their mother died two months ago with our last child still in her stomach. I will take the flogging that I deserve but please temper your justice with mercy, Great King."

Some spectators hissed. Trust shameless men to come up with excuses. Was he the first person to lose a wife?

But the king looked thoughtfully at both men. The rich man shook in his seat with righteous fury, the poor man grovelled on the ground with the pitiful ball of *fufu* clutched tightly in his hand.

After a period of silence, the king nodded and passed his judgment. "In this illustrious community of ours, we have no place for thieves. A man must tighten the strings of his trousers and eat from the sweat of his brow. Inasmuch as this poor man admits that he stole the smell of the rich man's soup, I hereby pronounce that his shadow be flogged forty times for the crime."

The poor man wept in gratitude. His accuser scowled. But he bowed before the king in acceptance of the decree and exited the court.

The punishment should always fit the crime, should it not?

Stepping out of Eniayo's room, I looked down the corridor. Aunty Adunni was sweeping Bros T's room. I heard the clock chime ten o'clock. Eniayo must have left for school. Hearing my footsteps, Aunty Adunni looked up from her sweeping. She stood still, watching me approach. Her face held no expression. She did not say a word. I kept quiet as well, stopping at the door of Bros T's bedroom and looking around. All his things were gone. Even the bed had been stripped of its sheets. It was as if he had never lived there. I turned and walked back to my bedroom. I could feel Aunty Adunni's bloodshot eyes boring into the back of my head.

"Morayo," she called after me.

I turned back.

"I am sorry," she said.

I nodded. I knew what she meant.

She swallowed hard. "Tayo was no good. He should never have been allowed to come back here."

From my bedroom window, I saw Aunty Adunni continue to sweep out into the courtyard of the compound. She stopped, staring at the pile of dirt, her hand wiping her wet eyes. She took a deep breath and continued to sweep along a straight path towards the gate. Then she opened the gate, sweeping the sand and debris and dirt from Bros T's room, pushing every presence of him out of the house and onto the road.

⚜

Daddy and Mummy drove Bros T back to his mother's home in Jos. It was an eighteen-hour round trip. Eniayo and I were in the sitting room when they came back late the next day. When Daddy opened the door and saw me, he stopped. His shoulders slumped as he turned his tired-looking face away. Mummy, who came in after him, stared at me with bloodshot eyes.

Eniayo ran to them. *"Ekaabo,"* she said with a smile. I stayed where I was and remained quiet. Mummy gave Eniayo a quick hug. *"Oya,* go and tell Adunni that we are back," she said. Eniayo ran to the kitchen.

Daddy walked towards the staircase leading to their bedroom, leaving Mummy and me alone in the room. Mummy's red-rimmed eyes filled with fresh tears. She looked at me and sighed. Then she too turned around, leaving the room.

I stared after them with my heart pounding in my chest. It felt as if it was going to break.

In the months that followed, I lived a double life. At school I pasted a happy smile on my face and pretended that everything was okay. Tomi was the only one who sensed that something was wrong with me. "Morayo, you are not talking much," she said one day after school. "And you always have something to do when I ask you to come and visit me. Is it because you are missing Kachi?"

I forced a smile to my face. "I am sorry I have not been coming to see you. I have not being feeling well lately. Maybe I *am* missing Kachi."

Tomi gave me an understanding pat on the arm. A part of me was glad that Kachi was not around. How would I have kept my secret from him?

Some days I wanted to tell Tomi what had happened with Bros T. My mouth would open and close several times. Yet I knew that I could not tell her anything.

If you don't want everyone to know your secret, you don't share it with anyone.

At home, I could not get away from the unasked questions in my parents' eyes as they lingered on my face. I no longer slept well at night, and my mind would play those questions over and over again.

Why did you not say something the first time?

Why did you let it go on for so long?

Why did you let this happen to you?

Even when I turned away from their gaze, I could not escape the shame that followed me around like a bad smell. I found the truth hard to admit even to myself: that after a while, Bros T's violation had lost its strangeness. It had become ... familiar. With each passing month, his hand at my neck became gentler and gentler, until there was no need for it to remain there. "This is what you want," he whispered in my ear on so many nights.

Crying, I would shake my head vehemently. "No! Please."

Bros T's response was always to stroke the inside of my thigh until I sucked in a breath and began to moan. "See?" he would say in a confident tone. "It is what you want. You just don't know it yet."

My body responded to the strokes and caresses of his rough hands in ways that I now wished I could forget. And after a while, I began to believe him. For what kind of girl has such feelings? Was it my fault too—could that explain Mummy and Daddy's unbroken silence? There were many days when every part of my body felt too heavy to move, when lifting an arm or a leg in the morning was painful.

Sitting back in the settee, Mummy opened the envelope and pulled out the letter. Eniayo and I sat across from her, wondering why she had summoned us. Reading the letter, she smiled. "Eniayo, it's from the Federal Government Girls' College in Oyo. You are admitted! You will be going to school this September."

My heart started pounding. *Eniayo was going away?*

"I am going to boarding school?" Eniayo asked. This was the first time we were hearing of this. I knew that Eniayo had written the admission examination for Federal Government Colleges, but so had I. I had always hoped she would join me at my secondary school.

"Yes. Your father thinks it will be good for you," Mummy said. "Oyo is not far away and your grandmother lives there." Eniayo's face fell. "Don't worry. We will come and see you during your visiting days …"

The words flew out of my mouth. "Mummy, why?"

She turned to me. "Morayo, what did you say?"

At first, I kept quiet. I had never questioned Mummy's

decisions before. At least not to her face. But I felt a strange boldness come over me. "Are you sending Eniayo away because of me? Because of what happened—"

Mummy snapped. "Morayo, stop it!" She glanced at Eniayo's curious face and then back to mine. "What is wrong with you?" Her hands fiddled with the admission letter. "You should be happy for your sister. Boarding school will teach her independence. She needs to be able to take care of herself."

I heard what she left unsaid: I had failed Eniayo as a big sister. I held Mummy's gaze.

She averted her eyes. "Things are different now ..." Her voice trailed off. "This is for the best."

The night before Eniayo left for school, she came to my bedroom after Mummy and Daddy had gone upstairs. "Morayo, Morayo. Are you still awake?"

I dried my eyes with my cover cloth before I faced her, but my swollen eyes must have given me away. "Morayo, why are you crying again?" she asked.

Looking at her worried pink face, I tried smiling through fresh tears. I was going to miss her so much. The lump in my throat grew larger. "I am not crying. It is just raining inside my eyes."

Eniayo gave me a puzzled look and then snuggled beside me in the bed, slipping her hand in mine. "Maybe it will make your pretty eyelashes grow faster?" she asked with a wobbly smile.

I shook my head and hugged her. Only Eniayo would say something like that.

We spent most of the night whispering about what life at boarding school would be like. Aunty Morenike had already told Eniayo that the food was going to be very small. Although Eniayo liked to eat, she was more worried about the fagging by senior students. Junior students had to carry out menial tasks for seniors, who took advantage of the system.

On one of her visits, Aunty Morenike told us that one night she had spent her entire prep time running around, killing mosquitoes in a senior class. If any of the seniors felt a mosquito bite, she got a knock on the head.

"Morayo, what if they don't like me?"

I knew what she meant—how would the other girls treat her as an *afin*?

I squeezed her hand. "They will like you, Eniayo. Remember, Aunty Morenike's friend is a teacher at the school. If you need help, you have to go and tell her, okay?"

Eniayo nodded. "Okay."

The next day, the picture of Eniayo's teary face stuck in my mind as we drove away from the school and back to Ibadan. The dark cloud surrounding me grew even bigger.

Back at home, the house felt empty and quiet.

The following month, Aunty Adunni finished her program at the catering school and announced that she, too, was leaving. Mummy tried to convince her to stay in Ibadan. Daddy even said they would open up a shop for her. But Aunty Adunni insisted that she go back to Ilorin. Her aging mother needed her. It was time for her to go.

Daddy bought her a brand-new oven and fridge along with other small items she could use to start her catering business. An overwhelmed Aunty Adunni knelt before Mummy and Daddy and wept with gratitude.

Before the bus hired to take her back home arrived, Aunty Adunni called me to her old room. She opened her handbag and brought out some money. "Take it, Morayo, and use it to buy something for yourself, okay?"

She reached into the handbag again and brought out a brown envelope. "This is Eniayo's money. Maybe you can buy something to take to her on visiting day."

Tears came to my eyes. "Thank you, Aunty." Aunty Adunni gave me a tight hug. "Be a good girl, okay? Don't let me hear that you are not behaving yourself. Promise me that you will ask to visit me in Ilorin."

Too choked up to talk, I nodded. Minutes later, after ten long years with us, Aunty Adunni too was gone.

Two weeks later we received Eniayo's first letter from school. She wrote that she had eaten all her provisions and wanted to come back home. She'd had to have all her hair cut off because she had caught lice from another girl in her dormitory.

Daddy sent his driver, Mr. Bello, to Oyo with a box of cornflakes, a tin of powdered milk, some *gari,* and a box of sugar. He also sent along a letter to Eniayo stating that she could not come home.

Most days after school, I was the only one at home. Mummy said that since I was now old enough to do all the housework, we did not need to have any house help. Although she did not say it, I knew no other relatives would come to live with us. Daddy and Mummy both spent more and more time away from home. They still did not speak to me about Bros T.

On Eniayo's first visiting day, Daddy drove us down to Oyo to see her. I had not seen her for almost three months. It was the longest time we had been apart. We waited for Eniayo under the shade of a tree near the administrative building. A carton of provisions and a basket of cooked food sat on a wooden bench and table. Mummy was able to find a student who knew Eniayo, and the older girl said that they lived in the same residence and would let her know she had visitors.

I finally saw Eniayo running towards us. But she was not alone. Another girl dressed in the same red-checkered daywear was trying to keep up with her. When Eniayo reached where I stood, she screamed and flew into my open arms. "Morayo!"

I hugged her and tried to blink back my tears. "Eniayo, you have grown taller!"

She laughed. "It is because of the beans and weevils they feed us."

After she knelt and greeted Mummy and Daddy, Eniayo motioned to her friend. The other girl had been standing aside and watching us. "Mummy, this is my friend Hauwa. Since her parents can't come for visiting day, I asked her to come with me."

"Good afternoon, Ma," Hauwa said in a shy voice.

Mummy smiled at the girl. "Hauwa, it is nice to meet you. Come and sit. There is plenty of food for all of us."

As I looked at the happy smile on Eniayo's face, I knew how special this friend must be for her. Hauwa was an *afin* too. Throughout the visit, they held each other's hand.

On our way back to Ibadan, I told myself that it was a good thing that Eniayo had found a friend. Still, I wondered—who needed me now? The cold knot deep inside me that had come after that first night with Bros T pulled tight until I could barely breathe from the pain.

※

"Morayo, are you ready?" Mummy asked as she popped her head into my bedroom. "We need to get going." A relative was having a twenty-year memorial party for his late mother. I did not know how to tell Mummy that I just wanted to be left alone.

Her eyes widened when she saw me. "You are not yet dressed?"

"No, Ma, I have a headache." I had started getting migraine headaches shortly after Bros T left the house. I did not have one, but Mummy did not know that.

Sighing, she left. She soon came back with a bottle of Panadol Extra and a cup of water. "Take this. It will help."

"Thank you, Ma."

Mummy watched me swallow the tablets.

Before she and Daddy left the house, Mummy came back to check on me. "Morayo?" I pretended I was asleep.

Later, I heard Daddy's car drive out of the compound. When I was sure they were gone, I sat up. I *was* beginning to develop a headache.

Seeing the medicine bottle on the table, I suddenly wondered what it would feel like to empty the entire bottle into my mouth. As soon as the thought came, my body became rigid. These thoughts had started soon after Aunty Adunni left. When I stayed awake in my room at night, I often wondered what it would feel like not to be trapped in this heavy body but floating around free.

Only last month, I had arrived at school to see a naked young man dangling from the wild mango tree. No one knew who he was. It was hard for me to concentrate on mixed cultivation methods when I could see his body swinging gently in the wind from our classroom window. That innocent mango tree bore the brunt of the community's anger. Its ripe fruit rotted on the branch. Even hungry birds shunned it. Then one morning, the tree was gone. Overnight, it had been hacked to the ground. But on windy days, I still saw that young man swinging gently from the tree branch. No doubt he longed to be free too.

Tilting my head back, I emptied half the bottle of Panadol Extra into my mouth.

Then someone started banging on the gate. Startled, I gagged.

Mummy! It had to be Mummy. She must have forgotten something.

Frantic, I ran to the bathroom and spat the chewed-up tablets into the toilet bowl. There was no time to fetch water outside to flush the tablets down. Wiping my mouth, I hurried outside to open the gate.

"Morayo!"

It was Aunty Morenike.

As I opened the gate, I saw the annoyance on her sweating face. I quickly knelt down to greet her, reaching for the travelling bag she was holding.

"Good afternoon, Aunty Morenike. I didn't know it was you."

"Morayo, if you did not know that it was me, *nko*?" Aunty Morenike pursed her lips, giving me a suspicious look. "What were you doing?"

I kept quiet.

Aunty Morenike took a deep breath. "Get up and let us go inside. The afternoon sun is merciless today. I need something cold to drink. I hope NEPA gave you people electricity. For the past two weeks our whole estate has been living in darkness." Still murmuring to herself, she walked briskly towards the house. I jumped up, carrying the heavy Ghana-Must-Go bag after her.

Later, as I set the tray of Coke and roasted groundnuts on the stool beside her, I asked after her son. "Aunty Morenike, how's Damilare?"

Instantly, her face lit up. "That boy. He is fine. You need to see the size of *amala* he is now eating. I can almost swear that his stomach extends into those little legs of his." Aunty Morenike stood up from her seat. She headed towards the toilet.

"Morayo!"

When Aunty Morenike screamed my name, I remembered that I had not flushed the tablets.

My heart dropped.

I could hear Aunty Morenike's footsteps as she hurried back to the sitting room. "What are those tablets doing in the toilet bowl?" she asked.

Looking down at my feet, I kept quiet.

I felt her gentle hand on my arm. "Morayo, please look at me." Her voice was low and soft. "How did those tablets get inside the toilet bowl?"

"I spat them there."

"*You did?*" Aunty Morenike took a deep breath. "Morayo, *kilo de?*"

"Aunty Morenike, Bros T ... He raped me." As I said the words out loud, I felt an intense sense of relief. He did not just come to my room at night. He did not just "touch me." He did not just lift up my skirts. I said it again: "He raped me."

I felt Aunty Morenike's body go rigid, and then she gathered me into her arms, resting my head against her chest. The pinching pain in my own chest made me gasp. "Aunty, nobody understands how much it hurts."

She whispered the words in my hair. "Morayo, I do."

When I felt teardrops on my forehead, I realized that Aunty Morenike was crying. As the tears sank their way through my hair to my scalp, I started to cry too. For what seemed like a very long time, we held each other and cried softly. When we both had no tears left, we sat on the settee and talked about what had happened.

I held onto her hand. "Please, don't tell Mummy about the tablets. I promise, I will never try that again, I promise!"

I saw the indecision in her eyes. "Morayo, you could have died today." I nodded.

That evening, Aunty Morenike did not leave until everybody had come back from the party. I knew that despite my promise, she was still afraid to leave me alone in the house. Later, when Aunty Morenike and Mummy disappeared into Mummy's room, I was sure that she was telling Mummy what she had seen that afternoon. Mummy did not discuss it with me, but from then on, she did not object any time I asked if I could go and spend some time at Aunty Morenike's flat. Any time I felt the sadness coming, I would jump onto a bus and take the twenty-minute ride.

During one of my visits, we lay side by side on the carpeted floor of Aunty Morenike's sitting room. The room was dark, and it helped that she could not see my face. We had been talking about Bros T. "But even though I didn't want him to come to my room, what he did felt good." My chest tightened and I whispered the words tainted by shame. "And I liked it."

Aunty Morenike sighed. "It still was not your fault."

"But ..."

"You know how you cry when cutting onions?"

I nodded. "Yes."

"It's because the vapours from the onions make you cry, even though you're not sad. Those feelings in your body were just like that: mere physical reactions. It does not mean that you wanted him to do what he did."

I blinked back the tears that came to my eyes. "But why did he do it?"

"Because he wanted to," Aunty Morenike replied in a soft voice. "It was his choice."

She reached for my hand. "It is okay for the sadness to still come, Morayo," she said. "One day it will all begin to feel a little better." That day seemed far away, but I never came back home as sad as when I left.

Aunty Morenike often said, with that enigmatic smile of hers, that one should always take care of one's own. Even a strong sieve cannot sift yam flour by itself. It needs a hand to hold it up.

Part Two

MORENIKE
1988

9

*A man does not get so angry at his head
that he then uses his cap to cover his buttocks.*

Morenike Balogun stared blankly out of the car window. Mr. Bello, Uncle Owolabi's driver, was taking her home. On their way to her flat in Orogun, they drove past the busy Sango Market. At seven o'clock, the market was still bustling with scores of people looking for last-minute bargains. Fresh produce sold for rock-bottom prices at the end of the day. Market women with tired babies strapped to their backs covered their goods with faded blue waterproof tarpaulin sheets and locked up their shops. Some were already hurrying off to the motor park to catch a commercial minibus. Hungry husbands and children were waiting at home.

Mr. Bello drove by the University of Ibadan campus. Morenike saw the silvery shadow of the university's ivory tower clock in the distance. She was happy when they drove by the bright streetlights. But she found the pitch-black darkness along the next stretch of road even more comforting.

Mr. Bello spoke up. "Please, I have to stop at the next petrol station."

Turning from the window, Morenike rubbed her red eyes. "I am not in a hurry to get home. Damilare is with Mummy Ibeji this weekend." Settling back into the seat, she tried to distract herself by staring at the colourful lights blinking on the car's dashboard. But her mind kept going back to the look on Aunty Bisoye's face.

When Morenike had told Aunty Bisoye about Morayo's attempted suicide, the older woman gasped and her legs buckled. As Morenike held her up, she could feel Aunty Bisoye's body trembling through her cotton *iro* and *buba*.

Sitting on the bed, Morayo's mother rocked back and forth, muttering and wringing her hands together. "How could I have been eating and drinking when my house was on fire?"

"Aunty, it is not your fault."

"Morenike—" Aunty Bisoye looked up in alarm. "Thank you for telling me. Now you must help me. Morayo's father must not hear of this. *He must not.*" She wrung her hands again, staring down at the bedspread as if she was berating herself. "He already told me that I was the one who brought evil into our home. My God, what have I done?"

In the back seat, Morenike found herself reaching for the door handle as the car swerved into a brightly lit petrol station, narrowly missing a little boy hawking Gala sausage rolls. Mr. Bello stepped out, locking the door behind him. The little boy knocked on the car window. He was wearing a grown man's long *buba*. His mouth parted in a smile; he pointed to the Gala. After Morenike shook her head, she watched the barefoot boy move on to the next car. A bus almost ran him down, but laughing, the little boy jumped between two petrol pumps. "Boy, *commot* for road!" the angry bus driver shouted.

The little boy was about the same height as Damilare. Morenike blinked away the tears at the thought of her son. *Damilare.*

"I don't know what to say to Morayo." Aunty Bisoye had held onto Morenike's hands, pleading with her before she finally took her leave. "Any time I try to speak to her about ..." Bisoye's hands waved limply in the air.

"Tayo," Morenike prompted.

Bisoye closed her eyes. "Yes," she whispered. "The words get stuck in my throat. *You* would know what to say."

Morenike nodded. Yes. She knew. In 1981, when she turned fifteen, her father's friend, Chief Komolafe, had raped her.

For years, Chief Komolafe and Morenike's father co-chaired the Oremeji Neighbourhood Landlord Association. She and her younger twin brothers, Taiwo and Kehinde, played with his children. Chief Komolafe owned some rental office buildings in Abeokuta and travelled there regularly. Morenike's father often asked him to drop Morenike at her boarding school in Abeokuta.

That fateful morning, years back, Mummy Ibeji woke Morenike. "Good morning, Morenike. *Oya,* get up. Chief Komolafe will soon be here. When you are done packing your things, bring the boxes to the sitting room."

By the time Chief Komolafe arrived in his silver Mercedes 280 S, Morenike was dressed in her white cotton blouse, blue khaki skirt, and blue beret.

Mummy Ibeji hugged her daughter tightly as Chief Komolafe's driver, Mr. Adeoti, arranged the cardboard boxes inside the boot of the car. "Morenike, when you are in

Abeokuta, remember whose child you are." She hugged her daughter again and then looked in her face. "Focus on your books and listen to your teachers. Have you heard me?"

Wiping tears from her eyes, Morenike nodded. Mummy Ibeji walked her to the car. "My dear, don't cry. I promise that I will come and see you. Don't forget to give your school mother the packet of cabin biscuits I bought for her." Morenike opened the car's passenger door and sat next to Mr. Adeoti.

She remembered how her mother stood by the house gates waving as the car headed down the winding, hilly street. It had been dark outside. The pre-dawn prayer, called out from the Oremeji mosque three streets away, roared from huge speakers attached to the tall building. Soft yellow lights shone from houses on the hill as the neighbourhood woke up.

Morenike gently tapped her feet to the music of King Sunny Ade playing on the car stereo. At the back of the car, Chief Komolafe was going through a pile of newspapers. It was just like all the other times. Soon they left the busy traffic of the city behind them, driving past little farming villages with endless fields of cassava plants. When they arrived at the town of Aiyetoro, Morenike could feel butterflies in her stomach. They were now less than forty kilometres away from her school.

As they drove past the crowded weighing centres for cocoa and cowpea, Morenike could see sweaty young men loading the brown sacks into the lorries that would take the crops to Lagos for shipping. Then she noticed that the cars ahead of them were turning around.

Mr. Adeoti frowned. "Shief," he said in his thick Ibadan accent, "I think I should find out what is going on-o. I can ask the drivers at the motor park, sir."

"Okay," said Chief Komolafe. He pointed. "Park under that tree."

Leaving the engine running, Mr. Adeoti crossed the road and spoke with some commercial drivers. They told him that a gang of armed robbers dressed in police uniforms had mounted roadblocks and were currently operating on the road to Abeokuta. Hearing the news, Chief Komolafe decided that it would be safer to spend the night in Aiyetoro. They would leave for Abeokuta in the morning.

They checked into one of the guesthouses along the road.

After their delicious meal of pounded yam and bush meat, washed down by ice-cold Maltina, Mr. Adeoti went outside to stretch his legs. Chief Komolafe and Morenike walked back to their hotel rooms. Chief Komolafe stopped in front of his. "Morenike, come to my room." He looked at his watch. "Let's say in about thirty minutes? There is something I want to discuss with you."

"Yes, sir."

Later, Morenike knocked on Chief Komolafe's door.

"Come in!"

Chief Komolafe was sitting on the bed. The small white towel wrapped around his short, stout body barely covered him.

Embarrassed, Morenike took a step backwards. "Sorry, sir. I did not know that you were not dressed. I will come back later, sir."

Smiling broadly, Chief Komolafe gestured with his pudgy hand. "No, no. Morenike, come in. Come and sit down beside me," he said, patting the spot next to him on the bed.

Morenike sat on the bed, her hands neatly folded in her lap. Although her mother had warned against being alone in a room with a male, she did not think she was in any danger. Was Chief not like her father? Still, her skin crawled when Chief Komolafe reached out and stroked the back of her neck. She shifted away from him.

"You are such a big girl now," he said, moving closer. "When did you become so beautiful?"

Morenike looked at him, unsure how to answer the question.

Suddenly, Chief Komolafe wrestled her to the bed and rolled on top of her.

His hairy, protruding stomach was as heavy as bricks.

When Morenike opened her mouth to scream, Chief Komolafe clamped his hand over her mouth. Panicking, Morenike jabbed him hard in his side with her bony elbow. Chief Komolafe grunted and moved his body away. As Morenike tried to wiggle out from under him, he slapped her across the face. Her head snapped backwards, hitting the wooden bedpost. As Morenike drifted away, she could hear his stomach slapping against her body.

When Morenike regained consciousness, Chief Komolafe was snoring next to her. She was naked, her torn dress flung to the floor. Sliding off the bed, she clutched the dress to her chest and tiptoed to the door.

She almost dropped the dress when she found Mr. Adeoti standing outside in the corridor. The pile of newspapers in his hands fell to the floor. *"Morenike?"* Moaning, Morenike ran barefoot to her room.

The next morning, Mr. Adeoti scowled when he saw Morenike standing by the car. Morenike gave him a weak smile. *"Ekaaro,* sir."

Mr. Adeoti ignored her greeting and slammed the car boot shut. She could imagine him thinking, *This small girl is following an old baba for money. What is this world turning to?*

Smacking oily lips from his breakfast, Chief Komolafe strolled majestically out of the hotel. Morenike sat in the front of the car with Mr. Adeoti, her arms wrapped tightly around her body. She could feel the waves of hostility radiating from the driver as he stared straight ahead. Chief Komolafe got into the car without looking in Morenike's direction. Morenike felt the hairs on the back of her neck stand up. During the drive to Abeokuta she was conscious of every move he made. Her body tensed up whenever he held onto her headrest to reposition himself.

They soon arrived at Abeokuta, driving past the ancient, crumbling mud walls that still surrounded parts of it. The sprawling city was right below the famous Olumo Rock. From Morenike's school in the heart of Abeokuta, the students could see the Olumo and the crowd of tourists that visited its caves and shrines.

"Adeoti, stop at that supermarket next to the school."

"Yes, sah."

On other trips, Morenike would skip out of the car and race inside with Mr. Adeoti to buy more cornflakes, powered milk, and bottles of Ribena. The extra provisions always came in handy during lean periods in the middle of the school term. But this time when Chief Komolafe pointed the wad of money in Morenike's direction, she froze.

He handed the money to his driver instead. "Adeoti, go and get some provisions for Morenike to take back to school."

Mr. Adeoti collected the money and went into the supermarket. Adjusting the folds of his white lace *agbada*, Chief Komolafe sat back in the plush leather seat and continued reading his newspaper.

Morenike stared into space. When they arrived at her school, she quietly opened her door and stood outside.

Without saying a word, Mr. Adeoti removed the heavy carton of provisions from the boot and dropped it right on Morenike's feet. Then he took the thick bundle of naira notes Chief Komolafe handed him and flung it inside the open carton. Morenike watched the car drive away, its spinning alloy wheels gleaming in the sun.

"Morenike!"

Morenike turned to see her friend Remi running towards her. Remi had already changed into their checkered blue house wear. The two girls had lived in the same dormitory room during the previous school year.

"Guess what? You are in my dormitory room again," Remi said with a giggle when she reached Morenike's side. "Aisha too." The girls hugged each other.

"I am so happy," Morenike told her friend as they each picked up a suitcase. Morenike balanced the box of provisions on her head and the two girls started walking towards their dormitory.

The brick school buildings were scattered all over the compound. The two-storey administrative building and classrooms were nearer to the school gate. The dormitories, the staff quarters, the dining hall, and the kitchen were closer to the back wall of the school. The general-assembly ground was right in the middle of the compound. By the time the two girls reached Queen Amina house, they were both panting from the long walk.

When the dining bell rang for their evening meal of beans and fried plantains, Morenike had already made her bed. Her provisions were neatly stored away in the little metal locker she had to share with her bunkmate. For the first time, Morenike was assigned to the lower bunk. The top belonged to a form-

one girl who had yet to arrive. As Morenike took her shiny new aluminum plate and cutlery out of the locker and headed out to the dining hall, she prayed that the girl was not a bed wetter.

Soon Morenike was standing at her table in the dining hall, singing the grace at the top of her lungs with the other girls.

"Some have food but cannot eat.
Some can eat but have no food.
We have food and we can eat.
Glory be to thee O God."

That night, alone under the cover of her mosquito net, Morenike was finally able to think about Aiyetoro. She told herself that the incident with Chief Komolafe never happened. She said it over and over again, night after night, until she started to believe it. And when she began waking up early in the morning to rush to the toilet and vomit, she told herself she must have eaten something bad.

Then one morning, Morenike fainted during the general assembly. The students, lined up according to their classes, were listening to the school principal, Mrs. Durotoye, call out the names of the students on the detention list and their offences.

"Folusho Ogundoyin. Leaving the school compound without permission."

Morenike took a deep breath and blinked. Remi's blue beret was swimming before her eyes. She blinked again. Maybe the unusually hot morning sun was to blame.

Mrs. Durotoye cleared her throat. "Mudina Abass. Stole three bowls of uncooked rice from the kitchen pantry."

Some girls at the back of the assembly ground giggled. Mudina's nickname at school was Recurring Decimal. She was always on the detention list for one offence or another. She was probably planning to cook the stolen rice on a contraband hot plate smuggled into the dormitory.

Suddenly Mrs. Durotoye's head divided into two as Morenike's eyes rolled back in their sockets. She reached out for Remi's shoulder, trying to steady herself, but she kept falling.

The next thing she remembered was cool water dripping on her face.

Nurse Ibidun was leaning over her. "Morenike, how are you feeling?" When Morenike tried to sit up, she vomited all over her.

"How long have you been sick like this?" the nurse asked.

Morenike thought. "Two weeks?" she said weakly.

The women in the room exchanged alarmed looks. They whispered fiercely among themselves, and that morning Morenike missed her classes. Nurse Ibidun sat next to her in the school's rusty Kombi bus as they drove her to the nearby hospital. In the packed waiting room, Morenike kept praying that she would not vomit on the tiled floor as bile rose in her throat. Nurse Ibidun's anxious eyes darted from Morenike's sweating face to the nurses' station.

One of the nurses finally called her name. "Morenike Balogun!"

Nurse Ibidun stood up, helping Morenike to her feet. "Present," she said.

The nurse closed the thin paper file. "The doctor is ready to see you."

Morenike and Nurse Ibidun followed behind the woman as she walked down a corridor. She opened the door with a sign that read "Examinations" and pointed to a metal bed with a thin foam mattress. "Lie down there. The doctor is coming."

The doctor's tired face broke out into a smile when he saw Nurse Ibidun. "Ah, I see you have come to visit us again."

"Yes, doctor. This is one of my students. She has been vomiting for the past two weeks."

The doctor's smile disappeared. "I see." He beckoned to Nurse Ibidun. "Please, can I see you outside?" Morenike heard some whispering, and then they returned to the room and there was some prodding by the doctor. After the blood test result came back, Morenike found out what the whole school would soon learn—but before that, the principal, Mrs. Durotoye, contacted Mummy Ibeji by telephone, asking her to come down to Abeokuta.

A couple of hours later, a worried-looking Mummy Ibeji sat beside Morenike in the school principal's office. Mrs. Durotoye sat behind her desk with a stern look. "Mrs. Balogun, I am sorry to tell you that Morenike has been expelled from school for getting pregnant. As much as this saddens me, the Ministry of Education regulation clearly stipulates that pregnant students be automatically expelled."

Mummy Ibeji jerked her body in the chair. Then she looked around as if she was just waking up from a dream. "Pregnant? Who is pregnant?"

Mrs. Durotoye's stern expression softened. But Morenike could only shrink back in her chair as Mummy Ibeji's burning eyes landed on her. Later, Morenike would think back on this meeting and wonder how many other mothers at Olumo Girls' Grammar School had sat in this very office, hearing this same kind of sad news. How many times had Mrs. Durotoye said these same words?

Mummy Ibeji stammered in confusion, "Ex ... expelled?"

Sighing, Mrs. Durotoye stood up from her chair. "It is a

pity, but my hands are tied. The Ministry of Education's policy on pregnant students is very clear. I have to say we are very surprised at this development because Morenike has been such an exemplary student. In fact, she was the likely candidate for the position of Head Girl next year. It would be such a pity if she does not further her education after …"

Her voice trailed off. In the office, Morenike could hear only silence.

Stumbling on a can that littered the ground, Morenike hurried after her mother through the busy Asero motor park. Mummy Ibeji was marching briskly ahead. Morenike balanced her cardboard boxes on top of her head. Her mother had yet to speak one word to her since they left the school compound.

Inside the green-and-yellow commercial minibus, Mummy Ibeji rocked back and forth. Morenike snivelled beside her.

Several passengers eyed them warily—it was plain to see something was very wrong. The elderly woman sitting next to Mummy Ibeji patted her on the arm when silent tears ran down her face. "Madam, whatever it is, please take it easy. Things always have a way of working themselves out."

Mummy Ibeji opened and closed her mouth like a mackerel fish pulled out of water. What could she say? The only way this pregnancy was going to work itself out was when a screaming baby was born.

When they arrived home two hours later, Morenike knelt in front of her mother. Her bony knees dug into the cement floor.

Mummy Ibeji was finally ready to talk. "Morenike, tell me the truth. Who is responsible for this?"

Morenike wiped her dripping nose with the back of her hand. "It is Chief Komolafe, Ma."

"*Chief Komolafe?* But how—?"

Morayo's voice fell. "He forced himself on me."

Mummy Ibeji bolted up from her chair. Her Ankara wrapper unravelled from her waist, whispering as it fell to the floor. "But when did this happen?"

Morenike explained.

"Are you sure of what you are saying?"

Morenike nodded. "Yes, Ma."

"Please my child, tell me the truth."

"I am telling the truth, Ma."

Mummy Ibeji stared into her daughter's eyes. Tying her wrapper unevenly around her waist, she did a little war dance, stamping her feet on the multicoloured linoleum tiles.

"Chief Komolafe has pulled the tail of a sleeping tiger! Get up!" Mummy Ibeji commanded, adjusting the *gele* on her head. "We are going over to his office. He has to tell me what demon possessed him."

Chief Komolafe's office was just down the street. As Mummy Ibeji marched ahead, Morenike struggled to keep up. The afternoon sun was very hot and she felt fainter with every step. She had not eaten all morning. She was also very afraid of what her mother would do. By the side of the road a sugar-cane seller glared at Morenike as she almost knocked over her tray into the sand. "Please, I am sorry," she mumbled as the woman hissed, "God gave you eyes, use them!"

Mama Atinuke, Chief Komolafe's youngest wife, sold cartons of frozen fish and turkey on the first level of his three-storey office building. Her co-wife, Mama Kike, had a hairdressing salon on the second level. Their husband's office was at the very top. As they approached the building, Morenike could see Mama Atinuke standing in front. A customer was loading her car with cartons of frozen fish. Morenike's heart sank. She started to pray under her breath that her mother would not address the woman. It would quickly turn into a public spectacle.

"Good afternoon, Mummy Ibeji," Mama Atinuke said in a respectful tone. "Did you come to pick up your turkey?"

"Turkey?" Mummy Ibeji glared at the woman and hissed. A look of surprise dawned on Mama Atinuke's face and she took a step back. "Mummy Ibeji, what is the matter? Did I offend you?"

"Go and ask your husband," she snapped, pulling on Morenike's hand and pushing her up the winding stairs by the side of the building. Chief Komolafe's secretary told them that he was busy and could not be disturbed. "Madam, you can wait in reception if you like." She pointed to the room across the corridor.

The room was empty and they sat in leather armchairs arranged in rows. The chairs felt cold from the window air conditioner that was blowing directly at them. Morenike's sandals practically disappeared inside the plush wall-to-wall rug.

It was Morenike's first time in the office. Looking around, she saw large framed photographs of Chief Komolafe all over the painted green walls. There were pictures of him on the day he received his chieftaincy title, and there was even one of him and Morenike's father as they received a joint award from the Oremeji Neighbourhood Landlord Association.

After sitting in the reception room for an hour, Mummy Ibeji's patience ran out. She stood and marched past the secretary—"Madam, you can't just go in"—and threw open the door to the office. Morenike followed her mother.

Chief Komolafe was sitting behind a huge executive desk. There were even more photos of him on the light yellow walls of the large room. A big television stood in one corner. Mummy walked up to his desk and crossed her arms across her chest.

His secretary hovered nervously near the doorway.

"Biliki, you go can go back to work," Chief Komolafe commanded in his gravelly voice.

The secretary quickly closed the door.

Tapping his fingers on the edge of the desk, Chief Komolafe gave Morenike's mother a half-smile. "Mummy Ibeji, I hope you have a good reason for just barging into my office. Is everything okay? How is my friend?"

"How is your friend?" she roared. "So you want to pretend you do not know why I am here?"

Chief Komolafe raised an eyebrow. "Is there a reason why I should know what goes on inside your head?"

"Very well, I will tell you." Planting her hands on the desk, Mummy Ibeji leaned over the piles of paper to stare into Chief Komolafe's face, her mouth twisted in a snarl. "My Morenike is pregnant. She tells me that you are the father of the child in her stomach."

Morenike's body tensed when Chief Komolafe looked at her and narrowed his eyes. He turned to her mother. "*And so?* Is that why you think you have the right to come into my office uninvited? Just because *you* neglected to teach *your* wayward daughter how to keep her legs together?" Chief Komolafe wagged his pudgy pointer finger. "Listen, the only reason why I have not called my security men to drag you out is my respect for your husband. I do not have time to listen to women who do not know their place. Leave my office."

Mummy Ibeji's hands flew to her head. "*Mo gbe!* Oh, so

you think that I am like one of those sheep-women you keep cooped up in your house?" She gave a bitter laugh. "By the time I am done with you, the whole of Ibadan will know that you are a shameless old man who cannot be trusted around a goat. You will live to regret the day you touched my daughter."

Mummy Ibeji grabbed Morenike's arm. "Let's go."

Mama Atinuke was now standing outside the building with her senior co-wife, Mama Kike. When Mummy Ibeji marched down the stairs with fire in her eyes, Morenike saw the women exchange worried looks.

Mama Kike bravely stepped forward with a pleading look. "Mummy Ibeji. *Please*, tell us. What is the matter?"

"Your shameless husband has impregnated my daughter," Mummy Ibeji announced in a loud voice.

Mama Kike gasped. Mama Atinuke's mouth fell open. Morenike felt as though she was about to faint. Mummy Ibeji marched straight ahead.

Later that evening, as soon as her father walked into the house, Morenike started crying again. She looked at her mother. "Mummy …"

He gave her a worried look. "Morenike, what are you doing at home? Are you sick?"

"Daddy Morenike, this is not something we should discuss in front of the twins," Mummy Ibeji said in a soft voice. "Please, let us go to your bedroom."

They should not have bothered leaving the sitting room, Morenike thought later, because no doubt Taiwo and Kehinde heard the entire discussion.

Her father's eyes bulged when he heard the news. "Morenike is PREGNANT?" Daddy Morenike shouted. He kept shaking his head in disbelief. "Komolafe? Komolafe? It cannot be so!

Gbanjubola, tell me, what would a man with two grown women in his house want with a mere schoolchild? Has Komolafe not been taking Morenike to school for many years? Gbanjubola, ask your daughter to tell you the truth!"

"Daddy, I am telling the truth," Morenike said.

Daddy Morenike turned around, wagging his finger. "You! Shut up. When did you become a stone-cold liar?" He faced his wife. "Gbanjubola, did I not warn you? Did I not warn you that you need to pay more attention to your daughter?" He mimicked Mummy Ibeji's high-pitched voice: "Morenike is a responsible girl. Morenike can be trusted. Daddy Morenike, you are too hard on her. Children nowadays need freedom to discover themselves." He threw out his hands. "Are you satisfied now? She has discovered that she has a womb and she has put it to good use."

"But, sir, I am telling you the truth," Morenike insisted.

Her father spun around, raising his hand. Mummy Ibeji jumped between them. Morenike winced as her father's hand connected with the side of Mummy Ibeji's head. She almost gasped, but covered her mouth.

The enraged woman spat her words. "Gbadebo! What has come over you? Have you forgotten that she is carrying our grandchild?"

"Grandchild?" Stepping back, Daddy Morenike laughed sharply. "Both of you open your ears wide. I will not raise any bastard child in my house." He pointed at his sobbing daughter. "Morenike, wherever you found this, your shameful pregnancy—you had better take it back there." The bedroom door shook on its hinges as he slammed it shut behind him.

Over the next two weeks Mummy Ibeji tried to get her husband to change his mind. One morning, he stormed out of the house with an ultimatum. "Woman, listen. Shut up and leave me alone, or leave with your daughter. It is your choice."

Mummy Ibeji kept her mouth shut. How could she leave the house when her sons needed her too?

Two days later, Mummy Ibeji called Morenike to her bedroom. "My child, you heard what your father said." Mummy Ibeji knew when she had pushed her husband far enough. He would not budge. "You will go and stay with your grandmother in Omu until your father's anger subsides. Before you know it, you will be back in Ibadan."

Morenike's large eyes widened in her thin face. Despite her mother's valiant efforts, she had not been able to keep any food down since she came home.

She looked at her mother, bewildered. "But …" Her voice was raspy from bouts of crying. "It was not my fault."

Mummy Ibeji wiped the tears off her daughter's face and wrapped her arms around her. Rocking Morenike back and forth, she kept whispering in her ear, "I know, my child. It is not your fault. Your mother knows it is not your fault. And I am so, so sorry."

Morenike ran into her grandmother's welcoming arms. "My child!" Mama Omu said happily as she hugged her granddaughter. She held Morenike at arm's length. "How is it that you grow more beautiful every time I see you?" she asked with a smile.

Morenike smiled back. "But I have not changed much since you last saw me." Mama Omu shook her head. "What kind of mirrors do they sell in that Ibadan? Even in the village we have better mirrors. Tomorrow, I am going to buy you a new mirror at the market." Morenike buried her face in Mama Omu's *buba*, breathing in the familiar smell.

In Mama Omu's eyes, Morenike and her brothers could do no wrong. Sometimes Morenike found it hard to believe that the small, smiling woman had given birth to her fiery mother. Even after a few moments she could already feel the sadness of the last few days starting to subside.

Mummy Ibeji knelt to greet her mother. "*Ekaasan,* Mama." Mama Omu turned towards her daughter. "Welcome, my child. Come. Let us go inside the house." Mama Omu was clutching her little purse. She had been on her way out when they arrived.

The next day, Morenike and Mama Omu walked Mummy Ibeji to the motor park from where she would travel back to Ibadan.

At first, Morenike missed the vibrant sounds of the city. For days she found it hard to sleep. At night all she could hear was the creaking of crickets and the croaking of frogs. Lying awake in bed, she wondered when she would see her brothers again. She missed school.

The small village of Omu boasted one church, one mosque, one school, and a little community clinic. The two partially paved roads that ran through the town made a T junction in front of the king's palace. From Mama Omu's little house in the middle of the village, Morenike could see the nomadic cattle rearers herding their cattle to the village's stream to drink water.

Morenike was two months pregnant when she arrived at Omu. As her stomach grew bigger, stares and whispers followed her as she walked along the village paths. In her head, she could hear the village women warning their teenage daughters.

Come here! Giggling like a fool just because that riff-raff boy looked at you sideways. Have you seen Mama Omu's granddaughter?

How many granddaughters does she have? Yes, the one who came from the city.

Aha, you see. Have I not told you? That is what happens when you let a boy ruin you. I hear she was so smart with her books, too. She could have been somebody in life. What a waste.

Every month, Mummy Ibeji came to Omu to see her daughter. She would arrive with provisions and little things in preparation for the baby's arrival. In one visit, Mummy Ibeji pulled out a purple shawl with a matching hat and booties from her bag. "Morenike, come and see what your Aunty Bisoye knitted for the baby."

Morenike took the items from Mummy Ibeji. She ran her fingers over the soft wool. "They are very nice. Please help me thank her," Morenike said.

"Don't worry, you will soon be back at home and you will thank her yourself."

In those early months, Mummy Ibeji kept assuring Morenike that soon her father would change his mind and let her return home. At every visit, she would look expectantly at her mother. "Mummy, when I am coming home?"

"Your father is still angry, Morenike. I am trying …"

Mama Omu stepped between them and smiled. "Soon, my dear. Just give your father some time." But Mummy Ibeji's excuses did not stop, and Morenike resigned herself to life in Omu.

Their day started early in the morning. Mama Omu had a little wooden shack at Oja Oba where she sold cooked *ofada* rice and black-eyed beans wrapped up in fresh plantain leaves.

In the mornings, she also sold tea and bread to commercial bus drivers and other traders in the market. Customers sat at the wooden tables and benches arranged inside and in front of the shack. Business was brisk, since Mama Omu was known in the market for her generosity. She would let her regular customers eat on credit. Even though she had never attended school, she kept an accurate record of who owed her and who had paid up. Soon one of Morenike's jobs was to visit those who were behind on their payments to remind them of their debt. The humiliation of having a child asking the debtors for money often loosened tight purses.

Bolanle, a distant relative, helped Mama Omu with the cooking. Although Bolanle was older than Morenike, she was much smaller. At the end of each day she would pack up the leftover food to take home for the rest of her family. At first, her dark, brooding eyes followed Morenike around. Realizing that Bolanle felt that she had come to take her place, Morenike made sure she did not touch anything without first asking her.

Most evenings Mama Omu and Morenike sat under the shea tree at the back of the house to enjoy the fresh air. There was no television in the house, but Mama Omu's ancient transistor radio worked erratically. On Friday nights they listened to Akolawole Olawuyi's investigative program, *Nkan Mbe*. The program highlighted true-life strange and mysterious happenings. Morenike would never forget the story about the woman who gave birth to a green-eyed boy with blond hair. The problem was that both parents had no white relative in their families.

Because the young mother worked with white male expatriates, her angry in-laws quickly branded her a whore and threw her and her newborn child out of their son's house. Even her own family turned their backs despite her loud cries of innocence. In desperation, the woman contacted the producers of *Nkan Mbe* for help.

Mama Omu held the transistor radio in her lap as she and Morenike listened to the woman swear that no other man had seen her nakedness since the day she entered her husband's house. The woman declared that she was ready to do anything to prove her innocence. Even if it meant swearing before the dreaded shrine of Ayelala.

As they listened to her trembling voice, Morenike and Mama Omu looked at each other. "Does this foolish woman want to bloat up and die?" Mama Omu muttered under her breath. Morenike's eyes widened. Everybody knew this manner of death was the fate of those who lie to the river goddess.

Morenike's heart raced as Olawuyi's calm voice narrated how the woman, accompanied by her husband and their family members, travelled to the shrine. True to her word, the young mother swore her innocence and lived. When the priestess shrieked that someone else was concealing a great secret, everybody was shocked when the husband's mother fell to her knees before the shrine, pleading for her life. The woman revealed that when she used to travel to London for her business, she would engage in prostitution to raise spending money. She had missed her menstrual period after one of those trips, but then her son was born with very dark skin nine months later. How could she have known that the birth of her grandson almost thirty years later would reveal that her husband's pride and joy was really a bastard?

Olawuyi's poignant voice came on at the end of the show. "Hmm … Strange things happen."

On one of their quiet evenings, Mama Omu talked to Morenike about the baby.

"Morenike, I have been watching you for some time now. Every time your mother and I talk about your baby, your face changes. It grows long and sad. Tell me, my child, what is the matter?"

Morenike did not know how to tell her grandmother that sometimes she prayed that the baby would die in her stomach so that she could be free. Every time the child moved, she remembered the father and the hatred in her heart grew. She could not bear to think of raising such a child. But what choice did she have?

It was as if Mama Omu heard her thoughts. She reached for her granddaughter's hand. "I know that this child was brought into your life by a painful thing," she said. "But I also know that good can come from evil. Remember, this child has a part of you too. Start with loving that part. Perhaps one day, your love for your child will grow stronger than your hatred for the father."

After Mama Omu went to sleep, Morenike stayed awake in her bed and listened to the hooting of the owl. Her stomach shook as the baby kicked and turned. For the first time, Morenike placed her hand on her stomach and sang softly to the baby inside.

On Wednesday evenings, Morenike went with Mama Omu to the Mission House. Mama Omu was part of a group of basket weavers. The money made from the sale of the colourful raffia baskets went towards taking care of the young orphans in the community.

The women sat in a circle on large mats in the courtyard of the Mission House. As their busy fingers bent the long raffia strips, they shared their stories. Morenike listened quietly.

At one meeting, one of the younger women spoke about her longing to have a child. She talked about the emptiness she felt, and the bitter tears that flowed in the quiet of the night while her husband slept peacefully beside her. As her fingers bent the raffia, the young woman shared the crushing disappointment that came every month with the stickiness between her thighs. "I was told to save myself for my wedding night, and I did. My mothers, what have I done wrong?" she asked.

Morenike saw the young woman take a quick, longing look at her protruding stomach. Feeling guilty, she bent her head before the young woman could see the pity in her eyes.

"You have done nothing wrong," Mama Omu said softly. "Remember that others have walked this path before you and now balance babies on their backs. Daughter, yours will not be an exception." The other women nodded their heads, echoing Mama Omu's words.

"The doctor says that my husband too must come to the hospital for tests," the young woman said, reaching for another raffia strip. "But I know my husband will not go. He insists there is nothing wrong with *him*. How could there be when his father had ten children? My mothers, what should I do?"

"Your mother-in-law, Ayoka, is my good friend," one of the older women said with a thoughtful look. "I know that she is a reasonable woman. The other day, she told me she needs some new chicken baskets. Next week we will weave her some beautiful ones. You will then visit her. After you present the baskets, you will discuss how the wise *dokita* from the city wants to see her strong, handsome son. Make sure you tell her there is nothing wrong, but that the *dokita* says that your husband must take some tests to ensure his well-being. I know she will tell you what to do."

A grateful smile beamed across the young woman's face. "My mothers, may you all live long."

When Mummy Ibeji visited and discussed preparations for the baby with Mama Omu, Morenike would stay silent. She did not feel any joy in her heart about the approaching birth of her child. She noticed that her grandmother would look at her with a worried expression.

During one of Mummy Ibeji's visits, she sat Morenike down to talk. "I can tell that your time is coming fast from the way you are carrying the baby so low. I don't want you to be afraid of the labour pains. It is different for everybody, but you are young and the baby will come quickly."

Two days before the baby arrived, Bolanle came to the house to braid Morenike's hair. Mama Omu sat nearby shelling melon seeds for their night meal.

Bolanle never hid her curiosity about Morenike's pregnancy. As usual, she started asking her questions about the baby's father. Who was he? Why had he not come to see her in the village? Tired and irritated with the questioning, Morenike told Bolanle that the baby's father had denied that the baby was his.

Looking around to make sure Mama Omu was not listening to their conversation, Bolanle lowered her voice. "I have heard that if one dips one's hand in the blood that comes with the baby and curses the father, he will know no peace until he admits publicly that the child is his," she said with a knowing look.

Morenike slowly shook her head. "Curse him? Me, I cannot curse anybody."

Bolanle hissed and gave her a pitying look. "So you want everybody to think that you don't know who the father of the child is?"

Morenike kept quiet. She had already said more than she intended to.

Her contractions started the following afternoon while they were still at the market. Morenike was giving a customer some change when she felt a sharp pain radiating from the base of her spine to her groin. She gasped, holding onto the pillar at the entrance of the wooden shack. "Are you okay?" the man asked as the tin of money fell from her hand, rolling on the ground. Before Morenike could answer, another wave of pain hit and she stared at the customer, unable to speak.

The man hurried outside, shouting at the top of his voice. "Mama Omu! Mama Omu!"

Mama Omu found her granddaughter holding onto the pillar with tears running down her face. She hurried to her side. "Morenike, what is the matter?"

"Mama, my stomach … my back …," Morenike croaked as pain shot through her sides.

Mama Omu, adjusting her *gele,* called out for Bolanle, who was washing dirty pots beside the shack. "Bolanle!"

Bolanle poked her head in through the window opening. Looking around, Mama Omu lowered her voice. "*Oya,* leave those pots alone. Please go to the Mission House and tell the midwives that Morenike's time has come. I am taking her home." Mama Omu wrapped her arms around Morenike's waist. "Bolanle, make sure you lock up the shop when you get back."

All night, the contractions came one after the other. There was no time for Morenike to catch her breath before another one hit. Groaning and kneeling at the side of her bed, she wondered why nobody had ever told her childbirth was this painful. "Please, Morenike, you have to walk around so that your body will be loose," Mama Omu begged as she gently rubbed Morenike's back. With Mama Omu's help, Morenike staggered up to her feet and slowly walked around the room. Soon, she began to feel pressure low in her groin.

When Morenike's water broke in the middle of the night, she thought that her bladder had failed her. Her eyes flew open and she tried to get off the bed without waking Mama Omu, who was lying beside her. But Mama Omu woke up as soon as Morenike moved. Embarrassed, Morenike told Mama Omu what had happened. Mama stood up from the bed and wiped Morenike's damp forehead. "It is your water that broke, my child. Now it is time to go to the Mission House."

They slowly made their way to the Mission House—on the other side of the village—with the help of Mama Omu's large kerosene lantern. The newly constructed two-storey building was the pride of the whole village. In addition to housing the reverend and his family, the building contained the maternity ward and a training centre for missionaries. Its vast grounds were often used for wedding receptions.

As they walked slowly along the empty village paths, they could hear the hoot of an owl and the flat-sounding quacks of the white-backed night heron. The dim light of the new moon left long shadows on their faces. For Morenike, the ten-minute walk from her grandmother's house felt like an eternity. Each step brought sharper pains. She almost fell when she stumbled on a tree root jutting out on the path. "Mama," she gasped, "I am tired."

"I know, but we are almost there, my child," Mama Omu whispered. "I promise—just a few more steps."

Morenike could also hear the roar of the Mission House's diesel generator in the distance. She kept her eyes fixed on the lighted compound, willing herself to take just one more step as her grandmother tried to prop her body up with her fragile frame.

When they arrived at the Mission House, the night watchman opened the gate at Mama Omu's urgent call. Two midwives quickly came down to escort them to the birthing room. Within minutes, Morenike was on her back and the urge to push was upon her. She tried as hard as she could, but nothing happened. "Again," the midwife said, squeezing her hand, and Morenike pushed. "Again." She pushed. But still, nothing. Beads of sweat soon gathered on her forehead and she thrashed her head from side to side and wailed. "Mama, I cannot do this again. I cannot. Please don't make me ..."

Mama Omu stood by her side, mopping her brow. "Yes, you can do this, my child. *You can.*"

Through the haze of pain, Morenike could see worried looks on the faces of the midwives as they moved around her bed. They were both praying furiously under their breath. When Mama Omu gave her a tiny sip of water, she could see their worry reflected in her grandmother's eyes.

Time seemed to slow down. There was a clock on the far wall, but Morenike was delirious. She could not see if it was only minutes or hours—or days—that had already passed. "She is losing too much blood," she heard Mama Omu say to the midwives. Morenike had never heard fear in her voice before. And then—who's this? Her friend Remi, from school, skipped happily around the room.

Remi gave her a hurt look. "Morenike, why didn't you tell me you were not coming back to school?" Then she smiled. "But guess what? Recurring Decimal was on the detention list again today."

"It is too late to travel to the teaching hospital," the head midwife whispered to her partner at the base of the bed. "I fear that she will not make it. Only God can help her now."

Morenike saw her father's stern face in the corner. He leaned his back against the wall, arms crossed across his chest. "All this is your mother's fault," he said with a scowl. "She should have taught you how to keep your legs together."

Morenike leaned back and closed her eyes. She felt the midwives down below; they seemed to have found out what was wrong: the baby was coming feet first. Mama Omu was now whispering to her. "My child, they will turn the baby around. You must listen for the baby's cry, okay?"

Morenike felt the bed creak. Turning, she saw her mother sitting next to her. Mummy Ibeji was smiling gently. "Morenike, your father just told me that you can come back home. I am sorry that it took so long. After the baby is born, we will go back to Mama Omu's house and pack your bags."

As the images and voices faded in and out, Morenike could feel Mama Omu's hand gently stroking her head, wiping the sweat off her brow. She kept whispering the same words softly into Morenike's right ear. "My child, you will live and you will not die. You will see the breaking of dawn."

When the midwives turned the baby around, Morenike screamed. She could hear Bolanle's voice in her head. *I have heard that if one dips one's hand in the blood that comes with the baby and curses the father, he will know no peace until he admits publicly that the child is his.*

At that moment, Morenike did not care if Chief Komolafe never admitted that the baby was his. Her body was tearing itself in half! She just wanted to curse him with every fibre of her being. Her trembling fingers moved towards the pool of blood beneath her. Just before her fingertips could touch the blood, she felt someone grab her hand. She looked sideways and saw Mama Omu's face. She tried to pull her fingers away, but Mama Omu would not let go.

"Mama, leave me. *Leave me. Please.* Let me …," Morenike cried weakly. But her grandmother held on tightly.

Finally, a screaming baby boy announced his arrival as the soft early morning light filtered into the room. Later, when one of the midwives placed her hungry son in her arms, Morenike took one look at him and laughed hysterically. The women exchanged worried looks. Was it possible that the pain had sent the young mother over the edge into madness? But Morenike ignored their confusion. She was laughing in delight, for the boy had a large nose and a high forehead—and a birthmark, that very same birthmark, on his left cheek.

The boy was the spitting image of his father.

Mama Omu showed Morenike how to place her new son at her breast. As the hungry baby latched on and sucked hard, Morenike winced. Her stomach clenched with each suck her son took from her—and she felt the hard edges around her heart begin to melt. Watching her son's face, Morenike wondered if her grandmother was right. Maybe it was possible that, one day, the love she could already feel bubbling in her heart for the child in her arms could be greater than her hatred for his father.

The next day Mummy Ibeji arrived in Omu to meet her grandson. When she saw the baby, she too began to laugh. She held onto the edge of her Ankara wrapper and danced around the room. Did she not say that her daughter was no liar? Now her enemies would have no choice but to eat their words in defeat. "And the irony of it all," Mummy Ibeji whispered to her mother, smiling with her, "is that none of that animal's wives has given him a son. And here ...!"

Eight days after the baby was born, Mummy Ibeji, Mama Omu, and Alagba Fakoya—an elder from Mama Omu's church—gathered for his naming ceremony. Holding the baby in his arms, Alagba Fakoya asked Morenike for the boy's name. "His name is Oluwadamilare: *The-lord-has-vindicated-me*," she told him quietly as Mama Omu nodded and smiled. "Yes, he has."

10

The aftertaste of the bitterleaf is sweet.

They called the boy Damilare, and Morenike stayed in the village for another six months. When it looked like Morenike's father would not let them come back to Ibadan, Mama Omu sent for him. She knew that he would not refuse her request. She did not tell Morenike that her father was coming.

When Morenike saw her father's car parked in front of the house, her heart began racing. Her mother had visited the week before. Why was she back so soon? She hurried into the house and stood still when she saw her father happily bouncing Damilare on his lap. She had not seen him or her brothers in over a year.

"*Kaabo,* Morenike," he greeted her warmly. "Your mother and brothers send their greetings."

Morenike stared at him in silence. Mama Omu, hovering in the background, chided her. "*Morenike.* Didn't you hear your father?"

Kneeling with a solemn face, she greeted him. "*Ekule,* sir."

"Damilare has been keeping me company," her father told

her with a smile. "He reminds me of Kehinde." Morenike did not smile back.

Shortly after her arrival, her father announced that he was leaving. Before he left, he called Morenike aside. "Your mother will return at the end of the month to bring Damilare and you back home," he said.

"Thank you, sir," Morenike said in a flat voice. A disappointed look flashed across her father's face. She knew that he was expecting a different response—perhaps a joyful, grateful one—but at that moment, all Morenike felt was a searing hurt that flooded her body.

The night before they left Omu, Morenike went looking for Damilare and Mama Omu. She had just finished packing their last bag. She found them sitting at the back of the house under the giant shea tree. Standing at the door, Morenike watched them for a few minutes. The dusky red rays of the setting sun had settled around their faces, turning their skin a magnificent mahogany shade. Damilare's chubby little arms grabbed at Mama Omu's face as she threw him gently into the air. His delighted laughter rang out in the still evening. Damilare had spent most of his short life riding on Mama Omu's back, watching quietly as they went about their day at the market. Morenike knew they would miss each other very much.

She sat down beside them, watching their play. Damilare, tired from his busy day at the market, soon fell asleep in his great-grandmother's lap. His snores brought smiles to both their faces. Morenike turned to her grandmother. "Mama Omu, I am afraid," she whispered, not wanting to wake Damilare up.

"Afraid? What are you afraid of, my child?" Mama Omu asked. "How can the daughter of the fearless warrior woman

Gbanjubola be afraid? Please do not let anyone hear you," she said in mock horror as a playful smile flitted across her face.

Morenike started to laugh. She knew that Mama Omu was secretly proud of her very outspoken daughter. Even if she did not understand her. Mama Omu had once told Morenike the story of how her mother used to wear trousers under her skirt when she was a little girl. She had decided that just in case she had to fight a boy, she did not want to be at a disadvantage. From a very young age, Morenike knew that her mother was very different from other mothers. Mummy Ibeji never failed to speak against an injustice. It did not matter if she was the only woman standing in the midst of a dozen men.

"Mama, don't our elders say that it is the child of the courageous one who turns out to be a coward?"

"You, my dear child, are no coward," Mama Omu replied, shaking her head. "What you have survived in this past year requires great courage. You are like me," she told her granddaughter with a smile. "We are the silent, strong women of Omu.

"Morenike," she continued, "you cannot hide here forever. Listen, my child, we do not abandon the business of living life just because of what people will say about us. Do people not even talk about the dead?" Mama Omu patted Morenike's arm. "It is time for you to go back home with your son. Go and finish your schooling. Become that teacher you have always wanted to be. I will be right here if you need me."

Mama Omu held her granddaughter's hand. "Promise me that one day, you will find it in your heart to forgive Damilare's father. Remember that Damilare's father is a part of him too. Please do not teach your son to hate a part of himself."

When Morenike walked into her father's house in Ibadan, it felt as if she had been gone a lifetime. Although she had come back home as a mother, she was still in a frightened young girl's body. Despite her mother's support, she worried about what was going to happen to her—to her son. Even when people quickly added two and two together after seeing Damilare's face, most people kept their distance. How could Chief Komolafe be a rapist? Was he not a prominent man in the community?

No. There had to be another explanation. It is widely known that if you walk across a woman's legs when she is pregnant, her baby will look like you. Morenike must have tricked this innocent man.

Damilare quickly established himself as the most important person in the Balogun household. Morenike often watched with a smile as her parents revolved around their active grandson. Three months after their return, Morenike decided that it was time for her to go back to school. She approached her father, and he nodded. Several days later, after their night meal, Daddy announced, "I went to see your principal yesterday."

Morenike and Mummy Ibeji exchanged surprised glances. They did not know he had travelled to Abeokuta to see Mrs. Durotoye. "She wrote you a very good letter of recommendation. I have also spoken to the principal of St. Louis Grammar School. You will be starting classes next week."

Morenike could not stop herself. She flung her arms around her stunned father while her mother laughed happily and knelt in front of her husband. "Daddy Ibeji, thank you. May you live to enjoy the fruits of your labour over these children."

Mummy Ibeji took care of her grandson when Morenike

started day classes at the secondary school. She went on to complete her teacher training diploma at St. Andrews College.

But after a while, Morenike found that she was no longer satisfied with just a diploma. She wanted to go to university. For a whole month, she struggled with telling her mother, who had already given her so much. Mummy Ibeji waved aside Morenike's apprehension. "If that is what you want, then go ahead and apply. Damilare and I will be fine."

When Morenike was offered admission to the University of Ife, Mummy Ibeji's joy knew no bounds. "You are worth a thousand sons," she said with tears in her eyes.

Morenike found the double degree program in English and sociology very stimulating, and the three years flew by. She tried hard to balance her responsibilities at school with coming home to see her son. Every time she returned to Ibadan and saw how much Damilare had grown in her absence, Morenike wondered if she had made the right decision. It was even harder when Damilare cried and held onto her clothes. "Mummy, don't go," he begged. Her heart broke when she had to hand him over to Mummy Ibeji. But she consoled herself that the sacrifice was for Damilare too.

One day in her third year, Morenike was walking down to the lecture theatre when she ran into her sociology professor, Dr. Lot. The middle-aged woman gave Morenike a smile. "I'd like to see you in my office after the lecture, please."

Morenike's heart pounded. "Yes, Ma."

After the lecture, she quickly made her way to Dr. Lot's office. She knocked tentatively on the door and heard a cheerful voice call, "Come in."

It was Morenike's first time in the office. Unlike other

professors' offices, this one was uncluttered and painted a soft yellow. It felt airy and welcoming. Academic certificates and pictures adorned the walls. Morenike tried not to stare at the personal pictures.

"Please take a seat," said Dr. Lot.

Morenike sat with her hands tightly clenched in her lap.

Dr. Lot gave her a reassuring smile. "Have you heard of BAOBAB For Women's Human Rights?

"No, Ma."

Dr. Lot stood up and walked over to the lone file cabinet in the room. She pulled out a drawer and removed some colourful brochures. "It's a national not-for-profit, non-governmental women's human rights organization." She handed the brochures to Morenike. "I just received a grant from the Women's Learning Partnership to partner with BAOBAB on their skills-building initiative." She sat back at her desk. "I have been very impressed by your performance and composure during my classes. Your analytical paper on the social, economic, and political status of women in contemporary Nigerian society was simply outstanding. That is why I want to offer you a research assistant position for the rest of the year."

Morenike's mouth dropped when Dr. Lot told her the stipend. She would be able to help her mother with expenses for Damilare. She fought back her tears. "Thank you very much, Ma. I accept."

Back in Ibadan, Mummy Ibeji listened with pride when Morenike shared stories of her experiences. "The Ife outreach team alone sponsors fifty widows with children to attend skills training. You should see the look on the women's faces when they find jobs or start their own businesses." She smiled at her mother. "One day, I too will make a difference."

"Of course you will," Mummy Ibeji responded. "You were always destined for greatness, my child."

In her final year, Dr. Lot encouraged her to apply for a master's program.

"I can't apply now," Morenike stammered. "I have a son to care for." Her fingers fumbled as she opened up her satchel to get a picture of Damilare. He was smiling inside the stiff three-piece corduroy suit Mummy Ibeji had bought him for Christmas.

Dr. Lot looked at the picture and handed it back. She gave Morenike an understanding look. "You have a fine son. When he is much older, please apply to a graduate program. We need all the female lecturers and researchers we can get."

After completing her one-year National Youth Service Corps posting in Kaduna, Morenike came back to Ibadan. Her mother insisted that it was better for her and Damilare to live at home, and so they did. She started teaching English at St. Louis, her old secondary school, and joined the local chapter of BAOBAB.

One Sunday afternoon, Chief Komolafe came knocking. Morenike's brother Kehinde was outside washing their father's car. Kehinde came in and nervously announced, "Excuse me, sir, Chief Komolafe and some other people are at the gate."

Mummy Ibeji looked at her husband as he silently signalled that Kehinde should let the group in. Mummy Ibeji immediately sprang to her feet and stormed out of the house. Daddy Ibeji hurried after her. "Damilare," Morenike told her son, "stay with your uncle Taiwo," and then she followed her parents. Kehinde was closing the gate behind Chief Komolafe and the people with him. Chief Komolafe had aged since the last time she had seen him. From their close resemblance, Morenike guessed that the other men and women were members of his family. The oldest member of the group led the way. A nervous-looking Chief Komolafe followed behind.

The little group stopped about two metres away from Mummy Ibeji. An elderly man who looked very much like Chief Komolafe stepped forward. He took off his cap to expose his greying head. Holding the cap in his hand, he quietly addressed Morenike's father.

"Daddy Ibeji, you know why we are here. We should have come a long time ago. Our brother has greatly offended you. Today we come with him to ask for your forgiveness. Please let us come into your home."

From where Morenike stood, she could hear her father swallow as he held on tightly to Mummy Ibeji's arm. She knew that her father wanted Chief Komolafe to acknowledge Damilare as his son. "Boys need their fathers to teach them how to be men, Gbanjubola," her father had said one morning as he and Mummy Ibeji argued over the matter.

"I know that boys need their fathers, but please tell me, what can that shameless man teach a child?" Mummy Ibeji asked with a hiss.

Out in the courtyard, the elderly man sighed. "Please, Daddy Ibeji, for the sake of the boy, let us make all necessary amends."

Glaring at her husband, Mummy Ibeji tried to pull her arm away. "For the sake of the boy?" she repeated incredulously. Finally breaking free from her husband's grip, she clapped her hands. "*Oh,* so now that his new wife just gave birth to his twelfth daughter, he thinks he can just walk in here one afternoon to claim a son?"

One of Chief Komolafe's female relatives tried to placate her. "Mummy Ibeji, we know that our brother has greatly offended you. That was why we agreed to come with him. We are here to discuss what needs to be done so this child can know his father. After all, if we do not eat yam for the sake of palm oil, we will eat palm oil for the sake of yam."

Mummy Ibeji looked at the woman as if she had suddenly sprouted horns and a tail.

"What is all this nonsense talk about yam and palm oil? Did you come here on an empty stomach? Does this shameless man remember that we entrusted our child to his care when he violated her? Does he?"

"Gbanjubola, Damilare needs to know who his father is," Daddy said in a quiet voice. "Please let them come into the house."

Ignoring her husband's plea, Mummy Ibeji faced Chief Komolafe. He was still cowering behind his relatives.

"*Agbaya!* So you now know the way to my house? Listen carefully. I am going to close my eyes. By the time I open them, if I still see you here, whatever happens to you is your own fault."

Morenike watched as Chief Komolafe's bulging Adam's apple moved up and down his throat.

"Gbanjubola, it is enough," Morenike's father stated quietly.

Mummy Ibeji turned to look at her husband. "*Enough?* When I have not even started? It will not be enough until I have dragged him on the ground, the same way he dragged my daughter's name in the mud."

Hearing someone sniffing behind her, Morenike turned to see Damilare standing in the doorway. She wondered how long he had been standing there. Damilare was staring at Chief

Komolafe with his mouth wide open. He was seeing his father for the first time. Damilare was already six years old.

Morenike quietly tapped Mummy Ibeji's arm. "Mummy ... please ... Damilare is watching."

The soft words cleared the angry haze from Mummy's Ibeji's eyes. She turned around and saw the scared look on her grandson's face. Damilare ran to his beloved grandmother, wrapping his arms around her waist. Morenike wiped her tears as she watched her son comfort Mummy Ibeji. "*E ma sunkun.* It's okay, Grandma."

Daddy Ibeji quietly asked the group to come back the next day.

That night, Morenike sat her son down to tell him his father was coming to see him. "Damilare, do you remember the man who came this afternoon?"

Damilare cocked his head to the side. "Is it that old man who looks like me?"

Morenike nodded her head. Damilare was still the spitting image of his father. "Yes, that old man." Morenike felt her pulse quickening. Her son had asked her about his father many times before, but she had always dismissed the question gently. Finally, he had stopped asking. "Damilare, that old man ... He is your father."

Damilare stared at his mother for a while. "Okay, Mummy," he said quietly. "Can I go outside to play now?"

Morenike watched Damilare skip happily out of the room. Her apprehension about his reaction had been for nothing. But later that night, he woke her up. "Damilare, what is the matter?" Morenike rubbed sleep out of her eyes.

"Mummy, do I have to go and live with the old man?"

Morenike sat up. "What old man?"

Scratching his head, Damilare whispered, "My father."

Looking at his wobbling chin, Morenike wrapped her arms around her son. "No, you don't have to go and live with him ... only if you want to," she added with her heart in her mouth.

Damilare looked relieved. "I don't want to. I will never leave you, Mummy," he said firmly. Blinking back sudden tears, Morenike hugged him tightly.

A week later, Morenike dragged a shy Damilare into her parents' sitting room. Head bowed, Chief Komolafe sat alone in the room. He looked up when he heard Morenike clear away the lump in her throat.

Damilare held onto his mother's skirt. "Damilare, go and greet your father," Morenike said in a soft voice. The boy walked over to his father and prostrated flat on the floor. "Good afternoon, sir."

Chief Komolafe placed a jewelled hand on Damilare's head. "Good afternoon ... my son." His hand lingered for a long time.

Morenike sat in a corner of the room and watched Damilare gradually warm up to his father. Several times, when Damilare looked in her direction, Morenike gave him a reassuring smile. Still, when she saw Damilare finally smile back at Chief Komolafe, Morenike wanted to run across the room and plant her body between the two of them. Damilare was hers. But she resisted—remembering the promise she had made to her grandmother years earlier. She would not teach her son to hate someone who was a part of himself.

As Damilare spent more time with his father, Chief Komolafe soon began to make demands. He wanted his son to live under his roof with his wives and daughters. He said that

Damilare was his only heir and should take his rightful place. But Morenike refused to listen to any pleas, even when Chief Komolafe's pleas became veiled threats.

"A child belongs to the father, and so Damilare rightly belongs to me. Even the law of the land recognizes this," Chief Komolafe said to Morenike as they stood in her father's sitting room.

Morenike held on tightly to Damilare's hand. "I don't care. I will not send my son to live in a den of vipers. It will be over my dead body."

This time, Morenike's father stood solidly behind her. Damilare stayed.

Part Three

MORAYO AND MORENIKE
1989~1991

11

Truth arrives at the market but finds no buyer.
It is with ready cash that people pay for lies.

Last month, I travelled to Omu with Aunty Morenike and Damilare. Mama Omu was very sick—one morning as she was stepping out of the cemented bathroom, she slipped and fell, breaking her left hip. The young girl who now lived at home with her found her when she returned from school. Mama Omu wanted to see her only great-grandchild again and sent word that Morenike and Damilare should come to her.

Damilare and I sat quietly in the room watching Aunty Morenike present the gifts we had brought. An overwhelmed Mama Omu started crying weakly. Aunty Morenike, who sat on the floor next to the bed, wiped her face gently. "Mama, why are you crying? Are you in pain?"

"I am not in pain, my child. I am just happy," she said, smiling through her tears. Mama Omu laid a trembling hand on Aunty Morenike's head and prayed for her.

"Morenike, as you have taken such good care of me, your child too will take care of you."

"*Amin,* Ma."

"May *Olodumare* always shield you from shame and make you deserving of mercy."

"*Amin,* Ma."

"May you always find favour in the midst of your enemies."

"*Amin,* Ma."

When Mama Omu finally fell asleep with Damilare curled up beside her, Aunty Morenike and I left the house and sat on a mat under the shade of the giant shea tree behind the house. We sat still as the golden sun gradually disappeared in a striking red- and orange-coloured horizon. For a long time, Aunty Morenike had her head bowed. I could tell that the sight of her frail grandmother had upset her.

When she finally looked up, she gave me a tired smile. "Visiting this place always brings back memories for me. You know, I was just two years younger than you when I came to live with Mama Omu."

My seventeenth birthday was coming up in three months.

"Morayo, there is something I have not told you yet," Aunty Morenike said softly. "I am sure you must have wondered about Damilare's birth?"

I slowly nodded my head. I still remembered those stories about Aunty Morenike's experience with men. As she started to speak about Chief Komolafe, and the time she spent living with Mama Omu, I swallowed hard. So many things made sense now. I had always wondered how she was able to know how I was feeling inside. As tears came to my eyes, I wondered how many other female cousins were carrying heavy secrets.

Aunty Morenike stared straight ahead and her mouth twisted in a bitter smile. "I still live in fear of the day when Damilare asks me how I met his father. Children want to know their parents wanted them. But where is my child's love story?"

I knew that Aunty Morenike was not expecting an answer. What could *I* say?

"But I remember something Mama Omu told me. She said that we do not abandon the business of living life because of what people say about us."

Turning, Aunty Morenike reached for my hand. "Morayo, also remember that we do not abandon the business of living life because of what people *do* to us. Do you remember what we read on the back of that lorry we saw on our way here?"

I nodded. The bright blue words spray-painted on the weathered wooden frame of the mammy-wagon lorry proclaimed "Man no die, Man no rotten."

That weekend, I was back in Aunty Morenike's flat for a visit. As I looked around the room—Aunty Morenike's bookshelves and Damilare's toys filled the small space—my eyes fell on the wooden plaque that hung over the shelves crammed full with books. Aunty Morenike had explained that the sentence carved in the plaque was a quote from Nadine Gordimer. I whispered the words under my breath: "The truth isn't always beauty. But the hunger for it is." Gordimer's novel *Burger's Daughter* was one of Aunty Morenike's favourite books. Her eyes shone brightly whenever she talked about it. "Morayo, it reinforced again for me that women have to be politically active in the issues that affect their lives, or we will suffer the consequences."

Crossing the room, I ran my fingers along the book spines

and picked out the play *Wedlock of the Gods* by Zulu Sofola. I shook my head when I saw the stick figures Damilare had drawn all over the first page. I quickly slid it back. It would be better for his mother to discover the artwork herself. "It is not from my mouth that they will hear that the teacher's mother had died," I muttered to myself.

"Are you talking to yourself now?" Aunty Morenike's amused voice called to me from across the room.

I turned around to see her looking at me with tired eyes. "Daddy says that it is a sign of intelligence."

"Just don't go and start talking to yourself at the bus stop," she said with a small smile. "You will probably find yourself in a straitjacket before you know it."

I smiled back.

She walked over and pulled out a book from the middle shelf. "I was thinking the other day that you are old enough to read this now."

I took the book from her and looked at it. The title was *Second-Class Citizen* by Buchi Emecheta.

"Life for us women has come a long way since that book was written in 1974. You were only three years old." She moved over to the settee and sat down. I sat on the chair opposite her. "One of my students asked me why we should bother to read old books, and I told her it is for the same reason that we study history. To know and learn from the past."

I looked down at the novel in my hand. It didn't look big enough.

Aunty Morenike visited a couple of weeks later.

"Aunty Bisoye," she asked my mother, "please can I take Morayo with me to a political rally at Old Dugbe Market?"

My face lit up. Aunty Morenike was the only woman I knew who really cared about politics. Her whole face glowed when she talked about political issues.

"Political rally?" Mummy said. "Madam Teacher, you did not tell us that you are now a political activist? *Abi,* you are now working for Chief Gani Fawehinmi?" Mummy knew how much Aunty Morenike admired the formidable lawyer and human rights activist.

Aunty Morenike's ringing laughter filled our sitting room. "Aunty, it would be a great honour to work for Chief Fawehinmi. But I am just helping my good friend, Mr. Tiamiyu." She took out a little flyer from her handbag and handed it to Mummy. "He is running for the post of Chairman of Ibadan North West Local Government. I am sure you must have seen his posters around your shop at Amunigun Market."

Mummy looked at the flyer and shook her head. "Honestly, my dear, I don't remember this face." She handed the flyer back. "But I have not been paying much attention to the posters. After all, what difference will my voting make anyway? Everybody knows these elections are always rigged. Last election, did Chief Omoniyi not win with over seven hundred thousand votes? The entire population of Ibadan North West Local Government, even counting the goats and chickens, is less than two hundred thousand." Mummy hissed in disgust.

"But Aunty, if we stay silent, all kinds of things would just continue to happen to us."

"Okay, Madam Activist. Let it not be said that I stood in the way of progress." Mummy turned to me. "Morayo, you can go with your aunty. Go and help this Mr. Tiamiyu. Maybe your generation can change this country for the better. As for me, my eyes have seen too much." I was thrilled, but her expression became serious, so I kept quiet. "Please, Morenike—be vigilant. You know how Chief Omoniyi's thugs are. Leave immediately if there is trouble."

Aunty Morenike nodded. "Morayo is just going to help us hand out flyers to the people that show up for the rally."

Eniayo, who was home for the long school holidays, quickly spoke up. "Mummy, can I go too?"

"Your aunty will be too busy to watch the two of you."

"But I want to—" Eniayo started to grumble.

"Eniayo, I will come and take you out another day," Aunty Morenike promised.

As Eniayo sulked further, Mummy called her name in a warning tone. "Eniayo!" My stubborn sister fell silent.

"You are so lucky," Eniayo told me later that day as we sat in my bedroom. "Mummy always lets you do whatever you want."

Looking at her, I shook my head. If only she knew.

I knew Mr. Tiamiyu very well. He often came to Aunty Morenike's flat during my visits. He and Aunty Morenike would spend hours arguing about one political issue or another, their voices rising as they each tried to prove their point. I liked the way Mr. Tiamiyu spoke to me like an adult, calling me "Miss Morayo" with a gentle smile.

When I overheard Mr. Tiamiyu and Aunty Morenike discussing his campaign strategies, I wondered where the small, slim man found the courage to run against Chief Omoniyi.

Chief Omoniyi was like a demigod in our local government. His family members and friends held all the top government positions. And his political thugs, notorious for their brutality, were his personal law-enforcement body.

Two years earlier, men riding on *okadas* had gunned down Chief Omoniyi's main opponent, Engineer Oluwalambe, and his pregnant wife in broad daylight. Chief Omoniyi's head thug, nicknamed Avenger, was seen riding one of the *okadas*. The year before, a man who publicly challenged Chief Omoniyi at a local government meeting disappeared. He was never found.

"Daddy Morayo," Mummy often said with a shake of her head, "Chief Omoniyi is the kind of tough meat reserved for seasoned teeth. Who can win against him?"

The next time I saw Mr. Tiamiyu was on Aunty Morenike's birthday. It was her twenty-third. Aunty Morenike had invited him over to her flat for a special meal. While I stayed behind at the dining table to finish my second piece of birthday cake, Mr. Tiamiyu and Aunty Morenike moved to the sitting room. I watched him pull out a piece of paper from his pocket. He cleared his throat. "Miss Balogun," he addressed her formally, with great respect, "I wrote this little poem yesterday. I called it 'The Tango.'" He gave a little nervous laugh. "I wanted to share it tonight."

"I will be happy to hear it," Aunty Morenike said with a soft smile.

Glancing towards me at the dining table, Mr. Tiamiyu slowly paced the small room. He had an intense look on his face as he began to read the words.

"Four eyes meet across a room and the ageless dance of love begins.

That instant recognition. The sensual softening of the gaze. The fluttering of long eyelashes. One pair looks away in suddenly remembered modesty. The other pair continues to stare boldly, leaving little doubt as to the brazen intentions of the owner.

As two dark eyes move closer, the other pair dims for a brief second, feeling quite faint from the anticipation. But wait, the brazen eyes move right by, leaving behind a pair clouded by bewilderment.

And then, a gentle tap on the shoulder, a slow turn, and there they were, those eyes from across the room. The Tango continues."

I was not surprised to see Aunty Morenike look away. When it came to Mr. Tiamiyu, she seemed determined not to see the devotion shining brightly in his eyes. For the remainder of the night Mr. Tiamiyu stared at her intently, but she would not meet his gaze.

The following Saturday, Aunty Morenike and I arrived at the school soccer field to find that Mr. Tiamiyu had already set up a wooden podium and loudspeakers near the goalposts. But the grass on the field was sparse and there were no benches. "Aunty Morenike, where are the people going to sit?"

She looked up at the overcast sky and frowned. "Mr. Tiamiyu could not afford to rent any chairs. The main problem now is this rain. God knows we need the water in this drought, but I hope the rain will wait."

When Mr. Tiamiyu saw us, he greeted us with that warm

smile that complemented the wide Oyo tribal marks on his face. He shook my hand vigorously. "Miss Morayo, so you were able to come. That is excellent. I can see that your aunty is determined to infuse some of her love of politics into you. Is that not so, Miss Balogun?"

Aunty Morenike rolled her eyes in response.

For two people who saw each other almost every day, the formal way they addressed each other was amusing to me. If I had been bold enough, I would have asked Aunty Morenike how she felt about him.

We quickly joined in the preparation for the rally. A little group of Mr. Tiamiyu's friends and family members were already at the soccer field. In the heat, thick sweat soon poured down my back. As more and more people joined us, Mr. Tiamiyu's junior sisters and I started handing out sachets of cold pure water from three large plastic basins filled with ice blocks.

Aunty Morenike and one of Mr. Tiamiyu's younger sisters decided to walk over to the nearby Amunigun Market and mobilize the market women for the rally. Before they left, Aunty Morenike gave me a packet of small flyers printed with Mr. Tiamiyu's picture and manifesto to distribute among the crowd. Walking between the people, my ears caught snippets of different conversations.

"Please, my people," said a tired-looking man, studying Tiamiyu's picture on the flyer. "Who is this Muffy?"

The woman standing next to him shrugged her shoulders. "I only came because I saw a crowd. Is he from around here?"

Another man peered closely at the flyer and exclaimed, "Wonders shall never end! Is this not Mufutau's picture?"

"Mufutau?" the tired-looking man asked.

"Yes! Mufutau, the only son of Baba Mufu. You should

know Baba Mufu now. He is the vulcanizer whose shop is on that little bend on Queen Elizabeth Road. It is just across from the cemetery."

I watched the other man peer at the flyer again. "You don't mean it! You are very right, my brother. You mean this is little Mufu who used to run around half-naked?"

"*Beeni*. It is the same one."

"Truly, the young shall grow. I remember him as a little boy." The man chuckled to himself. "His date of birth was tattooed on his stomach, right above his extra-large belly button."

The other man burst into laughter, exposing uneven teeth stained red by kola nuts. "Atanda! You have come again with this your elephant memory. I wonder if Mufu shows his stomach to prove his date of birth?"

The woman laughed, wiping the sweat on her brow with a stained white handkerchief. The flyer that I had just handed to her floated to the ground. She didn't seem to notice.

"Mufutau! So he now thinks that he knows more than his elders. These young people nowadays. Small book learning, one visit to the perimeters of an airport, and soon they think they know everything about the world."

"Thank you, brother, you are very correct. Imagine the audacity of the boy! Daring to run against a man of timbre and calibre like Chief Omoniyi. Was it not Chief Omoniyi who created the scholarship fund that sent Mufutau and three other students from our local government to the University of Ibadan?

Those standing around him nodded—Yes, it was.

The woman clicked her tongue in disapproval. "I have told my children they are not going to university. Too much book learning only corrupts the mind."

As the conversation ended, I almost ran over to tell Mr. Tiamiyu that we should just pack up and go home. There was no use talking to people who were obviously there just for the spectacle. But looking at Mr. Tiamiyu's earnest, sweaty face as he adjusted his polka-dot bow tie, I told myself that he probably knew his chances.

Aunty Morenike and Mr. Tiamiyu's sister soon returned from their quest with a few market women dragging their feet behind them. It was funny to see Aunty Morenike's petite, blue jean–clad figure marching ahead of the other women. When it was obvious that the crowd was not going to get any bigger, Mr. Tiamiyu stood up on the wooden platform. He addressed the crowd in both Yoruba and English, introducing himself as Mufutau Tiamiyu, a proud son of the soil who had big dreams for his people.

As Mr. Tiamiyu spoke, I pictured the vibrant vision he was trying to share. The crowd around me rumbled in agreement, too—but as he continued, our starved minds could not grasp his vision of constantly running water taps, safely constructed roads, and well-equipped maternity centres. Were such things even possible in this generation? But as Mr. Tiamiyu's face dripped with sweat and passion ignited his eyes, he transformed himself from the small, gentle man I knew. He reached out into the audience with his hands and his words. He walked across the little wooden podium, and even though the crowd was small, he spoke as if calling out to an entire stadium of listeners.

"For over a quarter of a century I have watched and listened to our people talk, shout, and cry about the injustice in our lands. We shout to the high heavens about the relentless treachery of one tribe and the unending domination of another. Yet we remain silent about our individual acts of injustice. Market women, you march on the streets protesting against the injustice of corrupt transporters. Yet you sell bottles of adulterated palm oil to unwary, hungry buyers with a friendly smile."

Looking around, I could see guilty looks on the faces of some of the market women. They tried to fade back into the crowd.

"And buyer, don't you dare shout that you have been violated. Remember, if you would, the many times you calmly asked for bribes before doing the job you are being paid a salary for. In our little corner, we must reflect the integrity we demand in our leaders."

Mr. Tiamiyu's voice broke. "My people, it is time we stop applauding and condoning those who steal our joint inheritance and toss us dry bones. If not, I fear that in another quarter of a century, we will still be talking and crying while our youth, the strength of our land, wander the world looking for a future. Our children will look around at the utter desolation and accept, yes accept that this catastrophe is their only reality. They will accept that for our land, indeed for our peoples, there can be no change."

When Mr. Tiamiyu ended his speech, I clapped my hands so hard my palms stung.

✂

During the weeks leading up to the election, every afternoon after school Mr. Tiamiyu walked around the constituency to meet with the people. He always had a megaphone and a little wooden stand in hand. He stood and talked about his manifesto with anyone who was willing to listen. Often his only audience was little children who saw him as a distraction from slow afternoons.

Mummy's fears about Chief Omoniyi's political thugs attacking Mr. Tiamiyu never materialized. They probably concluded that if his main audience was young children who had nothing else to do, he was no threat to Chief Omoniyi. I knew Aunty Morenike was worried that he would make himself sick before the elections, but Mr. Tiamiyu was determined to give the campaign everything he had.

12

Whoever wishes to die a decent death,
let him or her live decently.

Two very significant incidents happened shortly after Mr. Tiamiyu's political rally. The first took place on August 31, 1990, the tenth anniversary of the great *omiyale*, the day the Ogunpa River flooded its banks. Eniayo was home for the long school holidays. We were sitting at the dining table playing Monopoly when we heard a woman's frantic cries through the open window. It was one of our neighbours, Mama Afeez. She was shouting at the top of her voice in the rain, *"Odo Ogunpa ti ya o!"*

My hands flew to my mouth. The Ogunpa River had overflowed its banks? Eniayo bolted up from the dining table, knocking over the Monopoly board. I watched as the cards and game pieces scattered all over the floor. The Ogunpa runs through the densely populated eastern part of the city, and Mummy's shop was right next to the river at Amunigun Market.

I remembered the last time the river overran its banks, in 1980. It was the most devastating flood in the history of

Ibadan. That night we all sat in the sitting room, silently watching the news report on television. Hundreds of people died during the downpour, which lasted the whole day. Some were trapped inside commercial buses and drowned in the floodwaters, and others were crushed in rushing debris and collapsed houses. By the time the rain stopped, thousands were homeless.

Things could not get that bad this time, could they?

"Morayo, how are we going to go and find Mummy?" Eniayo asked. I bit hard on my lip. I honestly did not know. Daddy was away on a business trip and I had no way of contacting him. Seeing the tears welling up in Eniayo's eyes, I tried to assure her even as I blinked back my own tears. "Mummy is going to be fine. You will see, she will be home soon."

Hours later, we heard someone banging on the gate. Eniayo and I looked at each other and ran in our bare feet to the entrance. When I opened the gate, I saw that it was Aunty Morenike. When she saw us, she tried to smile. "Morayo, Eniayo, how are you?"

Seeing that it was not Mummy, Eniayo's mouth started quivering. "Aunty Morenike, Mummy has not come back from Amunigun."

Coming in, Aunty Morenike put her arm around her. "Eniayo, it is okay. Your mummy will be home soon. *Oya,* come, let us go back inside the house."

Aunty Morenike went into the kitchen and starting cooking. Declining my offer to help, she made us sit with her in the kitchen. As we forced the hot yam and eggs down our throats, my ears kept listening for a bang on the gate.

By nine P.M., even Aunty Morenike could not keep the pretense up. *Where was Mummy?* When Eniayo said that she wanted to go and sit outside, Aunty Morenike did not try to change her mind.

When Mummy finally came back home that night, she met us sitting outside the gate with our chins in our hands. Her clothes were caked with mud and her shoes were gone. She had bleeding gashes on her face and legs.

While Eniayo and I held on tightly to Mummy, Aunty Morenike quickly went inside to heat up water on the stove for Mummy's bath. After her bath, she sat with us in the sitting room.

"Why didn't you come home right away?" Eniayo asked.

Mummy gave her a gentle rub on the cheek. "I had to walk home. There were no buses."

"How is Mama Bintu and em … Mrs. Sokoya?" Aunty Morenike asked. The two women also had shops on Mummy's row at the market. When Eniayo and I visited, they would buy us bottles of minerals and groundnuts.

At first, I did not understand when Mummy slowly shook her head. "The water came too fast."

"Ah!" Aunty Morenike gasped. "They are both gone?"

Mummy looked away. "Within minutes, it carried everything in its path. People, cars, shops. Everything. I had just left to deliver clothes on the other side of the market, so I escaped the surge. We all tried to dig in the mud to find those buried alive …" She rubbed her hands over her face. I noticed the caked mud under her nails. *Everything was gone?*

Daddy came back in the middle of the night in a panic. We had waited for him in the sitting room. Eniayo was asleep with her head on Mummy's lap. Aunty Morenike had left to put Damilare to sleep in his own bed.

When he saw Mummy, Daddy stood at the doorway for a couple of seconds. Then he rushed from the door to her side.

"Bisoye, are you all right?" He sat down next to her, his arm around her shoulder. "Our manager phoned the office in Benin and asked them to tell me the news of the flood."

Mummy just stared at him with tears running down her face. "It is okay. I am home now."

The following week, Mrs. Adigun and Tomi came to our house to greet Mummy. From where we sat at the dining table, we could hear the adults talking about the flood. Over a hundred people had died that day.

"Mummy Morayo, we thank God for sparing your life. May we never see any such thing again. Yesterday when I went to deliver cupcakes at Bodija, one of my customers said the traditionalists insist the river goddess is unhappy that the market traders did not keep up with the required sacrifices since the 1980 flood."

I was surprised to hear Daddy's loud, bitter laugh. Usually when Mummy's friends visited, he would sit for a while and then retire to his room. However, since the flood incident, he has been staying very close to Mummy.

"*Nonsense!*" Daddy barked. "That is just another ploy by those leeches to make suffering traders part with money they don't have. Our people have a way of ignoring leprosy while we dedicate ourselves to the cure of ringworm. They will not stop throwing refuse in the river even when they know it blocks the river's path. When the river swells up during the rainy season, where do they think the water will go?" He laughed bitterly again. "For eight years, the rechannelization project has had no head or tail. The construction companies take the money and run. Even if those traditionalists sacrifice all their chickens and goats to the river, nothing is going to change. We are just going to have another flood and more people will die." He hissed in frustration.

Mummy sent her friend an apologetic look. Mrs. Adigun and Tomi left shortly afterwards.

The second incident came out of nowhere, just like the first. One month after the flood, my dear grandmother, Mama Ejiwunmi, died in her sleep. I came home from school to find Mummy rolling on the floor wailing. Mama Ejiwunmi had just left for Oyo the week before. When she heard about the flood, she had come to Ibadan to spend time with us. She had not been sickly when she left.

The period before the funeral was a whirlwind. The Service of Songs and Lying in State was taking place at Mama Ejiwunmi's house on a Friday. On Saturday, we would have the funeral service and commendation. The thanksgiving service was at Mama Ejiwunmi's church the following day.

I once heard Mama Ejiwunmi say that when she died, she did not want her body refrigerated. "Bisoye, I don't want a big burial," she had told Mummy. "There is no need to prolong things. You have taken good care of me as a responsible child should." But the strained relationship between Mummy and Aunty Tope dragged out the burial process for three months. Mama Ejiwunmi's body *was* embalmed when her oldest child said that she was not yet financially ready for a funeral.

Mummy, who has been steadily losing weight since the flood, was frustrated. "Daddy Morayo, what I am going to do?" she said one evening as we sat in the sitting room. "Sister *mi* is so stubborn. I know that she and Mama were fighting over Tayo, but how can she do this to her own mother?"

Daddy patted her gently on the arm. "It is okay, Bisoye. If

Tope does not agree to a date by next week, I suggest you go and talk to *olori ebi* Baba Muti. Let them call a family meeting. We are not rich but we can afford a decent burial. Mama Ejiwunmi was not a rubbish kind of mother."

A week later the two sisters finally agreed on a date, but that did not end their squabbles. First, they could not agree on the clothes to wear for the funeral. Then it was on the choice of the caterer, the food to serve at the reception party, whether they wanted to have a night party … the list went on and on.

I sat quietly at the back of the car when Daddy drove us to Sasa Market. We needed to buy cheap baskets of tomatoes and peppers from the Hausa traders. "Daddy Morayo," Mummy said, "all week I have been calling Sister *mi* to discuss the burial arrangements, but it is one fight after another. I am tired. She will not even tell me when she will be arriving in Oyo, or how many people she is bringing with her. How can I arrange their food and accommodation? It is almost as if we had not sucked on the same breasts!"

When the weekend of the funeral finally came, I was happy to leave for Oyo. On the way we would be picking up Eniayo from her school.

When Aunty Tope arrived late for the wake-keeping service, the elders in the family shot her a disapproving look. The sisters sat stiffly next to each other, staring ahead at the officiating deacon. When it was time for Aunty Tope's scripture reading, Mummy silently passed the program booklet to her.

Bros T did not come to Oyo with his mother. I had been thinking of what to do when I saw him. Several family members commented on his absence. After all, he was the only grandson. I overheard Aunty Tope tell one of the aunties that Bros T was out of the country and could not get back in time for the funeral.

Bros T was out of the country?

Later that night, as Eniayo and I snuggled up on a raffia mat in one of the bedrooms at Mama Ejiwunmi's house, she too asked after Bros T. "Morayo, why do you think Bros T did not come?"

I swallowed hard. "I heard Aunty Tope tell somebody that Bros T has travelled abroad."

Eniayo's eyes lit up. "Abroad? Did they say where he went?" I shook my head. "No."

"That Bros T is always enjoying life," Eniayo said with a tinge of envy in her voice.

"Do you think that *we* would ever go abroad? Me, I want to go to Australia."

I felt myself relax, glad that she had changed the topic. "Why Australia?"

"So I can see the kangaroos, of course."

I thought about this. "We can always go to Ghana," I suggested. "The buses—"

Eniayo looked at me as if I had gone mad. "How is that abroad? *Me,* I am going to the *real* abroad. With white people." She shook her head stubbornly, and I laughed out loud—but I stopped abruptly when I remembered that Mama Ejiwunmi's casket was in her sitting room just two doors down the corridor.

Earlier in the day, Eniayo and I had stood hovering by the door of the sitting room. This was different from seeing dead bodies abandoned by the side of the road. They were just a normal part of our days. My fingers tightened on the door as it swung open.

Eniayo, who started crying, would not go into the room. She ran off, leaving me at the door.

But I wanted to see Mama Ejiwunmi.

Stepping into the room, I walked slowly towards the open white casket. I stared at the stiff figure lying inside a red velvet lining trimmed with white lace. She was darker and smaller, dressed in a white lace *iro* and *buba*. I was there when Mummy had picked out the most expensive lace material at the market, her hand gently stroking the soft fabric in the car on our way home. Mama Ejiwunmi's hands were folded neatly on her chest. Tucked beside her head was a small white bible. Pieces of cotton wool peeked out from her nostrils and ears. Taking a deep breath, I touched her hand with the tips of my fingers. Her skin felt very firm and cool. Her body had always been warm and soft when she held me.

Back in the bedroom, I found Eniayo sitting up on the raffia mat. "Did you go inside?" she asked. I nodded, sitting down beside her.

"What did she look like?" Eniayo asked in a small voice.

"She was smaller and darker," I said. I knew that if I told Eniayo I had touched Mama Ejiwunmi's hand, she would run screaming from the room.

"I could not go in," Eniayo said as she stared down at her hands.

I wrapped my arm around her. "Mama Ejiwunmi would have understood."

Later, when I woke up to use the toilet, I walked past the room with Mama Ejiwunmi's casket. I glanced inside the room and saw Mummy and Aunty Tope. They were going to spend the entire night with their mother. But even with their dead mother between them, the sisters had their faces turned away from each other.

Mummy's stoic face was staring straight at the corridor, but I knew that she did not see me. Aunty Tope had her hands in her lap, wringing them together as her chest heaved up and down. She took sneaking glances at the casket.

On my way back to the bedroom, the room was still quiet.

The next day we woke up early to get ready for the church service. Late in the morning, Aunty Morenike, Damilare, and Mr. Tiamiyu arrived from Ibadan for the service.

I ran to the side of Mr. Tiamiyu's car. Eniayou skipped after me. "Aunty Morenike!" She stepped out of the car and hugged us both. "Morayo, Eniayo, how are you both?"

"We are fine, Aunty," Eniayo said as she held Damilare's hand. "We have been waiting for you!"

While Aunty Morenike went to help Mummy, Eniayo and I sat with Mr. Tiamiyu in front of the house watching family members and friends arriving for the funeral. Our sad faces brightened a little when Aunty Adunni and her mother arrived from Ilorin.

At the cemetery after the service, the gravediggers stood to the side, waiting for us so that they could finish their work.

Aunty Tope's hardened face finally melted when it was her turn to throw her fistful of dirt on top of her mother's coffin. From where I stood beside Mummy, I could hear Aunty Tope chanting to herself, "Mama *e jo e da ri ji mi*." She was asking for her mother's forgiveness.

Mummy moved closer to her sister, putting her arm around her. For a brief moment, Aunty Tope relaxed her body against Mummy, but then she jerked away. Family members gave each other puzzled looks. Mummy tossed her own fistful of dirt on top of the coffin. One by one, the rest of us followed suit.

After the thanksgiving service on Sunday, Baba Muti called a family meeting. He wanted to know why the two sisters were fighting. Sitting across from each other, the sisters refused to talk.

Aunty Tope left Oyo later that day.

Mummy and I stayed behind for a week to clean up the house. Eniayo's school allowed her to become a day student during that time, so that she could go to school in the morning and come back to Mama Ejiwunmi's house at the end of her lessons.

"We have to finish going through your grandmother's things today," Mummy said the day before we left Oyo. She handed me a wooden box with two elephants carved on the sides. "Look through it and take what you want."

I opened up the box and found that it contained some of Mama Ejiwunmi's jewellery. The two copper bracelets she had always worn were right on top. I picked them up. "My father, who was a coppersmith, made them for me," Mama Ejiwunmi had told me the day I asked her where she had gotten them from. "They make the aches in my fingers better."

I ran my own fingers around the bracelets. The etchings were worn out in many spots. I clinched them on. Turning my wrists to look at them, I smiled. The ache in my chest eased a little.

Back home in Ibadan, Mummy locked herself up in her room for hours. With Daddy away on his business trips most days, I would sit in the sitting room by myself, wondering when Mummy would start smiling again.

Meanwhile, Aunty Morenike came to see us frequently, and she gave me regular updates about Mr. Tiamiyu's campaign. With the December election quickly approaching, Mr. Tiamiyu was still going out every day to campaign. Aunty Morenike told me that she went with him as often as she could. "Morayo, I can't wait until the election is over," she said one evening. "This campaign is finally getting to me. Some days I don't know if I am coming or going. You should see Mr. Tiamiyu, he has lost so much weight. The other day he fell asleep on his feet while teaching at school. Just three more days now."

On the day of the election, I woke up bubbling with excitement. Aunty Morenike arrived at our house early in the morning.

"Aunty, will you be coming down to the voting centre later?"

Mummy shook her head. "*Me? Vote?* I am not coming to vote. I have yet to see one politican I can trust. When you strip off all the tribal and religious paraphernalia our leaders wear, they are identical—corrupt, manipulative, interested only in furthering their own personal agendas."

Laying a gentle hand on Aunty Morenike's arm, Mummy sighed. "Just help me greet Mr. Tiamiyu and tell him that Daddy Morayo and I are wishing him the best today. Please, if there is any trouble at the voting station, come back home immediately."

Aunty Morenike nodded. "I have heard, Aunty."

The voting station was at a primary school not too far from our house. Mr. Tiamiyu was already at the school compound with members of his family and some friends. Our little group of supporters stood on the right side of the compound while Chief Omoniyi's group stood on the other side. Some of Chief

Omoniyi's thugs were already present, with reddened eyes and bodies draped in amulets, swinging around their AK-47 rifles as they patrolled the compound. The amulets made their bodies impenetrable to sharp objects and bullets.

Aunty Morenike gave the thugs a wary look. "You can tell that they have sniffed their cocaine again." She tugged on my hand. "Morayo, please stay where I can see you."

Looking around, I was surprised to see two women preparing to fry *akara* inside the school compound. Wrappers tied to their chests, they were turning two large basins of blended bean mixture with long wooden paddles.

The delicious smell of *akara* soon filled the compound as the sweating women flipped over golden-brown balls in large vats of sizzling cooking oil. Not long after, we watched two young girls walk into the compound with wooden slabs piled high with freshly baked bread. Even though I had eaten breakfast, my mouth watered at the smell of the *akara*. Chuckling to myself, I tried to picture Aunty Morenike's face if I were to walk over to the enemy's camp to ask for food.

The news of the free food giveaway must have passed from mouth to mouth because more and more people streamed into the compound to cast their vote for Chief Omoniyi. I watched Aunty Morenike's face grow darker by the moment as she tried unsuccessfully to talk to some women walking into the compound. Mr. Tiamiyu tried to calm her down. He gave her a gentle smile. "Miss Balogun, it is okay. That is the beauty of democracy. We get to choose who we want. And we also get to live with the consequences of our choices."

"But that is where it is not fair," Aunty Morenike protested. "We all have to suffer the consequences of stupid choices."

Sighing, Mr. Tiamiyu kept quiet.

Two hours after the election was supposed to start, four electoral commission officials arrived with the ballot boxes and their other paraphernalia.

Shortly after their arrival, Chief Omoniyi marched majestically into the voting station surrounded by praise singers.

I watched the electoral commission officials prostrate flat on the ground before Chief Omoniyi. Relinquishing their tables and chairs to him, they moved their ballot boxes and sat under a nearby tree. The praise singers accompanying Chief Omoniyi were beating their talking-drums with such intensity that the veins on the side of their heads stood up.

"Omoniyi," the talking drums called. "He, who says that when you go out you will not come back, is whom you will not meet upon your return."

Chief Omoniyi sat down while a steady stream of people paid homage to him. Even Mr. Tiamiyu's elderly father went over and prostrated before Chief Omoniyi. "Shief, I am very grateful for all the business you have sent my way this month. May God continue to prosper you."

When Chief Omoniyi saw his opponent's elderly father flat on the sand before him, he turned and sent Mr. Tiamiyu a victorious look. Then he relaxed back in his chair and his wide mouth curved into a smile that did not reach his beady eyes. "Ha! Baba Vulcanizer, please get up. I am just a very young boy. I should be the one prostrating before you *ke*." But he made no move to stand up from his chair.

Baba Mufu picked himself up from the ground and dusted the sand off his body. After he replaced his cap, he hobbled back to his son's side of the compound.

His angry wife hissed at him. "Baba Mufu! Why would you

go and prostrate in front of that man? On today of all days! Rubbishing your only son in front of everybody."

"Must I join your son in biting the hand that fed him?" Baba Mufu snapped back. "When this madness of his is over, are we still not going to eat?"

The angry woman turned her back to her husband.

Mr. Tiamiyu looked at his parents and rubbed his hand over his head. Aunty Morenike placed a hand on his arm. I heard her whisper softly to him, "Your father meant no harm. He is just a product of his time."

Mr. Tiamiyu stared back at her with eyes that were full of hurt.

Shortly after Chief Omoniyi's arrival, one of his political thugs brought out a table from a school building and set up a food takeaway station right beside the electoral officials. Those lining up to cast their vote for Chief Omoniyi were each given a small loaf of bread, two *akara* balls, and a sachet of pure water. After casting their votes, they each received a numbered cardboard from Chief Omoniyi's men. With the piece of cardboard, the voters were entitled to a hot meal of *amala* and *ewedu* soup in front of Chief Omoniyi's home later in the evening. The political thugs soon ran out of the cardboard and started using ballot paper collected from the willing electoral officers.

As I watched men and women old enough to be my parents stand in line, I wondered if the food was a fair exchange for leaky primary schools, unsafe roads, and dry taps. Even we children knew that the money allocated for these programs and services went towards maintaining Chief Omoniyi's harem of women and sending his children to the top schools in the United Kingdom and the United States.

Despite the rising heat, Mr. Tiamiyu continued to smile, walking around to thank the few people who came out to vote for him. But it was obvious to all that it was Chief Omoniyi's day.

Aunty Morenike had not given up. She continued to whisper to the women as they walked into the school compound. "My sisters and mothers, let us show that we are not children to be bought with food. Whatever we eat today, we will purge tomorrow. But our problems will remain the same. This is our chance to fight for our children's future." She put her arm around their shoulders. "Come, let us cast our ballot for a new beginning."

By late morning, I was growing tired and hungry. Aunty Morenike had brought some food with her, but she was still talking to the women. Then something unexpected happened. An old blind man led by a young child walked into the school compound.

The little boy stopped in front of Chief Omoniyi's table. "Open your ears and listen!" he said. Instantly, the whole compound fell silent as if it was under a spell.

The blind old man turned his face in Chief Omoniyi's direction and began to speak.

"Omoniyi is the name your father gave you. Why do you live life as if your name is Shame? If truly your name is Omoniyi, you must know that your life comes with great worth and dreams. Why do you live as if it does not? If the name you were given was Strife, you could continue to live in conflict and blame it on the intense urgings of your name. But your name is Omoniyi. Your mother carried you gingerly on her back, danced around, and sang your name with pride. Why do you live your life as if your name is Greed? Living life recklessly as if you own tomorrow and snatching food from the mouths of innocent children. Feverishly building up wealth that brings no honour and only invites disgrace. Living life like the hunting dog who forgot his master's call. Living without purpose as if your name is Lost. Will you remember that your name is Omoniyi? A child of great honour and hope. To the promises of your name, you must be true."

The blind old man turned to the little boy. "Child, take me to Mufutau's table." Everybody in the compound watched in shock as the blind man pressed a shaking thumb into purple ink to cast his ballot for Mr. Tiamiyu. When he was done, the child quietly led him by the hand out of the compound.

The crowd continued to stare at Chief Omoniyi with their mouths wide open. What was he going to do? Who could have brought about this great insult to their benefactor?

Chief Omoniyi looked around like a cornered rat staring at the metallic gleam of a cutlass. Then he turned, looking in Mr. Tiamiyu's direction with smouldering eyes. Everybody in the compound followed his gaze. But of course! This had to be the handiwork of that defiant boy Mufutau.

An angry murmur swelled up from the crowd. Some men from Chief Omoniyi's camp moved purposefully towards Mr. Tiamiyu. Frightened, our little group moved back, huddling together. The crowd was grumbling: Did this young scallywag not go around shouting that he will bring running water to every household? Is that not foolish talk? How do you bring running water to streets with no water pipes?

To Chief Omoniyi's credit, it was not as if he did not try to bring water to his people. Did everybody not see the shiny new water pipes dropped off at the local government headquarters? Who could have known that armed robbers would raid the

warehouse just two weeks later? That poor night watchman—
both his legs were broken.

But even babies knew that this was the handiwork of Chief
Omoniyi's political enemies. It was also mere coincidence that
two months later, Chief Omoniyi's brother-in-law, Agbabiaka,
opened a shop where he sold brand-new water pipes at Ekotedo
Market.

No one said he was a saint. Who was?

But who could send this young man, Tiamiyu, with such
tender bones to the pack of jackals at the state house? Tiamiyu
would be torn to pieces in just a matter of months. Chief
Omoniyi—despite all his flaws—was the man with the wisdom
and stamina for the hard job of ruling the people.

Hearing the snarls, I looked around with concern. The only
exit out was blocked by Chief Omoniyi's thugs, who patted
down the men walking into the compound.

Chief Omoniyi sat back in his chair. The smug look on his
face told me he knew that the people whose stomachs were still
full with *akara* and pure water would fight his battle for him.

As the Chief's men moved closer, the men in our little
group asked the women and young children to move to the
back. My heart began beating very fast. The crowd was growing
irate, calling out for Mr. Tiamiyu's head.

Then Chief Omoniyi stood. "*My* people! Listen to me. This
is not the time for violence. You all know that I am a man of
peace."

The crowd stopped.

"It is true that the house mouse that spares the sheath but
eats the knife is bent on provoking one." He laughed mirthlessly
to himself. "But it is impossible for anyone to carry the wind.
Mufutau is like all my other enemies—he cannot succeed."

Flapping the arms of his stiff damask *agbada* as if he might take flight, Chief Omoniyi's voice shook as he sprayed those standing around him with a shower of saliva. From the looks of adoration on their faces, it could have been sprinkles of holy water.

"My faithful followers, instead of fighting with our fists and clubs, we will destroy our enemies with our ballots." He punched the air with a raised fist. "We will boldly stare down our enemies and we will WIN."

The people began clapping their hands, thumping their feet on the ground, raising clouds of dust into the air.

Chief Omoniyi's voice continued to rise. "We the great people of this local government will be a shining example to all others! We will show that right here in our great community, the dream of democracy that has eluded so many others is alive and thriving!"

The praise singers increased the tempo of their drumbeats, driving the crowd into a frenzied dance of victory.

Mr. Tiamiyu turned to Aunty Morenike. He whispered, "Miss Balogun, I think it would be wise for you to leave now with Morayo."

Aunty Morenike started to protest, but Mr. Tiamiyu shook his head. "Please, Miss Balogun. We were almost lynched. I am going to ask my mother to take my sisters home as well. I will come and see you later this evening."

He spoke quietly with his mother. Soon our little group of women and girls left the school compound. As we walked back home, we could still hear the people stomping the ground and chanting with one voice, "Shief! Shief! Shief!" As we moved farther away their cries sounded more like "Thief! Thief! Thief!"

Mr. Tiamiyu lost the election that day. I was at Aunty Morenike's house when Mr. Tiamiyu came to tell her that he was leaving Ibadan for good. He had accepted a teaching position at a secondary school in Abuja.

Aunty Morenike agreed to go out with him that evening. When she went to change her clothes, Mr. Tiamiyu gave me a weak smile. "So, Miss Morayo, did you enjoy your first taste of politics? Maybe you too can run for a political office in the future."

In that moment, I seriously doubted it. The truth was that I found the whole thing very confusing. It was obvious that in all the years Chief Omoniyi has been Local Government Chairman, our lives have not changed for the better. Yet, the majority of people were not ready to try something new.

When I told him this, Mr. Tiamiyu nodded. "You are right. We have become so used to accepting the pitiful crumbs thrown our way. The other thing our people know is that Chief Omoniyi is ready to do anything under the sun to stay in power. When our people see danger coming, we run away, saying to ourselves, *Ta ni fe ku?* Who wants to die? But are we not dying slowly anyway? The truth is, *Ta ni o ni ku?* Who is not going to die?"

A tired look came into his eyes. "Always remember that making change happen anywhere is never an easy thing. Sometimes it takes leaning far over the fire and getting burnt." He rubbed his hands over his head. "Take care of your aunty for me, okay?"

That was the last time I saw him.

Weeks later, I was back at Aunty Morenike's house. Aunty

Morenike sighed from her spot on the settee. "Morayo, is it only me or do you also miss all the excitement of the elections?"

I nodded in agreement. But I could tell she missed Mr. Tiamiyu more than the excitement of the elections. "Today at school, I really wished Mr. Tiamiyu was there. He would have understood exactly what I was talking about."

Other times she would flip through the pages of a book she was reading and sigh. "Mr. Tiamiyu would have loved to read this book too."

For the first few months after his departure, they exchanged letters regularly. "Morayo, Mr. Tiamiyu said that I should greet you," Aunty Morenike said as she scanned through one of his letters. "He has just been promoted to vice-principal at his new school. Can you imagine? A whole vice-principal in less than four months! He is such a smart man." Aunty Morenike's face beamed with a proud smile. "He has been given his own quarters inside the school compound. He said that you and I could come and visit him in Abuja. What do you think?"

I waited for her to announce that they were going to get married and that she was moving to Abuja. She never did.

There were days when I wanted to ask Aunty Morenike why she did not just marry Mr. Tiamiyu regardless of what anyone said. But as close as we were, I did not forget that she was still older than I. Because of that, I respectfully kept my mouth shut.

Two years later, during a visit to Aunty Morenike's house, I came across a dusty manila envelope while browsing through her bookshelf for something to read. The envelope was full of campaign flyers. Looking at Mr. Tiamiyu's picture, I wondered what life would have looked like in our city if people had given a young man named Muffy a chance.

13

The dance of a millipede does not impress
he who has seen the dance of a snake.

Life settled down to a new kind of normal. Mummy was
back at work in a new shop. Daddy travelled all over the country
selling pharmaceutical products and Eniayo spent more time
at school than at home. My visits to Aunty Morenike's house
remained one of the highlights of my weekends.

While my relationship with Mummy had improved since
Mama Ejiwunmi's death, Bros T's ghost still walked around our
house. There were days when it seemed as if Mummy wanted to
talk to me about it. She would pause, look at me awkwardly, and
take a breath—but then she would look away and the moment
would pass.

Mummy came home one evening and found me watching
a Nollywood home video. The films made by the emerging
Nigerian film industry had gradually weaned us off our
dependency on Indian and other foreign films. For me, they
helped to pass my lonely evenings.

After changing into her house clothes, Mummy sat quietly

next to me on the settee. When a sex scene came on, the atmosphere in the room became charged. I kept my eyes glued to the television screen.

I could feel Mummy's eyes boring into the side of my head. Finally! Here was the moment I had been longing for. Surely she would say something now. I squirmed in my seat when I heard her clear her throat. "Morayo …"

I slowly turned. "Ma …"

"There is something I wanted to talk to you about …"

My mouth suddenly went dry. "Yes, Ma …"

Mummy's left eye suddenly started to twitch. Her eyes flickered back from the images on the television screen to my face. "Em … I just remembered something I need to go and do. I will talk to you later." She stood up from the settee and left the room.

And that moment passed, just as others had before it.

During this time, my friendship with Tomi—my childhood train-waving comrade—flourished. In that final year of secondary school, Tomi and I shared a desk at school. We also spent most of our free time together. We were either sitting at Mrs. Adigun's supermarket waiting for customers or at my house talking about life after secondary school.

"Can you believe that in just three months we are going to be in university?" Tomi asked. We were lying on her bed, making our school shopping list. The first two items on our long list were blue jeans and penny loafers.

Dropping my pen, I rolled over on the bed, tucking my hands behind my head. "I know. I can't wait to leave Ibadan." My name had appeared on the admission list for the economics program at the University of Lagos, and I was ready for the bright lights of that bustling national capital city right on the edge of the Atlantic Ocean.

Tomi sighed. "I really wish that Mummy would have let me leave Ibadan. I am so tired of this town." Tomi had been admitted to the law program at the University of Ibadan.

"You can always visit me in Lagos," I said.

Tomi nodded. "That is true—" But I could still hear the uncertainty in her voice. Her mother had told her she was not moving to a residence hall. She was stuck at home.

"So what colour of lipstick are we going to buy?" I said, trying to get her back in a good mood. Tomi giggled. Our mothers had insisted that we could not wear makeup until we were in university. The only beauty product approved was loose white powder, and that too had to be used in moderation. Mummy once told me I looked like I had *elubo,* yam flour, pasted to my face.

That cheeky Eniayo had interjected, "But Mummy, Morayo does use *elubo* when she runs out of powder."

Mummy's eyes bulged. *"She uses what?"*

Only when Mummy saw Eniayo shaking with laughter did she realize that Eniayo was joking.

Tomi's voice interrupted my thoughts. "How about gold?" she asked.

On our list, I wrote down one gold lipstick, and just for the fun of it, I added one more colour—bright red. It was Mummy's least favourite colour. But I had no intention of wearing it at home. What Mummy did not know would not hurt her.

Tomi's mother or mine would often send us to Bodija Market on an errand. We loved haggling back and forth with the market women before agreeing on a price. And over the years we had built our network of regular market vendors. We chose our rice seller because her rice was usually cleaner. Our regular butcher often threw in some extra pieces of meat with our purchases. We had a regular fish seller named Morili. Morili was a beautiful young woman who could not have been a day older than twenty. While her prices were slightly lower, I have to admit that we bought our fish from her more out of curiosity than loyalty.

Morili's fellow fish sellers called her Morili *oloko kan*. By the tone of their voices, we knew they were not complimenting Morili. What could be wrong with being a one-man woman? Tomi and I wondered.

On a trip to the market, we finally summoned up enough courage to ask Morili. I was worried she would grow angry with us for being nosy, but she only smiled. "I think it will be better if you asked Mama Supo," she said, pointing to the woman whose wooden fish tray was right next to hers.

Mama Supo was more than happy to answer our question. She sprang up from her stool. "We call her Morili *oloko kan* because we just cannot understand why, when we are all on our second or third husbands, she is so determined to stick to just one." Then she and Morili burst into laughter.

Later that same week, I was back at the market with Aunty Morenike. She had come to visit us and we both had some last-minute purchases to make. Daddy had requested *amala* for his evening meal and I had discovered we did not have enough yam flour at home to make the dish. Since the sun was already setting, Aunty Morenike and I quickened our pace as we walked briskly through the market.

There is something almost magical about the open-air market as the sun goes down. Flickering paraffin lamps light every stall and the heady aroma of frying *akara*, mixed in with the mouth-watering smell of roasting mackerel fish, flavours the air. On our way to the grinders Aunty Morenike and I walked past the record store, right in the centre of the market. As usual, Old Soja was dancing in front. Fela's "Gentleman" was blaring from the mounted loudspeakers. Singing along in his husky—but terribly off-key—voice, Old Soja was contorting his hips wildly. The woman ahead of us quickly covered her young daughter's eyes.

Old Soja was the market's resident madman. For as long as I could remember he had been part of the market scene, with his deep-sunken, bloodshot eyes and dirty hair. A cigarette dangled from his blackened lips as he walked about in a dirt-brown *buba* and *sokoto* covered with holes. In his more lucid moments, he shouted greetings to people walking by. In turn they tossed him a coin or bought him cigarettes. Most often, though, he minded his own business as he walked up and down the market paths.

We were making our way back to the bus stop when the loud, angry cries of Mama Put interrupted my animated conversation with Aunty Morenike. Mama Put, who owned the little canteen at the centre of the market where most of the market traders bought their food, would have run me into the muddy path if Aunty Morenike had not pulled me aside at the last minute. As Mama Put stormed by, I could hear her panting heavily. Her ample bosom heaved up and down as she clutched desperately to her *ankara* cloth wrapper that threatened to blow away in a sudden gust of wind.

I looked around. Was someone chasing her? Then I saw Old Soja running far ahead with a pan of hot *akara* balls placed jauntily on his head. One hand held onto the pan of *akara* while the other hand tried to hold up his falling trousers. The whole market could see his scabbed, fleshy buttocks slapping against each other as he ran.

My mouth fell open. It was difficult to decide which sight was more hilarious: Old Soja galloping ahead with a wide, beautiful smile on his face or Mama Put chasing him in a see-through nylon slip.

Later, as we stood at the bus stop waiting for the bus back home, I chuckled to myself. Aunty Morenike shook her head. "Morayo, you are still laughing?"

"But Aunty, you have to admit that it was so funny. Why didn't Mama Put just let Old Soja have the *akara*? Who is going to buy them from her now?"

Aunty Morenike shrugged her shoulders, smiling. "I doubt she caught up with Old Soja. That man runs like the wind—"

Her eyes widened and she froze. I spun around. Engrossed in our conversation, we had not seen the Operation Finish Them truck approaching in a distance. The joint police-military task force had the mandate to deal with the rampant armed-robbery incidents in the state. But the dedicated officers always had time on their hands for personal business.

The crowd at the bus stop quickly dispersed. Like every one else in the city, I had heard the stories of missing girls and women, abducted at gunpoint from the roadsides. The task-force officers who went about under the pretext of ridding the streets of prostitutes abducted young girls in broad daylight. There were whispers of gang rapes at the barracks and mutilated bodies found in nearby bushes like unwanted trash. Frantic relatives of those who survived then had to pay exorbitant amounts of money to bail out victims held on charges of prostitution!

"Morayo, run!" Aunty Morenike shouted, grabbing my

arm and whipping me around. She pointed. "Fast! Run towards that bush."

Feeling my mouth go dry, I picked up my bag of yam flour and ran. Those ahead of me hurled themselves into the tall grass.

As I ran, I was sure that Aunty Morenike was right behind me. When I got to the edge of the bush, I stopped. She was not. She had tripped—and was sprawled on the muddy ground near the bus stop. The Operation Finish Them truck was fast approaching. I could not leave Aunty Morenike. I started running back towards her.

She saw me and tried to pull herself up. As she stood, she fell back. Her face looked pained, as if her ankle was sprained. She waved her arm above her head and screamed. "No, Morayo! Please go back! Go back!"

I kept running towards her. Grimacing, she pulled herself unsteadily to her feet and tried to stumble towards me. It was too late. I saw the truck pull up beside her and my heart dropped. I wailed, "Aunty Morenike!"

"Morayo, go back!"

Before I could take another step, two strong hands pulled me back. I turned around in surprise. The hands belonged to one of the women who had been standing with us at the bus stop.

"No, child," she whispered, holding tightly to my waist as I struggled to get away. "Listen to your sister. This is bigger than you are. You cannot help her. Please come with me," she pleaded.

Struggling in the woman's grasp, I called out again, "Aunty Morenike!"

"No, Morayo. Go back!"

Through my tears, I saw Aunty Morenike finally manage to pull herself up. She leaned against the cement wall of the bus-stop shelter and the lone, dangling light bulb at the side of the building shone brightly on her face. I swallowed hard when I saw glistening grains of sand stuck to her forehead.

Panting, the woman pulled me to the ground. We were only about four metres away from the bus stop. It was now too late for us to run back to the bush. The Operation Finish Them truck had parked right next to Aunty Morenike. Two uniformed men sat inside the vehicle. The man in the passenger seat opened the door and strolled over to where Aunty Morenike stood. I could see the gleam of his AK-47.

"Enter!" he barked. The gun muzzle pointed to the back of the truck.

Aunty Morenike stood still against the wall of the bus stop.

The yam sellers on the other side of the road started shouting at the top of their voices. *"Ma wole o! Ma wole o!"* Their voices were full of desperation as they warned her not to enter the truck.

Aunty Morenike stared boldly at the man towering over her. I tried to force the image of the bullet slamming into her skull out of my mind. I knew that Aunty Morenike would rather die by the roadside than allow the men carry her off.

"I said you should enter now!" the man with the gun barked again, waving the AK-47 wildly in the air.

Aunty Morenike turned her head in my direction. The look on her face scared me. I had seen it before in my bedroom mirror the day I emptied the bottle of pills in my mouth.

"Get in now!" the man shouted again. Bubbles of spit foamed at the corners of his mouth as his big Adam's apple moved rapidly up and down his throat. When he got no response he moved closer, placing the gun muzzle right against her forehead. "Woman, are you deaf?"

Aunty Morenike closed her eyes.

I felt hot urine slide down my inner thigh. I clamped my legs together as it pooled under me in the sand. My rescuer mumbled Arabic words frantically under her breath. *"Hasbunallah wa ni'mal wakil ..."*

The shouts from the market women died as we all held our breath. The driver, who had been watching the standoff between his comrade and Aunty Morenike with an uninterested look, called out to his friend. "Julius, *abeg*, make we *dey* go."

The officer ignored the request. With the gun muzzle still placed on Aunty Morenike's forehead, he shouted, "I said you should get into the truck now!"

"Julius, I say make we *dey* go!" the driver repeated.

Frustration clouded Julius's face. His eyes went back and forth from his comrade to Aunty Morenike. I saw his index finger quivering above the trigger.

He suddenly moved his head back and spat a big blob of blood-tinged phlegm in Aunty Morenike's direction. It landed right under her eye, but she did not flinch. The man turned on his heel and walked back into the truck. The truck sped down the road and ran down a man darting across. The young man's cries shattered the silence as those standing nearby hurried to his side.

The woman who held me down pulled me to my feet. Like cockroaches scurrying out into a dark room, our fellow travellers soon came out of the bush and headed towards the bus stop. I ran to Aunty Morenike. She was still standing by the wall of the bus stop with a vacant look on her face.

"Aunty Morenike! Aunty Morenike!"

Hearing me, she turned and held out her arms. As she held me tightly to her body, I could feel her heart pounding fast. The woman who pulled me down soon joined us at the bus stop. Hobbling, Aunty Morenike went over and thanked her. "*E se gan ni,* Ma."

Wiping the sweat on her brow, the woman smiled back at Aunty Morenike. "It is nothing. I have a daughter her age." I knelt down to thank the woman. The woman patted Aunty Morenike's shoulder. "Your mother's prayers were surely answered today. It will surely be well with you." Those standing around us echoed the sentiment as they looked at Aunty Morenike in wonder.

When the bus arrived, Aunty Morenike made sure I stepped on first. She assured me that she would be able to get back to her flat on her own. As I sat in the bus, I realized I still had the bag of yam flour clutched tightly in my hand.

But what would I do the next time the men in the white truck came hunting? I told myself that if this happened again, like Aunty Morenike I would choose to die by the roadside. At least my parents would have a body to bury. Mummy always said that the pain of a dead child is better than the unending anguish of a missing one.

Half an hour later, I dragged my tired body through the front door of our home. Mummy did not look too pleased when she saw me walk into the house. Kneeling down, I greeted her. "*Ekule,* Ma."

"Morayo! Where have you been? Did you stop at Tomi's house on the way back?"

"No, Ma. I came home straight from the market."

Mummy clicked her tongue. She did not believe me. "You know that your father will soon be home and he will expect his food to be ready. *Oya,* hurry. Go and put a pot of water on the stove so that I can quickly make his *amala.* The soup is already bubbling."

For a moment, I thought of sharing the events of the evening. But seeing her rush obliviously back into the kitchen, I kept my mouth shut. What difference would it make? Besides, there was no way she could prevent it from happening again—and she would only worry needlessly. I shuffled my tired feet to the kitchen. All I could think was that tonight a frightened girl or woman would be riding in the back of that truck.

Standing by the sink to fill the soot-darkened pot with water, I smelt the urine and felt the dampness between my thighs. Carrying the pot of water to the stove, my teardrops fell, one by one, into the pot.

14

*It is the fear of what tomorrow may bring
that makes the tortoise carry his house along with him
wherever he goes.*

In the weeks that followed our roadside encounter, Aunty Morenike changed. So did I. I guess there is no way one can catch a glimpse of death, even from a distance, and still stay the same.

On the days I saw Aunty Morenike, she often had a strange blank look on her face. "Aunty, what is wrong?" I finally asked during a visit. "You are always quiet now."

Her words came in a soft moan. "I don't know." She stretched her body. "I am just so tired."

I gave her a closer look. Her body did look deflated, and for the first time it struck me just how physically small she was.

What changed for me was the anger—a smouldering anger that woke up with me in the morning and stayed with me late into the night.

Before our roadside encounter, I had told myself countless times that when I became an adult I would be safer, stronger.

Just like my Aunty Morenike. But it seemed as if age or education made little difference. Now when I walked out of the house, I often wondered if I would come back. A new sense of urgency pushed me through the day.

I was not surprised that Eniayo was the only person at home who noticed that something was wrong. On one of her visits home from boarding school, she came to my bedroom early one morning and sat down at the table.

From where I lay on my bed, I could tell from the frown on her face that there was something on her mind. "Morayo, what did I do wrong?" she finally asked.

Swinging my feet to the floor, I sat up. "Who said you did anything wrong?"

"Because every time I have asked you to come and play *ayo* with me, you say that you are tired," Eniayo said. "On our last visiting day, Mummy said you didn't want to come to Oyo at all." There was a long pause before she whispered, "And I was waiting to see you."

Eniayo's visiting day at her boarding school had been just three weeks after the roadside incident. I had begged Mummy to let me spend the day at Aunty Morenike's house instead. "But you know your sister will be expecting to see you."

"I can see her when she comes for mid-term break," I pointed out.

Mummy's only response had been a long sigh and a silent nod of her head.

Now I looked at Eniayo's open, innocent face and acknowledged an uncomfortable truth. I was jealous of my sister. It was the kind of jealousy that made me question why my path had to be so hard.

I knew I could not tell Eniayo about what had happened.

Just as I could not tell her about Bros T. I wanted her to believe that life was kind. I wanted her to believe that all she ever had to endure were the *afin* taunts she already knew how to shrug off so well.

I patted the spot beside me on the bed and Eniayo came flying at the invitation. "I am not angry with you."

Instantly, her pink face brightened.

"I can never be angry with you." *Jealous, yes. Angry, no.*

We spent the rest of the two-week break playing *ayo* and helping Mummy at her new shop. Eniayo was still around when my admission letter to the economics program at the University of Lagos finally arrived. I was very relieved. Even though I had seen my name on the admission list posted up at the university, names of admitted students often disappeared from the list while unqualified names appeared instead.

As I held the letter in my hands, all I could think of was the anonymity that a move to Lagos offered. "Mummy, can I go and visit Morayo?" Eniayo asked. "And after, can we visit Bar Beach?"

"We will see," Mummy said. Eniayo and I exchanged looks. We knew this meant no.

"I am coming back home for holidays," I reminded Eniayo. "And you are at school most of the time anyway."

"Eniayo, what you need to do is focus on your books so that you can go to university like your sister," Mummy added before she stood up from the settee. "*Oya,* let us go and pack your bags. We have to leave home early tomorrow."

This time, I went with Mummy and the driver when Eniayo returned to school. On the hour-long drive, Eniayo and I amused ourselves by reading the inscriptions painted on the colourful mammy-wagon lorries. These passenger lorries were packed full of people and wobbled past us at a high speed on the narrow road. Mr. Bello almost drove into a ditch when he tried to avoid being run over by one of them. The irony was that the inscription on the back of the wagon read "Life Has No Duplicate."

The other mammy-wagons had statements like "The Rich Also Cry," "God's Case, No Appeal," "No Hurry in Life," and "No Food for Lazy Man." Eniayo's favourite was "No Telephone Line to Heaven." A large mural on the wooden frame of the lorry showed a man holding a red rotary-dial telephone with a dangling cut cord, while a puzzled face with a halo above his head peeked down from a white cloud. "Maybe somebody in heaven owed the man money," Eniayo said. We all started laughing.

Two weeks later, it was my turn to leave home for school.

I spent my last night in Ibadan at Aunty Morenike's house. She had braided my hair all day, and by the time we were done it was too late for me to go home. Damilare, who had been watching television, was fast asleep on the sitting room carpet. Aunty Morenike woke him up and followed behind him as he staggered half-asleep to his bedroom.

I turned my stiff neck to look around the room. The new colour television was the only thing that had changed in the years I had been visiting. "I am going to miss this place," I muttered under my breath.

Aunty Morenike came back and sat beside me on the settee. "So are you ready for school?"

"Yes, Aunty." I could not wait to escape my parents' awkward silences and make new friends.

"I was excited to leave for university too. But remember that with all that freedom comes responsibilities. There is no

Mummy or Daddy there to make sure you attend your lectures or do your assignments. It is all up to you now."

"I will remember."

"Good." Aunty Morenike cleared her throat. "I really should have brought this up earlier," she said in an apologetic voice. "I know that these past months have been really hard on you. And I have not been my usual self." She reached for my hand. "Morayo, I can sense your anger and it worries me. Especially now that you are going to be on your own. My dear, unchecked anger only erodes self-control. Please, you have to let it go."

A lump lodged in my throat. "Thank you, Aunty."

She nodded. "Come, let us go and sleep. Tomorrow is going to be a long day for you."

"Morayo, please take care of yourself," Mummy said before slamming the car door shut. "Make sure you warm that pot of stew tonight so that it does not go bad."

I smiled. "Yes, Ma." She had given me the instructions at least five times already. We had arrived in Lagos earlier in the day and spent most of the afternoon arranging my clothes and provisions at my residence room at Moremi Hall.

Mummy reluctantly agreed to leave after I reminded her that it was getting dark. The Lagos–Ibadan expressway was not the safest road to be on at night.

"Bye!" I waved as Mr. Bello drove away. For a fleeting second, I was tempted to run after the car. I squared my shoulders and watched until they were out of sight.

Since none of my new roommates had arrived, I sat in

the courtyard to observe the other students come in. It was possible to tell which ones were jambites, first-year students like me. They all had brand-new buckets and most had their whole families with them.

I became bored after a while and decided to go for a walk. Stepping out of the residence gate, I stood for a moment and then headed out. Eventually I found myself near the old Senate building, where I sat on one of the wooden benches and watched the students walking by. I looked around and saw the other benches occupied by mostly couples. I had obviously stumbled on a popular spot. I gave a startled cry when a young man crept up behind me. "Hello."

Stepping back, he held up his hands. "Eh, I didn't mean any harm. I just could not help wondering why a beautiful lady like you was sitting alone."

My heart gradually slowed down. I hated it when people snuck up on me. It had been one of Bros T's habits. I forced a smile to my face. "It is okay. I didn't hear you coming."

Obviously taking my smile as an invitation, he sat down. "I don't think I have seen you around campus before."

"It is my first day." I was hoping that my cold voice would tell him I was not interested in a conversation. It didn't work.

"Really? Then it is only right that I take you to a nice little restaurant at the Student Union building to celebrate." He grinned. "Consider it part of your orientation."

I grimaced. "Well …"

"If you have plans"—he moved closer to me on the bench—"you can just give me your room number and we can go out tomorrow night. Whatever you decide. You are the one in charge."

I looked at him from under my eyelashes. There was

something exciting about the uncertain expression in his eyes. He looked harmless enough, and for once I was the one in charge. "I think I would like to get a quick bite after all."

"Thank you." He linked his arm through mine. "By the way, my name is Borode."

My eyes roved over his angular face. "Nice to meet you." I got to my feet. "Let's go."

Part Four

MORAYO
1995~2005

15

The butterfly that brushes against thorns
will tear its wings.

"My dear Morayo, who is the flavour of this month?"
Aunty Morenike asked with a raised eyebrow.

I sat across from Aunty Morenike in her residence room
at the Henry Carr post-graduate hall. Hearing her words, I
groaned inwardly. *Not again.*

Ever since a relative named Mosun had moved into my
residence hall, she had made it her job to broadcast embellished
stories of my campus escapades.

The last time I was home, Mummy woke me up in the
middle of the night to talk. "Morayo, I saw Mosun's mother
at the market today," she said with a frown. "My ears are still
burning!" She glared at me. "Tell me, is it true that you are
sleeping around with different men?"

When I kept quiet, she hissed. "Are you deaf? Did you not
hear my question?" Mummy eventually left my bedroom when
I stayed silent. The next morning, I packed my bags and came
back to Lagos earlier than I had planned.

The truth was that my life in Lagos was a world apart from my life in Ibadan.

In Lagos, my relationships with men fluctuated between feast and famine. During my feasting seasons, I chose the men I wanted. If a boy at the library smiled at me, I smiled back and we would leave together. Saturday mornings often found me in strange beds after a night of clubbing in town. In Ibadan, I mostly stayed home or followed Mummy to the shop to help.

As far as I was concerned, what was really causing all this talk was the simple fact that I did not care about putting up the preferred facade of modesty. What no one understood was how much I needed to be in control. I wanted to be able to decide what happened. The irony was that when I lost interest in men during my famine seasons, it only intensified the chase. The fact that I did not need their sweet words or attention drove them crazy. I was like a new frontier they wanted to conquer. But if there was any conquering to be done, I was determined to be the one doing it.

I could feel the waves of disapproval from Aunty Morenike's icy eyes. Seeing the deep disappointment on her face, I fidgeted in my seat.

Aunty Morenike tapped her fingers on the bed. She had just temporarily moved to Lagos. During the Christmas holidays, she had told me that she was starting a post-graduate program at the University of Lagos. "Damilare will stay with Mummy Ibeji while I am at school," she said. "We decided that it would be risky for me to travel back and forth from Ibadan every day—especially with my evening lectures."

"Aunty, I am so happy!" I had not seen her as often since I began university, and now we could finally spend more time together. In that happy moment, it did not occur to me that my two very different worlds were about to collide.

"Aunty," I said now, "it is not like that."

Aunty Morenike sighed. She folded her arms across her chest. "Okay, Madam Morayo, tell me how it is."

"You know I am dating Ladi," I said quietly, "and I am not going after any man for money." It was the truth.

"I am not going after any man for money," Aunty Morenike mimicked. I hung my head. "Look at me," she snapped. My eyes flickered nervously to her face. "What difference has your relationship with Ladi made? Has your name not been in every campus gossip magazine since you entered this university? Did I not see an article about you at the Student Union building?"

I felt my neck growing warm. I had never expected that Aunty Morenike would read those kinds of magazines. A new edition of *Sensations,* the student gossip magazine, came out every month. It was entirely student-run, and its male editors saw themselves as the voice of conscience against immorality—notwithstanding the fact that most of them slept with the same girls they ridiculed. *Sensations* had just released its premium edition, which had targeted me and other female students. The exposé highlighted all our liaisons on campus and included detailed quotes from so-called anonymous interviews with past sexual partners.

"They even posted a buyer beware caption above your name. *Morayo,* what have you done to yourself?" Aunty Morenike placed a gentle hand on my arm. "I can't stand by and watch you turn yourself into a public toilet for the boys on campus. *Please.* When you get back to your room at Moremi Hall, ask yourself this question. Has jumping from one man's sweaty sheets to another's taken away your pain?"

A short while later, I left Aunty Morenike's room and strolled back to Moremi. It was about eight in the evening and the front hall was bubbling as usual. I could hear loud music blaring from the cars double-parked in front of the residence. Visiting hours for male students were between five P.M. and nine P.M. But most boys waited until it was dark so that fewer people would see them walking in. They would have taken a bath after classes and doused themselves with cologne before coming to see a girlfriend, a prospective girlfriend, or an "under-g," those girls they were discreetly seeing on the side. And there was always the odd glasses-wearing, portfolio-clutching bookworm who came to join a female bookworm in the common room for a study group. It was funny the way their eyes grew big behind their glasses when they saw the scantily dressed girls strolling about.

"Morastically Morastic!"

I turned and saw Dee's smiling face. He was sitting on the bonnet of his new red sports car, probably waiting for a girl. Dee and I had become friends in our second year after I helped him with a crucial term paper.

"Dee!" I crossed to his side of the road and gave him a quick hug. "You have come to mark register again?" Dee was a frequent visitor at the female residences on campus.

He smiled with his perfect set of white teeth. "Of course! What would you girls do without us?" Dee was an *aristo*. Not only did he have a silver spoon hanging out of his mouth, he had a silver fork and knife too. He spoke with an upper-class British accent acquired from his elite private school education. In our third year, Dee and I had had a very short-lived fling. Although we'd had fun, we were better at being friends. Besides, Dee's parents probably had his wife already picked out from one of the *aristo* girls who drove their sports cars around campus. As my roommate Ekanem often said, water finds its own level.

I raised an eyebrow. "Oh yeah? I am sure we will be able to manage just fine."

"I know you can manage. But for those girls who need a strong chest to lean on, your man Dee is up to the task." He puffed out a chiselled chest under a monogrammed Turnbull & Asser shirt.

Laughing, I shook my head. "It is good seeing you, but I am going inside. I have had a long day."

"But why? The night is still young." Dee winked. "Or is some gentleman visiting?"

Ladi was not coming that evening. "No. I am not expecting anyone."

Dee wrapped his arm around my waist and pulled me to his side. "Then stay with me for a while. We can go and buy some *suya* and just chill out here."

I gave him a skeptical look. "Aren't you waiting for someone?"

Dee laughed. "You know me too well. She told me to give her thirty minutes to freshen up, so I have some time to kill."

I thought about it. Why not? At least the mindless chatter would take my mind off my discussion with Aunty Morenike. "Okay. You better have some interesting gist for me."

I was still sitting outside with Dee when a car screeched to a stop near us. The woman behind the wheel parked in the middle of the road and flew out. She must have heard that her husband was visiting a female student at Moremi, because she walked straight up to an older man, who was dressed in a *buba* and *sokoto* and lip-locked with a girl. Screaming, the woman pulled the girl by her arm and gave her a dirty slap across her face. Before the woman's hand returned to her side, the girl slapped the woman back. The man at the centre of it all asked the girl to get into his car, and they drove off. The stunned woman just stood there.

Dee shook his head. "Error! That woman made a serious mistake. This is not her turf. She should have stayed home with her children and waited for her husband to come home."

I watched the woman's body gradually deflate as she walked back to her car. All eyes were on her. I felt sorry for her. She should have slapped her cheating husband, not the girl. But she probably knew her belongings would be waiting for her outside their house if she had dared.

By the time I finally walked into my residence room, I was too tired to do any thinking as I fell into a deep sleep.

The next morning, I huddled at the back of the lecture theatre with the other latecomers. With over two hundred students signed up for the course, finding somewhere to sit was always a problem. The economics professor continued with his lecture at the front of the hall. "Micro-loan schemes operate from the basic premise that economic growth starts at the grassroots level and that the poor have the capacity to lift themselves out of poverty. Can someone give me an example of an informal micro-loan scheme?"

One of those efficient frontbencher students raised her hand.

The professor gave her a smile. "Yes?"

"Would that not be *Ajo*?"

The professor nodded. "Excellent example. For those of you unfamiliar with the term, *Ajo* or *Susu* is an indigenous thrift collection scheme that offers an avenue for poor people to access non-collateral-based loans."

Shifting my feet, I noticed that the male student sitting close to me was trying to make eye contact. I kept my face turned away. Finally, he tugged on my arm and spoke in a loud whisper. "Fine girl, do you want me to make space for you on my lap?"

I glared at him and pulled my arm away.

He grinned, licking his big *kpomo* lips. "You don't have to be scared. Feel free to come and sit down. Didn't your mother tell you that you can't get pregnant by sitting on a man's lap?"

My eyes pinned him to his seat. "Actually, she did not. But I am not too worried about getting pregnant," I snickered. "Please correct me if I am wrong, but does it not take a *complete* man to get a woman pregnant?"

Everybody around us burst into laughter. One dark look from the professor killed the laughter, but Romeo's dark eyes flashed with anger. I turned to focus on the lecture.

The professor was still looking at the back of the class. I lowered my eyes and he continued. "As socially conscious economists, you must educate yourselves about the politics of giving, whether it's in the approval process of personal credit or the award of international aid."

Romeo snickered beside me. "Who cares about the politics of giving? In this world, it's every man for himself."

Clenching my teeth, I resisted the intense urge to grind my heel into his foot.

After the lecture, I went back to my residence hall and found an empty room. Apart from Ekanem, I shared the room with two other girls. We each had a single metal bed and a locker we had to bring from home. That school session we had even brought our own mattresses. A bedbug infestation the previous academic session had led to a huge bonfire of mattresses.

Dumping my handbag on the wooden table nailed to the wall, I knocked over a framed picture of Eniayo and me.

The picture was from my twenty-first birthday two years earlier. As always, Aunty Morenike had made my birthday cake. I smiled, putting the picture back on the table. In the past few years, Eniayo and I had seen each other infrequently because our school holidays were scheduled at different times. She was now seventeen and in her final year of secondary school. Mummy and Daddy were so proud when Eniayo announced that she wanted to be a doctor.

I turned when the door to the room creaked open and Ekanem strolled in. She was not only my roommate; we were course mates and friends. Despite our closeness, she did not approve of my lifestyle and never failed to tell me so. "Morayo, do you realize that you are putting yourself in danger? If you do not take care, one of your strange men will carry you off and use your dead body for money-making rituals!"

Ekanem was right about the risk. Women and girls were still going missing every day.

She flopped down on her bed. "Babes, your *Bobo Nice dey* wait you outside."

Bobo Nice was Ekanem's nickname for Ladi. As far as she was concerned, I had too many other *bobos* at my beck and call, and Ladi was just too nice for me.

Yawning, I glanced at my wristwatch. *What was Ladi doing here?* It was not yet visiting hours. I dressed up and hurried outside. As I walked through the quadrangle linking the new section of the residence to the older sections, my mind went back to the day Ladi and I met.

It was at the Faculty of Social Sciences library. The medium-sized room was packed full with students. That evening, Ekanem and I were studying for our macro-economics exam. Ladi sat at the table next to us. Several times during the evening I caught him staring. Initially I found the attention flattering, but it quickly became distracting. Standing up abruptly from my table, I walked over and sat on the chair across from him. I stuck out my hand and smiled. "Hello, my name is Morayo."

Staring at my hand, he quickly recovered his composure. "Ladi. My name is Ladi Thomas. It is nice to meet you, Morayo." His palm was surprisingly soft.

"It is nice to meet you too."

I bent over the edge of the table. Ladi's face was now mere inches away from the breasts peeking out from my low-cut blouse. I lowered my voice. "Em, Ladi, please can you do me one favour? I am trying to read and I find the way you are staring at me very distracting. Do you think that maybe later we can meet outside the building?"

Ladi's eyes yo-yoed from my chest to my face. He scratched his head, stammering, "Me ... meet you outside the building?"

"Yes. My friend and I will be leaving the library at eight. I'll see you outside by the computer lab." Not waiting for a response, I walked back, and when I sat down, Ekanem kicked me under the table. I winked at her and went back to my cramming. When I saw Ladi leaving with his bag of books, I glanced up. The clock on the wall said it was 7:55. I hid my smile behind my textbook. Ekanem and I had no plans of leaving for another hour.

A couple of days later, I ran into Ladi at the university's main library. I was walking down to the lobby from the Faculty of Medicine section on the sixth floor. When I had substantial reading to do, I would hide in one of the reading rooms. It was usually quieter there as the medical students were more serious about studying. With the number of textbooks I carried down to the main floor, it was one of those days I wished the old stone building had a lift.

I almost bumped into Ladi, who was walking up the stairs. When he saw me, he stopped. "Hello, Morayo. It is good to see you again."

I purposely gave him a quizzical look. "I am sorry, but I don't remember you." Of course I did, but I wanted Ladi to repeat the whole story again. He did, and quickly caught on when I started laughing.

That evening, we ended up sitting in front of the library and talking for hours. I found out that Ladi was also in his final year.

His expression became serious. "I would like to get to know you better, Morayo."

A coy smile curled my lips. "But I am not easy to get to know."

"I am willing to try."

For three months, Ladi came to see me almost every evening. Beneath his stiff exterior he had a great sense of humour. I told him I had no intention of joining his beloved Campus Christian fellowship—that going to church was no better than the weekly malaria pills we used to stuff down our throats—yet his persistence intrigued me.

We also had different convictions about premarital sex. After waiting patiently for him to make the first move, I had wondered if he was shy and needed some encouragement. One night as we sat outside Moremi Hall, I blurted out the question. "Ladi, when are you going to sleep with me?"

Ladi's jaw dropped. "What?" When he saw that I was

serious, he reached for my hand. "Morayo, I am not going to sleep with you."

I could not understand this. My eyebrow rose.

"I mean not until we are married."

"Married?" I started laughing. "Who said anything about getting married?"

Ladi went into a long speech about how much he loved and respected me. He felt that our relationship did not need sex to be meaningful. That night, looking at Ladi's earnest face, I vowed to make him so mad with desire that he would forget every word he'd just said. When Ladi gave me a chaste kiss on my cheek, saying, "Good night," I just smiled—and laughed inside. We were either going to play this game by my rules or not at all.

By the fourth month into our relationship I was wound up from sheer frustration. I wore tighter clothes, I changed my perfumes, I would touch him lightly—on his neck, his shoulders—every opportunity I had. I would deliberately make myself unavailable for his visits, and then at other times I would surprise him with small gifts. But Ladi seemed immune to all my highly potent charms.

Sometimes, I even let him catch me gazing at other men, dropping gentle compliments about the other boys in my classes. Ladi ignored these too. He was either made of stone or oblivious!

So I started cheating on him. The first time it happened, I was out with friends at one of the popular Lagos nightclubs. Through the haze of cigarette smoke I saw a good-looking man sitting alone at the bar. He returned my stare. The thump of the music made me feel braver than normal, and an hour later we ended up going back to his flat. The following week, another student caught my eye during lectures. I approached him and whispered into his ear. His eyes almost popped out. It was as if I was back in the nightclub again.

And each time, I told myself that it was all Ladi's fault for rejecting me.

Ladi sat on a bench outside the residence wall. His ebony face lit up when he saw me walking towards him. I sat down and gave him a teasing smile. "Ekanem said my *Bobo Nice* was waiting for me outside."

Ladi grinned. "Well, since I am definitely a fine *bobo* and I am nice, I guess that must be me." He laughed as I rolled my eyes. "Where were you last night? Didn't Ochuko tell you I came to the room?"

My roommate Ochuko and I were not on friendly terms. "Oh, she did not tell me. I went to Henry Carr Hall to see Aunty Morenike."

I had introduced Ladi to Aunty Morenike when she moved to Lagos. She liked him. During the previous year Aunty Morenike had suddenly became very serious about going to church, and so they had that in common. "Morayo, I really like this young man," she told me. "He is definitely better than the Sango worshipper I met on your birthday last year."

I laughed, remembering a former boyfriend, Tosin, who braided his hair and wore a stud earring. When she met him Aunty Morenike had smiled politely, but I could see the truth. I thought she was going to pin him to the wall with her disapproving eyes as he stuffed his mouth with cake.

"How is Aunty Morenike?" Ladi asked. "It has been a while since I saw her."

"She is doing fine. I thought you said you were travelling to Ikorodu today?"

"I know, but I have to submit my research proposal on Monday. Peter went with the rest of the band." Peter was Ladi's roommate, and the two of them played bass guitar in their campus fellowship band.

I squeezed Ladi's hand. We were both working on our theses. Ladi was having a particularly rough time with his chemistry professor. They had still not been able to decide on an appropriate research topic. "Is there anything I can do to help?"

"Maybe you can help me read through the draft tomorrow? Actually, I wanted to ask you if we could go out tomorrow evening. There is a stage performance of *Wedlock of the Gods* at the Arts Theatre." Ladi smiled. "I was thinking ... chicken and chips and then the seven o'clock show?"

I could feel a big smile spread across my face. Ladi knew how much I loved Zulu Sofola's plays. I was very touched by the gesture, for Ladi did not have a lot of money. Shortly after we met he told me how his mother back in Epe had to visit their rich relatives before every semester to beg for school fees. But it was not as if Ladi just folded his hands, waiting for a handout. He also worked part-time at the University Guesthouse maintenance department.

"Oh, Ladi!" I gave him a quick hug. "Thank you. I would love that very much." I smiled at his uncomfortable look. He did not like me hugging him in broad daylight, just in case his fellowship people were walking by.

When I got back to the room, Ekanem was cooking in our little kitchenette. Ochuko was also back. She was busy arranging provisions in her locker. Ekanem looked up from stirring her pot of fish stew. *"Bobo Nice don* go?"

"Yes, he is gone. He went to the library," I said, carrying my dirty dishes to the kitchenette. "Guess what? He is taking me to see the *Wedlock of the Gods* tomorrow."

Putting her spoon down, Ekanem clicked her tongue. "I really should go and wash this head of mine in the Lagos Lagoon."

"What do you mean?"

"I just don't understand this Ladi at all. When he can easily have any five-star, three-course meal—*you know*, someone like me—he cannot drag himself away from the fast-food leftovers of half the boys on campus."

"Ekanem! You are looking for trouble." Look at Ekanem with her stout, manly figure, I thought, comparing herself to a five-star meal. Talk about delusions of the highest order. Immediately I felt guilty. Ekanem had been a very loyal friend over the years. But I did not appreciate her discussing my business in front of Ochuko.

Ochuko, looking up from her task, faced Ekanem. "Babes, have I not told you to leave those two alone? It is not Morayo's fault now. The *bobo* has some fault in this matter. If Ladi's love is blind, is it deaf too? If he has not heard what the whole campus is tired of hearing, then maybe he deserves to have her."

Hissing, I turned my back to them and walked to my bed. I told myself I did not care about their opinions, especially Ochuko's.

The next evening, Ladi and I sat holding hands at the Arts Theatre. Ladi was completely engrossed in the play. In the darkness, I could see the gleam of his eyes and teeth as he watched Ogwoma declare her undying love for Uloko. I could not stop thinking about Ochuko's words. There had been days when I wondered why Ladi never asked me about the other men who flitted in and out of my life. Did he truly not know? On the other hand, Ladi and his friends seemed to live in their own world. I had come to realize that you could interview four students on campus and they would all describe a different reality.

Ladi turned, smiling indulgently at me. Sighing, I rested my head on his shoulder.

After the show, we walked leisurely back to my room. The skies opened and rain poured down. Ladi's Boys' Quarters happened to be close by, so we decided to head there to wait out the rain. By the time we got to his room we were both soaking wet. Ladi handed me a pair of his jeans and a T-shirt. He took some dry clothes for himself and went to change in the bathroom.

When Ladi came back to the room, he found me in his bed looking at some of his photo albums. Snuggled up, with our feet entwined, we talked about graduating in a couple of months. We hoped that our one-year National Youth Service Corps posting would be to the same state.

It suddenly struck me that I had never been in Ladi's room this late at night. "What would you do if Peter just walked in?"

Ladi gave me a puzzled look. "What do you mean?'

"Well, you do realize that I am in your bed wearing nothing but your clothes, O Virtuous Brother Ladi?"

"I know you are wearing my clothes, but I have nothing to be worried about. We are not doing anything."

"We could be," I said in a breathy voice as I wrapped my arms around him.

Ladi gently pushed me away, shaking his head. "Get your mind out of the gutter, woman."

I stuck out my tongue at him. Ladi tickled me with his foot.

From the warmth of the soft bed, I could hear the skies thundering. The rainstorm showed no sign of stopping any time soon, with the gusty wind splashing rainwater hard against the closed louvres. There was no way I could leave for my room just yet.

When Ladi's head started nodding off around midnight, I could still hear the rain pounding on the aluminum roof. Ladi untangled himself and staggered off to Peter's bed. I should have known that he would not sleep in the same bed with me.

Sometime in the middle of the night, the rumbling skies woke me up. I remembered where I was when I saw Ladi curled up in Peter's bed. I sat up, watching him sleep. He looked so peaceful. Taking off my clothes, I crept across the room and spooned my body behind Ladi. As I wrapped my arms around him, he stirred in his sleep but did not wake up. His left ear was temptingly close to my mouth. When I nibbled on it, Ladi moaned softly in his sleep. And when I moved on to nuzzle his neck, his eyes flew wide open. They were shining with desire.

Stretching his body, Ladi groaned. "Morayo ..."

As he turned around, his hand landed on my naked body. His hand recoiled as if he had touched a hot stove. "Morayo, why did you—"

"Shhh ... this is not the time for unnecessary questions," I whispered into his ear. Moving closer, I planted my lips right on his open mouth. Ladi didn't resist; we kissed deeply until he moved his head to the side and groaned. "Morayo, we really should not be doing this."

"Says who?" I said, planting feathery kisses along his neck.

"Morayo, please," Ladi groaned again as he tried to move his head away. "You are not playing fair with me at all."

But I was not ready to listen to his pleas. Before Ladi came along, I had resigned myself to the fact that there would be no one special for me. Who could truly want me?

If Ladi truly wanted to marry me, he had to experience and like all of me, and this was my chance to finally show him.

Before long Ladi's resistance melted. Soon, the only sounds in the room were the howling of the wind and our soft moans. Afterwards I fell asleep with a bright smile of victory on my face. Ladi was mine.

The next morning, my eyes opened to an empty room.

I got up, wrapping the bedsheet around me. I opened the door and peeked outside. Ladi was standing out on the veranda. Fully dressed, he was leaning against the building, shivering in the early morning Harmattan cold and hugging himself. He looked miserable. I could hear him murmuring to himself.

My heart started pounding fast. This was not the happy scenario I had pictured the night before. "Ladi …"

He slowly turned around. When I saw the tortured look in his eyes, my heart sank. "Morayo, please go and get dressed. I want to walk you back to Moremi before daybreak."

As I took a step forward, he turned his back to me. I went inside and paused in the hallway. His eyes—I suddenly felt my breath catch; I had to gasp for air. It was like looking into my own eyes the morning after Bros T first came to my room.

On our way back to Moremi, I sneaked side glances, but Ladi kept looking straight ahead. Walking me right up to the gate of the residence, he turned back without saying a word. With heavy footsteps I opened the side gate and walked inside the compound.

Everything was quiet. Most rooms in the buildings were still dark. I was grateful for the darkness. I could get to my room before anyone saw me walking in wearing men's clothes and clutching a bag of my own damp clothes.

But a hall porter was sitting in front of his lodge. He looked at me with unmistakable disdain.

I mumbled "Good morning" and quickly walked past him.

Behind me he cleared his throat noisily, spitting the pulp from his chewing stick.

"Miss Night Rider, bad morning to you," he said. "*Yeye ashawo* girl. *Na* book your papa and mama send you come university come read. *Na* so so man, you go *dey* follow." He spat again. "With this your *waka waka,* you fit get PhD degree for Man-ological Sciences." He laughed loudly at his joke and I recoiled as if he had slapped me across the face. He had called me a prostitute. Even worse, for the first time, I felt like one.

Ekanem and Ochuko were still asleep when I entered our room. I quietly changed into my nightgown and crawled into my cold bed. I dragged the cover over my head, stuffing the cloth in my mouth to muffle my crying. In the darkness, I could only see Ladi's sad eyes.

For two days I walked around the room like a zombie. I did not attend my lectures. I could not eat or bathe. I just wanted to stay in my bed. Ekanem watched me with concern, but I repeatedly told her nothing was wrong. Ochuko's dark eyes followed me around the room in silence.

On day three, Aunty Morenike came to look for me. Ochuko answered the door.

"Good evening, my dear."

"Good evening, Aunty," Ochuko said in a pleasant voice.

"Is Morayo in the room?"

"Yes, Ma. She is here."

I flung my cover aside. It was late in the afternoon and I was still in my nightgown. Aunty Morenike looked down at me in the bed. She calmly asked me to go and take my bath. When I got dressed, she told me to pack an overnight bag. All the way back to her room, she did not say anything to me. When we were in the privacy of her room, she sat me down. "Morayo, what is wrong?"

Suddenly I was a little girl again, back in Ibadan. It was the same question she had asked me the afternoon I tried to swallow the pills. Only I was not a vulnerable child anymore. I was an adult.

A huge wave of shame washed over me. "Something happened between me and Ladi," I finally said.

Aunty Morenike raised her eyebrow.

I whispered, "We slept together." Then I quickly averted my eyes. I could not begin to say what really happened—I had made him sleep with me.

After a long silence, she asked, "Didn't you tell me Ladi treats you like a princess?"

I held onto her arm. I was crying. "Aunty, please tell me what to do. I don't want to lose him. Maybe I should go and look for him?"

"Let him be. He will come and look for you when he is ready," Aunty Morenike told me firmly as she stroked my head. "Do you know the saying, *Folorunsho ti ofi okun ogede gun igi ope?*"

I nodded. Mummy said the phrase all the time. Folorunsho was the name of a mythical young man who had used a rope made from banana leaves to climb a palm tree. Of course, he fell and broke his neck. Folorunsho had arrogantly assumed that since his name meant "entrusted to God's care," he was immune to harm.

"Listen, Morayo, it is arrogance to tempt fate, saying, What is the worst that can happen to me?" Aunty Morenike said. "Plenty can."

I blinked back my tears as she wrapped her arms around me. "But even if Ladi does not come back, remember that not everybody who comes into our lives is meant to stay. Some people come just so that we can learn important lessons."

✄

Two weeks later, I found Ladi waiting outside my lecture hall. "Morayo, we need to talk."

As we sat on a bench in front of the main library, I knew what he was going to tell me. How ironic that we would end our relationship at the same place where it started.

But Ladi looked different now from the young man who had walked into my life. His hooded eyes were tired and red-rimmed. I could tell that he had not slept much in the days we had been apart. Neither had I.

Ladi covered my hand with his. "Morayo, I am so sorry."

I whipped up my head around. *He was sorry?*

"For the past two weeks, I have done nothing but think about us. All along, I knew about those other guys …"

"You knew?"

"Yes. But I thought that if I gave you some time, you would realize that they were not worth it. That I had something better to offer." His lips twisted in a bitter smile. "You never pretended about what you wanted from me. I really thought I had the power to change you because I had fallen in love with you." His voice broke. "I only ended up changing myself."

Ladi took a deep breath. "Morayo, I can truly say that this

past year has been one of the happiest times of my life. But I made a promise to someone else long before I met you." He took another deep breath. "I am sorry, but we have to go our separate ways."

He wrapped his arm around my shoulder. "Morayo, please don't cry."

Suddenly, I needed to run. I stood up from the bench, smiling at Ladi through my tears. I could hear myself speaking calmly. "It is okay, Ladi. I understand. Take care of yourself." I turned and walked away.

Behind me, I heard Ladi calling out my name.

16

If one has not fallen, one does not learn
how best to pack one's load.

Four months later, I wrote my last exam and moved back home to wait for my National Youth Service Corps posting. Aunty Morenike also completed her program and returned to Ibadan. In addition to her teaching job, she started lecturing part-time at the Ibadan Polytechnic.

Nothing had changed at home. Eniayo was away at boarding school. Mummy still had her tailoring shop and Daddy was still travelling around the country. Only now, he and Mummy were talking about his resignation and his plans to start his own business: a pharmacy supermarket. He would hire a young pharmacist and Mummy would manage the supermarket. "But Daddy Morayo, what will happen to my tailoring shop?" Mummy said.

"You can always hire another tailor to help at the shop. You can divide your time between both businesses."

I sat quietly as I listened in on their conversation. No one asked for my opinion. My relationship with both of them had not changed much over the years. Bros T's ghost still walked around the house.

One good thing was that for a short while, Tomi and I became close again. My visits back to Ibadan over the years had been sporadic, and we mostly saw each other during the Christmas holidays. When Tomi told me she was getting married, I was happy for her. She had been dating Timi since our second year at university, and I had met him a couple of times over the years.

Tomi and I were in her bedroom going through the wedding favours we had just bought at Aleshinloye Market. Tomi had decided that instead of giving her bridal party the usual plastic bowls or cups with the bride and groom's picture plastered on them, she would give out custom-made costume jewellery.

"So which one do you think I should give Sola?" Tomi said. Sola was her chief bridesmaid. I picked up a red coral bead earring and necklace set. "Hmm ... I like this one. I think it would go well with the yellow lace we are wearing for the night party."

"You are right. Thank you." Tomi moved over to the bed and sat down. "Morayo, I can't believe I am getting married."

"I know. It is almost like it was yesterday we were staring at Dotun from this window." We were all grown up. Tomi's brother Gbayi was a bigshot living in Abuja now.

Tomi sighed. "I still can't imagine what it will feel like living so far away from home. There are days I wish Timi had not accepted that transfer to Kenya. I am going to miss Mummy so much."

I sat next to her on the bed. "She can always visit you, and I am sure you two lovebirds will not miss anyone too much."

Tomi turned to look at me. "That is true ...," she said,

fiddling with her earring. "Morayo, when do you think you are going to get married?"

When I found out about Tomi's wedding, I had asked myself the same question. "Honestly? I don't know."

Trying to shake the heavy feeling that suddenly came over me, I stood up from the bed. "I promised Mummy I would be back early to cook the night meal, and we still have so much to do."

For a minute Tomi hesitated as if she had something to say, and then she stood up. "Okay, who is next on the list?"

Three months later, Mummy and I arrived back home from Tomi's wedding party. The wedding had been a success and I was exhausted. After changing from my party clothes, I sat alone in the sitting room. Mummy was still in her bedroom changing her clothes. Minutes later, she found me crying on the settee. The tears just came and I could not stop them. "Morayo, what is wrong?"

The question that came to my mind was, *Where do you want me to start?*

I looked at Mummy's worried face. "I am just tired."

Mummy did something unexpected. She sat next to me and pulled me to her. "I know you are tired. You have been working hard these past months." She started rocking me like a child. "Do you remember those times I used to tell you and Eniayo riddles?"

I gave her a puzzled look.

"You and Eniayo used to run around the house shouting the answers at the top of your voices."

As I remembered how Eniayo always wanted to win, a reluctant smile tugged at my lips.

"So, Morayo, what passed in front of the king's palace without stopping to greet the king?" Mummy asked as she rocked me back and forth.

"Hmm ... A fly?"

"No ... that is the answer to who came to eat with the king without being invited."

My eyes squeezed together as I tried to remember. I forgot how tired I was. "Hmm ... it's floodwaters!"

"You are right."

For the next hour, we sat there quietly. For the first time in so many years I allowed myself to relax in Mummy's company.

My National Youth Service Corps posting letter came three weeks later. I was not happy when I read that I had to report to Anambra State for the one-year period. I knew that most likely I would be sent to teach in a rural school. Daddy insisted it was good for me to experience living in another part of the country. "Morayo, you young people don't understand that the program became necessary after the civil war. If the government did not make it mandatory, how many young people would leave the familiarity of their towns to learn about their fellow Nigerians?"

"But Daddy Morayo, Anambra is too far," Mummy said with a sigh. "All these young people leaving home and travelling to these strange places where they speak different languages."

Daddy laughed. "Bisoye. They are university graduates, not children. And those strange places are part of their country. Are they not the ones demanding change? Let them go and discover the country first."

I listened to Daddy's words with mixed feelings. The program may have been started with good intentions, but I really doubted if it had significantly changed the level of distrust people from the different tribes had for each other.

The reality, though, was that unless I completed the one-year posting, no reputable employer would give me a job. I had to report for the three-week orientation camp at Umunya. From there, we would travel to our assigned stations within Anambra State.

Shortly before I left for Anambra, Eniayo came home on a mid-term break. I had not seen her since I moved back home. She had been in the middle of her final examinations and Mummy said she did not need any distractions. On her first night home Eniayo lay beside me on the bed. The only light in the room came from the full moon peeking in through the open window.

"Morayo …"

"Hmm …"

"Why are you sleeping around?"

Eniayo's words made my chest feel as if it could not expand to accommodate the air that my body needed. The painful sensation constricted my throat. My body jerked into a sitting position.

"I heard you and Mummy talking the other time I was home. Then Hauwa's sister brought home your university magazine." Eniayo's voice dropped. "Hauwa had seen your name inside."

My teeth clenched. "It has nothing to do with you."

Eniayo sat up, leaning her back against the headboard. The trembling in her voice became even more pronounced. "But it does. Should I not care when people call my sister an *ashawo*?"

I flinched. "I am not an *ashawo*!"

"But that is what the magazine said."

The shame I felt turned to anger. "All your life you've had

people protect you from everything. Eniayo should not hear this. Eniayo should not see that. What do you know about anything?" I pointed to the door. "Just leave my room!"

Her response came in a low voice. "I know about Bros T."

My hand fell to my side. "What?"

"I saw the two of you one afternoon in his bedroom. I was playing outside when I heard him moaning. I thought he was hurt and I peeked in through the window."

Eniayo shook her head. "I didn't understand what he was doing to you. But I was afraid to ask questions because he had warned me never to look through his window." Her shoulders started shaking. "Maybe if I had told Mummy or Aunty Adunni what I saw, it would have ended sooner. And when I understood what he had done, my guilt would not let me talk." She started sobbing. "I am sorry."

My anger melted away and I wrapped my arms around her. "But it is not your fault."

"It is not your fault either," Eniayo whispered.

But why couldn't I still believe that?

My arms tightened around her. "How did you get to be so smart?"

Eniayo wrapped her arms around me. "I have a really smart big sister."

I arrived in the city of Onitsha on a sunny September afternoon. Aunty Morenike had dropped me off at Molete at four o'clock that morning to catch a commercial bus.

Just before the bus left, Aunty Morenike gave me a tight hug. "Take care of yourself and be good, okay?" she said.

I swallowed the lump in my throat and nodded. "I have heard, Aunty. I will try and call when I can get to a payphone."

As we drove on the bridge from Asaba, I could barely contain my excitement at seeing the River Niger for the first time. I remembered the first time I read about the river in one of our primary school textbooks. When I pushed my head out of the window, its clear blue waters stretched as far as my eyes could see.

After I got off the bus at Upper Iweka Road, I half ran through the throng of people as I tried to keep up with the young wheelbarrow pusher I had hired to carry my suitcases. Weaving his way expertly through the crowd, he was shouting *"Uzo, uzo, uzo"* at the top of his lungs.

When he dropped my bags at the motor park, I ran into a group of fellow youth corpers who were also going to Umunya. Looking out from the commercial bus we hired, I noticed how different the soil colour was. I had never seen anything like it before: it was red compared to the brown sand at home. There were also signs of erosion everywhere. The deep gullies on each side of us forced the driver to stay in the middle of the road. We all had our hearts in our mouths when it looked like a collision with an oncoming car was unavoidable. Cries of *"Oga,* make you take am easy-o!" filled the bus. By the time the driver dropped us in front of the camp compound, we were all relieved. The majority of us were from the other side of the Niger, and this was our first visit to the East.

That first night at Umunya, I found it difficult to sleep. Apart from the fact that I was roasting inside my mosquito net, I was not used to sleeping close to so many people. My dormitory room housed nineteen other female corpers. Our bunk beds were arranged like sardines in a tin.

The next day we woke up at six for our early-morning drill. I joined a group of female corpers as we walked half-asleep in the dark to the parade ground. Before we headed out of the campgrounds for our endurance run, the officer in charge of our platoon did a roll call.

"Kachi Nwosu," the officer called out.

"Present, sir," boomed a voice on the other side of the platoon.

The sleep cleared out of my eyes.

Kachi Nwosu! I looked around, but it was still too dark for me to see. Could it be the same Kachi Nwosu from my childhood days? The first boy I had kissed—the boy whose letters were once hidden like precious gold in my mattress? Thinking about it, I laughed to myself. I was in the East now. There were probably a hundred Kachi Nwosus walking around the orientation camp. What were the odds that Kachi and I would be in the same batch of corpers?

But by the time we came back from our run to get ready for our day, I had forgotten all about the morning roll call.

I saw Kachi before he saw me.

Walking into the dining hall, I noticed a tall, light-skinned man standing ahead of me in the line. I watched him hand his meal card to the food server. There was something very familiar about him. Later, when he sat at the table opposite me, I kept trying to remember where I had seen him before.

"Kachi, I salute you-o." When the man turned in my direction to greet his friend, our eyes met. I watched him whisper something into the ear of the person he was sitting with. He got up and walked over to my table. After saying a few words to his friend at the other end of the table, he came to my end.

"Good morning, sister. I am sorry to disturb you, but I have a feeling we have met before." He stretched out his hand. "My name is Kachi Nwosu."

My heart started pounding as I shook his hand. "I am Morayo Ajayi."

Kachi's eyes widened. "It is a lie. *Morayo Ajayi?* Morayo from Eleyele?"

"Yes, the same one. How are you?"

Stunned, Kachi sat down beside me. "Morayo, it *is* you." He stared. "Oh my God, you have grown even more beautiful."

Laughing, I shook my head. "And your mouth, Kachi, has grown even sweeter."

"Morayo, please, let me go and tell my friend that I will meet up with him later. I don't think I can eat anymore." Neither could I. When Kachi came back, we decided to leave the dining hall and find somewhere private to talk. We walked over to the empty parade ground and sat on the cement floor. For the first couple of minutes, we just stared at each other. It had been ten long years.

I noticed a little scar about his right eye. He did not have one there before. "Kachi, where did you get that scar?"

"What scar?"

I reached out and touched it gently.

Kachi grinned. "I was trying to catch a soccer ball when I dived into the goalpost."

Smiling, I shook my head. "You and soccer."

Kachi smiled and reached for my hand. "Seriously, Morayo, I am so happy I found you again."

"Me too, Kachi."

Over the next three weeks, Kachi and I spent most of our free time together. Every morning he kept a seat for me at the dining hall, and after breakfast we would walk to the parade ground. Evenings we spent at the mammy market, sipping hot pepper soup. We would sit talking late into the night even after the shops were closed. We talked about Eniayo, his sisters, our parents, and university life. I did not ask him why he stopped writing me letters, and Kachi did not say anything about it either. But all that changed on the night of the campfire party.

"So, Morayo, is there someone special waiting for you at home?"

Instantly I thought of Ladi. I shook my head. "No. There is no one waiting for me."

Kachi smiled. The giant logs of wood crackled in the bonfire and the sparks rose up in the air like fireflies. I cleared my throat. "Kachi, I am redeploying back to Lagos State."

The smile left his face. "What? But why, Morayo?" He reached for my hand. "What about us? I thought we were going to spend the service year getting to know each other better."

Ever since Kachi and I met again, I had dreaded this moment. I knew he wanted us to pick up from where we left off. But in my heart, I knew that he was really enamoured with a childish dream. I doubted that Kachi would want a serious relationship if he knew about my sexual past. It was best for me to walk away now. I shook my head. "Kachi, it won't work."

He rubbed his head. "What if I disagree with you? Why do you think we met each other again? These things don't just happen."

I kept quiet.

"Fine," he said. "But I will not let you go again. I will come to Lagos to see you. I will write—"

"No, Kachi. We are both grown up now. Let's not make irrational promises." Kachi turned away from me. I sighed. "Please don't let us spend the rest of our time here arguing about this."

On the last day of orientation camp, Kachi and I stood in front of the gates to say goodbye. His eyes were hidden behind a pair of sunglasses. My own eyes felt gritty and dry from crying myself to sleep the night before. "I guess this is it, then?" he said with a pained smile.

Too choked up to talk, I nodded silently.

Just like the night in Eleyele, Kachi pulled me to him for a quick, tight hug. I clung to him. What I clung to was not this adult man I barely knew. It was what he represented. He had been part of all the days that were good. Loud whistles from a group of youth corpers passing by broke us apart. Watching Kachi walk away, I was sure he and I would never see each other again.

Back in Lagos, I was one of the lucky few who found a position at a new-generation bank. In addition to my youth service allowance, I received a generous stipend from the bank. My days were long and busy, but they left me with no time to think about Kachi. I lived with the family of one of my mother's cousins, Sister Bose.

About two months into the service year, Eniayo and Aunty Morenike came to Lagos for the day. "Morayo, we are here!" Eniayo called out as she knocked loudly on Aunty Bose's door.

"I am coming!" Laughing, I opened the door. "Eniayo, I am sure half of Lagos can hear you."

Aunty Morenike smiled as Eniayo and I hugged each other. "Aunty Morenike, welcome. Please come in. I am sure Eniayo has almost talked your ears off."

Eniayo turned to Aunty Morenike with a pained expression. "Aunty, see what I told you? Morayo is *always* trying to spoil my reputation."

"Morayo, please be nice to your sister." Eniayo stuck out her tongue at me behind Aunty Morenike's back. "Truth be told, she only talked one of my ears off."

"Aunty!" Eniayo pretended to pout.

Eniayo was on the admission shortlist for the College of Medicine and had come to Lagos for her entrance interview. The next morning, when we got to the university and found out that Eniayo needed to pay a fee, we ran to a nearby bank to buy a bank draft.

As I closed Aunty Morenike's car door, a blue Toyota Corolla pulled up right beside us. I turned when I heard a familiar voice. "Morayo Ajayi ... Is that you?"

I looked into the car and saw that round familiar face. It was Ekanem, my university roommate. I had not seen her since our graduation day. "Ekanem! Wonders will never end. So are you in this Lagos?"

Ekanem jumped out of the car and gave me a hug. "Morayo! *Na wa!* You just forgot about me."

I collected Ekanem's contact information, promising to get in touch with her later that week. In a happy coincidence, it turned out that she was also completing her youth service at another bank not far from mine. We decided to rent a flat together. But when I told Mummy about our housing plans, she immediately vetoed it. She insisted that I continue living with Sister Bose.

"But Mummy, why can't I just share a flat with Ekanem? After all, you like her."

Mummy pursed her lips with disapproval. "Two unmarried young women, living by themselves in *that* Lagos? You might as well put up a sign outside your flat saying that you girls are open for business."

"*Mummy. Haba!* What business is that one now?"

"See this child. Listen, you are not too old for me to put you across my lap for a good spanking, if you continue asking me foolish questions. You are going to stay with Bose for the rest of the service year and that is my final decision."

I started to tell Mummy that times had changed— but looking at her stubborn face, I just sighed. I saved my emancipation speech for another day.

As it turned out, my stay at Sister Bose's home was short-lived. One Saturday morning I woke up to the sound of Sister Bose's raised voice filtering into my bedroom from the courtyard. I could also hear someone crying. Alarmed, I slipped into my Dunlop slippers and hurried outside. I found Aunty Bose standing over her house girl, Abundance.

Sister Bose had one of her high-heeled work shoes in her hand. From the way the poor child knelt in front of her and rubbed at a bloody spot on her head, I could tell that Aunty Bose had beaten her.

"Madam, *abeg*. I no steal your pant," Abundance pleaded.

"Shut up your lying mouth!" Sister Bose snapped. "*Ole!* Thief! Every time you wash my clothes, one of my panties gets missing. Tell me, who else in this house will be stealing my underwear? Who else!"

My jaw dropped. All this was about some missing underwear? Abundance used her blouse sleeve to wipe her dripping nose. "Madam, I no know. I no know. Maybe it falls for ground and Madam Grace dog Bingo eat am. Ask Madam Grace. Bingo *don* eat her pant too before. I no *dey* wear any pant now. I no *dey* wear. In fact, make you ask *Oga* if you think say I *dey* lie."

Suddenly, a bigger question was floating around in the air. How would Sister Bose's husband know that Abundance the house girl wore no underwear? When Abundance realized what she had said, she pressed her hands over her mouth as if to contain her wayward tongue. But it was too late. The secret was out.

Abundance left their home that evening. Her worn travelling bags were piled high on her head. The sour-faced madam who had brought her to Lagos from the village came to pick her up, and within a week she returned with another child to work as the new house help—a young teenage boy. Three weeks later, Sister Bose asked me to leave too. With tears flowing down her face, she insisted it was nothing I had done. It was entirely because of her husband. "Now that I know he has this kind of *problem*," she whispered to me, "it is best to keep all temptation away from him."

Assuring her that I sympathized with her predicament, I packed my bags, and Mummy reluctantly gave her blessing for me to rent a flat with Ekanem. We were lucky to find a two-bedroom flat that was not too far from our places of work. The flat was in a newly renovated building, so everything was freshly painted. Mummy gave me the old sitting room furniture from home because she wanted to buy something new. We made a deposit with the carpenters for a dining set. Ekanem bought some Hausa leather pouffes and a raffia area rug. Aunty Morenike gave me her old standing mirror, and we both bought new beds. By the time we had arranged everything, it was perfect.

✂

Eniayo was ecstatic when Mummy agreed to let her spend the weekend with me in Lagos. But before Mummy left, she took me aside with an anxious look. "I don't want to hear that anything has happened to your sister."

I rubbed my temple, sorely tempted to say that she should just take Eniayo back home. I gave her a pained smile. "I have asked my men not to visit this weekend." Mummy's eyes flashed at my insolence. Eniayo's entrance into the room saved me from an immediate tongue-lashing. From the look she gave me, I knew Mummy would revisit the issue later.

Later in the evening, Eniayo and I sat outside on the balcony. NEPA had struck again, and with no electricity, the heat in the flat was stifling. "Morayo, I have to tell you something."

Whatever the matter was, it sounded serious. "What is it?"

"Tunde asked me out."

I shifted my chair so that I could see Eniayo better. "He did? When?"

"He came to see me at school on our last visiting day."

"Oh …" Despite Eniayo's outgoing personality, she had always shied away from boys. Partly because Mummy had always hovered around her like a hawk—but also because she was still so conscious of how she looked.

Tunde was the son of Daddy's childhood friend from Elewure. Because of his family status, our parents never complained when Tunde came to the house to visit. I think because he and I were age mates, Mummy assumed that he was coming to the house because he had an interest in me. I smiled. "So that is why Tunde has been coming to the house."

Eniayo nodded. "He said that he was just waiting for me to start university before he said anything."

"So what did you tell him?"

Her face turned red. "I didn't know what to say. So I said that I needed some time to think about it."

"Do you see yourself going out with him?"

"I don't know. He is nice, though … but I still think that I should wait and finish my first year of university before I start any relationship." Eniayo pushed her hair away from her face. "I heard that the first year is usually hard. I do not want any distractions. He can wait … and then we'll see."

I felt my chest swell with pride. "Eniayo, if he really likes you, he will wait until you are ready."

Tunde agreed to wait. I thought they complemented each other. Not only was Tunde as dark as Eniayo was fair, he was also quiet and well mannered. And both families would most likely welcome a permanent union. The Alabis had known Eniayo since she was a baby. For them, Eniayo being an *afin* would not be an issue. I had decided not to try to persuade Eniayo either way. I was no expert when it came to relationships.

Two months later, an old university classmate invited Ekanem and me to her birthday party. We showed up at the party hoping to catch up with other old classmates.

I was talking with the birthday girl when I heard a very familiar laugh. For a moment, I thought I was imagining things. I turned and saw Ladi, *my* Ladi, standing at the other side of the room. Immediately, I patted down my newly set hair, praying no spinach leaves were stuck between my teeth.

When Ladi looked in my direction, it felt as if we were the

only people in the room. I wanted to run towards him, but then I saw an intrusive dark shadow by his side. It turned out to be a pretty young woman. My eyes narrowed when I saw the way she was holding onto Ladi's arm as if it were a lifeline. I quickly turned my back, trying to hide in the crowd. As I thought of how to leave the room without walking by them, I heard my name.

"*Morayo?*"

I turned around slowly with what I hoped was a surprised look on my face.

"*Ladi?*"

"Morayo!" Ladi greeted me with a big hug. The pretty woman beside him gave me a slow look over. She cleared her throat when Ladi failed to introduce her right away. Ladi quickly put his arm around her. "Morayo, please meet Bimpe Adedeji. Bimpe, this is Morayo Ajayi."

Bimpe's smile dropped. So he had told her about me. But her smile came back when Ladi proudly announced, "Bimpe and I are getting married next February."

Somehow, I made it through the motions of smiling, shaking Bimpe's hand, and congratulating them. The smug smile on Bimpe's face told me that if my acting fooled Ladi, she could see right through me.

Ekanem and I left the party shortly afterwards. She could tell that seeing Ladi again had affected me. "Morayo, it is okay, cheer up now. I know that you really liked him." What she didn't know was that I had secretly nursed the fantasy that one day Ladi would come back and save me from myself.

Later that night, tears ran down my face as I scrubbed my body with a loofah sponge. I scrubbed until my skin felt raw from the soap and I had to clench my teeth from the pain.

Splashing my body with bowl after bowl of cold well water, my skin burned as if it was on fire.

Back in my bedroom, I stood naked in front of my full-length mirror, taking a critical look at myself. I saw a young, petite woman with full breasts, a narrow waist, and a generous behind. Her smooth ebony skin glistened with tiny droplets of water. But tonight, her large almond-shaped eyes were sad and bloodshot. Her chest heaved up and down as she fought hard against another bout of crying.

I looked away, disgusted by the image in the mirror.

Lying in bed, curled up in a fetal position, I made a promise to myself. There would be no more random men.

17

The thirsty fig sits and waits, waiting patiently
for the arrival of the rains.

Standing at Ekanem's office cubicle in the banking hall, I looked at the lingerie she had bought during our lunch break. Youth service had ended in 1997, and for the past five years Ekanem and I had been working at the customer service department of the Atlantic Bank. We were still roommates, but that would be changing soon: Ekanem was preparing for her wedding.

I shook my head. "Ekanem! Do you want to give Brother Ubong a heart attack? This teddy should come with a caution notice."

Ekanem smirked. "Heart attack? My friend, don't let Ubong's grey hairs fool you. He is the one who picked out these styles from the catalogue."

Our colleague Kafiyah laughed, white teeth flashing from a pretty Fulani face framed by a *hijab*. "*Kai,* Ekanem, so you want to tell us that Brother Ubong sanctioned this very unholy purchase?"

Ekanem raised her eyebrow. "Is Brother Ubong not a man with warm blood flowing in his veins? I am not going to stand by and let one small girl itching to reap where she did not sow bamboozle my husband with some overexposed wares. Spirituality aside, my sisters, we have to stay hot."

We did not hear our boss, Mr. Idris, coming. "What is going on here?" he asked. "You women do know that this is a place of serious business and not a marketplace where you can stand around gossiping?"

Ekanem slowly dropped the bag of lingerie on the floor and kicked it under her desk. "Sorry, sir," she said with a sweet smile. "We were just discussing the importance of safeguarding vital economic assets, particularly in these very volatile markets."

I started coughing. Kafiyah patted me gently on the back.

"I am sure you were, Miss Bassey," Mr. Idris said with a sneer before heading for his office. We stared at his back, watching his funny walk. When he was out of earshot, Kafiyah clicked her tongue. "*Walahi*, I can almost bet my entire salary that the man has a bad case of untreated piles."

Ekanem and I exchanged looks. "*Haba*, Kaffy, that almost sounds personal," I said.

Kafiyah rolled her eyes. "In this country, is everything not always personal?"

There was no love lost between Kafiyah and Mr. Idris. Mr. Idris's secretary had walked in on him chasing Kafiyah around his office desk. Within minutes, the entire banking floor heard what happened. Some colleagues even joked that Kafiyah would need to invest in some roller skates so that next time she would be able to run faster. Others joked that Kafiyah could now consider herself properly welcomed to the department.

Hours later, I covered my yawn as Kafiyah and I dragged

our feet towards the gate. Even though it was already seven P.M., poor Ekanem was staying behind to complete her end-of-month financial report.

Walking past the security post, Kafiyah and I greeted the bank gateman, Mr. Pius.

Mr. Pius saluted us. "Good night, madams. Em, Madam Morayo, please wait."

Kafiyah, who was in a hurry to get home, left to catch her bus. I waited for Mr. Pius and gave him an inquiring look.

"Madam, em, *abeg* no *vex-o.*" He scratched his head nervously. "You know say I like you well well. This is why I been wan talk to you since about this your problem."

I looked at him in surprise. "My problem?"

"Yes, madam. If no be say you be better woman with proper home training, I for no open my mouth. You no be like that *yeye* Madam Clara *wey dey* proximity banking. That one, if goat wear trouser, she go follow am." From the way I narrowed my eyes, Mr. Pius knew I was not in the mood to engage in any office gossip. He quickly changed the topic.

"*Em,* madam, I been know one prayer mountain for around Okokomiko area. This mountain *na* original sure banker. My two sisters *wey dey* look for husband like you, *dey don* marry since *dem* come down the mountain. Madam, I swear," Mr. Pius said, licking his pointer finger and waving it up high in the air, "one of *dem sef,* na for inside the same bus *wey dey* carry am go house the next morning, she meet her husband. Her husband na *de* the bus conductor. In fact, this very last week, *na* twin boys my sister born for the man."

After congratulating him on the birth of his twin nephews and promising to discuss the prayer mountain offer on another day, I headed to the bus stop.

I did not know whether to start crying or laughing. I had to have "desperately seeking a man" stamped on my forehead. Why else would my office gateman be offering me solutions to "my problem"? On the other hand, if Mr. Pius could guarantee the instant result his sister got, maybe I should give this prayer mountain offer of his some consideration.

Mr. Pius was not the only person concerned about my unmarried state. For a second, I wondered if Mummy had paid him to talk to me. I would not put it past her. She had just been in Lagos the previous month for my thirty-first birthday. Every month Mummy came down to Lagos on those covert visits—and I saw right through her. She disguised her visits as shopping trips for tailoring supplies. But please, how many bags of buttons can one tailor use in a month?

The visits were part of Mummy's mission to save her daughter from the perils of spinsterhood. She was absolutely convinced that I was purposely causing her heartache by refusing to get married. "At the very least, you should be the mother of two children by now," she said with a sigh. "Mrs. Adigun just came back from visiting Tomi in Kenya. She is pregnant with her third child." She pursed her lips. "Morayo, time is passing you by. Find someone."

"Mummy, I have heard." Though I would never admit it to my mother, there were some nights when I heard my own biological clock ticking so loudly that it managed to drown out the deafening noise of our landlord's diesel generator.

⚜

On Eniayo's twenty-fifth birthday, Tunde proposed to her. She said yes. It did not come as a surprise to me. As far as both families were concerned, she had been off the market since the day they started dating. Tunde's parents, the Alabis, had quickly scheduled a date to meet with our parents. We were promptly summoned from Lagos. "A woman marries the man *and* his people. Which is why they too must come to ask for her hand," Mummy said.

The Alabis had been to our home innumerable times over the years, but Mummy still had the entire house thoroughly cleaned. She also insisted that Eniayo cook the meals for the reception. "Let me know that their son won't starve when he marries you."

Tunde attended with his parents and an older married brother. Dressed in a form-fitting, navy-blue sequined dress Mummy had made for the occasion, Eniayo walked into the sitting room to serve her new family-to-be with bottles of Coke. Then she and I watched the meeting through the kitchen pass.

Once they finished their drinks, Mrs. Alabi started the discussion. "The reason we are here is that we saw a beautiful rose growing in your garden and we came to ask for permission to pluck it."

Of course, Mummy was willing to play her friend's traditional marriage guessing game. "A beautiful rose? Since I have more than one beautiful rose in my garden, you have to be specific."

In the kitchen, Eniayo rolled her eyes. "Do they think they are acting out a 1920s Yoruba stage play?" She mimicked Mummy's voice. "Please tell me? Is it the glasses-wearing rose flower or the flower with a K-shaped stalk?"

I gave Eniayo a playful shove. "Please leave my K-shaped stalk out of this discussion."

Mrs. Alabi smiled. "Of course we are here for our fair princess Eniayo. Our son Tunde told us that he loves your daughter very much and wants to marry her. That is why we came to seek her hand in marriage."

Eniayo covered her giggle.

Daddy spoke up for the first time that afternoon. "You do know that Eniayo is still in school?" Eniayo had just started her Pediatrics internship. "It is very important to us that she complete her education."

"We know," Mr. Alabi said. "And we are prepared to wait. We just don't want our case to be like that of the patient dog that finds no bone. That is why we are here now."

"She is worth waiting for," Mrs. Alabi quickly added.

"In that case," said Daddy, "we accept the proposal. May the union of our families be sweet, fruitful, and long-lasting."

"Amin!" everybody chorused.

Mummy quickly pointed out that Eniayo had cooked the meal when our guests were being served. Mrs. Alabi exchanged a smile with Mummy. "We know you trained her very well," she said. "Beauty, brains, and manners. Now that is the original triple threat." The men joined in the laughter.

I watched Eniayo exchange a shy look with Tunde as she placed dishes on the table. The only time he had spoken up was when he greeted Mummy and Daddy.

Before the Alabis left, both sets of parents prayed over Eniayo and Tunde that their love would survive the years still ahead.

"Morayo, do you want your younger sister to get married before you?" Mummy asked me later that night.

"There is nothing wrong with Eniayo getting married first." I shrugged my shoulders. "We came into the world separately."

"Morayo, how can you say that? Do you even care about my feelings?"

"But Mummy, this is about my life."

Mummy almost bit off my head. *"Your life?"* she snapped. "That is where you are wrong, my child. This is *our* life. It became our life the day I gave birth to you. Whatever you do or whatever happens to you affects my life. Our lives are intertwined. So don't tell me it's just your life."

As always, I ended up apologizing.

Mummy spent the rest of the weekend lecturing me on how my good years to find a husband and have children were passing me by. By the time I left for Lagos, my skin had broken out in giant hives.

When Aunty Morenike visited Lagos the following month, I complained about Mummy's behaviour. "Aunty, I really wish Mummy would just let me be."

Aunty Morenike gave me a sympathetic smile. "I am probably not the best person to talk to about marriage. One of my fellow lecturers even suggested that I find an older widower with children who is looking for companionship. When I asked her if there were any eligible men in her family, her mouth snapped shut." Aunty Morenike's eyes became serious. "Morayo, I know that Aunty Bisoye can overdo things sometimes, but she loves you. Believe me, she does."

Apart from Eniayo and Kafiyah, who visited when their busy schedules allowed—and Aunty Morenike's rare visits too—I hardly received any visitors anymore. I kept turning down invitations to attend parties, and after a while, people got the message. Morayo the party girl was gone. Despite my deliberate self-destructive acts, I had made it through. Not only did I no longer need someone to save me, I knew I was worthy of being loved.

One afternoon after work, the rickety bus's sudden halt jolted me out of my light sleep and my head bounced against the side of the vehicle. "Maryland! Maryland bus stop!" the bus conductor announced in a singsong voice.

I was grateful for the darkness inside the Molue bus as I quickly wiped away the pool of drool by the side of my face. Reaching into my bag, I took out a two hundred–naira note and handed it to the conductor.

The bus fare was one hundred naira. The conductor frowned when he saw the currency in my hand. "Aunty, I no get change. Why you *wan* cause trouble for me now?"

My heart sank. The end of the month was still two weeks away. I needed to stretch my money, but I knew my options here would be to forfeit my change, which meant paying double the fare, or be "married" to another change-less passenger disembarking. We would then have to find a way to split the two hundred–naira note. At that moment, the man sitting next to the driver got off the bus and handed him another two hundred–naira note.

The conductor complained yet again about having no change. Then he grinned cheekily, handed me back my money, and said to the man, "Uncle, I go marry you with this, my fine Aunty, *wey dey* for back here."

I made my way out of the Molue, resigning myself to looking for change with this stranger. It did not help that on my way out, my skirt latched on to a jagged piece of metal jutting out of the body of the bus. Hearing the material rip as I tried to unhook myself, I hissed in frustration. That month alone, it would be the third skirt I had to patch.

Stumbling out of the bus, I almost fell into the arms of the male passenger. Embarrassed, I held onto the side of the bus, steadying myself on my high heels.

"Didn't I tell you that one day you are going to stop running and marry me?"

I looked up. "Kachi?"

"At your service, Princess Morayo," he said, and bent down to give me a quick hug.

The bus conductor looked at the two of us in surprise. Then he smiled with satisfaction. You would have thought he had just brokered a peace agreement between the federal government and the Egbesu boys. "*Oga* make we *dey* go," he said. And the rickety bus moved on to its next stop, leaving Kachi and me standing by the side of the road, smiling at each other.

Suddenly feeling shy, I looked away.

Kachi pointed to the two hundred–naira note in my hand. "I guess that is going to be your first soup money."

"*Soup money?*"

"Yes, now. Since we have now been married by the bus conductor, are you not going to be cooking for me?"

I rolled my eyes. "If this is the amount of money you intend on giving your wife for soup money, I pity her."

"In that case, my dear wife," he said, "I hope you have a very good job where you are earning plenty of money. Don't you women say that what a man can do, a woman can do better?"

I rolled my eyes. "Kachi Nwosu, you really need to move along with the times. That was back in the 1970s. This is 2002. The proper saying is, What a man can do, why should a woman bother?"

Kachi's robust laughter filled the air. "Seriously, Morayo," he said, "it is so good to see you again. Are you in a hurry to get home?"

"Well, it is getting dark and Eniayo is coming to stay with me tonight. I have to be home when she arrives."

"Ah!" He brightened. "Well, I can walk you home. I live close by at Williams Estate."

I looked at him in surprise. "Me too!"

Kachi was living just two streets away from me. As we walked towards the estate gate, I noticed that he kept trying to look at my hand, no doubt for a wedding ring. I purposely kept it hidden in the folds of my skirt.

Eventually he was forced to ask, "So, Morayo, are you married now? Before we reach your house, you better let me know. I don't want anybody chasing me with a cutlass because they saw me following their wife."

I laughed. "So you are now afraid of a common cutlass?"

Kachi raised an eyebrow. "Woman, when did a sharp cutlass become common? *Please*. I don't want any marks on my handsome face."

"Okay, Mr. Universe, there is no need to worry. I am not yet married. I am sharing a flat with a friend."

We stood outside my house gates to talk. It was too late to invite Kachi into the compound. Baba Landlord was very particular about us bringing back men to our flat, especially at night. Ekanem had officially introduced her fiancé, Ubong, to our landlord before he could stay past seven P.M.

Kachi and I were still standing outside talking when Eniayo arrived on an *okada*. After paying the *okada* man, she walked over. I saw her sizing up Kachi. From the look on her face, I could tell that she was dying of curiosity, but I kept quiet.

She moved closer and stuck her hand out. "Hello, I am Morayo's younger sister, Eniayo. You are?"

He shook her hand with a straight face. "My name is Kachi. I have to say that there is a striking resemblance between the two of you."

"That is very observant of you. In fact, people often think that we are identical twins," Eniayo replied, glaring at Kachi. Her undisguised sarcasm dripped from every word. "So, Mr. Kachi, please tell me, what are your intentions towards my sister?"

"Eniayo!" I felt heat radiating all over my face.

"Well if you must know, I have very dishonourable intentions towards her." He covered his mouth with his hand. "Oh, did I really say that out loud? What I meant to say was that I have very honourable intentions towards your sister. The same ones I have had since we were ten years old."

Eniayo looked puzzled.

Kachi shook his head. "Don't you remember me? I am Kachi from Eleyele, Adanna's brother."

She covered her mouth. "It is a lie! Oh my God, I would never have recognized you! How is Adanna?"

Watching the two of them talk, my heart swelled. I have always been in awe of Eniayo's self-confidence. Now a woman, the shy girl was gone—she walked into rooms with the air of someone comfortable in her own skin. She had grown immune to the stares and the whispers.

When Kachi had to leave, he gave me a pointed look. "I hope I will be seeing more of you."

Inside the compound, Eniayo turned to me impatiently at the front door.

"My dear sister, why do you have that grin on your face? You look like an ant frolicking inside a box of sugar."

I started laughing and made a point of trying to open the door.

"Okay, okay," she said. "I know you are not going to tell me anything. In that case, let's go and talk about all those fine clothes that I will be taking back to school with me."

When Eniayo saw me fold my arms across my chest, she quickly added, "Did I say take? I am sorry, my dear *working* sister. Let me rephrase the sentence. I meant borrow," she laughed, "and never return."

Laughing with her, I opened the door to the flat.

18

He who loves the vase also loves what is inside.

The next week, after I had folded and unfolded the slip of paper with his number a thousand times, Kachi called me at the office and said that he had grown impatient waiting for my call. He was coming to see me. When Ekanem heard Kachi was coming, she packed a small bag and said she was going to spend the night with Kafiyah to give us some space.

I changed my clothes more than five times before Kachi finally knocked on the door. Over the rice and *dodo* I served, he quickly made it clear what he wanted from me. "Morayo, listen. I am not looking for any casual relationship. That time has passed. What I am looking for is a wife."

A wife?

"Em … Kachi, don't you think that you are going a little too fast?"

"I don't," Kachi insisted.

"Well I do. Marriage is not something that you rush into."

"Morayo, I am not going anywhere," Kachi said with a determined look.

"Well, we'll see."

Between Kachi's long hours at his engineering firm and mine at the bank, we did not have that much free time. Our limited time together became very precious and we mostly spent it indoors at my flat or his, watching videos or playing board games. I kept declaring that Kachi and I were just friends. But Ekanem and Kafiyah, his loyal fans, insisted that I give him a chance to prove himself. And Eniayo bluntly told me, "Morayo, you are really not fooling anyone but yourself. If Kachi is just a friend, then I am really just an undercover European spy."

In truth, I was scared. Scared of what Kachi's reaction would be when I told him about my past. I had promised myself years ago that I was not going to hide anything from the man in my life.

Two weeks later, I was back in Ibadan for a weekend visit. On the Saturday afternoon, I took a bus to Aunty Morenike's flat. Although my relationship with Mummy was gradually getting better, I knew she would not have understood. Apart from Eniayo, Aunty Morenike was the only person from home who had met Kachi.

Aunty Morenike and I sat in her sitting room. On my visits, it always struck me how everything had remained the same. Of course, Damilare was now a big boy and his toys no longer cluttered the room, but Aunty Morenike had just acquired another bookshelf and crammed it full of even more books. "Morayo," she would say, "some women collect shoes, I collect books."

"Aunty, I am afraid that one day Kachi is going to regret falling in love with me."

"Why would he do that?"

"He would when he finds out the kind of woman I am."

"No, Morayo, the kind of woman you were. But why are you borrowing extra worry from tomorrow?" Aunty Morenike asked. "You have not even told him anything yet."

"I know. But what if Kachi stops loving me when I tell him?"

"Then he stops loving you," Aunty Morenike said in a firm voice. "That is his decision to make. That does not stop you from loving yourself." She sighed. "I know it is not easy. You love him."

I nodded. I did love him.

"You know, a long time ago, there was someone special for me too," Aunty Morenike said with shining eyes. "His name was Dehinde. Dehinde and I met after youth service. I really thought he was the one."

"So what happened, Aunty?"

"His mother happened. I told Dehinde about Damilare the first day he came to see me at home. Amazingly, he did not mind. By the end of that year, we were already talking about marriage. We were both so ready. One evening Dehinde picked me up to spend time with him. He was still living with his parents. We met his mother at home. I sat with her in the sitting room while Dehinde went to get something for me to drink. As soon as Dehinde came back, his mother sent him away on an errand. It turned out she just wanted to talk to me alone. Dehinde had told her about Damilare earlier that day."

Wrapping her arms around her legs, Aunty Morenike smiled. "Oh, Morayo, you should have seen the look on her face. I thought she was going to pass out on her chair when I told her that I had Damilare when I was fifteen years old. She lifted the *gele* perched high on her head and set it down beside her on the chair. Honestly, it would all have been very funny if we had not been discussing how Dehinde's family could never accept my son."

Aunty Morenike wrinkled her nose as she repeated the devastating words spoken to her by Dehinde's mother. "We want a woman whose womb is still fresh to give us grandchildren." Aunty Morenike paused. "Morayo, I could not believe my ears. There I was, just twenty-four years old, and my poor womb was already too old."

My chest felt heavy. "Oh, Aunty …"

"Poor Dehinde could not understand why I suddenly wanted to go home or why I told him the relationship was over." She closed her eyes for a brief moment. "If I had told him what his mother said, he would have still married me." Her lips pulled into a sardonic grin. "He had always complained about how he had to constantly prove to his mother that he was a grown man. Still, if I had made him choose between me and his mother …" She shook her head. "It would have been only a matter of time before I lost out. And my Damilare would have suffered for my choice."

She shrugged her shoulders and reached for my hand. "Please, my dear, don't let life pass you by because you are afraid to come out from the shadows. I do enjoy my life, but it is a lonely one. Tell Kachi and let him decide."

Suddenly Aunty Morenike swayed in her seat and shouted out in pain.

"Aunty Morenike, are you okay?"

She caught her breath. "Oh yes. It is nothing."

I pressed her again. I could see beads of sweat pooling fast on her brow, but she just shrugged her shoulders again. "There is this swelling under my armpit and sometimes the pain radiates to my chest. But it will pass."

I stood up and sat next to her. "Swelling? How long has it been going on?"

She reclined back in her seat, waving her hand. "Morayo, I said it's nothing. It's probably a boil that is not yet ripe."

"Aunty, is it not best if you just go and see a doctor?"

Aunty Morenike licked her dry lips and laughed. "I should go and see a doctor over a boil?"

"But you look as if you are in serious pain."

She held up her hand. "Okay, I can see that you won't stop worrying about this. If the pain comes back, I will go to the hospital."

The following weekend, Kachi and I were sitting out on the balcony of my flat. There was no electricity and it was too hot inside the house. I had to talk above the honking sounds of the busy Lagos city traffic. "Kachi, there is something I have to tell you."

Kachi looked a little worried. "What is it?"

I kept my eyes locked on his face and I started from the very beginning. I told him about Bros T, about my life at the university and the men—faceless and nameless now to me—that had passed through my life. I told him about Ladi, about the numbness and the shame.

When I was quiet, Kachi hung his head.

As I waited for him to talk, every passing second felt like an hour. He finally looked up at me. "Do you still love Ladi?"

I had since come to the drawn-out conclusion that what I had felt for Ladi was not love. It was something sick that had me twisted and that had ended up almost destroying us both. "No, Kachi, I don't love Ladi. It is you that I love."

Kachi inhaled sharply. This was the first time I had ever said those words to him.

"I love you, Kachi."

Looking away from my face, Kachi stood up and backed away towards the door. "Morayo, I need to think ..." He paused. *"Okay?"* He looked around as if he was confused. "My keys?"

"Your keys are on the dining table." I forced myself to remain sitting where I was. He would come back when he was ready, or perhaps not at all. "Kachi ..."

The front door slammed shut. He was gone.

19

A person who has only one set of clothes
does not play in the rain.

*I*n the months that followed, there were days when I wondered if I had made a mistake in telling Kachi about my past.

Kachi came back to my flat days later, but there was an unfamiliar guardedness in his eyes. It was as if he was not sure who I was.

While we were out together, I found myself explaining how I knew each man that greeted me. It was not as if Kachi said anything to me. Maybe that would have been better. But his body would tense up while his eyes darted back and forth from their faces to mine. I would quickly stretch out my hands to male friends to avoid any hugs.

Then he suddenly started dropping by at my flat unannounced at different times of the day. At first Ekanem did not say anything. But she too started to resent the intrusion. "You know how men always say they want to know all about your past? And they swear that they won't hold it against you?"

Ekanem asked as she turned off the gas cooker to look at me. "Trust me, they don't really want to know. All that knowledge just eats them up alive."

Turning off the tap, I drained water from the rice I was washing. "So what did you tell Ubong about your past?"

Ekanem raised an eyebrow. "You know I have very few skeletons in my closet. Ubong knows that I had boyfriends just like he had girlfriends, and we are leaving it at that. What do you think would happen if we start discussing numbers and my exes are more than his? Then Ubong will start wondering if he is marrying a second-hand woman. What is past is past. I have learned from my experiences and I am wiser for it. There will never be another man for me, and I pray every day that I am enough woman for him."

Even though I did not regret telling Kachi about my past, I resented the fact that overnight I seemed to have lost all his trust. I also knew that I could not spend the rest of my life explaining the identity of every man we met.

Things finally boiled over about a month later. Kachi was walking me back to my flat from his. I stopped by the side of the road. "Kachi, I can't do this anymore."

He gave me a puzzled look. "You can't do what?"

"Kachi, I love you but I can't make you trust me, and a relationship is not worth much without trust."

"Morayo ..."

I shook my head. "Kachi, let me finish. I have worked so hard at not hating myself. I ..." Nothing was going to take me back to the days after Ladi. "If you can't live with my past," I told Kachi, "please let me go."

"Oh, Morayo ... I am sorry." Kachi gathered me in his arms, weaving his fingers through mine. He placed both hands right above his heart and tilted my chin up so that I could see his face in the evening sunlight.

"Kachi …"

Kachi interjected. "Morayo, *ahuru m gi n'anya*." The words were in his native Igbo.

Although Kachi was very fluent in Yoruba, I did not understand his language. "What does that mean?"

"It means I love you, Morayo." Kachi paused, looking into my eyes. "Don't you know that you are the only cube of sugar in my tea?"

I was silent. I wanted much more than sweet words.

"Morayo?"

I took a deep breath. "No more third-degree interrogations?"

Kachi nodded. "No more."

"Are you sure you still want to be with me?"

Kachi stroked the side of my face. "Yes, I am sure." A little smile tugged at the side of his mouth. "I figured someone has to take you off your father's hands. I am selflessly volunteering for the job."

I buried my face in Kachi's chest. As Kachi gave me a hug, that knot deep inside me twisted even tighter. I wondered how long he would wait.

Six months later, Kachi was still around.

In those months, my feelings for Kachi deepened as we navigated through our relationship. I soon found out that under his calm, smiling exterior was a quick temper. The good thing was that most times, it went as quickly as it came.

So that afternoon when Kachi walked into my flat with a dark look on his face, I knew there was trouble.

He sat across from me on the settee. "Morayo, we need to talk." His voice was low as he rubbed his head repeatedly. "Listen to me. For a year I have been asking you to marry me. I am not saying we should get married tomorrow. You know I am not a rich man. Neither is my father. I will need time to gather money for our wedding. But all you say is no. Morayo, don't you love me?"

"Kachi, I do, but I need some more time." As I reached for him, he jerked his arm away.

"Then why—?"

When I did not reply, he stood up and started pacing the room. "There has to be something else you are not telling me," he muttered. He stopped suddenly. "Or is there someone else? I will have you know that I am a fine, upwardly mobile young man. In fact, today on my way here, five girls whistled at me on the street."

I forced a smile to my face. "See me, see trouble. Who are those jobless girls whistling at my man? These young estate girls better not try me."

But Kachi did not look amused. I could tell he was getting very impatient with me.

"When you are ready to tell me the real truth, you can come and look for me." Kachi flung the words over his shoulder as he stormed out of my flat. I did not go after him. He needed some time to cool off. But when I did not hear from him for days, I started to panic, and yet I could not bring myself to call him. I still had no answer for him.

"Aunty Morayo!"

Turning around, I saw Bisi, one of my landlord's teenage daughters, hurrying towards me. I could hear the Dunlop foam slippers flapping against the soles of her feet. "Good afternoon, Ma," she greeted, pulling out a crumpled envelope from her skirt. "Uncle Kachi came to look for you. He asked me to give you this envelope."

I smiled at her. "Thank you. When did he come?"

"Not too long ago, Ma."

I opened the envelope in my bedroom. I smiled when I saw the title on the note.

Obi m. My heart. Kachi's special Igbo name for me.

> *Obi m,*
>
> *I have gone to Awka. I got an urgent message yesterday that Papa is sick. He wants to see me. While I am away, please think about our discussion on Saturday. I will call you before the end of the week.*
>
> *Yours always,*
> *Kachi*
>
> *P.S. Nobody whistled at me all week. What have you done to those pretty girls?*

Reading the postscript, I smiled again. The next morning I woke up from a restless night's sleep. Kachi was right. There was something important that I had yet to tell him—but first, I had to go home. I could not put it off any longer. It was time for me to tell Mummy that despite Daddy's clear warning against inter-tribal marriages, I had fallen in love with an Igbo man. Since Mummy so desperately wanted to see me married, she had to change Daddy's mind.

⚮

During one of my visits home soon after I had started work at the bank, Daddy called Eniayo and me to the sitting room. He had a map of Nigeria open on the little stool in front of him. "Two of you, listen. I know that you are growing older and soon you will be telling us that you want to get married."

Eniayo and I watched in stunned silence as Daddy took a red marker and drew a thick line along the state boundaries of Lagos, Ogun, Oyo, Kwara, and Ondo.

"Before you bring a man to this house, you better make sure that he is from one of these states. I do not want to see anybody from any other state. Marriage is hard enough when you marry someone from your own tribe. When you marry someone from a different tribe …" He did not finish the sentence. He just said, "Have I made myself very clear?"

"Yes, sir," we chorused.

"Good," Daddy said as he folded the map neatly and handed it over to me. "Morayo, when you no longer need the map, you will pass it to your sister. The two of you can go."

Kachi was from the eastern part of the country—definitely not an approved geographical region.

When I arrived at my parents' home after I had received Kachi's letter, I sat with Mummy in her bedroom as she hemmed one of Daddy's trousers. "Mummy, there is something I have to tell you."

I saw cautious hope jump into her eyes. She carefully laid the trousers on her bed.

"Mummy, I met someone."

She crossed her legs. "Someone?"

"Yes, Ma. A man."

"A man?" Mummy asked in wide-eyed wonder. You would have thought I'd just told her I had seen a unicorn with Oyo tribal marks hawking roasted groundnuts at the motor park. From the gleam in her eyes, I could already see the mathematical wheels spinning. Man plus marriage equals grandchildren.

"His name is Kachi Nwosu."

"Oh." She ran her hand slowly over the creases in her wrapper. I waited. "Is he Igbo?"

"Yes, Ma."

"I see. So where did you meet this Kachi?"

"Do you remember the Igbo family who owned that kiosk where we used to go and grind pepper?"

Mummy frowned as she tried to remember. Then she snapped her fingers. "Em … Mama Chukwudi."

I smiled. "No, Mummy. It was Mama Kachi."

"Chukwudi and Kachi, are they not the same thing?" Mummy said with a wave of her hand. "But didn't they move back to the East?"

"They did."

Her eyes narrowed. "So where did you two meet again?

"I met him when I went to Anambra for Youth Service camp. Then again in Lagos almost two years ago, and we have been …" My voice trailed off.

"So are you telling me that you have been seeing this young man for almost two years now?"

I nodded my head.

She took a long look at me. "You say this Kachi wants to marry you?

"Yes, Ma. We love each other."

"Love?" Mummy clicked her tongue. "I know you think the cow eyes you are making at each other is love. My child, the trials of marriage and life are what produce real love."

I was not surprised. I had heard her express those sentiments many times before. "Mummy, he is a good man and I want to marry him."

"He is a good man," Mummy echoed. "Okay, my dear, I have heard you. Tell this *good man* that your mother wants to meet him."

I felt hope spark inside me.

"After I meet him, I will then talk to your father about this marriage business. And we will see."

When Kachi returned to Lagos, I told him that Mummy wanted to meet him. His travel-weary face beamed. I laughed when he picked me up and swung me around.

A few weeks later, when Mummy visited Lagos, Kachi arrived dressed in a starched shirt and trousers. I covered my smile when I opened the door. He looked pale and he was sweating. He prostrated flat on the floor to greet Mummy. A smile tugged at the side of my mouth when Kachi greeted her in fluent Yoruba. "*Ekaasan,* Ma."

Mummy watched him, stone-faced. She pointedly answered him in English. "Good afternoon, young man. You are welcome."

Kachi sat on the chair across from Mummy, his hands folded neatly in his lap. He looked like an errant student summoned to the school principal's office. I sat next to Mummy to watch the drama unfold.

After a few awkward minutes, Kachi bravely started the conversation.

"How was your journey down from Ibadan, Ma?"

Mummy gave him a quick smile. "It was fine. Thank you."

"How is Daddy doing, Ma?"

"Daddy is doing fine. Morayo told me you went home to see your sick father. How is he doing now?"

"Papa is doing much better. Thank you for asking, Ma."

Mummy cleared her throat loudly, looking Kachi squarely in the eye. "You know why I asked to meet with you today."

Kachi nodded. "Yes, Ma, I do."

"Morayo told me that you want to marry her. Is this true?"

"Yes, Ma, I really want to marry Morayo."

Mummy pursed her lips. "So have you told your parents about Morayo?"

"Yes, Ma. I told them about her last Christmas."

"So what did your parents say?"

"They are looking forward to meeting Morayo soon. They were very happy."

"Happy?" Mummy gave him a skeptical look.

Kachi nodded. "Yes, Ma."

When Kachi had told me about his parents' reaction, I did not believe him either. He was their only son. He later admitted that his mother had expressed some reservations when he first told them—but that they still wanted to meet me.

The damp patch under Kachi's armpits grew larger.

I was surprised when Mummy suddenly changed the topic. "Morayo, is the food ready now?"

"Yes, Mummy. Should I go and set the table?"

Mummy faced Kachi. "Young man, I hope you have a strong

stomach. You might change your mind about the marriage business after you eat Morayo's *egusi* soup."

My mouth opened. "Mummy!"

But Kachi burst into laughter. And for the first time, Mummy smiled at him warmly. Thankfully, my *egusi* soup passed the taste test, and the rest of the afternoon went very well. They chatted amicably at the dining table, and I could tell Mummy liked what she saw of Kachi. I could not have been happier. Before Mummy left, she assured me that she would talk to Daddy but that she needed some time.

Three months later, Mummy told me to bring Kachi to Ibadan. Eniayo insisted that she come along. "I have to see this meeting with my own eyes," she said.

From the way Kachi clenched his teeth all the way to Ibadan, I could tell that he was very nervous. During the drive we could barely get him to talk. Just before we arrived at Ibadan, Eniayo was finally able to get him to laugh. "So, Kachi, did Morayo tell you to wear a bulletproof vest?"

Kachi's mouth fell open as he stared at Eniayo through the rear-view mirror. "Bulletproof vest?"

Eniayo turned to me. "Morayo! You didn't tell him?" She smacked her forehead. "Don't tell me you forgot the helmet, too? Kachi, since I like you, I have to warn you." Her eyes twinkled. "There is an old hunter-slash-sniper on our street who wants Morayo as his fifth wife. Why do you think she has stayed single this long? The one and only suitor she brought home is still missing an ear. Luckily for him, the hunter has shaky hands."

I could not believe my ears. "Eniayo!"

By the time we drove down our street, Kachi had begun smiling again.

But the smile quickly disappeared when we walked into the house and met Daddy in the sitting room. Daddy was watching television.

Kachi quickly prostrated his long body in greeting. Even I was impressed at the way he landed gracefully on the floor. "Good afternoon, sir."

Daddy pushed down his bifocal glasses to stare at Kachi.

"Good afternoon, young man."

"*Ekaasan,* sir," Eniayo and I chorused, kneeling to greet Daddy.

Mummy came out of the kitchen, beaming from ear to ear. "*Ekaabo!* Kachi, welcome to Ibadan! How was your drive from Lagos?"

As it turned out, there was a soccer match between the Manchester United and Liverpool football clubs airing on the television. Both men were ardent soccer fans, and watching the game helped break the ice considerably. Eniayo and I watched in wonder as they continued their discussion over lunch. In one afternoon, Kachi had walked into our home and broke the sacred rule of no talking during mealtime. Mummy glanced at me, smiling with her eyes.

After the meal, Daddy asked Eniayo to put some chairs out on the veranda. He wanted to talk to Kachi away from our listening ears. From inside the house, we soon heard laugher drifting in through open windows.

Mummy gave me a triumphant smile. "I will start making my lists," she said.

By the time Kachi and I left for a quick visit to Aunty Morenike's flat late that afternoon—Eniayo was staying behind in Ibadan to tax Mummy and Daddy for more pocket money— we were both feeling giddy with excitement.

I had called Aunty Morenike the previous day to let her know we were coming. She looked worried when she came to the door. Her expression changed, though, when she saw the broad smiles on our faces. "Everything went well?"

I nodded. "Mummy is busy writing a wedding list as we speak."

Squealing like a little girl, Aunty Morenike ushered us into her flat. She pulled our hands as she headed for the settee and then sat down between us. "Tell me. Tell me."

After Kachi recounted how Daddy had asked him about his future plans and how they talked about Daddy's travels to the East, Aunty Morenike gave a contented sigh. "I am so happy for the both of you." She squeezed our hands and got to her feet. "This definitely calls for a celebration. I have a bottle of fruit wine chilling in the fridge. I am coming."

Kachi and I reached for each other's hand.

We were both exhausted when Kachi dropped me off at home later that day. He gave me a quick hug before he left for his flat. *"Obi m,"* he whispered into my ear.

"Hmm …"

"We are going to get married."

"Yes, Kachi," I said. "We are."

Two months later, it was my turn to feel apprehensive when Kachi drove us to his parents' home in Awka. His sister Adanna was having her *Igba Nkwu Nwanyi,* the wine-carrying ceremony that is the Igbo traditional marriage. As Kachi explained it, the groom and his family bring palm wine to the bride-to-be's family and both families are formally introduced. The bride-to-be, a cup of palm wine in hand, would then walk among the crowd, pretending to search for her groom. When she finds him, she offers him the drink and brings him to her father, who blesses them when they kneel before him.

Mama Kachi danced to my side of the car. She embraced me as soon as I stepped out and tried to kneel in the loose red soil. "Good evening, Ma," I managed to say.

"Welcome, my daughter. We have been anxiously waiting!"

Kachi's sisters, Adanna, Ogadinma, and Dumebi, also came out to greet us. "Your father and your uncle Ekene are inside the house," Mama Kachi told Kachi after he gave her a big hug.

We found Kachi's father, Papa, and his younger brother in the sitting room. I knelt to greet both men. "Good evening, sirs."

"*Ada nno-o*," both men chorused in Igbo. "Welcome, my daughter," Papa said in English. "You are welcome to our humble house."

I sat in one of the floral upholstered chairs, my eyes respectfully lowered.

Dumebi took our bags inside the house. She soon returned with plates of freshly washed *ube* and roasted corn. Nne told me that I would be sharing Adanna's room during my stay. A short while later Ogadinma announced that a bucket of water was placed in the bathroom—just in case I wanted to take a bath.

When I joined Kachi's sisters at the back of the house, they were shelling baskets of melon seeds for the ceremony. I sat on the stool Adanna placed for me beside her, listening to her talk animatedly about her groom, Obinna.

Kachi came out and pulled me aside. He was leaving the house with his father and uncle. There were some last-minute details that needed attention before we left for the village. "Are you going to be okay?" he whispered to me with a worried look. "Papa insisted that I had to come. We should be back soon."

"I will be fine." Smiling, I squeezed his hand. "Your sisters are about to start cooking. I am sure they will let me help."

Kachi's eyes widened as he shook his head. "Help with cooking! Please, no. I already told my mother to keep you away from the pot of soup."

As my jaw dropped, he gave me a quick kiss on my forehead.

Behind us, his sisters started giggling.

The next morning, we left Awka for the short drive to Kachi's village, Ezinifite Nnewi. Both his parents were born there. Dumebi, my self-appointed translator, provided me with a steady stream of information as we drove through the village. The family's large gated compound was right in the middle of it. The compound had three houses with a big quadrangle in the middle. The massive blue glass building was Uncle Ekene's village home. The building towered over Papa's two-storey building. Their late father's modest bungalow looked like a poor cousin beside both buildings.

Nne took me to meet Kachi's ninety-year-old grandmother, who lived in her husband's house. Kachi's grandmother did not speak English and I did not speak Igbo, but she pulled me to her frail body in joy after Nne said something to her.

During the five days we spent in the village, I barely saw Kachi. He and the other men went about their own preparations while I stayed with the women. The day before the ceremony, the *nwunye umudi* came to help with the necessary tasks. I lost count of the number of hugs I received as the women welcomed me as the newest wife of the clan. On the day of the ceremony, we woke up very early. Adanna had barely slept from all the excitement. "Adanna, you are going to need the energy," Mama Kachi kept repeating until she ate some food.

The groom, Obinna, and his family were coming from the neighbouring village of Ekwulumili. The large party tents set up in the quadrangle quickly filled up with family members and guests from various parts of the country. Mama Kachi, who knew that this was my first time attending an Igbo wedding, told me to go and sit with Kachi. That way I would not miss any part of the ceremony. Adanna and her group of young maidens, made up of her sisters, cousins, and friends, were going to be making their entrance much later.

Mama Kachi made her own entrance with her entourage of friends and family members. She danced into the circle, and guests and family members got up to shower her with naira notes. Some notes stayed plastered to her face, held down by her glistening sweat. After the mother-of-the-bride dance, Adanna danced into the circle with her group of maidens. They all looked beautiful in their matching gold-lace outfits, but Adanna rightly stole the show. When I saw her, I gasped quietly. Kachi was pleased at my reaction, and his eyes moved between me and his sister. Adanna was stunning in her gold-lace puffed blouse and navy-blue George wrappers. The blue and gold damask head tie fanned out from the top of her head like a satellite dish. Heavy gold trinkets, flashing from her ears, neck, and wrists, complemented her fair skin. Yet Adanna's dazzling gap-toothed smile still far outshone the flash of gold.

After her dance, Adanna knelt before Papa as he handed her a cup of palm wine. Soon we were all laughing at Adanna's theatrics as she danced around in her search for Obinna. One of her friends even handed Adanna a pair of binoculars. When Adanna eventually "found" Obinna in the crowd, she offered him the cup of palm wine, which he gladly gulped down. Adanna then brought Obinna back to Papa for his blessing.

I sat up in my chair to watch the colourfully dressed *Egedege* dancers. The muscles of the young male dancers rippled and shimmered with beads of sweat. The female dancers moved their beaded waists with captivating elegance, challenging every woman watching to move in her seat. The sounds of the *Oja* flute and the drums spurred an energetic dance that made me tap my shoes to the beat. The dancers' feet sent a fine cloud of red soil up into the air.

Ogadinma and Dumebi pulled me up from my chair to dance with them. I knew that I would pay later for trying to force my stiff body to do such vigorous dance moves. Kachi joined me on the dance floor, showering fistfuls of naira notes over me. Kachi's childhood friend, Nnamdi, also came to the dance floor to spray me with some dollar notes. When I woke up the next morning I was sure I had pulled several muscles, but the pain was well worth it.

Three days after the ceremony in Ezinifite, Kachi and I returned to Lagos. After he dropped me off at my flat, I took a cool bath and went straight to my welcoming bed. I soon fell asleep, and that night, the haunting *Oja* flute played on in my dreams.

20

*Borrowed trousers: if they are not too tight around
the legs, they will be too loose around the waist.
Only one's own things fit one perfectly.*

The following months flew by. Kachi's parents came to Ibadan and met Mummy and Daddy. At the small introduction ceremony, both families agreed on a wedding date and the preparations began in earnest.

Between work and travelling back and forth from Lagos to Ibadan, the days preceding the wedding ceremonies were very busy. Kachi had his own work cut out for him as he tried to coordinate the accommodation arrangements for his family and friends travelling down from the East for the wedding.

I quickly found out that Mummy had her own ideas about what she wanted her first child's wedding to look like. Her ideas were usually the opposite of mine.

"Morayo, why do you want to wear a pink wedding gown? All your other cousins wore white dresses. Why do you have to be so difficult!" she shouted in frustration on one of my visits home.

She was right that all my married cousins wore white, even the one that was already seven months pregnant, and another one whose two children were the ring bearer and little bride! I wondered what Kachi and I would have done if we were marrying in the time of our grandparents. What poor animal's blood would we have needed to sprinkle on the white cloth spread on the wedding bed to show that I came to my husband's home a virgin?

"Mummy, honestly," I said before I could control my tongue, "I am sure they all know I am not a virgin."

Mummy's mouth fell open. "*Morayo!* What has come over you? If you do not care about yourself, please think of your sister. What do you want the Alabis to think of our family?"

We finally compromised on an ivory-coloured wedding dress.

Many weekends I had to escape to Aunty Morenike's house when the tension between Mummy and me became too much. Aunty Morenike would listen to my complaints and smile gently. "Morayo, do you know how long Aunty Bisoye has been dreaming of this day? A little compromise would go a long way, you know."

During those trips back home, I noticed that Aunty Morenike seemed to be looking sicker and sicker. "Aunty, I am really getting worried about you. Have you gone to see the doctor?"

Aunty Morenike gave me a sheepish smile. "I did not go." Her face became serious. "Truth be told, I am beginning to get worried too. All these symptoms started just after that poisoned beans episode, but I didn't think ..."

My heart jumped. "Ha! Aunty, you have to go to the hospital today. *Please.* I will go with you."

Months earlier, a gang of armed robbers had attacked a semi-trailer truck carrying sacks of fertilizer-treated beans to a farm in Ogun State. The thieves sold the stolen sacks of beans. By the time the public realized what was happening, scores of people had died and hundreds had fallen sick from the poisoned beans.

Aunty Morenike yawned. "Mummy Ibeji too has been complaining. She is dragging me to the hospital next week." Stretching her body, she changed the subject. "So have you and Aunty Bisoye gone to pay the deposit for the reception hall?"

When I returned to Lagos, Kafiyah, who knew how stressed I was over the wedding, insisted that we needed a movie night. On our way to Silverbird Cinemas, she said we had to make a quick stop at her house. I had no idea that she had other plans.

"Surprise!"

Startled, I took a step back from the doorway. Kafiyah laughed as she gently pushed me into the room. Eniayo and a beaming Ekanem were among the small group of women. Balloons with wedding bells and streamers were everywhere. Eniayo handed me a sash with "Mrs. Nwosu" printed on it to wear over my clothes. Kafiyah had organized a surprise wedding shower.

Ekanem and I flew into each other's arms. I had not seen her since her own wedding. She was glowing. "Ekanem, you came!"

"Bride-to-be!" Ekanem said. "You know I would not miss this for the world."

Later Kafiyah teased, "Okay now. Morayo, let us see what Ekanem bought you." When I unwrapped Ekanem's present, I recognized the gift box. It was from one of the exclusive lingerie stores on Victoria Island.

Ekanem smiled at me. "Morayo, do you remember that conversation we had about getting ammunition for our marriage arsenals? I bought you some essentials. I know Kachi has been waiting impatiently all these years." My neck grew warm when everybody started laughing.

Lifting up the tissue, I saw a matching pink silk and lace bra and panties. The women all hooed and haaed as they passed the lingerie around.

"That, my friends, is known in select married circles as the grenade," Ekanem said. "Small but mighty, guaranteed to produce an instant reaction."

"Eky Baby!" Kafiyah said with a laugh.

"Trust me, Kaffy; I am a true Efik woman. My mother shared the notes she took down inside the fattening room."

"Morayo, please bring out the next item for viewing," Ekanem said. It was a red silk chiffon teddy with shiny gold silk threads.

"Aha!" Ekanem exclaimed. "The Tear Gas. Grown men have been known to weep at the sight of this little mama."

Eniayo's face was now almost as red as the teddy.

"Ekanem," I laughed, "I beg you, please don't kill my sister."

"Eniayo, close your eyes," Kafiyah commanded. Eniayo covered her eyes with her fingers, but I saw her smiling anyway. After all, her Tunde was patiently waiting for her to finish school, and someday she would be unwrapping such gifts too.

I pulled out the last item from the box. It was a backless lilac nightgown with a plunging neckline and a matching robe. Ekanem bowed her head. "Last but definitely not the least.

Behold, the Rocket Launcher M4 Special Edition. The ticket to that guaranteed honey pot in the moon."

"Honestly, Ekanem, you missed your calling," Titi from head office said. "You should be on stage doing stand-up comedy."

"Or selling lingerie to premium ladies of the night along Allen Avenue!" Kafiyah said.

Ekanem narrowed her eyes at Kafiyah. "Kaffy, I guess you will be public relations officer for the lingerie business?" Ekanem laughed when Kafiyah visibly shuddered. "My sisters, it is good to know I have some options if this banking career becomes too much for me to handle. Very soon, I don't think I will be able to find any more family members with money to deposit at our bank!"

The rest of the evening passed quickly as we ate, laughed, played some games, and danced.

On our way out of the house, we went to greet Kafiyah's aunty, Hajia. "Hajia, thank you for your hospitality."

Hajia wove her dainty fingers in the air. "It is nothing, my dear. I am happy you enjoyed your evening."

As we walked out of the room, Hajia called my name. "Morayo."

I turned. "Yes, Hajia."

"I would recommend that you start with the Tear Gas," she said with a shy smile.

Ekanem's hearty laughter echoed throughout the house.

A week before my wedding, Eniayo and I travelled to Ibadan. The house was already bursting at the seams with relatives who had come to help with the preparations. And there were also those cousins and aunties I saw only at family weddings. Mummy walked around the house with a radiant smile.

Kachi had left for Awka the week earlier. He was to arrive with his family entourage the day before the engagement ceremony.

The wedding ceremonies were planned to go on for three days. Friday was for the *idana,* our traditional engagement ceremony, the Yoruba version of the Igbo wine-carrying ceremony. Saturday was for the church ceremony, reception, and night party. The wedding thanksgiving service on Sunday was at my parents' church.

Kachi and I would then travel with my new family to spend a week in Awka before going away for our honeymoon. Nne and Papa planned a small reception the following weekend for their friends and family members who could not attend the wedding. From Awka, Kachi and I would travel to Obudu for our honeymoon at the Obudu Mountain Resort.

On Thursday, Kachi arrived with his entourage. His sister Adanna and her husband, Obinna, had arrived earlier in the day.

During the *idana,* my father returned the bride price that Kachi's family had brought as part of the required gifts. "My in-laws, we are now one. We give our daughter to your family in love." Daddy turned to look at me. "Please take good care of her."

When I knelt before him during the ceremony, Kachi stuffed my handbag full of money to show that he was able to take care of me financially. He bent his head closer to my silk *gele* and whispered, "You better make sure this soup money lasts a long time."

It started to rain as the engagement ceremony ended and

guests were heading home. Within a short time, the little drops of rain turned into a torrential downpour.

All night the howling wind kept me up, until shortly before dawn, as the wind subsided, I finally fell asleep.

In my dream, it was our wedding morning. Kachi stood at the end of the aisle waiting for me. As I floated towards him, I wondered why he was wearing a top hat and tailcoat with a pair of shorts that showed off his long hairy legs.

Soon I was standing beside Kachi, listening to Pastor Adeojo ask anyone who had any objections to the wedding to speak up or forever hold their silence. Mummy stood to her feet, fiery eyes scanning the church. Just as Mummy sat down and Pastor Adeojo opened his mouth to continue the ceremony, the church door swung wide open.

In walked a pregnant woman with a baby strapped to her back. Clutching the hands of two toddler boys, she walked straight to the front of the church, every pore of her skin shouting, I object! But it turned out that the woman was looking for another man. Her well-wishers had given her the wrong time; her husband had married his new wife earlier in the day.

The ceremony continued, but then the church door swung open again with a crash and Bros T came running down the aisle, headed straight towards Kachi—

I sat up in bed, gasping.

I looked around the quiet room, hearing the light rain outside. Then I lay back, waiting for my fast-beating heart to settle, and fell asleep. Later that night, deep in my sleep, I felt pressure on my arm. Mummy's calm voice woke me. "Morayo."

She was sitting beside me on the bed.

"Good morning, my dear. I just wanted to talk to you while the house is still quiet."

Rubbing the sleep out of my eyes, I yawned. I sat with my back propped against the wall.

"Morayo, since the day we brought you home, you have been a joy to your father and to me. You have grown into a responsible young woman and we are proud of you. You are our precious Adunni. Adunni who stands tall in the marketplace, walking with elegant steps as people stare at the velvety sheen of your skin and think that surely you must be the beloved daughter of a king. If only they knew that God Almighty blessed you with his beauty."

Her soft voice washed over me and I started to cry. These were the words I had wanted to hear for years.

Mummy tilted up my chin. She took the edge of her wrapper and wiped my face. "My daughter, no more tears. This is your season for laughter. Today is your day of joy. Only happy tears are going to grace our faces."

By the time Mummy left the room, I could hear her prized Fulani rooster crowing. It was dawn.

It was still dark outside, but I was too excited to go back to sleep. I got up and opened the frosted louvres. For as long as I could remember, a large piece of rock had stood in a corner of our compound. For the first time, I noticed that a little tree was growing right through the rock. Somehow the tree had pushed its way through the rock, cracking it. What had once seemed so invincible was actually conquerable. I smiled, sharing in the tree's victory.

"Morayo?"

I turned to find Eniayo rubbing her eyes. "Good morning, Eniayo."

"Good morning, Miss Ajayi. So are you ready to become Mrs. Nwosu?"

I took a deep breath. "Yes, I am."

One of my battles with Mummy had been over our wedding vows. It took some time to convince her that I needed to say the marriage vows I wrote for Kachi. She wanted to know why the vows said for generations were suddenly not good enough for me. We finally agreed upon another compromise. I would say the vows that I wrote and then Kachi and I would say the traditional vows. That way everybody would be happy, except perhaps the guests who had to listen to the vows twice.

"Maybe Mummy is worried that your written-up vows won't be binding and Kachi's family can return you when they are tired of you," Eniayo teased.

When Daddy walked me down the aisle, I felt his arm trembling slightly through the folds of his *agbada*. He laid his palm over both our hands before he sat next to a beaming Mummy and Aunty Morenike. Aunty Adunni and her family sat in the row behind them.

Against Mummy's wishes, Daddy had sent a wedding invitation to Aunty Tope. But she did not attend. I knew that she would not. She and Mummy had not spoken to each other since Mama Ejiwunmi's funeral. Still, Aunty Tope had sent me a wedding present—an exquisite gold and silver jewellery set. When I showed Mummy the jewellery, she hissed, "I see she still thinks money can solve everything."

When she stormed out of the room, I looked at Daddy. "Your mother misses her sister," he said quietly.

Eniayo, who was my chief bridesmaid, winked when I handed my bouquet to her.

I said my vows in as clear and strong a voice as I could manage. "I, Morayo Adunni Ajayi, choose you, Oyedikachi Michael Nwosu, to be my lawfully wedded husband. To say that I fell into this love suggests a series of coincidences or just pure luck that takes away from the responsibility of my choice. For if our days are long or our nights bleak, when life springs unpleasant surprises along our way, I will remember that loving you was my choice. I will remember that love is much more than intense feelings. For feelings can be fickle and change so swiftly just in the course of one day. Know this then, my love. Know that this choice to forever link my life with yours was mine alone to make. With my eyes wide open and clear, in the presence of God, our families, and our friends, I choose to spend the rest of my life with you and with you alone."

Soon Kachi and I were having our first dance as a married couple. As Kachi held me in his arms, he sang the P-Squares' "No One Like You" into my ear, and I forgot that over two hundred people were watching us. In that moment, it was just Kachi and me, dancing on our private love island as the silky voices wove a magical web around us.

Part Five

MORAYO AND KACHI
2005~2007

21

*What is the value of the bitter kola? We tried to split it open,
it had no lobes. We ate it, it left a bitter taste; even its tree
branches are not useful for cooking.*

Kachi and I drove down to Ibadan. This was our third visit
home since our wedding seven months earlier. That weekend,
we were having a memorial ceremony for Mama Ejiwunmi. It
was 2005—hard to believe that fifteen years had gone by since
she passed away. Mummy had asked us to stop in Ibadan to help
transport some items to Oyo.

Walking into the house, I could sense some tension.
Mummy had her head bowed while Daddy had an anxious look
on his face. He pulled me aside. "Your Aunty Tope called me
this morning. She is already in Oyo."

No wonder Mummy looked so distressed. When I told
Eniayo the news, she sighed. "Maybe Aunty Tope is now ready
to talk."

I clenched and unclenched my fingers. "I really hope so.
Their feud has gone on long enough."

Kachi gave me a hug when I told him. Then a worried look came into his eyes. "Are you going to be okay?"

I nodded. "I will be fine. I am more worried about Mummy." It was obvious that the news had destabilized her. She was still barely speaking to us.

Kachi and I left for Oyo ahead of the others. As soon as Kachi parked his car in front of Mama Ejiwunmi's house, Aunty Tope came out. I was surprised to see two young children by her side. As she walked towards us, I saw that she was now looking more like her mother.

A big smile beamed across her face. "Morayo! Is this your face?"

I knelt to greet her. "*Ekaasan*, Aunty Tope."

Hugging me, she turned to Kachi, who prostrated in greeting. "Good afternoon, Ma," Kachi said. "It is good to finally meet you."

"Ha, you have to be my new son, Kachi. Welcome."

After shaking Kachi's hand, Aunty Tope called out to the children who were standing under the house veranda. "Abby. Jaden. Come and say hello to your aunty and uncle."

The children skipped over and stretched out arms for hugs. "Hello, aunty and uncle," they chorused. Despite their milky skin, the girl's face looked very familiar.

After giving them hugs, I turned to Aunty Tope with a puzzled look. She pulled them close. "These are Tayo's children."

Before I could say anything, Daddy and Tunde's cars pulled into the compound. Kachi reached for my hand when Aunty Tope walked towards the cars. "What did she just say?"

My throat suddenly started itching. "She said they are Bros T's children."

Kachi's face darkened. He looked around. "He is here?"

We soon found out that Bros T and his wife had brought their children to Oyo. Aunty Tope, who kept up a nervous chatter, told us that they had left to run some errands for her.

The rest of the afternoon was a blur.

Daddy hid his face behind a newspaper. Eniayo, with a worried look in her eyes, tried to keep the children occupied. Kachi sat close by. Tunde seemed oblivious to the underground currents. Mummy and Aunty Tope spent hours talking in Mama Ejiwunmi's bedroom. Sitting at the edge of my seat, I kept waiting for shouts from the room. When they eventually came out, both sisters had red eyes.

Daddy and I exchanged looks when Mummy announced that they were walking to Baba Muti's house for a quick family meeting about the memorial ceremony.

When Bros T and his wife, Arianna, arrived later that evening, Eniayo, Mummy, and I sat in the bedroom talking. I did not want to go downstairs while Bros T was there. Aunty Tope brought Arianna to the bedroom to meet us, and looking at her pleasant face, I told myself that she probably did not know what kind of man she had married.

"Happy to meet y'all," she said with a soft American drawl.

Mummy gave her a hug. "Welcome, our wife."

With small tight smiles, Eniayo and I shook Arianna's hand.

After a period of awkward silence, Aunty Tope headed towards the door. "Arianna, let us go and see what those children are up to."

When they left, Mummy turned to Eniayo. "Please go and ask your father what he wants to eat tonight."

Eniayo stood up. "Yes, Ma."

After she left the room, Mummy sighed. "Morayo, Tayo is in the sitting room."

"I know." Even though my head felt as if it had doubled in size, strangely, my voice was calm.

Mummy gave me a concerned look. "Do you want me to get Kachi?

Shaking my head, I stood up. "No, I am fine." Clenching my teeth, I left the room and walked down the corridor as Mummy followed me.

As soon as I stepped into the sitting room and saw him, I felt as if I were submerged in water and my lungs deprived of oxygen.

I will not faint.

I will not faint.

Bros T was dressed in a starched shirt and jeans. I could see the highly polished shine of his Italian leather shoes reflecting light as he tapped them on the floor. He looked just as I remembered him, except for the touches of grey at his temples, which only made him look more distinguished. When he saw me, his expression did not change. It occurred to me that he might not recognize me. After all, it had been almost twenty years.

"Morayo, how are you?" Bros T greeted me with a smile. "I can't believe that you are this grown up now. It is so good to see you again."

I wanted to slap the smile off his face. "I can't say the same." The words flew out of my mouth before I could stop myself.

Arianna, who sat next to her husband, looked puzzled. Not too long after, she gathered her children, saying that they had to leave for their hotel since it was past the children's bedtime.

That night, Kachi stayed up with me as I paced the room and stared at the ceiling.

Luckily, the next two days were very busy, leaving me no

time to think. During the day Kachi hovered around me with fire in his eyes, and Bros T kept his distance.

On the Sunday afternoon before we left Oyo, Arianna found me in Mama Ejiwunmi's room. She gave me a hesitant smile. "Jaden and Abby just showed me the beautiful fabric you gave them. Thank you."

"You are welcome. I found it here at the house. I thought it would be nice for them to have something made by their great-grandmother. They are good children. You must be proud."

"I am." Her voice became softer. "You are … you are very kind."

Startled, I looked into her gentle eyes, but they gave nothing away. We both heard Abby cry out. Arianna's eyes darted towards the door. "I need to go find out what's going on."

After she hurried away, I escaped outside. I needed some fresh air. When I saw the row of tall clay pots propped up against the side wall of the house, I felt a little smile tugging at the side of my mouth. Mama Ejiwunmi used to soak her fabrics in the pots. They were now in various stages of disintegration. The one complete pot had deep cracks running along the sides. I ran my hand around the rim. Indigo dye flakes crumbled into my hand.

I heard footsteps behind me.

"Morayo …"

It was Bros T's voice.

My hands began to sweat. Turning, I saw that he had a cautious smile on his face. He held up his hand. "I did not mean to scare you. I just wanted to talk to you." He started walking towards me.

I shook my head. "We have nothing to say to each other."

Bros T continued to walk towards me. "Please, just hear—"

I backed away, bumping into Mama Ejiwunmi's clay pot. It crashed against the wall and smashed into pieces.

I gasped and Bros T stopped. "Morayo …"

"Leave me alone!"

He left.

I did not tell Kachi about this brief encounter until we were back in Lagos. I was afraid of what he might have done. It turned out that I had made the right decision. Kachi was furious.

"How dare he …! You should have told me in Oyo."

I shook my head. "No, Kachi. I did not want to ruin the weekend for everybody else, especially for Mummy."

"But he could have hurt you again." I tried not to flinch as Kachi's fingers reached over to stroke my cheek. I could not tell him that the touch of his fingers grated on my skin like sandpaper.

Then the nightmares returned. At first I did not tell Kachi about them, but the flashbacks soon began to threaten the intimacy we had worked so hard for.

On the first night of our honeymoon, Kachi had watched me curl up on my side of the bed to cry. By the third night, he was frustrated. "I am not a robot, Morayo," he shouted. "I have feelings too. How do you think I feel when I make love to my wife and she spends half the night sobbing?"

Kachi had quickly learned that any random grabbing for my body in the middle of the night made my blood run cold. I had woken up screaming one night when I felt a hand stroking me. For months, we slept with the bedroom light on just so that I could see his face.

And even though I had tried so hard, now we were back at the starting point.

Kachi's frustration grew daily. "Morayo, you know I can't bear to see you like this again. Please let me help you," he pleaded. "Just tell me what to do."

But how could I tell him what to do when I didn't know myself?

"Soon, I am going to be fine," I kept repeating. "Was I not okay before? It was just because I saw him again. It is all over now."

The look in Kachi's eyes told me that he felt differently.

Rubbing my aching back, I stepped out of my office lift. My slightly protruding stomach strained against my skirt band. I needed to buy some maternity clothes, but shopping was the last thing on my mind.

Kachi and I had just come back from Ibadan. We had gone to visit Aunty Morenike, who was in the oncology ward at the University College Hospital. Five short months ago, we found out that she had stage-two breast cancer.

After our wedding my trips to Ibadan had been infrequent, and although Aunty Morenike and I kept in touch over the phone, she did not tell me what was going on. Any time I commented on how tired she sounded, she would make up one excuse or another.

The only time Aunty Morenike had visited us in Lagos I noticed that she looked very pale, but she told me it was a minor reaction to medication she took. The important thing she neglected to add was that the medicine was actually part of her chemotherapy treatment. Shortly after that visit, Aunty

Morenike collapsed while she was teaching. The cancer drug had affected her platelets and her period had lasted for one whole month. After her hospital admission, she could no longer hide her condition.

The following weekend, Kachi and I drove down to Ibadan to see her. During the hour-long drive, I kept whispering the word over and over: *Cancer, cancer, cancer.* I felt so guilty. How could I not have known that she was so sick?

As Kachi and I walked into the hospital towards the female oncology ward, I wanted to turn and run. That sickening smell of chlorine bleach seemed only to have become more pungent. I held onto Kachi's arm, trying not to dig my nails into his skin. I should not be coming to see Aunty Morenike at a hospital. "She does not deserve this, Kachi. After all she has been through ..." I bit hard on my lip.

Sighing, Kachi kept silent. "No one deserves cancer, Morayo," he finally said.

When we finally walked into the room, Aunty Morenike was awake and sitting up in her bed. "Morayo!" she cried weakly when she saw me. I clung to her, looking at her face. She looked a little tired, but she did not look that sick. Not *cancer* sick.

"Aunty, how are you?" Kachi asked.

"I am better now," she said, smiling and trying to change the subject. But when she sneezed, I clenched my teeth: droplets of blood were on the handkerchief.

Before we left, Aunty Morenike hugged me and said, "Morayo, people fight and beat cancer every day."

What about the millions who do not, I wanted to ask. But I forced a smile to my face. "Yes, Aunty."

I had a feeling she knew more than she was sharing.

She stayed at the hospital for about a month and then

went home. A couple of weeks after her discharge she started another round of chemotherapy, and the hard battle for her life continued. What we did not know in the beginning was that the cancer had already spread through her body. The double mastectomy that followed failed to contain the cancerous cells. Since the cancer had spread to her lymph nodes, the aggressive cancer cells reappeared in her lungs and then her liver.

Mummy Ibeji fell sick from having to watch over her daughter night and day. It became obvious that Aunty Morenike was going to need more care than her mother could provide. She soon went back to the hospital, and became weaker from the stronger drugs used to prevent the cancer from spreading further. Her hair fell out in clumps, and yet she would smile every time I walked through the door.

Damilare, who was now a graduate student at the University of Ilorin, travelled down every weekend to see his mother. My weekly visits stopped, though, when I announced I was pregnant. Aunty Morenike and Mummy insisted that it was not safe for me to travel every weekend. "Please come every other weekend," Aunty Morenike said. "I don't want you on that death trap of a road." I knew she was right. Every weekend, Kachi and I saw the charred remains of what used to be a minibus by the side of the expressway.

Walking into the office now, I looked forward to hearing about any news Kafiyah may have. During my week at work I would mentally hoard all the funny things that happened so that I would have something uplifting to share during our visits with Aunty Morenike.

Kafiyah was seated in her cubicle. Her face lit up. "Morayo! I was just thinking about you. When did you get back? How is your aunty?"

I tried to stifle a yawn. "We came back very early this morning. She is holding up. What is going on?"

Looking around, Kafiyah lowered her voice. "Clara secured the Phillips Oil account last night."

My jaw dropped. "You don't mean it?"

"Babes, *for real*. All morning Mr. Idris has been floating around the office with a big smile on his fish face."

Clara worked as a priority-sales support officer in our proximity banking division. The bigger the deposits secured by the officers, the better. Their monthly target alone ran into millions of naira. Last year, a newly hired support officer had only six months to meet a target of three hundred million naira. Even in our department we had monthly targets. When I first started at the bank I had to beg Daddy and some of his friends to move their accounts to our bank so that I could keep my job.

The main job responsibility of the officers, usually females, was to source for rich customers. Female officers were encouraged to visit hotels and nightclubs. I had even heard that Clara, who was one of the most aggressive officers in the division, worked as an escort at exclusive dinner parties just so she could meet a targeted customer. Most times, she got the account.

Eagle Oil was a major importer of petroleum products, with brand-new petrol stations springing up all over the country. The company had been around less than a year, and the rumours were circulating that the CEO, Mr. Phillips, was publicity-shy because he fronted for a group of ex-politicians laundering stolen government money.

I whistled. "*Na wa-o*. How do you think Clara pulled that one off? I heard the CEO is not accessible like that."

Kafiyah snickered. "Girl, wake up and smell the *kunu*. What do you think happened? I will just say that I am certain

Clara used all her GGGs to make sure she did not miss this opportunity. I have already heard whispers that she is getting a brand-new official car."

I smiled. GGG is Kafiyah's abbreviation—God Given Gifts.

Walking to my cubicle, I heaved a sigh of relief. Just last week Mr. Idris was threatening to send us all to the streets to find depositors. Maybe this mega account would take some pressure off his neck, and ours. But just before the lunch break, Mr. Idris came to my cubicle. "Mrs. Nwosu, I would like to see you in my office."

Puzzled, I followed him. Closing the door behind us, Mr. Idris pointed to a chair. I started to sweat. It is rarely a good thing when Mr. Idris calls you to his office. He sat behind his desk, rubbing his hands together. "I am sure you have heard of the acquisition of the Eagle Oil account?"

"Yes, sir. I have."

"Good." He started tapping his fingers on the desk. "So have you met Mr. Phillips before?"

"No, sir. I have never met him."

Mr. Idris sat back in his chair, looking at me under hooded eyes. *"Is that so?"* he said. "Well, Mr. Phillips is coming to sign some papers later this afternoon. We will be meeting with him. He has asked that you be assigned as his personal banker."

"He did?" I could not hide my surprise. It was an unusual assignment. Premium accounts were given to one of the three senior personal bankers.

"Mrs. Nwosu, I want you to know that I am putting a lot of trust in you. You must do everything within your power to ensure Mr. Phillips's satisfaction with our bank." Mr. Idris glared at me. "I know it is not necessary for me to explain what would happen if Mr. Phillips decided to move his account to one of our competitors because of the quality of your customer service."

I nodded. A colleague once told a major account holder that picking up girls was not part of his official job duties. He lost his job the following day, and had to resort to using his car as a taxicab when things became hard for him.

Two hours later, Mr. Idris and I were walking towards the executive boardroom. Halfway down the corridor he swore under his breath. "*Shege*. I forgot some documents that Mr. Phillips needs to sign. You can go ahead and meet with him. Tell him that I am on my way."

"Yes, sir."

I walked into the boardroom with a bright smile. But that smile faded. Mr. Phillips of Eagle Oil was none other than Mr. Eyitayo Phillips, my cousin, Bros T.

The room suddenly spun around. The papers in my hand fell, scattering all over the floor. This time, instead of feeling the urge to run, I was angry. But before I could open my mouth, Mr. Idris opened the door. His bright smile faded for a minute when he saw the scattered papers, but he stepped around them and extended his hand to Bros T. "Mr. Phillips, I am so sorry for keeping you waiting. I hope Mrs. Nwosu conveyed my sincere apologies."

As I bent to pick up the papers, Mr. Idris looked at me for confirmation. I could not utter a word. There was a buzzing sound in my ears.

Bros T shook Mr. Idris's hand and lied with a smile. "Not to worry, Mr. Idris, Mrs. Nwosu explained that you were delayed by an important matter."

Mr. Idris sent me a pleased smile. I just stared back at him.

While Bros T signed the documents, Mr. Idris kept glancing

at my sweating face. "Mr. Phillips," he said with a nervous laugh, "I can assure you that you are going to be in very good hands. Mrs. Nwosu is one of our top personal bankers. She will take very good care of you."

Bros T smiled. "Mr. Idris, I have no worries about that. From what I've heard, her performance speaks for itself."

Later that evening, Kachi and I were lying in our bed. He was reading a report he had brought home from work.

"Kachi, I saw Bros T today."

Kachi's glasses fell on the bed. "Where did you see him?"

After I recounted our meeting, a worried look came onto Kachi's face. "Can you ask Mr. Idris to reassign him to another worker?"

"Kachi, Bros T asked for *me*. Mr. Idris wants that account badly. He is not going to jeopardize it."

Kachi rubbed his head. "Then you have to tender your resignation ..."

I had anticipated this reaction. "Please don't ask me to resign," I snapped.

Kachi glared at me. "Why not?"

"Why? Please tell me, how are we going to raise this child? How will we be able to contribute money towards Aunty Morenike's medical treatment?"

Kachi sighed. "Morayo, Aunty Morenike would never ask you to offer yourself up as a sacrificial lamb. It's not wise for you to be close to this dangerous man." He reached across the bed for my hand. "Please, *Obi m*," he pleaded. "Let me ask around. We may be able to find you a position at another bank."

Maybe he was right about Aunty Morenike. But I could not spend the rest of my life wondering when or where Bros T was going to pop up again. I shook my head. "No, Kachi. I am done running. I am a big girl now. I can take care of myself."

"Morayo. This is not going to end well. I just know it." Kachi stormed out of the room. That night, for the first time in our marriage, we slept in two separate rooms.

The next morning, Kachi left for work without talking to me. When I came home in the evening, he was not yet back. In the past I would have called Aunty Morenike for advice, but this was not something I could discuss with her. I tried to cook and ended up burning the pot of stew—I was so distracted, I did not notice the room starting to fill up with smoke. I threw the pot in the dustbin and went to the sitting room.

I curled up on the settee and fell asleep. When I woke it was almost midnight and Kachi was still not home. I tried to call him on his cell phone but it went straight to his voicemail.

At midnight, I jumped when I heard the warning gunshots of the vigilante security group patrolling our housing estate.

By the time Kachi finally returned home at two in the morning I was about to tear my braids out. As soon as he walked into the house, I could smell alcohol on him. My jaw dropped. Kachi had never been much of a drinker. The most he would have was a couple of glasses of wine at home on special occasions.

Kachi flung his blazer on the nearest chair and walked unsteadily to the settee. Sitting down, he put his arm around me. "Morayo, I am sorry. Please stop crying. I love you. I am so sorry. Please stop crying."

As Kachi held me in his arms and stroked my head, I wanted to give in and tell him that I would leave my job, but I could not.

When we visited Aunty Morenike the following weekend, she noticed that Kachi and I were barely speaking to each other.

"Morayo, are you two fighting?"

I continued arranging the provisions inside her little locker.

"Morayo, look at me," Aunty Morenike said in a firm voice. "I may have lost all my hair, but my eyes are working just fine. What is wrong?"

Looking at her gaunt face, my shoulders sagged. She did not need to expend her limited energy worrying about me. "Aunty Morenike, please don't worry. We just had a little argument over something inconsequential, we will be fine."

Aunty Morenike looked concerned. "Is it about all the travelling you have to do? You know you don't have to come and see me so often. All this driving on those unsafe roads worries me. I have told Damilare the same thing, but he is just like you. Stubborn."

I shook my head. "No, Aunty. You know how much Kachi loves you." I sat at the edge of her bed. "You are worth everything we do. We only wish we could do more."

On our way back to Lagos that evening, I kept glancing at Kachi's stony face. All my previous attempts to start a conversation had been unsuccessful. "Kachi ..."

"Yes." Kachi kept staring at the road.

The words came out in a soft whisper. "Kachi, I have to do this. I can't keep running. I am going to be fine."

For a brief second Kachi turned to look at me with red eyes, and then he faced the road again. "Morayo, do you really think I will stop worrying?"

"But I am going to be fine," I insisted.

Kachi kept quiet.

Through Mr. Idris, I learned that Arianna and the children were back in the United States. Since Bros T often travelled back home, over the next couple of months my interactions with him were limited to delivering money to his office and making sure his business accounts were in order. We were never alone, and soon enough, I stopped jumping any time he came too close to me.

Kachi finally accepted that I was not going to resign from my job. But even when we stopped arguing about it, every other week he would tell me about a new job opportunity he heard about.

"Morayo, I saw a job posting in *The Guardian* today," Kachi said as he watched me change into my nightgown. As I looked at his face, I felt a twinge of guilt at its hopeful expression. Sitting on the end of the bed, I reached for his hand. "I will take a look at the posting tomorrow."

He gave me a skeptical look. "Promise?"

"I promise."

Smiling, Kachi gently pulled me down onto the bed.

The following afternoon, I was sitting at my desk when Mr. Idris appeared beside me.

"Mrs. Nwosu."

I looked up from my computer. "Yes, sir."

He held out a piece of paper. "Mr. Phillips just called. He needs some money urgently. He wants the money delivered to his house. I have some business to discuss with him, so we will go together. Go down to the banking hall and make sure we have enough foreign exchange. His driver will be coming to pick us up."

"Yes, sir."

Thirty minutes later, I was sitting in the back of Bros T's bulletproof silver Jaguar as it sped towards Banana Island. Two brown leather briefcases sat between Mr. Idris and me. Head tilted back on the plush leather headrest, Mr. Idris had his eyes closed. I knew he was not asleep. I was just glad he did not want to talk. The morose-looking driver stared straight ahead. The only sound was the soft purring of the car's engine.

This was my first visit to the artificially created island on the Lagos Lagoon. The banana-shaped island was home to the super-rich. Kafiyah, who has a relative living on the island, told me it was impossible to get a plot of land for less than one hundred and fifty million naira! As we drove through the slums of Obalende, I could see the desperation stamped on the faces that flew by my tinted window. I wondered how the rich people in the mansions slept comfortably at night when they had thousands of neighbours living in abject poverty. It had to be like dancing *bata* in a minefield and hoping that the vigorous steps would not set off a bomb.

After navigating through the waterlogged potholes on Onikoyi Road, we drove through the gates of Fairview Estate and turned into a side street. The Jaguar stopped in front of a massive black and gold gate. The driver honked his horn and a uniformed security man opened the gate. He saluted as we drove by.

Tall palm trees lined both sides of the winding driveway leading to the house. My eyes widened when the car turned the corner and I saw the house. I had seen mansions before, but this was a monster. The huge white marble building gleamed in the bright sunlight.

The driver stopped the car. Stepping out, he opened Mr. Idris's door. "Thank you, Johnson," said Mr. Idris as he slid some money into his palm. A wide smile appeared on Johnson's face. If I had not been looking, I would have missed the exchange. It was the smoothest tipping I had seen so far.

Coming around, Mr. Johnson also opened my door. Thanking him, I swung my purse on my shoulder, stepping out of the car with the suitcases. Mr. Idris headed up the steps, and I hurried after him.

Right on cue, a blank-faced, uniformed butler opened the door. He watched us walk up the stairs. "Good afternoon, sir ... madam. Mr. Phillips is waiting for you." Mr. Idris acknowledged the greeting with a nod of his head. I followed suit.

We stepped into a massive foyer with vaulted ceilings and a crystal chandelier. A long spiral staircase faced the main entrance door. The butler led the way. I could see my reflection clearly in the polished marble floors, and in the silence I heard the ticking of a giant antique clock at the top of the staircase. My sweaty fingers clenched the bone handles of the suitcases. They each held a quarter of a million dollars.

The silent butler turned down another corridor and stopped in front of a beautifully carved oak door. He knocked quietly and I heard Bros T's voice say "Come in."

The butler opened the door and stepped aside. The door clicked shut behind us.

Bros T was sitting on a bar stool at the other side of the large room. He was replacing a bottle of brandy at the bar. As we walked towards him, the only sounds I could hear were my heels clicking on the marble floor and the sloshing of ice cubes as Bros T swirled the glass of brandy in his hand. After a quick sip, he placed the brandy glass on the bar.

He smiled. "Mr. Idris … Mrs. Nwosu … I hope you found the drive here okay?"

Mr. Idris shook the offered hand profusely. "Everything was excellent." He pointed to the suitcases. "The money you requested is all there. I can have Mrs. Nwosu open the suitcases …"

Bros T waved his hand dismissively. "That will not be necessary. I am not worried about it. I am sure Mrs. Nwosu did her due diligence."

Dropping the suitcases on a nearby table, I turned to the men. "If there are no other banking services I can offer today, I would like to return to the office, please—" It was already five P.M. and Kachi was picking me up after work.

Mr. Idris frowned. "We will be returning to the office together. I have not yet discussed my business with Mr. Phillips."

"Yes, those documents I talked about are in my home office, just down the corridor." Bros T pointed to the door. "I am sure Mrs. Nwosu can wait here for us …"

After the men left the room, I sat down with a thud. As I crossed and uncrossed my legs, my cell phone rang. I looked at the caller ID. It was Kachi. "Hey, what are you doing? I am going to be about thirty minutes late. Something just came up. Do you still want me to pick you up?"

My mouth went dry. "I am actually not at the office right now, so it should be fine."

"Oh, okay. So where are you?"

"I am on Banana Island … at Bros T's house."

Kachi was silent.

"Kachi?"

His words became clipped. "Are you there by yourself?"

"No. Mr. Idris and I came together."

"Oh …"

I heard footsteps. "Kachi, I can hear them coming back. I am sure we will soon be leaving. I will call you when I get back to the office."

"Call me immediately when you get there. *Okay?*"

"I will." As I switched off the phone, Bros T walked into the room. "Ha, Morayo. Sorry for the wait."

My eyes darted to the door and I waited for Mr. Idris to walk in. He did not.

Bros T rubbed his forehead. "Em … Mr. Idris received an important phone call during our meeting and had to rush home." The tip of his tongue flickered over his lower lip. "When my driver returns, he will take you back to the bank."

My heart started racing. *Mr. Idris left?*

I flew up, holding on tightly to my handbag. "I am sure I can find a taxicab in front of the house. I will be leaving now." Bros T held out his hand and then brought it back to his side. He had a pleading look in his eyes. "Em … actually, since you are here, I was hoping that you and I could talk."

As soon as I heard the words, I began backing away towards the door. "No. We have nothing to talk about."

His voice was soft but firm. "But we do. I heard that Aunty Morenike has cancer."

I stopped, drawing in a quick breath.

Bros T took a step forward, his eyes darting from my face to a spot above my head. "I have already spoken with a friend of mine. He's an oncologist at the M.D. Anderson Cancer Center in Houston, Texas. He is willing to see her if she can be brought to the United States." He licked his lips nervously.

"I will arrange the medical visas for her and her mother. I am also willing to pay for the treatment and their care while they are there."

I stared at him with my mouth open.

Bros T took another step closer. The hems of his long navy-blue Senegalese robe swished against the floor. Despite the coolness of the room, beads of sweat appeared on his forehead. He held out his hand. "Morayo, please listen to me."

Even as I felt the short hairs on my neck standing up, my feet did not move. It was as if they suddenly had a mind of their own.

Bros T rubbed the side of his head. I watched him swallow hard. "I was young ... selfish ..." He stopped. Bros T was now standing in front of me. He was so close I could smell that familiar musky scent.

I jerked my head back. A numbing coldness took over my body and I started to shake. Another flashback came. A picture of me arching up my back while Bros T's hand ran down the length of my leg. There had been no pushing or biting on my part, just acceptance. Hot tears ran down my face.

"Morayo, you did nothing wrong ..." Bros T reached out his hand. "You were a child. It was my fault. It was all me."

The touch of his fingers on my skin felt like hot oil. "Don't touch me!"

Backing out of the room, I ran for the front door.

It had begun raining. Heavy raindrops splattered on my face as I stepped out of the house onto the steps. Hearing footsteps behind me, I jumped and slipped down the marble stairs. Just before my head hit the last step, I saw Bros T's shadowed face staring down at me. I heard a gasp and he hurried down the stairs and cradled my head with his hands.

Then it went all dark and I felt nothing.

My eyes opened to a bright white light. There was a fluorescent tube right above the bed. Turning my head, I saw Kachi sitting in a chair. His head was in his hands. I licked my dry lips. "Kachi …"

Kachi bolted from the chair. "Thank God, you are awake!" he said, hurrying to my side. I winced at the pain in my head as I tried to sit up. "Morayo, lie down. Let me go and call the nurse."

When Kachi left the room, I rubbed my hand on my stomach. I could not feel any movement. Was the baby okay?

Kachi soon came back with a nurse. "Please—the baby?"

The young nurse walked over the bed. "Madam, you don't have to worry. The baby is fine. I will let the doctor know that you are awake." She took my temperature and adjusted my IV.

I turned to Kachi. "How long have I been here?"

"Two days," Kachi said. He sat next to me on the bed.

"Who brought me here?"

"He did," Kachi said bitterly. Not making eye contact, he rubbed his head and got to his feet. "I need to go and buy some phone credits so that I can call Ibadan and Awka to let them know you are okay. Eniayo was here earlier today."

"Aunty Morenike?"

"She is fine. We did not tell her anything."

When Kachi left, I fell asleep. By the time I woke up, the friendly young nurse was back in the room. She smiled at me. "Madam, your husband said I should tell you he went home to cook some food for you." She smiled again as she helped me off the bed. "You are a very lucky woman, madam. Your husband has not left your side since you were admitted."

When I came back from the toilet she was changing the bedsheets. "Madam, I am almost done." She dropped the sheets into the laundry bin. "If not for God, your husband would have beaten that rich man who brought you to the hospital into a coma. Four security men had to pull him off." She gave me a curious look. "Did he hit you with his car?"

I coughed loudly, pretending not to have heard the question.

When Kachi returned to the hospital, he did not say anything about his encounter with Bros T. He handed me some peeled oranges, and I noticed the bruises on his knuckles. I did not ask him about them.

The next morning, when I heard a knock on my door, the last person I expected to see was Mr. Idris. "Good morning, Mrs. Nwosu," he said as he strolled into the room.

He walked over to the bed. "The doctor called to let me know you were now awake. Mr. Phillips told me that he brought you here after you fell at his house. That was very unfortunate."

"Mr. Idris ..."

He held up his hand. "Please, hear what I have to say. I understand that you may need a week or two at home to recuperate, but I don't see why you cannot come back to your position." He gave a nervous laugh. "Em ... I also met with Mr. Phillips before he travelled out of the country yesterday. He has created a joint charitable foundation with the bank. He specifically wants you in charge of disbursing the funds to grant recipients. In fact, we have already compiled a list of orphanages in the community." Mr. Idris hesitated. "Em ... As you know, this will be very good public relations for the bank. But most importantly, it will benefit those poor children."

So that was why he was here. I finally found my voice. "Mr. Idris, I am not coming back to the bank."

All I had thought about since waking up was how, in my stubbornness, I had almost let Bros T take something else that was precious to me. If I had lost the baby, I would never have forgiven myself. I shook my head. No. I was done with him.

The expression on Mr. Idris's face changed from disbelief to anger—then desperation. "Mrs. Nwosu, I don't want you to make any rash decisions." He forced a smile. "As a person who cares very much about your well-being, I have to let you know that what you are doing is professional suicide." He lowered his voice. "In fact, I spoke to the managing director this morning. He has given the go-ahead to double your salary and give you a company car. You just have to let me know what kind of car you want." Mr. Idris licked his lips.

"Mr. Idris, you left me behind at his house."

It was as if he did not hear me speak. He blinked rapidly. "I hope you know that we will not give you a good reference if you abandon your duties in this manner …"

"Mr. Idris, please leave my room."

"Mrs. Nwosu …"

"Leave!"

One of the nurses poked her head into the room. "Madam, is everything okay?"

Mr. Idris quickly stepped back and left. The next day, Kachi personally delivered my resignation letter to the bank.

A solemn Kafiyah brought my personal belongings from the office when I returned home. All she knew was that I had fallen at Mr. Phillips's house. Despite my insistent questioning, she refused to tell me what was going on at work. I worried that Mr. Idris would take out his frustration on her.

I shook my head when she handed me the cold bottle of *kunu* she had brought with her. "So you won't forget the taste of *kunu* or me," she said.

"Kafiyah, honestly, I could not forget you even if I tried."

When she was leaving, Kafiyah gave me a tight hug. "I'll miss you at the office, but this is where you need to be. I'll come and see you next week."

When Kachi found out he had to attend a meeting at Lokoja, he worried about leaving me alone. He asked if I wanted to spend the week in Ibadan. I did. Eniayo, who was in the middle of her medical board examinations, could not come to stay with me, but Mummy and Aunty Morenike were ecstatic when I called to let them know I was coming.

The day after my arrival at Ibadan, Eniayo's fiancé, Tunde, who was now a radiologist at the hospital, picked me up on his way to work. Aunty Morenike was still asleep when Tunde and I arrived at her room. Mummy Ibeji had been sleeping at the hospital, and we could see that she needed a break. She could barely keep her eyes open during her conversation with us. Tunde and I were finally able to persuade her to go home. I promised to stay until she came back.

Sitting on a chair next to the bed, I watched Aunty Morenike's chest move up and down. Minutes after my arrival, a familiar-looking nurse came into the room. I had seen her before on one of my visits. "She is still sleeping?" the nurse asked in a low voice.

"I was told she was up all night," I whispered back.

A look of pity flitted across the nurse's face. "The night nurse said so. But it is time for her chemo."

The nurse rolled the IV pole aside. I watched as she deftly administered the medication through a large syringe into the tube leading to the port located just below Aunty Morenike's right shoulder. While the nurse injected the medication, Aunty Morenike stirred but did not open her eyes.

Five minutes later, the nurse was done. "Madam, I will come back and check on her condition later." Nodding, I mumbled my thanks under my breath. She closed the door quietly behind her.

Listening to the rhythmic sound of the IV pump, I found myself cheering for the Adriamycin as it made its way into Aunty Morenike's cells.

The pump continued to hum as I stared at her face. I was still staring when she woke up an hour later. When she opened her eyes, it was as if she had forgotten where she was. I watched as her mouth parted in a little whimper. Her startled eyes looked frantically around the room until she saw me. When she focused on my face, she smiled, stretching out a frail hand. "Morayo, when did you get here? Where is Mummy Ibeji?"

"She left not too long ago. Tunde and I begged her to go home and rest when she told us that she did not sleep all night."

"Thank you, my dear. She needs the break."

I propped Aunty Morenike up in her bed with pillows as she suddenly started gagging. While I helped to clean her face after she had vomited, she kept staring at me. "Morayo, you look very peaceful today. I am happy." I smiled back at Aunty Morenike. In the weeks since I had left the hospital, I did feel more at peace with myself. I felt—less empty.

When her chest rattled from a bout of coughing, I wanted to hold Aunty Morenike and cry. Instead I sat next to her on the bed, talking about Kachi's new business venture, about the movies I wanted to see, and all those other mundane, pointless things that came rushing out of my mouth—anything so that I would not have to admit out loud how scared I was of losing her.

Hours later, Damilare arrived at the hospital with Mummy Ibeji. Aunty Morenike's eyes lit up when she saw her son. "Good afternoon, Sister Morayo," Damilare said as he gave me a hug. I am always amazed at how tall he has grown.

"Good afternoon, Damilare." I picked up my handbag. "Aunty, I will come back and see you tomorrow."

After a quick knock, the door opened and Aunty Morenike's doctor came into the room. "Ha. I see you have visitors."

His excitement was obvious as he stroked his moustache. "Well, I have some good news for you." Mummy Ibeji and I looked at each other with wide eyes. Damilare held onto his mother's hand.

"Early this morning, our medical director received a telephone call from the Anderson Cancer Center in Houston. I won't bore you with the details, but you have been chosen as the first Nigerian patient to benefit from this new cancer treatment." He smiled. "I should add that all this is at no cost to you. A cancer charity will be sponsoring everything." He looked at Mummy Ibeji. "They will even pay for one family member to accompany you. Given your condition, the arrangements have to happen as soon as possible."

Aunty Morenike was staring at the doctor with her mouth wide open. It was as if she could not believe her ears. "People who do not know me would do all this for me?

"Please think about it, and we can talk some more tomorrow."

Aunty Morenike wiped the tears on her face. "Thank you, doctor."

After he left, Mummy Ibeji fell to her knees and started rolling back and forth on the floor. Hands lifted up in the air, she mumbled to herself. "*Olodumare!* So you have not forgotten me ..."

Aunty Morenike and I kept staring at each other as I sat on the edge of her bed. Already I could see her eyes brightening. All these months, I had not told her about meeting Bros T again—and no doubt he was behind this miraculous offer. But I could not tell her; she might refuse his money.

The following evening, as I walked towards the women's oncology ward, I could hear someone singing. Moving closer, I realized that it was Aunty Morenike. She was singing a familiar hymn:

"Abide with me; fast falls the eventide;
The darkness deepens; Lord, with me abide ..."

I glanced into the room through the open window. Aunty Morenike was alone. She was sitting up in bed, tears rolling down her gaunt cheeks. Leaning against the wall, listening to her voice, I began to sob quietly. But Aunty Morenike would worry if she saw my tears, so I wiped my face with the edge of my *boubou* sleeve. Coughing loudly, I knocked on the door and stepped inside with my fake bright smile.

Aunty Morenike greeted me with twinkling eyes. The tears I had seen through the window were gone. Tonight her bald, shiny head was exposed. I swallowed the lump in my throat, remembering her long thick hair I had envied as a child.

When Aunty Morenike pulled me close for a hug, I could feel bony ribs sticking into me. She seemed to have lost more weight just from the day before. Her petite frame looked more like that of a child than a woman. But she had a look of happiness on her face as she rubbed her hand gently on my protruding belly. "This is my way of getting to know the baby," she said, and we both laughed when the baby kicked hard, bumping against her hand. "My little Morayo—a mummy!" She was speaking slowly, for the ulcers in her mouth made talking very painful.

"Yes, Aunty. You are going to be around to carry the baby in your arms and dance with me at the naming ceremony."

"God willing, Morayo, I will."

The tone of her voice scared me. "But you are going to Houston next month." My voice broke. "Aunty, I am not yet ready to let you go."

Aunty Morenike's grip on my hand was surprisingly firm. "My dear Morayo, I am not saying that I want to die. I am only thirty-nine years old." Her body shook from another bout of coughing.

I picked up the cup of water beside the bed and put it to her lips. She took a tiny sip. "Thank you, my dear." Her hand tightened on mine. "When your time is running out, those regrets come up. Like rejecting Mufu's marriage's proposal." I looked at her with surprise. She had not brought up Mr. Tiamiyu's name in years. "I had always wanted more children." She sighed. "I want to hold your baby. I want to see my Damilare's children. I should be the one to bury my mother. But does the basket dare tell the basket weaver what length or colour or type of raffia to use?"

Aunty Morenike stroked the side of my face. "Oh, my dearest Morayo." She stretched out her arms. "Come. Today, you don't have to be strong for me. It is okay for you to cry."

Laying my head on her chest, I let myself cry until I had no tears left.

After the week had flown by, Kachi and I stopped by the hospital again before leaving for Lagos. As I gave Aunty Morenike a goodbye hug, we both felt the baby kick again. We laughed. It was as if the baby too was telling her goodbye. I kissed her on the forehead and promised that I would be back to see her in two weeks. We were going to celebrate her fortieth birthday.

Three days later, Aunty Morenike died in her sleep.

22

It is the same moon that wanes today
that will be full tomorrow.

Damilare called Kachi at the office to let him know the
news, but Kachi could not tell me himself. I later found out that
he called Mummy and begged her to come to Lagos. As soon
as I saw Mummy's eyes that evening, I knew something was
wrong. When she sat me down on the settee and told me, I fell
to my knees and wailed.

The next morning, when I woke up to the sound of a bird
singing loudly outside my open window, I wanted to pluck that
bird from its nest and fling it to the ground. How dare this
happy bird disturb my grief? Did it not hear that my Aunty
Morenike was gone?

Kachi refused to listen to my pleas to attend Aunty
Morenike's burial. "You cannot travel," he told me, and I
grumbled bitterly when Mummy told me she supported his
decision.

On the morning of the burial, Kachi left for Ibadan
with Eniayo. Mummy stayed with me. She had to abide by

our traditions. She was not allowed to attend the funeral of someone younger than her. I cried all day as I imagined Aunty Morenike's body lowered into a grave. I could not even be there for Damilare.

That same night, I started spotting. I was worried, but I told myself it would stop, so I said nothing to Mummy. Why worry her unnecessarily? But later that night the spotting turned into a steady flow. I had to tell Mummy. She was already asleep in the guest room.

"Mummy. Mummy."

As I tapped on her arm, her eyes flew wide open.

"I have been seeing blood."

She bolted right up. *"Blood?"*

"Yes, Ma. The flow is a little heavy."

She tied her wrapper to her chest and swung her legs off the bed. "When did this start?"

"It started some time ago."

Hissing, she got to her feet. "And you are just waking me now!"

"I did not want to disturb you."

She changed her clothes. *"Disturb me?* Did I come to Lagos to sleep?" She was rushing around the room. "Now what am I going to do at this time of night? Who am I going to call for help now?"

"Our upstairs neighbour is a nurse. Maybe I can knock on her door?"

Mummy's eyes pinned me to the spot. "YOU want to go and knock on her door? Go," she ordered. "Lie down." She stormed out of the apartment, calling back, "I will take care of this."

Mummy soon returned with Nurse Tawa. I could tell from the look in Nurse Tawa's eyes that she was worried. She advised me to lie in bed with my legs elevated. It would be best for me to see a doctor, but it was too late for a pregnant woman and an old woman to head out to a hospital.

Mummy stayed up all night pacing the room and looking at the clock. I drifted in and out of a restless sleep—at one point, I woke to see Mummy watching me in silence. I had never seen her gaze at me in that way. When I tried to sit up, she came to my side. "Stay," she whispered. "I'm here."

Kachi finally got home late in the morning, and we rushed to the hospital. When the doctor ordered bed rest for the rest of the pregnancy, I thought I would pull my hair by its roots from frustration and grief.

"Morayo, *please*. It is just for a little while," Kachi pleaded.

But nothing Kachi or Mummy said helped. Part of me realized I needed to listen, of course. I did not want to harm the baby. But I was still mourning the loss of Aunty Morenike, and being trapped in my bedroom stifled me.

Frustrated, Kachi asked his mother to come to Lagos. Mama Kachi, who had just returned from Abuja where she had gone to take care of Adanna's new son, packed her bags again. She and my youngest sister-in-law, Dumebi, arrived the following week.

A reluctant Mummy returned to Ibadan. "Morayo, I know your other mother will take care of you. I will come back before the baby comes."

During those three months, Mama Kachi and I became close.

On the days I did not feel like eating, she would cook different dishes just to tempt me. "See what I made for you today, my child," she would say with a smile. "This yam pottage has no master. Ask your husband. When he was a child, he would eat and eat until he could not move from his seat. When you are on your feet, I will teach you how to cook it. Trust me, when Kachi puts that food in his mouth, he will hand over his entire salary without complaining."

Kachi laughed quietly behind his mother's back. I narrowed my eyes at him. Cooking was still not my favourite thing to do.

"I will definitely learn how to make the dish before you leave. There is one piece of land I have been eyeing at Banana Island."

"Nne, see what you have caused now," Kachi said as he swung his arm around her shoulders. "You women always gang up against me."

Squinting his eyes at me, Kachi snorted. "I hope you remember that you didn't marry a rich man. Banana Island *ko*, Pineapple Peninsula *ni*."

We all started laughing. Suddenly I froze. I looked down: my water had broken. It was still three weeks before my due date. The baby was clearly not waiting for Mummy's return.

Mama Kachi stayed with me throughout the whole ordeal, as Kachi and the other fathers waited in the reception area. I had mentally prepared myself for a long labour. I was told first babies generally take their time—but not mine. This child was eager to come out. Everything happened so fast. Before the nurses could wheel me to the delivery room, I felt the tremendous pressure. I was ready to push! "I think the baby is coming!"

Mama Kachi looked frantic. "Wait, my daughter, we are almost there. Madam Nurse, *abeg*, push the chair faster oh!"

After a dash to the delivery room I was carried onto the bed, and after that hard final push, I heard one of the midwives shout, "*E ku ewu omo!* Congratulations! A girl!"

When the nurse handed my daughter to me, I looked closely at her face. She looked just like her father. She was long and light-skinned, with Kachi's slanted eyes—the same eyes he had inherited from Mama Kachi, who was standing by with happy tears.

I stared at my daughter. What was this new love? It seemed different from what I felt for her father. This love was ... fierce. As if a piece of my heart had broken off and implanted itself into the baby I held in my arms.

I turned to Mama Kachi. "Nne, here is your granddaughter," I said.

When she took the baby from me, her fingers tightened on mine for a brief second. It was the first time I had called her *Nne,* mother. "My child, you have done well," she told me in a quavering voice.

A few moments later, I watched my husband—trying hard to hold back his tears—balance his *Ada* in the crook of his arm. She looked so tiny. I closed my eyes: was this how my own parents—how my mother—had stared in wonder when they first held me?

Even in the midst of this joy, I remembered my dear Aunty Morenike. She would never hold this child in her arms to dance with me. I had lost one joy and gained another, but as Aunty Morenike would have said, Who is the raffia strand to question the basket weaver?

Epilogue

A person who rises in the morning without washing his face sees things with yesterday's eyes.

Kachi and I brought our beautiful daughter home three months ago. We named her Anuli Morenike. Her grandparents, aunties, and uncles also gave her names—between both families, I think she has fifteen!—but we chose Anuli because it means joy in Igbo. Now when I hear the little birds singing outside our bedroom window, I smile, welcoming the sweetness of their songs.

Dumebi left when the school holidays were over, but Nne stayed with us for another two weeks. During those two weeks, all I had to do was rest and feed Anuli. Nne would not let me do anything in the house. She called Kachi aside one day to tell him it was time for her to return to Awka. She was leaving to allow Mummy come to Lagos. Even though I was happy to hear the news, I cried when Nne left. In the four months she stayed with us, she had truly become my *nne*.

Mummy has been staying with us for the past six weeks, but she too is going home tomorrow, since Daddy keeps demanding his wife's return. Although Mummy clicks her tongue after his telephone calls, I can tell she is happy that her husband misses her.

Today, we are celebrating Anuli's arrival into our lives. Our family members and friends have been coming to the house all day. Tunde and Daddy drove to Lagos this morning. Papa, Nne, Ogadinma, and Dumebi are also here. They all came from Awka yesterday.

The caterers have been cooking since they arrived at dawn. Nne also insisted on cooking some special soups for the day. Large platters of tantalizing Igbo and Yoruba dishes have been set out in chafing dishes under the big party tent outside. Eniayo hired some uniformed service staff to help with attending to our guests. They have been very busy.

Kafiyah is sitting next to me. Her kohl-lined eyes twinkle as she tells us about her encounter with a romantic camel on her holiday trip to Dubai. "That camel just planted his mouth right on my own. I wanted to die from all that saliva. Honestly, I don't know how female camels manage."

I shake my head at her. "Kaffy! I can see Ekanem gave you some lessons during your visit to Calabar." Kafiyah laughs. Ekanem is expecting her second child and could not travel down to Lagos. I miss her bubbly presence.

Kafiyah, who left the bank shortly after I did, now works for a travel agency specializing in honeymoon travel packages. It is a perfect fit for Kafiyah, who is still searching for her dream sheik—a monogamous one.

Eniayo and Tunde just bought their honeymoon package to France from Kafiyah. I teased Eniayo when she told me about their plans. "Eniayo, so you are finally going abroad."

Eniayo laughed. "Yes, I am. On our next trip I am going

to Buckingham Palace. I figured it is time I introduced myself. They don't call me Lady Eniayo for nothing."

Eniayo and Tunde are getting married at the end of the year. Mummy, of course, is floating around with a contented look on her face.

I feel Anuli squirm in my arms. She is waking up from her afternoon nap. Her plump arms rise up in the air as she stretches her little body. When Anuli opens her gorgeous brown eyes, my heart flips. Here is the child who will bury me one day, I think. The child I will love for the rest of my life.

Anuli smiles back at me with those dimpled cheeks that are just hers. She holds onto my hand, curling her little fingers around my thumb.

We gaze at each other and I make my daughter promises that I intend to keep. "I promise that for *you*, there will be fewer secrets. I promise to talk about whatever causes you pain. To talk about shame. I promise to listen even when I do not understand. I promise because you are worth it." Anuli's gaze softens and her mouth opens in a smile.

"Sister Morayo." I look up to see Damilare walking towards me. "Sister Morayo, I have to go. I promised Mummy Ibeji that I would come back before it gets dark."

When Damilare walked into the house earlier in the day with three boxes filled with Aunty Morenike's books, I cried when he told me that he just had to come and see Anuli. I had not seen him since Aunty Morenike died.

"Please wait, let me walk you to the car." I walk over and hand Anuli to Aunty Adunni, who eagerly stretches out her hands with a smile, saying, "I have been waiting to carry my little princess all afternoon!"

Just before Damilare gets into his car, he brings out an

envelope from his pocket. "For Anuli," he says. I give him a hug and ask him to greet Mummy Ibeji for me. Later, as I put the envelope away in my wardrobe, I notice the script on its front. My heart skips. It is Aunty Morenike's handwriting. Tearing open the envelope, I find a bundle of crisp thousand-naira notes and a folded letter.

As I read, I can hear Aunty Morenike's voice clearly in my head.

> *My dearest Morayo,*
>
> *I decided to write this letter because something tells me that I will not be around to celebrate your motherhood.*
>
> *There are no words to tell you how much being your sister has enriched my life and how much I love you. As you read this, know that I am sad that I did not get to hold our baby and dance with you, but I was determined that I too would give this child of ours a name.*
>
> *My name for the baby is Opemipo: I have many things to be thankful for. I chose Opemipo because I hope that it will remind you that despite what you and I have been through, we can still give thanks. My life was not in vain. Yours will not be.*
>
> *My dear, please remember to be kind to yourself. I know we both tend to be so hard on ourselves. One thing I am sure of is that you will need that kindness in the many days and years that are still to come for you.*
>
> *Use the money to buy something special for my baby. I know you will decide on what to get.*

"Morayo!" It is Eniayo's voice.

I am shaking. Aunty Morenike found a way to be a part of my day. "I am in our bedroom," I shout back.

I hurriedly put the letter and money back into the envelope. I am just closing the wardrobe door when Eniayo walks in with Anuli in her arms. "I was wondering where you were," she says.

"Is Anuli okay?"

"She is fine. She just needs her diaper changed. I told her I don't do diapers." Anuli gurgles in Eniayo's arms as if she understood what her aunt just said.

"Even Anuli thinks you are funny." I point to the changing table. "You better start practising now. I am sure Tunde is eager to start a family."

Eniayo grins and walks over to the table. I watch Anuli coo and wave her hands as her diaper is changed. Eniayo turns to me.

"Morayo, I can't believe how much bigger she is now."

"They really do grow up fast."

"I still remember holding her in the hospital and thinking to myself that I was an aunty."

I nod. "Yes, you are. And aunties are the best."

We exchange a long look. Anuli's loud burp makes us smile. Eniayo wrinkles her nose at the sour milk smell. "You really are your mother's daughter."

I glare at her. "Eniayo!"

Laughing, Eniayo hurries out of the room with Anuli in her arms. I follow. As we step back out into the sunshine, I can see Kachi's tall figure out in the dance area between the tents. It's hard to miss the bright red *obi* hat bobbing up and down on his head as he break-dances to the music. When Kachi sees me, he walks over to the DJ and says something to him. As the DJ starts playing "Let Me Love You" by Bunny Mack, Kachi makes his way towards me with a serious look on his face. Reaching my side, he stretches out his hand to take mine. "*Obi m,* come. Dance with me," he says.

I take his hand.

As our eyes lock, I remember the shy young boy who kissed me tenderly with the taste of menthol on his lips. And the knot unravels some more.

As Kachi and I dance in the midst of our family and friends, I feel the waning sunrays warming the right side of my face. A blustery evening breeze passes through the tents. The wind breaks off some of the pink balloons tied to the tent posts, making the children shriek in delight as they chase the runaway balloons. I watch Aunty Adunni's youngest son, Tamilore, run ahead of the others. His bowed legs cross each other as he looks back to see if the other children are catching up to him.

I smile as the breeze ruffles the stiff edges of my red damask *gele.* It cools my skin and sends delightful tingles down my spine.

I continue to dance.

Acknowledgments

It truly took a village of people to help me write this book. Thanks to my many beta readers for their invaluable feedback: Jolade Pratt, Oyindamola Orekoya, Tiwalade Nwogu, Stella Toyin Jonah, Ulo Adefarasin, Dupe Bewaji, Tinunola Adelakin, Karen Warren, Susan DeKoter, Donna Chartier, Kimberly Garant and last but definitely not least, Genevieve Gagne Hawes.

I'm deeply grateful to my agent, Dan Lazar at Writers House, for believing in me and this book from the very beginning. Your dedication and positive energy made all the difference. Onward!

My gratitude to my editor, Adrienne Kerr, for loving this book and making it shine. My thanks also go to Karen Alliston, Mary Ann Blair, Barbara Bower and everyone at Penguin Canada who worked hard to make this book a success.

Many thanks to family and friends too numerous to list for cheering me on. I appreciate you all.

Special thanks to my parents, Prof. and Mrs. David Omobamidele Alonge, for buying those first books that opened up my world and for modeling the dignity of hard work. To my other parents, Mr. and Mrs. Amos Fehintola Kilanko, for welcoming me into their hearts.

Finally, to my A-Team, my husband Oladele and our children, Fikunmi, Kishi and Demilade. I could not have written this book without your steadfast love, understanding and support. We did it.

Daughters Who Walk This Path

About the Book 332

An Interview with Yejide Kilanko 333

Discussion Questions 337

Readers Guide

ABOUT THE BOOK

Set in modern-day Nigeria, Yejide Kilanko's debut novel, *Daughters Who Walk This Path*, tells the coming-of-age story of Morayo, a smart, determined girl growing up in the city of Ibadan. She is close to her family and friends but her young life is changed forever when her older male cousin, Bros T, comes to live with her family and begins to sexually molest her. Trying to protect her beloved sister, Eniayo, Morayo tells no one at first, partly blaming herself for the abuse. When she finally tells her parents, their silence and judgment only intensify her sense of shame and worthlessness.

Morayo turns to an older female cousin, Morenike, for support as she tries to make sense of her feelings and comprehend the sexual abuse she has suffered. Morenike's story is told alongside Morayo's and reveals that she, too, was raped by someone close to her family, resulting in the birth of a child. Unlike Morayo's mother, Bisoye, Morenike's mother isn't silent or ashamed; she takes matters into her own hands and succeeds in holding the rapist accountable for violating her daughter.

Through their close relationship, Morenike makes Morayo feel less alone and less of an outsider. Morenike is a strong and positive presence; she is an academic who is politically engaged, and becomes a mentor of sorts to Morayo. They attend political rallies together and talk honestly and openly with one another. They even share one harrowing scene in which even more violence is directed towards Morenike.

However, Morayo's relationship with Morenike can't heal all wounds, and by the time Morayo reaches university her sense of worthlessness starts affecting her behaviour towards men. Her mother worries she will never marry and her father remains on the fringes of Morayo's life. By chance, Morayo becomes reacquainted with her first love, but questions of honesty, vulnerability and trust threaten to destroy her fragile confidence.

After university, while working at a bank in Lagos, Morayo comes face-to-face with Bros T once more. It is at that moment that Morayo is forced to deal with the residue of the past while still reaching towards the possibility of a bright, loving future.

Spanning three decades, *Daughters Who Walk This Path* delves deeply into cultural traditions, patriarchal attitudes, and sexual superstitions. The novel also examines the sisterly bonds that develop between women and how these bonds provide the strength needed to move forward and find happiness. ■

AN INTERVIEW WITH YEJIDE KILANKO

Q: When you started writing *Daughters Who Walk This Path*, did you know that you were going to tell both Morayo's and Morenike's stories? In your mind, were their lives always interwoven?

In the beginning, *Daughters Who Walk This Path* was Morayo's story. The poem that inspired the novel, "Silence Speaks," was in her voice. Morenike's character evolved after I made the decision to explore challenges around raising a child conceived as a result of sexual assault. By the end of Morenike's first scene in the novel, I knew that this fierce young woman was going be an important part of her younger cousin's life journey. The novel then became about both women. ■

Q: Why did you decide to start each chapter with a proverb? Does this reflect the importance of proverbs in Nigerian society?

I find proverbs fascinating. They are little kernels of knowledge that succinctly capture complex emotions, ideas and advice. The proverbs used as chapter headers provided the right backdrop and gave the reader something to ponder on and walk away with. I was particularly thrilled to hear a Canadian reader say that when she washes her face every morning, she remembers the last proverb, which talks about unwashed faces and seeing things with yesterday's eyes. In this digital age, oral traditions have lost some of their importance among younger Nigerians. However, given the dearth of historical documents, it's important that we pass them on. ■

Q. The novel delves deeply into issues surrounding gender inequality and female sexuality and is very much a woman's story. While you examine the deep bonds created between women, you also present some significant male characters. How difficult was it to get into the minds of these men?

It was very important to me that I had three-dimensional male characters. As I wrote, I drew a lot from my personal experiences with male relatives, friends and acquaintances. It was also very helpful that both my husband and agent, Dan, read every manuscript change and offered me their perspectives. A reader had noted that there was no suggestion in the narrative that men should show solidarity, support, justice, or even accountability with regard to the issues discussed. In hindsight, exploring this would have strengthened the discourse, which is why I want to stress that when it comes to discussions around gender inequality and other important issues, male allies are needed at the table. ■

Q. Morayo and Eniayo's mother, Bisoye, seems caught between abhorring superstition and respecting long-held customs. Is this a generational phenomenon? Through your depiction of the younger characters, are you suggesting that blind obedience to tradition may well change with each new generation?

The conflict Bisoye experienced was definitely a generational phenomenon. Even though a part of her was able to accept that Eniayo's albinism had a medical explanation, she couldn't talk to her children about sexual safety. And her inability to respond appropriately to Morayo's abuse contributed to Morayo's suicide attempt. I do believe that younger Nigerians, like my characters, are beginning to question blind obedience to traditions. I'm not advocating the annihilation of traditional norms and values on the altar of modernity, only that we critically examine each one on its merits. ■

Q: Personal politics meet public politics in Morenike's relationship with Mr. Tiamiyu. His campaign is met with serious
dissent come election day, resulting in a sense of pessimism
about the role politics can play in bringing forth societal
change. If not through political means, how do you see
change occurring in modern nations?

I have lived under military dictatorships and democratic govern-
ments and it's hard for me to see how lasting, meaningful, societal
change can occur through anything but political means. Advocating
for change through revolutions and coups only offers short-term
fixes to deep-seated, multi-faceted problems. Social/political insti-
tutions that will serve a society cannot be established overnight.

With respect to Mr. Tiamiyu's story, while the situation remains
daunting, it is important to note that 51 years ago Nigeria was still
a British colony. Canada became self-governing in 1867; the United
States declared independence from Britain in 1776. Both of these
older democracies, like many other modern nations, still deal with
the issues of political apathy and low voter turnout. One thing I
do think would make a difference is informed political engagement and participation. When voters understand the real issues at
stake and how voting choices directly impact their lives, change can
happen. ∎

Q: At the end of the novel, Morayo makes a series of promises
to her baby daughter: to have fewer secrets, to talk and
to listen. What do these promises reveal about Morayo's
relationship with her own mother, as complicated as that
is?

I once heard someone say that you can only teach what you know
and you can only reproduce what you are. Bisoye, Morayo's mother,
struggled with helping her daughter because she, too, never had
those discussions with her mother. By the end of the novel, Morayo
had made peace with her because she acknowledged and accepted
her mother's limitations. Morayo wanted a different kind of
relationship with her daughter and she knew this would not happen
without an ongoing dialogue about the difficult subjects of life. ∎

Q. Did you travel to Nigeria while writing the book? Were there parts of the story that required further research?

I did travel to Nigeria while writing the book. It was a hurried ten-day visit that left little room for research. Because the novel was set in Ibadan, the city where I was born, and events took place during those years when I too came of age, I was able to mostly draw from my memories and personal conversations. Social media has opened up a whole new world when it comes to researching ideas and making connections with the right people no matter where they reside. I'm very grateful for this. ■

Q. You've said that in your younger years reading was a means of escape. Do you still feel this way? Have your feelings changed now that you've written a novel and know what that process entails?

Reading still offers a means of escape. It's the best way I know how to relax. The difference with being a published novelist is that now I read to learn the craft. As a writer, I want to know what worked when I read a book and can't put it down. I am especially delighted when I meet someone and they tell me, "I couldn't put your book down." It's the ultimate compliment. ■

Q. What kinds of stories do you find yourself drawn toward? Who are some of your favourite authors?

I find myself drawn to character-driven stories. Plot-driven stories have their day depending on the genre. What I'm most interested in are stories that make me think, teach me something new and yet also make me laugh. Growing up, a lot of the books I read came from the African Writer's Series. From these, the works of Buchi Emecheta, Cyprian Ekwensi and Ama Ata Aidoo really made me think about issues of gender roles and societal expectations. During my teenage years, I started watching and reading theatrical plays. Zulu Sofola and Athol Fugard are my favourites. I'm glad I later discovered Nadine Gordimer, Toni Morrison, Chika Unigwe and

Khaled Hosseini. I recently read Lillian Natel's *Web of Angels* and Chevy Stevens' *Never Knowing* and I'm looking forward to their next books. ∎

What are you working on now?

I just completed a manuscript for a second novel. The novel follows the lives of two young women who leave Nigeria to join new husbands, men they barely know, in the United States. While it draws on familiar themes from *Daughters Who Walk This Path*, this novel focuses on the alarming increase in domestic violence deaths among Nigerian-American couples. ∎

DISCUSSION QUESTIONS

1. In your opinion, what is the "path" these daughters walk?

2. How does the relationship between Morayo and her mother change throughout the novel? Why do you think Bisoye reacted the way she did to Morayo's assault, and what kind of ripple effect does it have on the family?

3. Stories, tales, and fables play a big part in the novel. How did you respond to them? Did they make you see the characters and their situations in a new light?

4. Morenike and Morayo both experience undeserved abuse, but their families' reactions are very different. Why do you think this is the case? Did reading Morenike's story affect your understanding of Morayo's situation?

5. Did your perception of modern-day Nigeria change after reading the book? If yes, in what way? Did any specific passages or sections of the book stand out to you?

6. How did you react to Bros T's acts of contrition? Do you think he truly regrets his past behaviour, or do you think he is still trying to exert his control over Morayo? Explain.

7. The author repeatedly explores forgiveness and its repercussions throughout the novel. What kind of a role does

forgiveness play in Morayo's later life? Whom does she have the most difficulty forgiving?

8. How does Morayo evolve throughout the book? Is there a pivotal moment that revealed to you that she had developed into a woman?

9. Some of the cultural traditions explored in the novel make the emotional pain of sexual abuse even more severe. Were there also rituals and traditions in the book that ended up serving women rather than oppressing them?

10. How would you compare the contemporary views of sexual violence in Nigeria with those in North America? What are the similarities and differences? Do you see a link between Nigerians' attitudes toward governmental politics and the sexual politics found in the country?